^{T H E}Smoking Gun

By Nigel Hastilow

Sir Reginald

Best Wishes

Nigel.

Published by
Halesowen Press
WR11 7SA

www.thesmokinggun.co.uk

Printed by
Book Printing UK
Remus House
Woodston
Peterborough
PE2 9BF

Smoking calms me down. It's enjoyable. I don't want politicians deciding what is exciting in my life. – David Hockney

A custom loathsome to the eye, hateful to the nose, harmful to the brain, dangerous to the lungs, and in the black, stinking fume thereof nearest resembling the horrible Stygian smoke of the pit that is bottomless. – King James I

Smoking kills. If you're killed, you've lost a very important part of your life.
– Brooke Shields

Tobacco, divine, rare superexcellent tobacco, which goes far beyond all panaceas, potable gold and philosopher's stones, a sovereign remedy to all diseases.
– Robert Burton, Anatomy of Melancholy

Cast of Characters

Acton Trussell, MP
Clarissa Trussell, his wife
Olivia Trussell, his daughter
Sam Trussell, his son
Hilda, his ageing Labrador

Vernon Small, Acton's agent
Daphne Beauchamp, Acton's mother-in-law
Linda, the Trussells' cleaning lady, also employed by Reg and Gloria Wootton
Amanda, Acton's constituency secretary
Polly, Acton's Westminster secretary
Mick Allardyce, Acton's gardener

Julian "Stud" Lee, bassist from The Wreckage
Marinka, his girlfriend, a Slovenian model
Mrs Dorsington, his housekeeper
Arthur "Arty" Welford, his solicitor

Aston Cantlow, a schoolboy computer hacker

In the Barset constituency association

Clifford Chambers, estate agent, chairman of the association
Samantha Chambers, his sister
Quentin Quinton, Treasurer
Gary Atherstone, Deputy Chairman
Councillor Sue Alne, St Thomas ward
Tony Grafton
Sonny Hatton
Trevor Lancaster
Jim Dutton
Sally Hardcastle
Councillor Terry Page, council leader
Councillor Langley Claverdon, head of housing

Morton Morrell, a PR man
Mavis Murcot
Henry Hardcastle
Mr & Mrs McPherson
Sybil and Beryl
Steve Prince
Steve Blunt
Pinky Green

In the village of Howard Michael

The vicar, the Rev Mrs Morris
Mrs James, face-painter
Mrs Hughes, a flower show stalwart
Sid Shipley, the former landlord of the Fox and Trumpet
Cordelia Quint, a young mother
Mrs Cullompton, a neighbour

In the town of Barset

Tanya Arden, a peripatetic music teacher
Hampton Arden, a wealthy car dealer, her cousin
Sir Oliver, chairman of the cricket club
Lord Percy de Vere Percy, Viscount Preston
Miles, his butler
Reg Wootton, retired schoolteacher
Gloria Wootton, driving force in the annual arts festival
Chatham Smith, businessman
Molly Merchant, music and dance festival secretary

Mandy Black, a council tenant
Derek Black, her husband
Kelly (7), Dean (16) and Hayley (14), her children
Degsie Brown, who lives with Hayley
Jean-Luc "the Camel" Faivre, ex-striker for Barset Albion (The Stokers)
Bill Rogers, council housing officer
Steve, manager of the Barset Working Men's Club
Finola, his third wife

Party candidates

Lucy Loxley
Robin Loxley, her brother
Richard and Ann Loxley, her uncle and aunt
Joanna, her lover
Sir Edmund Loxley, her father

Maggie Pride, housewife, mother and former dancer
Doug Pride, her husband

Viv(ek) Arnold, a London lawyer.

Sharon Duggan, a council leader
Conor George, son of an Earl
Parvinder Singh, a party employee
Wesley Small
Helen Panesar, businesswoman
Antara Muthupalanialpan
Sonia Prassana, lecturer in economics.
Ravi Viraj, another London lawyer
Colonel Tim Buckley

Government Ministers, spin doctors and gofers

Richard Justin Glengarriff Brandon (Dick), Prime Minister

Compton Dundon, party fixer
Amelia Browning, chief whip
Derek Browning, her husband
Natalia, her PA
Tina Bell, her Secretary
Marcia the Marvel, her hairdresser
Hugh Chipping-Compton, her PPS

Harriet Standing, deputy chief whip
Quentin Marsh MP, shares Polly with Acton Trussell
Bud Brooke, Chancellor of the Exchequer
Rick Pickering, Home Secretary

Steve Thomas, a media manager
Sir Michael Watford, the leader's "special envoy"
Ms Petula Cross, Speaker of the House of Commons
Steve Hassleman, transport minister
Denzil Duxford, Number 10 press officer
Dev (Dave) Hersey, party chairman
Gervaise Thynne, editor of itsmyparty.com website

Journalists

Jimi Hunt, reporter on the Barset Chronicle (the Chronic)
Newbold Whitnash, editor of the Barset Chronicle
Sophie Hicks, reporter for "Lorry World"

Election candidates

Mrs Abbey Luddington, Labour
Mick Mickleton, Communist
Cherry Bussage, Independence for Britain Party,
Senor Philosophus Mayhem, Totally Monstrous Raving Mad Party

The Police

Chief Constable Bingley Ortega
PC Sandy Freshwater, his girlfriend
DCI Hazel Snitterfield
DC Yardley Wood

Chapter 1

Trafalgar Square was sealed off. Smokers had rights too.

It was the last great rally, the 'Charity Smokeathon' organised by the Liberation Association which fought the rearguard action against the Government's total ban on the use of tobacco products of all kinds. At mid-day there would be the Great Stub Out followed by a funeral pyre of cigarettes if the mourners hadn't managed to finish them all first.

Gathered in the square were people who had spent most of their adult lives enjoying what they regarded as the innocent pleasure of a cigarette, a cigar or even a pipe. They had assembled from all corners of England and included enforced exiles from Scotland and Wales, where the ban had been imposed a year ago. Some said they would move to Northern Ireland, where there was no ban, or to France, where the ban was universally ignored.

The Government said only 50,000 people would be permitted to take part in the "Smokeathon" – everyone was sponsored, the money raised would go to Third World projects – but it looked as if at least 250,000 had turned up, with gatherings of smokers all down Whitehall and outside the Houses of Parliament as well.

They were lucky with the weather. February was an inhospitable time and it was still very cold but at least the snow had gone and it wasn't raining. From time to time, a thin sun peered through grey clouds. It was difficult to tell whether the clouds closer to the ground were formed of smoke or people's breath.

On the fringes of the crowd stood health workers handing out Government-approved nicotine patches and nicotine chewing gum as well as leaflets on how to kick the habit. On the platform outside the National Gallery a series of speakers testified to the intolerance of a society in which such a freedom could be removed.

The most frequently-quoted phrase was Edmund Burke's maxim, 'All that is necessary for the triumph of evil is for good men to do nothing.'

Standing outside the smokers' enclosure, a tall, thin man wearing a suit and a pale blue bow tie, remarked to his short, fat, dapper companion, 'They always use that phrase when they want to pretend they're better than the rest of us.'

'Yes,' the shorter, fatter man replied, 'It's like they think if only they'd had the chance they'd have stood firm against Stalin, Hitler and Thatcher combined.'

'Good Lord,' the thin man said, indicating a group of musicians away to his left. The three men and one woman were entertaining those on the periphery of the crowd with a medley of jigs and reels. 'That one on the left, the girl playing the fiddle, that's Olivia Trussell, isn't it? I'd never have thought she'd get mixed up with these losers. She doesn't even smoke.' She was furiously scraping her bow across the fiddle in an accelerating frenzy while one of the youths strummed a guitar, another seemed to be hacking at his banjo and the third youth plucked his double-bass unperturbed. They were wrapped up against the cold but the young woman's thick red hair seemed to be flying in all directions as she stooped and rose onto her tip-toes along with the feverish folk music.

The two men turned away. The protesters tried to drown out the speeches and the music. 'Scum! Scum! Murderers!' they continued.

Acton Trussell, secretary of the Liberation Association's parliamentary committee, was enjoying a Marlboro Light with Rick Hatton, the trade union leader. They were discussing the difficulties faced by the Government in cracking down on the black market which was already in existence. The average price of a packet of 20 had reached £35 and was bound to soar higher as the risks of smuggling tobacco into the country continued to grow.

'You'd think the police had better things to do than harass the ordinary working man,' Hatton complained.

'I don't understand why the Antis are out in such force or why they still seem so angry,' Trussell replied, pointing down from the platform across the heads of the smokers to the angry faces five deep behind the police cordon and the crash barriers.

'It'll be alcohol next,' warned Hatton.

'You know, it's funny. Do you remember the hunting ban? In those days, everyone said it would be shooting next, then fishing. Yet this Government, the same one which is now banning smoking, has restored the right to hunt with hounds.'

'Your Government,' Hatton growled. 'OK for the upper toffs to have their pleasures, not OK for the working man.'

'Actually it's a Coalition Government,' Acton Trussell reminded him.

'We're all liberals now.'

'Well if you call this liberal I hate to think what a Fascist State would be like,' Hatton grumbled.

Acton Trussell had been in politics long enough to know there was little logic to many of the decisions Governments made. They had very little to do with belief or conviction. In the case of the smoking ban, it had become clear tax revenues from the sale of tobacco were in decline. The law of diminishing returns applied: the higher the tax, the fewer people paid it. A tax-free black market already flourished. Smuggling cigarettes had become big business. And, it was true to say, fewer and fewer people actually smoked these days. The long Government campaign against the habit had taken its toll.

The Coalition needed a source of revenue to replace the billions they used to receive in tobacco duty. The answer was a 'green' tax on flying. It worked because they could say the aim was to reduce the number of flights and, therefore, cut greenhouse gases. The tax was needed to save the planet. It doubled the cost of most flights and did, as promised, reduce the number and duration of flights. But its main aim was to re-fill the Treasury coffers as the income from tobacco withered away.

It was the brainwave of a Liberal-Democrat think-tank made up of Cambridge University Old Etonians to link the green tax on flying with the ban on tobacco. It made the Conservative Prime Minister Dick Brandon look caring and progressive though right-wingers like Acton Trussell said it was just another example of the Lib-Dem tail wagging the Tory dog. But it pleased The Guardian, the BBC and the health and environmental lobby groups. Dick's poll rating rose six points when he made the announcement at the party conference.

Now, at five minutes to mid-day, Acton took another Marlboro Light from the pack in his suit pocket and offered one to everyone else on the platform. Unfortunately, they were all doing the same thing. Kent, Camel, Gauloises, Rothman's, Embassy, John Players – the endless variety of nicotine sticks on offer made him tempted to take one of each, secrete them about his person and savour them later. But he knew everyone who left Trafalgar Square would be searched. On-the-spot fines would be imposed on first offenders found in possession of any tobacco product.

Lord Henley d'Ardencote, the 35-year-old entrepreneur and former chairman of the Empire Tobacco Company, once of Nottingham, now of Kenya, was declaring the countdown between drags on the largest Cuban cigar Trussell had ever seen.

'It's the end of an era,' he yelled into the PA system. Drag, cough. 'It's the death of a great British industry.' Cough, drag, billow of smoke. 'It's the loss of liberty and the triumph of political correctness.' Examination of the finely rolled brown rocket in his hand. 'This ban is a triumph for oppression. Nobody is safe. We were born free but are everywhere in chains.'

Lord Henley took a deep draw on his cigar, as the crowd went silent and the chimes of Big Ben could be heard in the distance. He took a last lingering look at his half-consumed Cuban cigar and ostentatiously stubbed it out in a silver ashtray held aloft by a slim, attractive young woman in the bright green uniform of his railway company, Whizz Trains, which owned the franchise on all the routes to Europe.

Lord Henley looked out over the crowd, pointed in the direction of the Houses of Parliament and declared, in a sonorous voice which, he was certain, would make him the lead item on the news for most of the day, 'To lovers of liberty in Britain and around the world, I have this one message, this one message only: "Send not to know for whom the bell tolls, it tolls for thee".'

On his way out of Trafalgar Square, having stubbed out his cigarette in a giant bin described by the Smokeathon organisers as The National Ashtray – contents to be recycled for composting – Acton Trussell was delayed by supporter after supporter wishing to shake his hand, congratulate and commiserate with him on the campaign he had been part of, and to wish him well. One or two suggested locations where cigarettes could still be purchased and smoked. Acton smiled but waved away any suggestion he would be smoking on the sly.

He didn't really notice the young man wearing the Knights of St George hoodie and, later on, he never remembered their first, brief encounter. The young man, though, took it to heart because the MP had smiled kindly at him and said, 'Thank you.'

Chapter 2

Three months later, Clifford Chambers swung his bright red Audi Attractive through the imposing gates of Preston Hall. His i-Pod was playing 'Songs from the Shows' but Clifford wasn't enjoying it. He was thinking back on a recent phone call with one of his contacts. Clifford prided himself on his extensive range of contacts. They were always useful. This one had bought a house from Alveston Pinks, the estate agency in Barset where Clifford worked.

Morton Morrell wanted to know if Clifford had heard anything about Acton Trussell.

'Should I have?' Clifford asked, reminding himself that the tactic when you know nothing is to bluff. Pretend to be in-the-know by sounding wary. Thus ignorance is regarded as discretion and you enhance your reputation while, at the same time, encouraging indiscretion in the person you're talking to. Clifford found it easy to give nothing away when, actually, he had nothing to give anyway. But he was angry with himself – was it possible he wasn't in the loop? 'What's the latest, then?' he said, as if he needed no background information because it was all at his fingertips.

'The latest? Well, you know he's in trouble?'

'Obviously.'

'I thought you would. Nobody else in the party seems prepared to say anything. But when the shit hits the fan, which it will do any day now, we need to prepare our dispositions.'

What was this 'we' and what were these 'dispositions'? Clifford could make no sense of it. As they were speaking, he Googled 'Acton Trussell, MP for Barset', to see if there was anything new. It was just the usual "They work for you" clap-trap, the occasional rude blog comment, the BBC report on his fact-finding mission to Kenya, a couple of bits and pieces from the local paper, his fight against the smoking ban – nothing new, scandalous or juicy.

'He'll have to go,' Morrell said with great certainty.

'Morton, I think you are being a bit premature, don't you?' As the Barset Conservative Association chairman, Clifford thought a little loyalty was called for at this stage. It would do no harm.

'Premature? Only by a few hours, is my guess. He can't survive a scandal like this for long. It's not as if he's been shagging his secretary or pocketing taxpayers' money. This time he's up to his neck in it. Even an apology won't do him any good now the BBC's got hold of it.'

'The BBC?' Clifford went onto the corporation's web-site. Nothing. Not yet, anyway.

'They were there.'

'Were they?'

'Local radio.'

'Local radio.' Clifford was dismissive. BBC Radio Barsetshire was only interested in road accidents and missing parakeets. Nobody listened to it. Everyone preferred 104.8fm Radio Quark and its daily 'Sounds of the Seventies' show. 'Do we need to worry?'

'We will when it all comes out. Believe me. I've got a nose for this sort of thing.'

Clifford remembered. Morton Morrell was a public relations man. Very successful by all accounts. He acted for various public bodies, quangos and corporations. He kept well into the background but he understood the game, knew who was who, what was what. He'd made a great deal of money when he sold his agency. At 43, he was semi-retired and living on a small country estate (valued by Clifford at £2.3 million but actually sold for £2.9 million, which was embarrassing) with his surprisingly plain wife and three horses.

What, exactly, had their MP said that was so career-threatening? Clifford Chambers could not bring himself to let Morrell know how ignorant he was. Best to cut short the conversation, find out more elsewhere and regroup. 'Morton, look, I can't say much at this stage but I hear what you say. I'll come back to you in due course. OK?'

'OK Clifford. But we must keep in touch. Lunch tomorrow?'

'I'll call you back.'

Clifford loved arriving at Preston Hall for one of his committee meetings. He treated the place as if it were home, the servants as old retainers, Lord Preston as his father. Leaving the Audi Attractive under the gaze of the hall's great Georgian windows, he adjusted his yellow bow tie and bounced two at a time up the steps to the first floor front door where Miles was already waiting to welcome him in. 'Mr Chambers,' Miles murmured. 'First as usual. Let me show you into the library.'

They walked across the echoing stone, past the cold and unlit fireplace, into the chilly library with its three walls of unread books, its mobile steps and its view out across the park towards the motorway. Miles went over to the drinks tray as Clifford asked jovially for 'a wee glen' and made his way to the chairman's seat at the long, leather-topped table in the centre of the room.

Miles poured as Clifford sought out his papers and placed them neatly in front of him. He extracted his fountain pen from his jacket pocket – a double-breasted number today which made him look a little like a young Cary Grant he thought – and placed it precisely parallel to the papers and exactly an inch to their right. He adjusted the placement of the whisky glass until it was just so, laid his hands carefully in his lap and waited calmly for his committee to assemble.

Among his many hats, Clifford Chambers was the Chairman of the Barset Festival of Music and Dance. This was only his second year in charge. Last year had not been an unbridled success. Clifford didn't understand modern dance – he preferred ballet or pole. The former was too expensive. And so was the latter, really. The Indian gyrations he had subjected himself to last June were more than flesh and blood could bear. Or they would have been if the Xtreme Dnce Trpe, apparently a group created under some rehabilitation of offenders legislation, hadn't been even worse. Tonight, Clifford planned a two-pronged attack: firstly he would demand that they dropped dance from the festival altogether but, failing that, he would suggest a public participation event in pole-dancing, it being a wholesome recreation these days and not a sleazy sex show.

He waited. He could hear Lord Preston's voice booming. Percy was obviously on the phone. 'No I damned well don't,' shouted Lord Percy de Vere Percy, Viscount Preston. 'I don't give a damn for the damned man anyway. Just another of those shitty politicians. Can't stand any of 'em. No. No. No. Goodbye.'

Viscount Preston hobbled into the room. He was only in his early 70s but he was thin, small and unsteady on his feet. Clifford remained at the head of the table while Preston staggered over to him and sat down with a groan.

'Bloody cheek,' he said. 'Bloody papers. Some damned reporter from the 'Chronic' wanting to know about Acton bloody Trussell. Did I know anything about some damned scandal about him.'

'Really?' Chambers feigned surprise. 'What's he done?'

'Haven't a clue. Nor did the bloody reporter. On a fishing trip, apparently. Little runt.'

The music festival committee began to assemble. Clifford greeted them as if he were their host.

First was Tanya Arden, a youngish woman with long, greying hair and an intense expression. She played the violin, badly but with a passionate intensity, and worked as a peripatetic music teacher. She was married to Hampton, a very rich local car dealer who did not care for any music other than Meatloaf and who did not understand why Tan wanted to spend her time traipsing from one inner city comprehensive to another trying to interest wannabe rap-artists in string quartets.

Old Reg Wootton was a retired schoolteacher who devoted his days to the church choir and to a composition which, by his own admission, would never reach fulfilment. Reg played the organ occasionally, enjoyed conducting and spent much of the rest of his time humming quietly to himself on his allotment. His wife, Gloria, was the life and soul of the post-festival party and was already planning the next one.

Chatham Smith and Maggie Pride arrived together in his Jaguar Jugular. Chatham was the festival's main sponsor. He persuaded himself this would help towards his knighthood. Chatting up Maggie Pride was less likely to assist him in that ambition but he thought it didn't do any harm.

She wasn't all that attractive anyway. Maggie had been a dancer with a fairly well-known troupe before she married a TV producer at the Beeb and had babies. As a result of her seven appearances as one of eight young women in 'TnA' (an abbreviation of Tits and Arse) on 'Rock Week', she was the festival's dance expert. She said the festival was what kept her sane when she was trying to deal with her four-year-old twins and her baby son, Georgie. Maggie was a real right-winger: hang 'em, flog'em, cut their hands off, deport 'em. The works. It was reassuring, Chatham thought, to find a woman married to someone at the BBC who didn't automatically adopt their left-wing views. It was a pity she'd grown plump over the years and that the curvaceous body he remembered leering at when she was dancing to Ian Dury and the Blockheads' "Hit Me With Your Rhythm Stick" was no longer as sexy as it once was. That was the way of all flesh but he vaguely hoped she might encourage his advances if he was prepared to overlook the fact that she wasn't exactly 19 any more. Somehow it didn't seem terribly likely.

Last, as usual, and late, as usual, was Molly Merchant, the only member of the committee who did any work. In Molly's view anyway. She bustled in with her ring-binder full of letters, notices, contracts and schedules. 'Sorry Mister Chairman, sorry. I was just negotiating with the Vale Symphony Orchestra and the Choir of St Saviour's for the Monday afternoon slot. I know they're only amateurs…'

'Rank bad amateurs at that,' interrupted Lord Preston.

'...but they deserve another chance.'

'After last year's debacle?'

'Yes but actually they weren't bad.' This was Maggie's first contribution to the evening. Everyone turned to her. Molly saw Maggie as an ally; Tanya couldn't stand the woman.

The meeting went on for two hours. By half past eight, Preston was damned if he'd offer the buggers a drink but he desperately needed a Scotch. As usual, Chambers was allowing everyone to waffle. He was too weak to be a chairman but there you are. Nobody else wanted to do it so.

The meeting was shuffling along like a group of old ladies on the seafront at Blackpool when Chambers finally said, 'Now, as for dance. I think we should have a public participation pole dancing event.'

'Pole dancing?' asked Reg Wootton because he had no idea what Chambers was talking about.

'Pole dancing!' exclaimed Tanya Arden with disgust.

'Hmmm, pole dancing,' said Lord Preston with some relish.

'Not lap dancing?' said Chatham Smith in a voice which was intended to express comic disappointment.

'Pole dancing?' asked Molly Merchant, because she had every idea what Chambers was talking about.

'It's not about sex, it's about fitness,' Chambers replied to Molly's question.

'It's disgusting. It's degrading. It treats women as sex objects. It's not what you should have in an art and dance festival. It's not art or dance.'

'I think it's a good idea,' said Lord Preston. 'Best idea I've heard tonight. Nothing wrong with a few fit young women displaying their wares.'

'There,' said Tanya in a fury, 'That's precisely why it is a disgraceful idea. Disgraceful.'

'I'd like to know where we get the poles from,' said Molly. 'Won't there be some sort of health and safety issues. What if one of the girls slips and hurts herself?'

There was a pause. Chambers turned to the woman on his right, the only one not to have spoken. 'Maggie?'

'Well, as a former professional dancer, I can confirm that pole dancing is a valuable fitness regime for many women. It can be highly attractive and sexy but it is not disgusting, as Tanya would have us believe. And, after all, anyone taking part would do so freely, they wouldn't be forced into it.'

'I can't believe it,' said Tanya. 'You are a traitor to your sex.' Tanya stood up to leave.

Reg Wootton intervened. 'I suggest we discuss this again at the next meeting when we have had a chance to consider the implications further.' Everyone looked grateful. Chambers quickly dealt with any other business and the date of the next meeting so things broke up more or less amicably though Molly scuttled off with a frowning Tan in tow.

As Maggie and Chatham were heading towards the door, Reg Wootton declared to Lord Preston, so everyone else could hear: 'We'll be electing a new Member of Parliament soon, then, I hear.'

Chatham stopped in his tracks. Preston pressed on out of the room in search of privacy and alcohol. Chambers and Maggie both reacted. She was inquisitive, he was embarrassed. Did everyone know about this except him? 'Oh do tell,' said Maggie. 'What's the news? Is the old fool dead?'

'No, he's just got himself into terrible trouble. Career-threatening, they say.'

'Really, what's he done?'

'Well I don't actually know what he's supposed to have done. Probably an affair. That's what happens to most of them, isn't it?'

'Acton Trussell? Who'd have him?'

Chatham chuckled. 'Well they say power is an aphrodisiac.'

'And so it is,' Maggie assured him. 'But it's debatable if a backbench MP like Acton Trussell could ever be said to have any power. He's just lobby fodder. Who told you about it, anyway, Reginald? Hear it on the allotments?'

'Well actually,' he lowered his voice and moved closer to the others, 'Actually it came from our cleaning lady Linda. She does for the Trussells as well as us. She said there was a bit of a commotion. The press, you know.'

'No?' Maggie was all ears.

'Well, according to Linda, the phone has been ringing all day but poor Clarissa is spending all her time at the General with her mother, who's got cancer. Lungs but it's spread. Apparently she's riddled. Riddled. Terrible shame.'

'Yes but what about Chez Trussell?' Chatham asked with a hint of irritation. Wootton was not the sort of man he usually had much time for.

'Oh yes, well, according to Amanda their secretary, the constituency one, Polly Something-or-other, the one with the Prada bags, you know, anyway, Polly has been 'fielding calls all day long' while Acton is nowhere to be found and Clarissa is at the hospital and out of contact.'

'Did Amanda say what it was all about?' This was Clifford's first contribution to the debate. And he expressed himself in such a way it could be interpreted by the others that he knew all about it and was testing the water to make sure the news hadn't leaked yet.

'No. Something to do with one of his speeches, apparently. The BBC seem to have recorded him saying something he shouldn't have. But I've no idea what.'

'Don't you know, Clifford, you're a local Tory big-wig?' asked Chatham.

'Of course you are,' Maggie declared with a charming smile.

'Well, you know how it is,' said Clifford, enigmatically and finished packing away his papers.

*****

Lucy Loxley was sitting with her toes in the Indian Ocean, one hand round a gin and tonic, her girlfriend Joanna at her side, enjoying the sunset when her brother, Robin, rang.

'Luce, have you heard?'

'Heard what? We're in India, remember? News travels slow in these parts.'

'About Acton Trussell?'

'Who?'

'Trussell. Dinosaur for Barset. On his way out.'

'Oh, that Trussell?'

'How many Trussells do you know, then?'

'Several. Went to school with most of them. Slept with at least one of them.'

'Male or female?'

'Anyway, why are you calling me? What's so urgent?'

'Thought you'd be interested.'

'Why?' Lucy sounded sulky. Her brother bridled.

'Why?' Robin sounded incredulous.

'Yes, why?'

'Do I have to spell it out for you? Acton Trussell is the MP for Barset. He has a majority of over ten thousand. It's one of the safest seats in the country. He is in deep trouble. My guess is he'll have to resign within the next couple of days. If I were you, I'd come home. Now. There will have to be a by-election. You could be an MP by the end of June.'

Lucy sipped her gin and tonic as the sun disappeared in a streak of orange fire and the afterglow lit up the sky. Joanna shivered and stood up. 'I'm going in,' she said. 'Don't stay here getting bitten.'

Lucy nodded. 'Are you still there?' Robin asked.

'Yes. I'm looking at the sunset.'

'Lucy, this is no time to be looking at sunsets. You've got to get organised. Get going. Get over here. Now. Stake your claim before it's too late.'

'I'm not sure, Robin. I don't think I want to become an MP. I think I might move over here, buy a house, have servants, snorkel, read books, drink gin and tonic. It's medicinal, you know? Anyway, what's he done?'

'Trussell? Finally sealed his own fate. The old fart.'

*****

Clarissa Trussell was sitting at her dying mother's bedside wondering whether it would be better to go home and get Acton his supper or sit around flicking through 'Hello!' and 'Country Living' all evening while Daphne struggled for breath. She'd be happy when this performance was over. Acton had voted against euthanasia in the Commons for some spurious reason to do with the sanctity of life. But if you looked at Daphne now you'd wonder what was worth preserving in this frail old frame wheezing and whistling its last breaths. You wouldn't be this cruel to a horse, why did you have to be cruel to the people you loved? Not that Clarissa would say she loved her mother, exactly. They were never what you would call 'close'. But they were related and that was that. Clarissa didn't worry too much about emotion. She knew her duty, it was her up-bringing.

In the past, when people were less sentimental and the countryside wasn't seen through the green-hued spectacles of suburbanites, you could wring an animal's neck, hunt a fox, shoot a pheasant or even kick a dog if you had to, without anyone threatening you with five years' imprisonment. 'These days…. Just don't get me started,' was how Clarissa dealt with the subject in polite society.

There was commotion in the corridor. A door slam. A raised voice. Heavy feet on plastic tiled flooring. Her husband's voice, the words indistinct but the gruff contemptuousness clear as a bell. His bald head appeared round the door of her mother's private room.

'Cliss, Cliss,' hissed Acton Trussell.

'Acton?' She was irritated with him. She was always irritated with him. He was a very irritating man.

'Cliss. Thought I'd find you here. Shit and fan, Cliss. Shit and fan.'

'What are you talking about?' Clarissa reluctantly got up from the bedside and came towards her husband. She was ushering him out, backwards into the corridor. 'Come on, out. Out. Back, back.' She was waving her long arms at him as if he were a badly-behaved Labrador. 'And shush up. She's sleeping.'

'Oh. Yes. Cliss. Sorry darling, but shit and fan, dear. Shit and fan. Bloody BBC. Bloody, bloody BBC.'

'Acton, what are you talking about? What on earth are you talking about? Sit down here. Take a deep breath. And another. Now wait.' She went to the machine and slowly poured herself a plastic cup of very cold water. She needed a moment. A pause. Acton really was the end.

He was feverishly checking his Blackberry when she came back and sat next to him, his fat fingers stumbling over the tiny letters. The corridor was deserted. It was half past nine. Most visitors had gone home long ago. Most patients were trying to sleep though they could hear the murmur of TV from some of the rooms.

'Now,' she said with a sigh.

'Bloody BBC. Bloody, bloody BBC.'

'Tell me.'

Acton Trussell was not exactly a friend of the party leader. Indeed, the Prime Minister would willingly have got rid of Trussell many years ago. Trussell was not just an old-school politician; he was an old, old-school politician. Hanging and flogging were bad enough from MPs in their 40s. Trussell was 65 if he was a day. He was a hangover from the Thatcher era when he had been young, thrusting and had a whole career ahead of him. He was an out-and-out Eurosceptic. One of the last survivors of the rebellions of John Major's disastrous years in office (but not in power).

These days he was known to the leader and his friends as 'a bed blocker' keeping a perfectly nice constituency out of the hands of someone younger, more subtle, less antediluvian, more female, less heterosexual and less white. And he openly despised the Coalition Government of Conservatives and Liberal Democrats.

Trussell was lucky. He survived the great 2009 expenses cull. For reasons best known to the old fool, he had chosen not to claim expenses on any second home. He had not charged the taxpayer to clear his moat (he didn't have one anyway) nor had he tried to get the public to fund a duck house on his duck pond (not that he had either of those either). He hadn't even bought porn on the taxpayer.

Curiously, Acton Trussell had failed to take advantage of the lax regime of expenses and perks available to every Member of Parliament until they were finally exposed in a series of embarrassing revelations which put paid to the careers of several of Trussell's greedier contemporaries.

The scandal – which somehow left the leader's favourites unharmed – led to resignations in safe seats up and down the country. Into these the leader inserted his most trusted friends and allies, while concentrating on the appointment of women and members of various ethnic minorities.

Yet through it all, Acton Trussell sailed on. The worst that the press could say about him was that he claimed a first class return rail ticket from Barset to London every week when the House was sitting. He was one of those few MPs who took seriously the idea that the money made available to them had come from the pockets of his much-poorer constituents and he should not spend it without good cause.

Admittedly, it helped that Acton came from a pretty wealthy family and had inherited a decent amount of money when his father died. But that hadn't stopped a number of millionaires from making the most of the opportunities presented to them as elected politicians. Even the leader charged the taxpayer for his rhododendrons.

The party couldn't find a way of getting rid of Trussell, though it wanted to dispose of the seat elsewhere. Indeed, because he emerged from the expenses scandal without a stain on his character, Trussell was hailed in the media as one of the truly 'honourable members'. Even the 'Barset Chronicle' was obliged to be nice about him.

The party fixers hoped Acton Trussell would die. Soon. A heart attack would be nice. A scandal was not something the new Government wanted. The Prime Minister, The Rt Hon Richard Justin Glengarriff Brandon– 'just call me Dick' – and his public school 'friends of the people' in both of the parties which ran the country were more than anxious to maintain the façade. They didn't want scandal – especially after the various disasters of the Blair-Brown years.

Trussell had been offered a knighthood to quit before the last General Election. He held out for a peerage. Some thought he did this for honourable reasons, which is to say he did so knowing he wouldn't get one; others accused him of having ideas above his station.

The fixers wouldn't give him the time of day, let alone a place in the House of Lords, so they turned him down. Much to Brandon's annoyance. The leader thought booting people upstairs to the Lords was a perfectly sensible thing to do because that way the fools in the Party – the members, that is – could be persuaded into thinking it was old-school business as usual. A puffed-up Acton Trussell receiving undue reward for services not rendered was a small price to pay. But negotiations broke down and he stayed put, plain Mister Trussell.

A few months later, the Barset constituency was fought and won again by the incumbent MP. Elsewhere half a dozen of Trussell's contemporaries were now enjoying their first few months in the Other Place and in the boardrooms of Britain, where, despite the credit crunch, the expenses scandal and the recession, a title and access to the corridors of power still commanded a reasonable stipend.

'Now tell me, Acton,' said Clarissa. But at that moment, her mother stirred and asked for some water. The daughter turned her attention to the patient. Her husband patted her gently on the shoulder and stole away.

*****

'Bugger, bugger, bugger, bugger, bugger. I'm taking the dog for a walk,' Acton Trussell called to the empty house.

Trussell clicked his fingers and his black Labrador, Hilda, came trotting to his side as he marched out of the back door and headed up the hill. He was upset. He had received an e-mail from the Chief Whip, one of The Leader's 'cuties'.

The e-mail was to the point: 'Acton, Please attend a meeting with the party chairman and myself on Tuesday at 6pm in the House. In the meantime, maintain a low profile, do not speak to the press and refer any calls to party headquarters. Please confirm that you will make this meeting. Thank you. Amelia.'

Amelia, he kept thinking, What kind of a name was that for a Chief Whip anyway? Amelia Browning. Claimed to be a descendant of Elizabeth Barrett and Robert Browning. At least that's what the papers always said in their profiles of "The Leader's kitchen cabinet" or "The Leader's harem" or however the tabloids were referring to the bevy of beauties he surrounded himself with, claiming it was in the interests of giving the Party a modern, 21st century image.

Not that Mrs Browning could ever be counted among these alleged beauties.

So far nothing had appeared in the papers and even though he had taken a few phone calls from various journalists, they knew even less than he did. But there was trouble brewing, it was only a matter of time. The news was bound to filter out, if not in a newspaper then on some anonymous dickhead's blog. That still wasn't the same as seeing it spread over two pages in the 'Mail on Sunday' or the 'Daily Mirror' but it was where it started. He'd Googled his name and the usual rubbish came up. Nothing new. Nothing scandalous.

Even so, he realised he had to consider his future rather more seriously than he'd done since he gave up his dull career as a stockbroker to become the MP for Barset. 'Bugger, bugger, bugger, bugger.'

The woods outside the village of Howard Michael, where Acton Trussell lived, were empty. It was a working day in the middle of May and few people were around. The woods had been treated with suspicion since three bodies had been uncovered there early on in Trussell's parliamentary career. It was a good place to march through with the dog, swearing out loud with nobody to take offence.

Apparently from nowhere, two men appeared. They were wearing suits and ties though they were also shod in Wellington boots. One was Compton Dundon, the other was someone Trussell vaguely recognised but couldn't place.

'Good Lord. What the bloody hell are you doing here?'

'Hello Acton,' said Compton Dundon cheerfully. 'You know Steve Thomas, don't you?'

Thomas held out a hand to shake. 'What? What? We're not at Westminster, you know. You have ambushed me. Accosted me. Hilda, sit. What the bloody hell are you doing here?'

'Acton. How nice to see you. Steve is one of our Coalition partner's senior media managers.'

'A bloody Liberal is he?' Thomas smiled.

Trussell marched on, increasing his pace. Though old and overweight, he didn't tire and enjoyed long walks with his Labrador. The others fell into step, Dundon at his side, Thomas a few paces behind.

They walked on in silence for a minute or two, following a clear path which wound slowly but inexorably up hill. Trussell stopped suddenly, flung his arms wide and declaimed: 'OK if you've come to kill me, get on with it.'

Dundon was embarrassed, Thomas grim-faced, as if there might be some merit in the suggestion.

'We haven't come to kill you Acton. My God, what do you think we are? Anyway, you've made a pretty good job of burying your political career already.'

'We're just the undertakers,' Thomas chipped in.

Dundon tried not to chuckle. 'We need to cut a deal, Acton. Today, before you see the whips tomorrow. So we can agree an exit strategy.'

'What are you talking about?'

'Your departure from the House of Commons.'

'What are you talking about Dundon, you bloody poof? What departure from the House of Commons?'

'Come on now, Acton, we both know you can't carry on. Not now.'

'What on earth do you mean?'

'Your little *faux pas*. Your inadvertent slip. Your support for criminal activity. Your failure to back a major plank of the Government's legislative programme.'

'I don't know what you are talking about.' Trussell turned and stomped off. The others chased after him.

'Of course you do. You have been checking the internet almost hourly. You were even checking the BBC web-site while you were sitting with your grieving wife at your dying mother-in-law's bedside.'

'How do you know that?' Trussell stopped, turned, came close and menacing towards his tormentor. Dundon was a small, round man with wet, clammy hands and a flamboyant handkerchief at his breast pocket but he was not intimidated. 'Oh what's the use? There's nothing damaging anyway. Hasn't been for days, months, years even.'

'No, Acton, but there will be. Won't there, Steve?'

Thomas, tall, thin, young and with very greasy skin, smiled again in his gruesome way. 'Well, let's be honest, there isn't at the moment. And there might not be. But there could be. There would be. If…'

'If you don't agree to our proposal, Acton.'

'Bugger off.' Trussell stomped on again, increasing his pace even further. The dog trotted along at his side. Dundon and Thomas waited a moment before following him. Dundon was texting someone.

The path reached a plateau with a view over the surrounding countryside. Away to the left were the pylons and power stations of Barset. To the right, the river. Ahead, rolling fields full of filthy sheep. The trio marched on in crocodile for some time. The two men in suits struggled to keep up but, because they were much younger, they assumed their quarry would tire first.

He didn't. Trussell's only thought was how to shake them off – out-run them, or out-walk them anyway. Or at least lead them deep into the heart of the woods and lose them. Or get them lost so they couldn't find their way out.

They walked this way for three-quarters of an hour. Dundon and Thomas passed landmarks they thought they had seen before. They called out to Trussell on two occasions to stop and talk. He ignored them.

Eventually, they reached a clearing where a fallen tree had obviously been used as a bench by years of walkers. Cigarette ends littered the area. There wasn't even a bin though there were a few used condoms in the gorse. Trussell sat, gave the dog a biscuit and extracted a packet of Marlboro Lights from an inside pocket of his Barbour. The younger men stood before him, trying to catch their breath.

'This isn't doing you any good,' says Dundon. 'This isn't helping. You know very well what we're talking about and you know very well the game's up. Now if you want to go quietly, with some honour and dignity, we can arrange it. Plus the K you were promised nine months ago. But if you don't, things will get nasty. Very nasty indeed.'

'Nasty,' Thomas added.

'You look as if you should be wearing Gestapo uniform, you little shit.'

'So?'

'So what?'

'Will you come quietly?'

Trussell drew deeply on his cigarette. He paused, exhaled. He drew on his cigarette. He paused. He drew on his cigarette again. He took out his mobile phone, which had been turned off. He turned it on. He listened to a message. He fumblingly replied to a text. He drew deeply on his Marlboro Light. He looked up at his inquisitors. They were still awaiting his reply.

Trussell shrugged. Stood up. Stubbed out his cigarette. Said, in a tone of reasonableness, 'OK look, just let me call Clarissa and I'll come back. I suppose I have to announce I am too unwell to continue. Something unmentionable, is that it?'

They nodded assent.

'Hang on a minute while I call Clarissa.'

Trussell took up his mobile and made a show of checking for his wife's number. He made a show of hitting the green button, waiting for the call to be answered. He started to speak, 'Cliss, Cliss, it's me... Yes, I know...

How's your mother? Oh. Oh. I am sorry. Now listen, Cliss, there's something I have to tell you...'

Trussell wandered away from the clearing, into the thickets, closely followed by Hilda. He kept talking. After a minute he turned to check if he could see his persecutors any more. He couldn't. He put the phone in his pocket and broke into a trot, thinking how extraordinary it was to be capable of jogging at his age and wondering if his heart could stand the strain.

It was only a couple of minutes before Compton Dundon and Steve Thomas realised Acton Trussell wasn't coming back to finish their discussion.

At much the same moment, it started to rain.

Chapter 3

Lucy Loxley lay on the sun-bed as the warm day was filtered through the swaying palm trees and basted some more factor 30 onto her long, slim legs. She looked at Joanna, sitting cross-legged on her sun-bed poring over her Powermac. Joanna could never stay still. What the attraction was in computer games, Lucy had no idea. But Joanna seemed to enjoy them. They kept her happy, which was all that mattered.

Lucy was brooding on her brother's phone call. Should she go home straight away and stake her claim? Should she wait and see? Joanna was horrified at the whole idea and threatened to leave if Lucy seriously set out on a career in politics. Joanna thought it was just a hobby Lucy would grow bored with. It never occurred to her that Lucy might actually become an MP.

'But why do you think I became a councillor?' Lucy asked over dinner. 'Why did I go through the candidate selection process? Why have they made me a vice chairman of the party?'

'I didn't think you were serious,' Joanna insisted, looking increasingly grim and smoking furiously, even during the main course. Lucky they were outside in the warm Indian evening, Lucy couldn't help thinking.

'Well I think I am.'

'You think,' Joanna declared triumphantly. 'Either you are or you're not. You can't just think you are.'

'Then I am.'

'You think.'

'Jo, look, you know I've always been interested in politics. You know that most of my friends are involved in politics…'

'I'm not.'

'No but Graham, Tarquin, both the Harrys. Most of the people who have been my friends in the past few years are involved in politics. We're in Government; there's a proper job to do. I don't want to be left out. I want to play too.'

'It's not a game, you know.'

'Well, maybe not. Anyway, there isn't a vacancy at the moment. Robin just said Acton was in trouble. Poor old fool. But if he is going to resign and there's a by-election, I will be in there. It might never happen. I don't even know what Trussell has actually done. Something Thatcherite, I suppose.'

'Thatcherite?'

'You know, old-Tory. The Leader can't stand Thatcherites. He wants to get rid of them as quickly as possible so we can unite with the Liberal Democrats. Even the ones still in the Cabinet are past their sell-by dates. William himself has seen better days – American ambassador any day now, I shouldn't be surprised.'

'It is a vile business. I don't know what you see in it, everyone stabbing each other in the back.'

'It is the only way to improve our country. Politics. It affects everything. Without politics we have anarchy.'

'And without politicians?' Joanna looked over the top of her sunglasses.

'Without politicians we have no fun at all,' said Lucy. Joanna laughed, despite herself. Lucy was keen on 'fun'. It was what made her interesting to be with. 'And it will be fun, Jo. I promise you. We'll be Britain's First Lesbian Couple. Think of all the free make-overs. Think of the photo-sessions. Think of the publicity.'

'You are a whore,' Joanna laughed. Lucy was looking particularly attractive with her rosy glow from the day's sunshine and the evening's candlelight. This was how she liked her best. How could she refuse her? 'But I suppose you'll get what you want just like always.' Lucy gave her one of those mischievous grins she loved so much.

Now Lucy lay back in her sun-bed, wriggled and squirmed to get comfortable, half-closed her eyes so she could gaze through the palm leaves at the bright blue sky and plotted. She would not rush home. Partly because it would upset Joanna, partly because she didn't want to leave Goa, but mainly because she didn't see any advantage in dashing back before the MP announced his resignation. If he ever did.

There would be plenty of time to get into pole position for a by-election. It wouldn't do to seem over-eager. She'd have trouble enough with the party ladies without coming over all ambitious and uncaring. Lipstick lesbians had to tread carefully if they were to take advantage of the dice loaded in their favour. There were still Thatcherites in the Party who were not to be trusted.

Lucy imagined her first speech in the House of Commons. She would enjoy calling it her 'maiden' speech. Everyone would enjoy the *frisson*. She would wear a summer dress with her hair down. She would look girlie and endearing so the fat backbench men could sit there drooling. She would speak in support of the Leader's policies and the wonders of the Coalition, whatever they might be at the time, because she expected to be made a Minister almost as soon as she entered Parliament.

Lucy wanted to be an MP because she was scared of being bored.

She looked across at Joanna, still playing on her computer. The short dark hair, the brown eyes, the large breasts – she and Jo made a great couple. It was a pity Joanna wasn't interested in politics and didn't enjoy the limelight. Never mind, she'd learn.

Lucy wondered where in Barset she should get a house. She knew the town quite well because an uncle and aunt lived there. Uncle Richard was a local architect and general big-wig. He'd be a useful contact. Perhaps she should call him.

Barset itself was a dump. She wondered if the surrounding villages were inside the constituency. If they were, that would be ideal. If not, could she get away with buying somewhere there rather than in the middle of that urban sprawl? Probably not. How would Joanna take to provincial life? Not well. She had already refused to accompany Lucy on the rubber chicken circuit of dinners at Party associations up and down the country because it was too tedious. Even if Lucy became an MP, Joanna was unlikely to change her attitude towards the boring bread-and-butter of political life. Joanna was a city girl and a city girl she would remain. She wouldn't be leaving the house in Chelsea any day soon.

Mind you, perhaps if they had a civil wedding in Barset? Before or after an election? Lucy drifted off as the water lapped the shore, the breeze ruffled the awnings of the restaurant, the keyboard of Joanna's lap-top tapped away and the splash of the swimming pool faded into a contented murmur.

*****

'Jimi? Clifford.'

Jimi Hunt took his feet off the desk, sat up and started searching under the chaos of press releases on his desk for a viable Biro. He had no idea who Clifford was but clearly the bloke on the phone knew him well enough to use his mobile and refer to him in fairly familiar terms. Jimi's by-line was always Jonathan Hunt. He'd been Christened Jimi, thanks to his stupid, drugged-up hippy father. Dad thought it would be amusing to name a child born in 1984, at the height of Frankie-Goes-To-Hollywood mania, after the dead guitar hero Jimi Hendrix. It wasn't. He couldn't stand all that sixties psychedelic rubbish. He preferred dance, trance, hip-hop and rap. It was one of the reasons he didn't speak to his father any more.

'Clifford.' Jimi tried to sound interested. Already the voice on the other end was starting to bore him.

'Jimi? What do you know about Trussell?'

'Fat boring Tory MP of this parish. Knight of the shire only without the knighthood. What else is there to know?'

'He's in trouble.'

Jimi was interested. 'What sort of trouble?'

'That's for me to know and you to find out. I am not one to spread gossip about the party's stalwarts.'

The penny dropped. Clifford Chambers. Of course. Wasn't he a local bigwig. 'Is this call official? On the record?'

'Come on Jimi, you know me better than that.'

No I don't, Hunt thought. I can't remember ever meeting you and I have no idea what you look like. Still, here goes: 'Yes but in your capacity as a very senior officer in the Party?'

'In my capacity as chairman of the constituency association?'

'Yes.'

'I have no comment to make. None at all.'

'How do you know he's in trouble?'

'Just take my word for it. Have you really heard nothing? The BBC tape?'

'The BBC tape?'

'The BBC tape.'

'Sound or vision? Is it on the internet yet?'

''Course not.'

'No.' This conversation was going nowhere. If he couldn't make something out of it, Jimi Hunt would have to go back to studying the papers for the Barset Council social services committee in the hope of finding child neglect, maltreatment of old people or, at the very least, waste of public money. He'd far rather break a scandal about the local MP. 'So what can you tell me?'

'Off the record?'

'Off the record.'

'I think you should ask Acton if he's got any meetings planned with the chief whip.'

'A bollocking?'

'Or worse.'

'Worse?'

'Could be.'

When he rang off, Clifford Chambers felt he had advanced his cause somewhat. He now had a real contact with an influential and rising local journalist. He had provided a valuable tip-off. Unfortunately, the conversation had not been as successful as Clifford had hoped. Hunt knew even less about the alleged scandal than he did. If the press didn't know what was going on, who the hell would?

He dialled again. 'Compton? Clifford.'

Compton Dundon was in no mood to talk. He was soaking wet and trudging down a filthy country footpath finally in the direction of his car. Steve Thomas was at his side cursing with every step. They were both furious with Acton Trussell, each other, the Party and life in general.

'Not now, Clifford. Not now, OK?'

'Yes but what about Trussell?'

'What about him? He can go to hell as far as I'm concerned. I've done with the little bastard. It's out of my hands now and it serves him right. I have to go. Bye.'

'Where are you? Sounds like rain.'

'It is bloody rain. I am in the bloody rain. Steve and I are in the rain.'

'Steve?'

'Thomas. We are walking in the rain and it's too wet to talk to you. I am going now. Goodbye.'

The plot thickens, Chambers thought. Why is a gay London good-time boy like Compton Dundon traipsing around in the rain cursing Acton Trussell? And why is Steve Thomas with him? Thomas, the slimiest little reptile the Liberal Democrats had ever employed?

Clifford Chambers knew what he had to do. He had to call the MP. After all, wasn't he chairman of Trussell's local party association? The office was empty; it was time to shut up shop. Should he call now, or later, from home? What was his sister doing tonight? What, indeed, was he doing? Chambers consulted his organiser. She was at a bridge night. He was on his own – not even a Rotary Club committee meeting to attend. Might as well go home and enjoy a glass of that Penfolds Grange Shiraz. Obviously not the 1990 but quite palatable. He'd opened it the other day and shared a glass with Sir

Oliver when they met to discuss the pavilion extension at the cricket club. It would do nicely for what Clifford Chambers had in mind.

He strode with his customary military bearing – a leftover of the Combined Cadet Force at Fladbury, his minor public school – to the Audi Attractive, climbed in, turned up the volume on his 'Songs from the Movies' CD and sang along to "Somewhere Over The Rainbow" as he made his way through the evening traffic back to the home he had shared with his sister Samantha.

When Clifford turned 18 and Samantha was 27, their parents had taken them out for dinner and announced that they were leaving home to live in Argentina. They were tired of England and tired of their responsibilities. They had made enough money and they wanted a new life. They did not give their children the option of going with them, though they did leave them the house, 15, Rosepetal Avenue. Clifford and Samantha had scarcely seen their parents since. He didn't mind, at least he had a respectable house of his own without a mortgage and his sister looked after him pretty well.

Tonight it was cold and cloudy. He had a drink to pour and a call to make after first checking that Samantha had left him something substantial in the oven. She had. Lamb casserole.

As he sat in his favourite armchair savouring the heady bouquet of his 2005 Grange Shiraz, Clifford looked across to the mantelpiece at the photograph of his father with a young and intelligent-looking Acton Trussell. Father was congratulating the new MP on his election. The two men were clasped in a joyful embrace – they had been colleagues and friends since school.

Clifford couldn't speak for his father these days but the MP had thickened out, gone grey and jowly, lost his sense of humour and developed his sense of self-importance. He figured prominently in Clifford's early years. He was, after all, the young man's godfather.

He dialled Acton's private home number. Clarissa answered, which was awkward because Clifford wasn't used to talking to strange women – though Clarissa was hardly a stranger. He asked after their daughter Olivia. He forgot to ask after their son Sam, who was gay and worked in America.

Eventually Clifford got round to asking to speak to Acton only to be told he was on his way to London. Before ringing off, he remembered to ask after Clarissa's mother. She was still hanging on.

Phone calls when one of the participants is using a mobile on a train are more or less impossible. Acton Trussell was, to make matters worse, beginning to lose his hearing. He blamed it on Led Zeppelin, who he had seen three times in 1969, and The Wreckage. The conversation, at least on the part of the MP, was conducted at such a volume the other three passengers in first class could hear everything he said. For this reason, among others, he said nothing, at least nothing of interest to Clifford Chambers, whose excuse for calling was to discuss the Barset Literary Festival.

'Just thought I should make sure you're all teed up for it. Ready to do battle with Lord Natch, Rapsters XI and Minnie Mouze are you, Acton? It seems the aim is to get down with the kids this year.'

'Poets are the unacknowledged legislators of the world,' Trussell replied.

'So you're alright for Friday night then are you?'

'Yes of course I am…'

'Only I'd heard…'

'Heard what?'

'That there were issues.'

'Issues?'

'Difficulties.'

'Had you?'

'Is that wrong?'

'Nothing we can't handle.'

'I was talking to Jimi Hunt on the "Chronic". He seems to think it's a problem. For you, personally.'

'Does he? Does he?'

'Acton, I really do think you need to remember what the best interests of the party are likely to be in this sort of a situation.'

'What sort of a situation would that be, Clifford?'

'This sort, Acton. You know, where something's going to get into the papers, be on the TV and all over the internet. You know once it's on the internet you're dead, don't you? You may not use it much at your age but, believe me, it can be lethal. People of your age may not understand that.'

'Is that right?'

'Yes it is, Acton. The difficulty for the party is in defending the indefensible. You know… Acton? Acton?'

There was a crackling noise and the line went dead. Trussell stopped blowing air out of his mouth in imitation of a storm, sat looking at the perfect signal bar on his phone and wondered why they hadn't strangled the arrogant little shit at birth, when they'd still had the chance. His father would have despised him. He had his father's confidence in his own righteousness without his father's intelligence or, for that matter, his mother's good looks.

*****

The Chief Whip had two offices. One in the corner of the Members' Lobby just outside the main entrance to the Chamber of the House of Commons. This is where she and her acolytes sat sipping whisky and spinning webs of intrigue to entrap passing backbenchers. Today, though, the Chief Whip was in her other office, where the secrets were kept, more whisky dispensed and surrender documents signed.

It was a dull, functional affair with a large Melamine desk, a dreary swivel chair for the Chief and half a dozen wooden, straight-backed school chairs for her acolytes and victims. By the gas fire were a couple of sofas which held their own secrets, should cushions talk.

The half-light from Westminster Bridge filtered palely in through net curtains.

The Chief Whip's sole purpose, apart from obtaining promotion to one of the great offices of state for herself and those drones who served her with unquestioning loyalty, was to ensure that all those troublesome, under-worked MPs who did not have jobs in the Government would not go around causing trouble for the Prime Minister and his Coalition colleagues (unless, of course, it was convenient to encourage them to upset the Lib-Dems, though that was not a weapon to be used lightly).

The Chief Whip herself, Amelia Browning, was a small, plump woman of middle age, whose opinions were as settled as her waistline. Her walk was more of a roll. She had fat, stubby fingers which were expensively and ostentatiously manicured by the beauticians in the high street of Thor-pethwaite, the main settlement in her largely rural constituency. It was during these sessions that Amelia held court and conducted what she laugh-ingly referred to as her constituency surgeries. Everyone in Thorpethwaite knew where to find her on a Saturday morning and she paid above the going rate to get her nails done because Marcia the Marvel, who did her nails and her hair, was tolerant about the habitual importuning which took place between 9.30 am and 11 am each week. Marcia saw this both as her contri-bution to the cause of less regulation on small businesses – once Amelia's specialist subject – and as a marketing opportunity. About one-third of Amelia's supplicants ended up buying something from the salon during their visits. It was good for trade.

Today, though, Mrs Browning was not her usual expansive self. She had returned from an early meeting in Downing Street with her instructions. Grim-faced, she prepared for her meeting with Acton Trussell.

He was a difficult man. She had never liked him, not since the days when he sat behind her in the Commons when she was a shadow trade minister hissing instructions down her ear. He sometimes had bad breath. Not as bad as some she could name but noxious enough. And that was before he'd had a drink.

She couldn't understand how such a dinosaur had survived so long. He was very Old School – his views on women, workers' rights, immigration, the European Union; you name it, the man was stuck in the Middle Ages.

Mrs Browning asked her secretary, Natalia, if she would make some coffee. Natalia's English was coming on well.

Her Lib-Dem deputy chief whip, Harriet Standing, came panting into the office, all blowsy skirt and lipstick, closely followed by the tight-lipped upper-class tones of Hugh Lighthorne, the tall, thin, young and dim son of the former Lord Chancellor. They exchanged greetings, took out notes and waited for Natalia to present them all with their neat cups and saucers of weak, watery Nescafe and eventually got down to the main business of the day.

'He is coming?' Mrs Browning asked Lighthorne.

'I spoke to him first thing this morning, Chief Whip.'

'And Lucy? Is she on stand-by?'

'Lucy, Chief Whip?'

Harriet and Amelia exchanged glances. 'Yes, Hugh, Lucy Loxley, you remember,' said the Deputy Chief in her surprisingly gruff voice. 'The Chief asked you to make contact with her immediately now that a vacancy is due to arise.'

'But she's on holiday, in India.'

'This is the 21st century, Hugh. It is possible to communicate with India these days quite easily. Where do you suppose all those call centres are?'

'Shall I call her now?'

'Yes, alright. Even if it is the middle of the night. Remember. The Chief Whip and the Prime Minister would like her in Barset by the weekend.'

'Today's Tuesday.'

'Yes, I know that, Hugh. Now, off you go.'

Lighthorne got up to leave but hesitated on the threshold, straightening his yellow tie and adjusting the yellow handkerchief in his breast pocket. 'Yes?' the Chief Whip looked up from her papers.

'You don't happen to have her number do you?'

At that moment Natalia reappeared, her apparently-endless legs looking luscious to all those present, with a slip of paper which she handed to Lighthorne without a word. 'Thanks, Natty,' he said with a smile he liked to think of as winning and followed her out of the room.

'My God how much longer do we have to put up with him, Amelia?'

The two women sat in silence for a moment sipping their coffees. They had worked hard to make it to this uncomfortable little office just across the corridor from the Prime Minister's Commons sanctuary. But while Harriet Standing had been brought up fighting battles with argumentative Conservative councillors on her local authority in the North West of England, Amelia Browning was not used to meeting bad temper, ill-discipline, argument or intrigue. Amelia expected everybody to love her and do what she wanted them to do. It had always worked in the past. It worked when she was secretary in her husband's screw-and-fasteners business and it worked with her local constituency association. It worked with the voters and it seemed to work with the Prime Minister. But it didn't always work with her colleagues. Harriet didn't make it easy for her; in fact, Harriet seemed to go out of her way to make life difficult sometimes. But Amelia knew she had the confidence of the Prime Minister and that was all she needed. For now, at any rate.

That and some tactic for dealing with Acton Trussell.

As if reading her thoughts, Harriet fixed her over the rim of her coffee cup and asked with that pleasant smile of hers: 'So, how are you going to handle Trussell?'

'Well, I thought you might like to do the talking, Harriet.'

'I'm not really sure that's my role, Chief Whip. I think an issue like this needs the full authority of the most senior Minister, the Cabinet Minister. Someone in his own party.' Harriet smiled again. Amelia could see the red lipstick stain on the other woman's mug. She noted that Harriet's nail varnish was chipped and flaking.

'We're all in it together,' Mrs Browning joked, adding with a sigh, 'Well if I must, I suppose, only I thought maybe it would be better to keep me in reserve. A second line of defence, Derek would call it.'

'How is Derek?'

'Golfing in Portugal. What do you think our tactics should be?'

'Perhaps we should just play it by ear.'

Very helpful, thought Mrs Browning, as she agreed to the suggestion and turned to the second reading of the EU Integration (Amendment) Bill which was coming up later in the day.

*****

Acton Trussell was late. He walked across Hyde Park enjoying the London light. He had read 'The Times' and checked if there was anything in it about him. He had hidden behind the gents like a gay politician looking for rough-trade as he snaffled up another no-label cigarette, keeping a furtive eye out for the park police, then he finally forced himself to march on in the direction of the Palace of Westminster.

Even now, he relished all that pomp and circumstance as he walked through the members' gates past the concrete tank traps and machine-gun-toting police officers, through the metal detectors and the inevitable frisking by tough female coppers.

He reached the Chief Whip's outer office where Natalia and her older secretarial companion, Tina Bell, were dismantling the printer as usual. Mrs Bell looked up, recognised the MP for Barset, greeted him cheerfully and went off to inform Amelia Browning of his arrival. Mrs Bell had always rather liked Acton Trussell; she certainly didn't enjoy working for Mrs Browning.

Mrs Bell smiled pityingly as she led Acton into the office. Amelia sat behind her melamine desk. She did not move towards the sofas where most meetings took place. Harriet Standing was looking out of the window at the traffic going over Westminster Bridge.

Acton held out a hand to greet Mrs Browning. She did not acknowledge this gesture but continued to look at him. She did not offer him a seat but he took one anyway. 'Morning Hattie,' he said, surprisingly cheerfully. She turned, smiled weakly, muttered a good morning and took up position on a seat at right angles to the other two.

'Acton, you know why we have convened this meeting,' the Chief Whip began. 'I won't beat about the bush. You've been in this game long enough. You know the score. The way things have to be.'

Acton did not react. He neither nodded nor murmured. He smiled slightly and studied the back of his left hand. There was an awkward silence.

'We are pretty sure this story will hit the papers any moment and we need to be prepared for it. Or, indeed, act in advance. Damage-limitation, you understand.'

Pause.

'Acton?'

'I was just wondering, Amelia.'

'Wondering what?'

'How many clichés you would use. The count is six so far, if you can call "convened this meeting" a cliché. I'm not sure, it may just be a figure of speech. If I give you the benefit of the doubt, it's only five. Still, in two sentences that's an impressive score. Well done, Amelia. By the way, where's the Party chairman? Or do I mean chair?'

She sighed. Harried Standing shifted in her upright chair, which creaked. A phone rang in the outer office. Another pause in the proceedings.

'Very well. Cutting to the chase…'

'Six. Did you know, by the way, that "cutting to the chase" is a Hollywood expression? It relates to deleting the boring bits from a film so the director "cuts to the chase", chase scenes being *de rigueur* in crime films.'

Angela Browning sighed. 'Cutting to the chase,' she said, 'The Prime Minister, the party chairman and their senior colleagues believe your behaviour to be unacceptable. They require your resignation forthwith.'

'Resignation? From the party?'

'From the House of Commons.'

Acton Trussell laughed. It was a growl of a laugh. Not entirely bitter; partly incredulous.

'If you were to see that this is the only real option, the party would be willing to do everything in its power to protect you in the subsequent days.'

'Protect me? From what, exactly?'

'From the adverse reaction your behaviour will engender in the voting public. Not to mention the media. And even in the police.'

'Ah so it *is* blackmail,' Acton said. 'There isn't any adverse publicity yet because you have made sure there isn't. And there won't be any if I co-operate. Is that it? Blackmail, pure and simple. Bugger off and you escape the full glare of media publicity but if you don't accept our offer then we throw you to the wolves. That's it, isn't it?'

There was another silence broken eventually by Harriet Standing, employing her pleading primary-school teacher's voice. 'It's not blackmail really, Acton. I can see you're taking it badly and maybe you need time to think about it a little before you decide. But you know there's nothing we can do to help you if you tie our hands.'

Acton was surprised how calm he felt. Somewhere in the back of his mind he had the feeling he still had a trump card but he couldn't work out what it was or how to play it. For the time being, the best thing was to say little and do less.

'Of course,' the Chief Whip resumed, leaning forwards across her big desk, for emphasis, 'The fall-out could be very nasty. Criminal proceedings might be involved. It would be tragic if your eminent career ended in ignominy. And, of course, a Member of Parliament who is debarred as a result of criminal activity loses all his rights and privileges – including his pension. Which, at your age and with your many years of service, would add up to a tidy sum of money. Never mind your own pride, think of Clarissa, Acton. Think of Clarissa.'

'I am thinking of her. Thank you, Chief whip, for your valuable advice.'

'When can we expect to hear from you again, Acton? We really cannot wait.'

He got up to leave. He looked at Harriet Standing, who looked up at him with an apologetic smile and a slight shrug of her shoulders. He looked down at Amelia Browning. 'Never glad confident morning again,' he said.

'What was that, Acton?' She looked up, confused.

'"Never glad confident morning again," I said. You should know it, Amelia. It's by Robert Browning. Your ancestor. Supposedly.'

*****

Clarissa was at home when Acton rang. She was arranging the roses she had brought in from the garden, rescuing a few blooms from the heavy summer rains. She needed cheering up. The dog had been sick, her mother was no better, and her daughter Olivia's car had broken down somewhere the other side of Bristol and she was somehow expected to do something about it. They'd had a bit of a row.

Acton asked how things were and she told him. It took her longer than he had expected. Eventually she asked how he was and he described, briefly, his interview with the Chief Whip and her deputy.

'These bloody interfering women,' was Clarissa's first reaction, followed by a simple question: 'What is it you've done wrong, Acton? Why do they think you can't survive? You haven't been having an affair, have you?'

He laughed. 'I wish I had been, dear.'

Clarissa did not laugh. 'Actually Acton, you are too old, too fat and too slow all round to be attractive to anyone. I only stick with you because, like Hilda, nobody else would want you and I feel sorry for you.'

She said this regularly. He laughed again. 'Woof! Woof!'

'Oh for goodness' sake, Acton, I'm in no mood for your idiocies today. Haven't I explained that already? Now just tell me. What is going on?'

At that moment, the front door bell rang. Clarissa, who was still holding some roses in one hand, placed them carefully on the draining board, wiped her hands on a towel and strode off to the great oak door to answer it while her husband wittered away. She wasn't really listening. Hilda was getting under her feet, the Hoover (actually the Dyson) was still on the hall floor where she had half-heartedly been cleaning, and the bell was clanging again with an annoying impatience. She threw open the door to discover a smiling old lady with a large bunch of flowers wrapped in old newspaper. It was Mrs Collumpton, the old biddy from down the road, come about her sweet peas. She would be wanting a tour of the garden and, to Clarissa, this was preferable to listening to Acton droan on about meeting the Chief Whip.

'Hold on a moment, Mrs Collumpton. No, not you Acton, except yes, actually, you Acton. Mrs Collumpton's here about the sweet peas – they are lovely – so I will have to go. If you want to resign, dear, resign; if you don't, tell them to bugger off. You what? Sorry, I didn't catch that, darling. Say that again. You think you'll force a by-election. Say sod the lot of 'em? Is that it? Yes. Yes. Sleep on it. Yes. Bye.'

Acton Trussell was sitting in his poky office overlooking a concrete wall, a place he had been allocated some years ago and not bothered to argue over. He reasoned that the less time he spent in the office the better he was doing his job, therefore an office with no view at all and almost no natural light would deter him from sitting in it and force him to work quickly and effectively. Most of his colleagues, and his succession of bewildered secretaries, thought this was nonsense and fought tooth and nail for larger and more impressive accommodation. But it suited Acton. It was a useful hidey-hole. Nobody disturbed him, least of all his secretary, Polly, who he shared with a colleague and who only ever worked for him if she was specifically asked to do something, though he paid half her salary.

She wouldn't want him to go. Nobody else would give her such an easy life. But that can't be helped, he thought.

He sat in front of a plain sheet of House of Commons notepaper and scribbled his signature a few times, as if he were a schoolboy. He stared at the blank concrete, idly wondering why some patches were damper than others. He stood up and squinted into the small mirror hanging on the back of the door. It was a depressing sight: thinning hair, thick double chin, chubby cheeks with the typical ruddiness you expect of 'knights of the shires'. No wonder people think I'm a bumbling old fool, he thought, examining the bags under his eyes. He was past his sell-by date; the time had come to throw in the towel.

But what about a final farewell performance? Surely he couldn't go without a swansong. Maybe that was the thing to do – go out in a blaze of glory. An act of defiance. A show of, well, not exactly force, but at least independence. Integrity. Something.

A curious feeling was swelling up in his overweight frame. Acton felt bold and even angry. What was the point of being an MP if your only mark on the entire fabric of the nation was to have been one of those hundreds who loyally trooped through the voting lobby whenever your party told you to and whose greatest achievement had been to introduce legislation keeping the streets more free of chewing gum? It wasn't much for over 30 years as one of the nation's legislators.

Perhaps he should make a farewell speech. Perhaps he should. But would it be before, or after, he responded to the Chief Whip? Before. Bugger her. She could find out at the same time as everyone else.

So when should it be, he wondered? Well, no time like the present, he thought, why not?

Acton Trussell took one more look at his old, sagging face, stuck out his tongue to examine the orange film left by his recent cup of tea, gurned to emphasise his ugliness and turned to look at the TV monitor on the wall. The House was debating EU truck legislation. Could he twist a resignation speech into a debate about congestion charging for foreign lorries? Of course he could. He straightened his tie and set off with a purposeful stride for the debating chamber of the House of Commons. On the way, he saw his secretary Polly and her other boss, Carl Marsh. 'Carl, Polly, you must be the first to know. I hope to catch the Speaker's eye. I have something to say.'

Marsh, a young and ambitious backbencher, was sprawled out over his leather swivel chair while Polly sat on a corner of his desk with a notebook in her hand. They smiled vaguely at him as he swept though. 'Anything interesting?' Marsh called after him.

'Resignation,' he called back over his shoulder.

Marsh sat up immediately, calculating. He called the deputy chief whip. 'Harriet, Trussell. Chamber. Five minutes.'

The green leather benches of the House of Commons were, as usual, almost entirely unoccupied. This was a dull debate on a subject which would win no headlines. The Minister, a Liberal Democrat, sat in front of the despatch box looking through his typewritten speech and underlining a word here or there. A colleague sat behind him looking bored and scratching his arm. Two civil servants sat in a box behind the Speaker's chair waiting to issue urgent instructions to the Minister if someone asked a difficult question.

A couple of MPs sat on the Opposition benches. One seemed to be asleep while the other looked as if he were doing a newspaper crossword.

Trussell found his usual place almost as far from the Speaker's chair and the centre of the action as he could get, on the left of the entrance, three rows back. He had the bench to himself and sat ready to leap up and "catch the Speaker's eye" as soon as the fool on his feet had finished droning on about tonnage, something apparently called the "Eurovignette rules" and whether they should apply to vehicles of 3.5 tonnes.

It was an archaic system, having to catch the Speaker's eye. But it shouldn't be too difficult, he considered, given that there was scarcely anyone else in the Chamber.

The droning Labour MP announced he was turning to a discussion of one of the main A roads in his constituency.

There were four people in the public gallery, almost certainly road industry lobbyists, and two in the press gallery. He recognised the man from "The Times". The other would probably turn out to be from a trade publication concerned with lorries.

There was a flurry of activity behind the Speaker's chair and Hugh Lighthorne bustled in from the Whip's office, stared about him, caught sight of his quarry and sidled towards Acton Trussell. Carl Marsh arrived shortly afterwards and took up position close to the Minister. A couple of other MPs drifted in. Then an Opposition MP or two. Word had got out that something interesting was about to happen yet, in the press gallery, the man from "The Times" departed, leaving the field open to a young woman from the trade press.

The Speaker, Ms Petula Cross, stirred from her somnolence and raised an eyelid in the direction of the Minister who was, unlike everyone else in the Chamber, preoccupied with the debate and failed to register her significant eyebrow.

The Labour MP ground to a halt. There was a pause. The debate had run its course but there was still some time to go and the Minister was expected to rise to his feet and pad it out for another 25 minutes or so. He was too slow. Acton Trussell got there first and, waving a piece of paper in front of him to ensure the Speaker saw him, he called out 'Madam Speaker' in a clear, firm voice, expecting her to invite him to speak.

But she did not. She gazed benevolently on Grant Hassleman, the junior Transport Minister, as he tried to sort out his bits of paper and called out, 'Mister Hassleman...'

There was a further pause as he crouched forward, tried to lift his papers to the dispatch box in front of him and saw several sheets flutter gently to the floor.

'Madam Speaker...' cried Acton impatiently.

'Mister Trussell, I am afraid I have already called the Minister to reply to this debate. MPs who wish to contribute to debates of this nature know very well it is courteous, to say the very least, to make the effort to attend the whole debate rather than arriving at the last minute and expecting to be given a hearing.'

'But Madam Speaker...'

'No, Mr Trussell. Minister.'

Finally Hassleman was ready. He looked up at his benefactor and told her how grateful he was before going on to outline why the EU truck legislation, while technically an imposition on the UK and therefore, arguably, in theory, a diminution of British sovereignty, was in reality nothing of the sort.

'Oh hard luck, Acton,' Lighthorne whispered to him before scuttling off to inform his boss that nothing of any interest had occurred.

Acton felt honour bound to sit out the rest of the debate and even vote for the Government motion. When it was over, he stood at the Members' Entrance to the House of Commons wondering whether to press the bell to summon a taxi and wondering where he would want it to take him. Before he could decide, the young woman from the Press Gallery approached him. She introduced herself as Sophie Hicks and asked if he could tell her anything more about his planned intervention in the debate. He ended up accepting her invitation for a quick glass of Chardonnay.

*****

"Unfortunately I am not sure I have anything interesting to say about lorries at all," Acton told the young woman.

"You certainly looked as if you wanted to say something, Mr Trussell."

"Yes I did." Acton thought a moment. He wasn't born yesterday. He knew a young and pretty reporter was not buying him late-night drinks in the hope of sleeping with him. Those days were long gone. "You're looking for a story, aren't you?"

"That's what journalists do, Mr Trussell."

"Ah but can I trust you?" She tried to answer but he replied for her. "Of course not. You're a journalist. You want a story and you don't realty care where it comes from, what it's about or who is involved."

Sophie frowned and her dangling gold-coloured ear-rings shook wildly with her. "Oh really, Mr Trussell. We're not all unprincipled bastards, you know."

"Yes you are and you are no different. I do not complain and I am making no accusations. It's what makes you want to become a journalist in the first place – power without responsibility, the prerogative of the harlot throughout the ages."

"Yes, I've heard that before. I've always thought it over-estimated the value of prostitution."

"Well, I know I can't trust you. But I also know you are no more untrustworthy than your contemporaries. And you are far better looking. The truth is that I was going to announce my resignation."

Now he had her attention. She was scrabbling for her notebook and pen. "Your resignation? As an MP?"

"Yes, I'm afraid so."

"Why? When? Oh my God, won't there have to be a by-election? Who else knows?" She couldn't keep anxiety out of her voice.

"Nobody, not even my wife."

"So?"

Speaking at dictation speed, Acton went on: "It would appear the party requires my seat in parliament for one of its favoured friends. It has been put to me in very clear terms that my own political career is, to all intents and purposes, at an end. There is a pretext for this abandonment but nobody has had the courtesy to explain to me what it is I am supposed to have done wrong. However, it has been made clear to me that my best, indeed my only, course of action is to resign. That is blackmail and while I would usually refuse to submit to blackmail, I have decided to call their bluff. If I am to be held to ransom by my own party then I say 'publish and be damned'. I don't want anything more to do with any of you. Damn the lot of them."

"Can't you give me some idea what you're resigning about."

"I am being forced out by that dreadful woman the Chief Whip and her cronies."

There was a pause. Acton finished his wine and started looking for his briefcase. Sophie was desperate to get away and call the "Daily Mail" newsdesk but didn't want to be too rude about making a hasty escape.

"I suppose I shouldn't have said 'dreadful woman and her cronies' should I? Never mind. I'm off home for some whisky and a good night's sleep." He shook Sophie's hand and threaded his way towards the door.

Chapter 4

'Bloody beautiful. Can't be bothered to do anything but am checking e-mails while Joanna's off doing whatever it is boys do when they get bored in the sunshine.' Lucy hit send.

She was sitting cross-legged on a sun lounger, smoking a cigarette on the veranda of what the website called her "Indian Ocean holiday paradise". Actually, it was quite nice. Joanna was somewhere out in the sandy blue waters snorkelling. Lucy began a second reply to her brother's question asking if she was having fun: 'Can't find anything about this alleged scandal. What's he supposed to have done? Is it in the news? Not on the BBC web-site or the "Daily Telegraph" or even the "Barset Chronicle" where they have a pic of him beaming at the local rugby club. What's he done? What by-election? Whatwhatwhatwhatwhat???'

It was early but Robin was already at work dealing with Hong Kong. He replied: 'Still no news but let's just say I know. If I had shares in Trussells I'd be off-loading them as fast as I could. BTW you ARE a paid-up member of the party aren't you?'

'Course I am. Gave Ken and Shel a grand this year. Am a councillor you know. Anyway, tell me tell me tell me tell me now.'

'Don't know what he's done. Just that he's in trouble. It's all going to hit the fan.'

'Compton?'

'Compton.'

'Phew, hot. Am swimming.'

Lucy looked out Compton Dundon's e-mail address. She decided not to use his official work address. This wasn't for party headquarters. This was private. Really very private.

'Compton my darling. What's this about an impending by-election? BTW when are you coming to Devon with us again? You know how much Joanna misses your cooking??????'

Then she sent another e-mail. This time to her Uncle Richard in Barset: 'Rich, how are you? Joanna and I were thinking of coming over to visit you in a couple of weeks' time. Are you around?'

And a third: 'Cherry, greetings from Goa. Hope the office is quiet. Could you do some discreet investigating for me? I need to know all there is to know about Barset. My Uncle Richard has a business deal that may or may not come to something and I need as much info as poss. Also check out the MP. What do we know about him? This is just research – don't kick down any doors.'

Then Lucy went for a swim.

*****

'"That dreadful woman".' Amelia Browning frowned. '"That dreadful woman".' She tried the sound of it again.

'"And her cronies",' added Harriet Standing.

'Ah well. Now, has that idiot Lighthorne got hold of Lucy Loxley?'

The view in Howard Michael was similarly matter-of-fact.

'Acton,' Clarissa called down the phone to her husband. 'Is this right, what it says here?'

'Yes, dear.'

'Good. About time too.'

'You're not cross?'

'Why should I be cross? Those people have had it in for you ever since you turned down their knighthood. About time too if you ask me. But you haven't been filmed with some little totty have you Acton? That's not it, is it?'

There was an element of menace in Clarissa's voice. A tone he recognised and was wary of. 'No dear, of course not. I'm far too old for that sort of thing.'

'With your wife, maybe. But I know these young women…'

'Well the answer is still no. Unless they've dug something up from the 1960s which I rather doubt.'

'So what is it they've got on you, Acton?'

'I dare say we will find out today. That's all the hacks want to know about. That and when the by-election's going to be and who's being lined up for my job. I haven't actually resigned yet.'

'The King is dead….'

'…long live the King. Yes, I know. Has Clifford Chambers been on the phone yet?'

Clifford Chambers was in his bedroom busily dispatching e-mails to his contacts. As chairman of the constituency association, Clifford would come into his own. He would be in charge of the selection process and then run the election campaign. Victory was not in doubt. The Government was still popular, everyone loved The Leader, it was a safe seat made doubly secure thanks to the electoral pact with the Liberal Democrats which meant the two parties would not fight each other in seats they already held. The only difficulty would be persuading people to turn out. But they were pretty loyal in Barset. It should be simple enough. What really counted was the candidate.

In his e-mail to the Chief Whip, copied to the party chairman, the party chief executive and to short, fat, gay Compton Dundon, Clifford wrote: 'We will hold a paper sift within six days of the resignation with a view to two rounds of the selection process within a fortnight of that date and therefore the appointment of the candidate within three weeks of the resignation. If you have any special instructions, please feel free to contact me…'

In an e-mail to Chatham Smith, he wrote: 'As you will know, a generous donation towards the campaign fund would be most welcome at this time. Our coffers are low and we intend to fight a vigorous campaign on the record of our Government. Of course, Chatham, the party will be grateful for any support you may be able to offer. We estimate it will require £100,000 to secure victory.'

He said much the same in an e-mail to Hampton Arden. And to Morton Morrell. But to Maggie Pride he wrote: 'Mags, this is your chance…. Throw your hat into the ring. You know you have my backing. Meet later…'

Robin Loxley was in his office overlooking Canary Wharf watching a barge of some description move slowly up-river while a stream of worker ants emerged from the station. 'Get your arse down there this second, Luce,' he ordered. 'This is it. We need to secure you the nomination. I'll call Dick.'

The Prime Minister's personal, private mobile phone number was known to very few people. It was changed every ten days. Nobody except his wife was given the new number. It was astonishing how quickly news spread, though. Loxley had a number that was already six phones out of date. He tried and failed to contact the Prime Minister several times during the next 24 hours. His boast that he had a hot-line to Downing Street was not something he was willing to abandon without a struggle.

Meanwhile, Acton Trussell was persuaded to turn out on Westminster Green, the piece of grass round the corner from the Commons and next to the Abbey which was traditionally the hunting ground for TV crews and gawping tourists.

They all insisted on having their own reporter ask the same questions in order to broadcast the same sound-bites in the same way at the same time. More did not mean better, Acton reflected to himself as he was manhandled by production assistants and made to wait until the Danish team had finished doing their report on fish quota negotiations.

'No, I do not regret calling the Chief Whip a dreadful woman. She is a woman and she is dreadful. I do not accept that there is anything remotely sexist or old-fashioned about it,' Trussell explained. Yet again. 'If she is offended then I am delighted. I did not mean to be polite towards her. Or her cronies. They are a coven. And I am delighted to be rid of them. I shall apply for the Stewardship of the Manor of Northstead today and, hopefully, I shall leave this place for the last time tomorrow.'

They all asked the same question: 'Why are you resigning, Mr Trussell? Surely it's not just because you and the Chief Whip don't like each other?'

'They want me out,' he replied and, in response to the next question, added: 'My face and philosophies no longer fit. I am too old and too old-fashioned. I have gone way past my sell-by date and they made that very plain.'

'And why not wait until the next election? What will you do now?'

'Why wait? As for what I shall do now, I dare say I shall do what most retired men do which is prune the roses, mow the grass and learn to play golf.' And with that he would smile brightly, as if the prospect promised hope, freedom and satisfaction.

'But was there something specific which prompted your resignation?'

'A smoking gun?' Acton would smile at the idea.

'That sort of thing, yes?'

'I think you will have to ask the Chief Whip that question.'

Soon the TV crews had their two minutes' worth of Acton Trussell and he was free to go. He wandered slowly towards Pugin's magnificent neo-Gothic mausoleum of a Parliament building, admiring yet again its intricate stonework and regretting yet again the concrete lumps all round it to keep out suicide bombers. Big Ben struck the hour. Some of Trussell's colleagues were scurrying to work. It was a Wednesday – Prime Minister's Questions. Some of them were vain and ambitious enough to think they could make their mark, gain promotion or even solve the world's woes with an appropriately framed question. They were hoping to come close to the top of the list of those who could be called. They were rushing in to rehearse their spontaneous quips.

Acton walked alone. Several MPs he knew quite well passed him. At pace. Feigning haste. They had no wish to stop and talk to a marked man. In the Commons, disgrace is contagious. Even old Stringer – whose by-election victory Acton himself had engineered in his younger days – passed by on the other side of the corridor with nothing but a curt nod of acknowledgement.

Trussell went in search of newspapers and a late breakfast. The thing to do was behave normally. Don't even look at the "Daily Mail". Avoid reporters. Talk to friends. If there were any, which there were not.

In the central lobby of the House, with its little Post Office and its corridors going west to the Lords and east to the Commons, Acton Trussell bumped into a puffing young man in a black T-shirt carrying a large box of papers.

'Mr Trussell, Mr Trussell, thank God. Thank God.' The T-shirt was clean and newly-pressed. The youth was surprisingly sweaty for such a cool morning.

'Mr Trussell. I'm Aston Cantlow. I live in Barset. I'm a technology adviser. We met last summer at the symposium.'

Trussell had no idea what symposium that might have been. He immediately slipped into his "constituency MP" persona, grinned falsely, stuck his hand out and said, 'Yes, of course, delighted to meet you.'

Aston Cantlow was unable to offer his hand to shake without risk to the box file he was clutching to his chest. Acton realised the difficulty. They nodded at each other instead. Paused. Trussell did not want a conversation with a fat, spotty youth clutching what would almost certainly be computer print-outs with complicated calculations proving the existence of UFOs. 'I'm a bit busy this morning.'

'That's why I'm here. I have something for you.' The youth plonked the box down on the decorated stone floor of the lobby and opened its over-stuffed lid. He started rummaging through the papers inside. Acton noticed his T-shirt. It displayed a picture of a knight on horseback slaying a dragon which was threatening a young woman with unfeasibly prominent breasts who had been tied to a tree by someone, presumably not the heroic knight. The shirt had a prominent slogan: 'The Knights of St George' on the front and 'For Freedom' on the back.

'You need to see this,' the youth announced, holding up a home-made DVD as if it were Excalibur emerging from the lake.

'What is it?' Trussell asked.

'The smoking gun.'

*****

Clifford Chambers, who had donned an especially flamboyant red bow tie for the occasion, was presiding over lunch. Or, actually 'a' lunch. Lunch is something you eat, 'a lunch' is a meeting with food. You don't really care about the food or drink at 'a lunch', though it is often over-priced and it is possible to consume too much of both without noticing. What matters is the usefulness of your guests. You don't invite them because you are interested in them, their lives, their families or the state of their health. You invite them because they will be useful to you. And they accept because you will be useful to them. There's no such thing as a free lunch and everybody knows it.

Clifford was in Barset's newest and most empty Italian restaurant. It had enormous glasses with small splashes of house red in them. It had knives and forks which would not lie flat. It had sea salt in glass containers but no pepper because that would, in due course, be flamboyantly ground out from a two-foot-long pot. The lights were bright, the windows wide, the furniture velour, purple and uncomfortable.

On Clifford's left sat Newbold Whitnash, editor of the "Barset Chronicle". Newbold was a rotund man in his mid-30s. His hands were so podgy they felt like dough when Clifford shook one of them. He wore a sports jacket, grey trousers, black shoes but no tie. A red handkerchief disported itself from his breast pocket. He was known in Barset as an intellectual. Chambers assumed Whitnash would be picking up the bill for lunch because he could reclaim it on expenses. Whitnash assumed he was Clifford's guest and was not used to paying for anything, expenses or otherwise.

Opposite Clifford was Chatham Smith, who arrived late and planned to go early. He was a busy man. Smith wore an immaculate suit and a pastel-shaded but very expensive tie. He was getting on these days but his blond hair was still thick and gave him a youthful look enhanced by his recently-acquired tan from sailing in the Mediterranean. He was there because he needed to know how much money Chambers wanted from him. He knew it would be substantial but he didn't mind. What he really wanted was some kind of undertaking about a knighthood. Unfortunately, now he had seen his fellow guests, it was clear this lunch would not provide him with any answers or reassurances. He was irritated at this waste of time and constantly consulted his Zombiefone, which had recently been put on the market by one of his companies.

The reason Chambers wanted his money sat beside him. Maggie was loudly but somewhat shabbily dressed in a pair of black trousers, low heels, a turquoise jumper and a purple jacket which didn't go. Chambers noted that he would have to take her to task for looking slovenly. She needed to sharpen up.

'Anyway, Chatham,' Maggie was saying, 'The by-election won't happen for weeks yet. There's the summer. They never call by-elections in the summer.'

'Ah yes,' Whitnash interrupted, wiping his face with his napkin as he chomped his steak, 'But that was BD.'

'BD?' Clifford conveniently asked.

'Before Dick. Now we're all democratic and responsive and localised. So you can't leave a constituency without its official social worker and spokeswoman.'

'True,' said Chambers. 'All the more reason why we need to get on with the selection process, eh Mags?'

'I suppose so.' She was excited and couldn't sit still. Since she gave up show-business and had babies, Maggie had lost her suppleness and gained weight. She needed something to do. She thought becoming an MP could be the just the thing. 'I'm not sure how up-front to be about it. Should I admit to this as an ambition and openly campaign? Or should I be more restrained? A bit more like 'I couldn't, I couldn't... Well, if you insist'?'

'Up front,' said Whitnash.

'You need to make the people who matter know what's going on, Mags. That way they're primed and ready. I'll introduce you to them. Though of course the two most important people you need to meet are already here. The editor of the "Barset Chronicle" and the town's leading industrialist, who also happens to be the party's biggest supporter.'

Chatham Smith smiled wanly and looked at Maggie. 'It's not people like me you have to win over, Maggie,' he said.

'No,' added Whitnash. 'As I said in today's leader, Barset needs a new kind of politician for a new era. Someone who is committed to re-inventing Barset and making it fit for the 21st century. Someone with enterprise and compassion, someone with hope and realism, someone with boldness and caution, someone with the same vision as the Prime Minister himself. A vision for Barset.'

Chambers nodded. 'Yes, indeed. A vision for Barset.'

'Well, I have lived here for seven years,' said Maggie. 'And in that time I have helped build the music festival into a must-see event in the regional calendar. Now we must take the town and place it on the national, and indeed, the international map. Barset must take its rightful place on the world stage. We can achieve that through events like the music festival. But I would like to see so much more than that.'

'Why don't you write an article "My Vision" for the "Chronic", Mags? I'm sure Newbold would be happy to publish it. Wouldn't you, Newbold?'

The editor had his mouth full of potato. That did not prevent him spluttering an enthusiastic response. 'We need vision, definitely. Vision for the future. But if you're going to give us your vision, Maggie, you need to tell us what you would do with the Rec, the castle grounds and the riverside walk. You should also address the question of the motorway toll road and, of course, the industrial park.'

Everyone looked at Chatham, who was fiddling with his Zombiefone and not eating much. He had heard this, he just didn't want to comment but there was an expectant hush. 'Sorry?' he said.

'Newbold was saying Maggie should have a vision for Barset which includes her vision for the industrial park.'

'Ah yes,' said Chatham. Everyone knew he owned the industrial park. They also knew he had a plan in hand to re-develop it into an eco-town. He couldn't see why anyone would object, especially as most of the industrial units were run-down, neglected and empty. An eco-town would bring a new lease of life and new jobs to the area. Yet objectors had lined up against it and so had the local paper.

'Well, perhaps we should not mix politics and business over lunch,' said Chambers, trying to head off any unpleasantness. He didn't like unpleasantness. He found it bad for the digestion. Almost as bad as spilling sauce on his bow tie, which was why he ate with his napkin tucked into his collar.

Maggie wanted to tell him he looked like her seven-year-old but she didn't want to risk offending her patron.

'Well I suppose we do need a candidate,' Chatham said, looking particularly at Clifford, 'Who acknowledges the benefits that the eco-town will bring to Barset. I am sorry, Newbold, that the "Chronic" is not prepared to see which side its bread is buttered. I can't understand why anyone would want to cling onto a run-down industrial estate dating back to the 1950s. I dare say whoever we select will have enough good sense to realise what's best for the town.' He let this sink in before adding, as he turned back to the Zombiefone, 'Just like poor old Acton did.'

*****

Acton Trussell knew what he had to do, he just couldn't bring himself to do it. To resign from parliament, officially and for all time, he had to go through one of those bizarre old rituals which make the British political system inexplicable to everyone outside Westminster and cherished even by the most left-wing firebrands once they have been caught in its Byzantine mysteries. As he had to explain to Polly, who was most put out by his decision, MPs were not allowed to dash off a furious letter of resignation and walk away. They hadn't been allowed to do that since March 1623 and no exception would be made for the MP for Barset. He had to apply for 'an office of profit under the Crown'.

This led, unavoidably and inevitably, to an interview with the Chancellor of the Exchequer, Bud Brooke. Apart from his first name, which Acton thought ostentatiously American – the man's real Christian name was Bernard but he had decreed it to be excessively patrician – he disliked the Chancellor because he was only 33 years old, had never held a 'proper' job in his life, had inherited a fortune from his mother's brewery and refused to cut taxes which, in Acton's mind, is the only job of a proper Tory Chancellor.

By convention, Acton had to call Bud Brooke's office, explain his intention and arrange for a personal meeting with the youth. Acton thought the system absurd. If you wanted to resign, you should be allowed to do so. Other people walked out of their jobs all the time, why did MPs think themselves so special? It was the only escape, though.

He thought of the DVD that scruffy youth had thrust into his hands. He wondered if he should have a look at it. What had that fellow Cantlow called it? 'The smoking gun'. Ah yes, I suppose so… He slipped it into the DVD drive.

'Acton, can I have your desk?' Carl Marsh asked as the phone started to ring.

'Acton, what shall I do with these letters?' asked Polly, the secretary he shared with Marsh, adding, 'I suppose I'll have to start looking for someone else for the extra hours now, won't I?'

The phone was ringing. Acton heard Clifford Chambers asking how he could possibly have left the party in the lurch and plunged the constituency association into an unwanted by-election it could ill-afford.

Acton put the phone down without responding to his old friend's pompous son. He said, 'I don't really mind' to both Marsh and Polly.

Acton dialled Bud Brooke's office and asked if he could speak to the Chancellor of the Exchequer. Acton explained who he was and what he wanted. He repeated himself several times as his call was passed up the chain closer to the seat of power. Eventually he was told the Chancellor was in his constituency and would not be back before the weekend. Trussell said he couldn't wait that long. He would call Mr Brooke on his mobile phone if they would be kind enough to let him have the number. Brooke's secretary would do no such thing. She did think she might be able to get a message to the Chancellor asking him to call Mr Trussell in due course, if he liked. That was the best she could do unless he wanted to make an appointment to see the Chancellor next week. Wednesday morning at 7.15am was still free if he only needed a quarter of an hour. Trussell gave her his mobile phone number.

The call finally came through late in the afternoon as he was having a nap in what used to be the Members' smoking room at the House of Commons. Even then it wasn't the Chancellor in person. It was a disembodied voice asking Acton if he was, indeed, Mr Trussell and telling him to wait while she put him through to the Chancellor.

'Acton, how are you?' The Chancellor sounded cheery.

He should be, Acton thought, cosseted in his brand new hybrid Oxygenius limo with his chauffeur and his secretary being whisked from one important meeting to another. Jealous? Trussell wondered. Am I jealous? He dismissed the idea and launched into a protest: 'Bud, you might pick up the phone and dial the number yourself. Don't you know how bad mannered it is to get other people to make your calls for you?'

'Acton, what can I do for you?' Brooke replied cheerily.

'The Manor of Northstead.'

'You're applying? I had heard.'

'Had you?'

'Yes I had though I'm still not sure why. If I'm to grant you the stewardship, I think it's only right you tell me why you want it, don't you, Acton?'

'Not really, Buddy boy. Ask the Chief Whip.'

'She doesn't know.'

'What do you mean, she doesn't know? She summoned me.'

'Acton, she knows you've done something terrible but she doesn't know what. And you didn't actually tell her or admit to anything, did you? Apart from calling her an old harridan, of course.' The Chancellor chuckled pleasantly.

'Well, I await formal notification of my offence. But I do know everyone thinks it's a resignation issue. And, let's face it, you've been wanting to get rid of me for a long time now.'

'True, Acton, very true. We could do with your seat. Got a decent majority, haven't you? Anyway, have you got the paperwork for Northstead? Fax it over to the office, I'll sign it and they'll let you know when you are formally appointed and you are therefore no longer a Member of Parliament. We'll sort it out tomorrow, OK?'

The train home was unusually quiet. Acton Trussell finally turned on his laptop and decided to watch the DVD he had been given by the youth he bumped into in the Members' Lobby of the House of Commons. The machine was slow. It whirred and wheezed and eventually a picture appeared. Trussell watched it for a few moments. He chuckled.

Chapter 5

The summer monsoons had started. The harvest was flattened in the fields. Holidaymakers pretended they were not cold as they walked around in T-shirts and shorts. The crashing waves carried a few foolhardy and unsteady surfers towards the rocks.

Clifford Chambers and Maggie Pride had slipped away for the weekend. Her husband was on location for the BBC in the Niger delta. Maggie was enjoying a one-to-one political briefing from her constituency chairman. Chambers was carrying a map in a special case he had purchased on-line from Harrods.

They descended the cliff path beside The Bodens, a Victorian merchant's home now transformed into what was apparently known as a boutique hotel. Chambers had secured them rooms there – he had been at school with the under-manager. They marched down to Aga Point, with its spectacular sea views, and followed the cliff path high above Labrador Bay all the way to Trollop Head. The wind and rain whipped their faces furiously. Maggie wondered whether Clifford expected a reward for all this attention.

He'd driven her down to North Cornwall from Barset in his Audi Attractive. He insisted on paying for everything, even though this was a seriously expensive hotel. He booked separate rooms and registered each of them in their own names. He showed no signs of interest in her body or even, come to that, her mind. He was interested mainly in giving her the benefit of his opinions.

Maggie didn't mind. She liked cliff walks, even in monsoon weather. But she was shocked when they stopped in an old coastguard lookout hut to discover the building already housed two other people: Robin and Lucy Loxley.

Clifford knew them immediately. He had never met either but he had seen several pictures of Councillor Loxley on the internet, together with various articles describing her as the future for the party's lesbian tendency. He assumed, rightly, that she would not be out on her own with a man unless it was her brother. Clifford was also aware of Robin's reputation in the City and had been angling to meet him for some time. He liked rich people.

The coastguard's hut just about accommodated four people. It had a glassless window and the door was stuck ajar in the mud. The wind was loud but at least the hut was dry.

The Loxleys, dressed in expensive but worn walking gear, were taking a breather. They were about to head off again into the wet but politely stood aside to allow Chambers and Maggie inside. Clifford was too quick for them.

'Lucy Loxley!' he exclaimed. 'And this must be the famous Robin Loxley. Clifford Chambers and this is Maggie Pride. Maggie's a dancer.'

'A very ex-dancer.'

'Ah, Chambers. I know that name,' said Robin.

'Ex?' asked Lucy.

'Yes, I gave it up some time ago now. It's a young woman's art, I'm afraid.'

'Do you?' asked Chambers.

'Estate agency?' replied Robin.

'How clever of you.' Chambers was flattered.

'Barset?'

'Indeed.'

'Well, well.'

'What sort of dancing do you, did you do?'

'Oh very much contemporary.'

'She was in TnA,' Clifford interrupted with a laugh.

'TnA?'

'Yes, on "Rock Week". You know, the TV music show.'

'Oh God! TnA. Tits and Ass. Yes of course. God, I wanted to be a T and A dancer when I was a little girl. It looked such fun. Do you still keep in shape?'

'I try. And I am still involved in the arts.'

'Down here for a holiday, Mr Loxley?' asked Clifford Chambers.

'Robin. Yes. Just a couple of days. The family place over at St Bernard's.'

'Near Trenglower?'

'Trenglower House.'

'Of course.'

'What about you? How do you keep fit?' asked Maggie.

'Sex and holidays.' Lucy laughed.

'Sounds like the ideal combination.'

'Come on, Luce, let's get moving. By the way, Clifford. Can I call you Clifford? Why don't you come over for dinner? Lucy gets a bit bored when it's just the two of us down here for one of our long weekends. Too much walking, not enough talking, she usually says. Do come over and cheer her up. Both of you, of course. Can you get over tomorrow night? That would be marvellous.'

'Oh what a pity; we're going back to Barset tomorrow,' Maggie smiled apologetically at Lucy.

'Well I know *you* have to be back, Mags, but I could stay down another day or two I expect. I tell you what, Mags, I'll put you on the train at Bodmin tomorrow. You'll be back in Barset quicker than we can drive there. Then I can get over to Trenglower. Oh,' Clifford interrupted himself, suddenly aware of a snag in this plan, 'Assuming The Bodens has a room for tomorrow night.'

'Don't worry about that, old boy. Stay with us. Tell you what, clock in about tea-time. Be marvellous to see you. Wouldn't it Luce?'

'Lovely. Lovely. Well, bye then. See you tomorrow.'

'You know where Trenglower is, don't you Clifford? How to get there?'

'Doesn't everybody?' he grinned.

Chambers watched the Loxleys turn right out of the coastguard's hut and march into the wind, away from Labrador Bay in the direction of St Bernard's. Lucy was giggling.

'Well,' said Chambers, rubbing his hands together.

Only Maggie left the coastguard's hut feeling she was at a disadvantage. She couldn't work out how, or why, or what she had to complain of. Except Clifford's willingness to change his plans at her expense. Was that all? She didn't think so.

Back at the hotel, Maggie was confused. Was Clifford throwing her over for that Loxley woman or even for her brother? And was that political or personal, or both, or neither? She was just as confused about his intentions towards her. Why ask her away for a weekend and not take advantage of the situation? She wouldn't mind if he did – she'd not slept with a younger man before. He was quite good-looking in an old-fashioned way even if he was a bit pompous.

When she dressed for dinner, she decided on her sexy black lingerie just in case.

On the outside she wore a long, Indian-looking cotton dress in purple, with beads and bangles to match, and a bright pink shawl in case it was cold. Clifford wore a blazer and his yellow and red MCC bow tie, for all the world like an old colonel retired on half pay. All he needed was a moustache,

Maggie thought.

After dinner, he invited her up to his room 'for a night-cap'. Maggie had never before heard someone use the expression seriously and laughed before agreeing.

In room 204 with its high four-poster bed, chintzy furniture and what the brochure called a "side sea-view", which meant a clear view over the car park, across the tops of various houses and, in the corner, some cliffs and a bit of blue, Clifford produced a bottle of brandy and two tooth glasses. As he handed Maggie hers, he leaned in towards her, inhaling the perfume from her neck and declared: 'You smell good enough to eat.'

He kneeled at her feet, took her left hand in both of his, and began to kiss it. She watched him, mildly amused. He ran his lips, but not his tongue, she noticed, along her arm, and began on her neck. One hand was now sidling towards her breast. Nothing much was expected of her so Maggie closed her eyes and tried to persuade herself this was enjoyable.

What was she was doing there anyway? A younger man, an unexciting younger man at that. What would her children think? What would Doug think? Why was she doing this? She loved Doug, didn't she? Well, when he was at home, anyway. And he hardly ever was. Was she doing this to punish Doug?

She tried to concentrate on Clifford's explorations. It was all a bit half-hearted, she thought, especially as he hadn't actually tried to kiss her on the lips yet.

'Shall we?' Clifford asked, indicating the four-poster.

Maggie stepped back and sat down at the end of the bed. Clifford slowly removed her sandals and began kissing her legs. He stopped at the knees, stood up, carefully removed his jacket and bow tie, removed his shoes, which he placed neatly side by side at the foot of the bed, before throwing his socks with a devil-may-care flick into a far corner. He folded his trousers and placed them in the press, which he set to warm for 20 minutes, then returned to bed in his shirt and boxer shorts.

Maggie shuffled up to rest her head on the pillows and watched this performance with mild amusement. He was by no means urgent in his love-making.

Clifford eventually climbed up alongside her and resumed pecking around her shoulders. This went on a long while though Maggie tried to encourage him with mild moans to explore a little further.

His hand reached up inside her skirt and found its way towards her knickers. She tried to reciprocate but was stayed by his other hand firmly holding her wrist. Clifford began to grope inside her knickers and to moan. Maggie arched her back and opened her legs a little to confirm, if confirmation were needed, that he had no reason to hold back.

With his head on her breasts, Clifford concentrated his efforts on trying to please her but Maggie, for all her theoretical willingness, felt nothing.

Eventually Clifford sat up, having removed his hand from up her skirt, announcing, 'I'm sorry Maggie, it's just no good.'

She wanted to be sympathetic, motherly even. She thought maybe they should discuss it. But Clifford was already off the bed and heading for the bathroom with the words, 'I'm sorry, Maggie. It's not me, it's you. You have some kind of a smell, a scent, I don't know what to call it, an aroma. It put me off. You'll have to go.'

*****

Julian 'Stud' Lee was bass guitarist in The Wreckage when they were big in the Seventies. The band split up when the lead singer went into rehab and the keyboard player broke his neck jumping from the roof of the tour bus. Both these events occurred on the same tour of Japan in 1976.

Luckily, The Wreckage had no fewer than three classics and Julian had been credited as a co-writer of these songs though he could remember nothing about the composition of any of them. Even so, 'Yeah Babe', 'High Wire' and especially the worldwide mega-hit 'I Love You For Your Mind Not Your Body' – not to be confused with a different song with the same title which won minor airplay a couple of years later – with its distinctive guitar riff, secured the financial future for Julian Lee and bought him the leisure time to indulge his passion for fox hunting and actually learn to play the guitar.

Nobody called Lee by his Christian name. He abandoned that in his second year at public school in 1967. It was then he enjoyed the first two or three of his many female conquests and was awarded the nickname Stud by his drinking companions. He exploited this to the full during his days with The Wreckage, when he would appear on stage in his jodhpurs and riding crop and the groupies would queue up for a beating later.

Stud had been a friend of Acton Trussell's since the pair met back-stage at a Wreckage concert in 1972. Acton was an ambitious politician, a councillor with an active interest in noise pollution and had taken it upon himself to police the concert at Barset Free Trade Hall.

Somehow he'd been led into the band's changing room. Somehow Stud was both sober and women-free. The band wasn't due on stage for another two hours and while the others were ferociously consuming whatever came to hand – lager, chocolates, young women, LSD and so on – Stud and Acton embarked on a lengthy conversation about political revolutionaries.

By the time The Wreckage took to the stage, Councillor Trussell's concerns with noise pollution were a thing of the past. He was rocking in the wings with a young woman who was hanging around there and later joined the band in their hotel suite.

From that day on, Acton and Stud became firm, if unlikely, friends. Stud bought a farm in Acton's constituency and Acton often turned out to see off the hunt with Stud prominent in the party, a leading light in the countryside rebellion against the anti-hunting legislation. Indeed, Stud had managed the almost miraculous feat of re-forming The Wreckage for a one-off concert to raise money for the Countryside Alliance.

It had been a great success with fans and media and raised almost half a million pounds for the cause. But, as Stud and Acton agreed later, the magic had gone. Alf, the drummer, was almost an Alzheimer's case. Dave, the keyboardist, had kept himself well and looked every inch the elderly rock star. It was just a pity he'd been on bail at the time and was now serving seven years for various dubious sex offences. As for Rich 'Richie' Rich, the lead guitarist, lead singer and focal point of The Wreckage, well the sad truth was that he'd put on so much weight that his louche, dishevelled, dissolute, youthful innocence had been well and truly dissipated. His voice had more or less gone too – he certainly couldn't scream out the chorus of 'Mind Not Your Body' any more, or hit the high notes on 'High Wire', which was why the band needed the support of three young women in the chorus – much to Stud's delight.

When Acton called, Stud was in his drawing room gazing idly out of the window across his manicured lawns, over the ha-ha towards the park where his three favourite horses were grazing lazily in the declining light of a chilly July evening. Acton was in one of his Westminster pin-stripes; Stud was in jeans, a cowboy shirt and cowboy boots, as if the '70s had never ended. The drawing room was comfortable and old-fashioned with thick, squashy sofas, a big fireplace and portraits on the walls.

After they rapidly downed a gin and tonic each in companionable silence, Stud poured a second and led Acton onto the terrace where he proceeded to light two large cigars and hand one to his friend.

'So, tell me, Acton. Are you still an MP?'

'Resigned this afternoon. Applied for the Stewardship of the Manor of Northstead.'

'Wherever that may be. And?'

'And what?'

'And what now?'

Trussell was non-plussed. 'A quiet retirement, I suppose. Got enough to live off, just about. Not like an ageing rock star, obviously. But we'll get by.'

'Is that it then? Acton Trussell MP resigns mysteriously and goes off quietly to grow old and die?'

'I suppose it is, yes. Not much alternative, really. Celia's a bit taken up with her mother at the moment but she's had enough of politics anyway and would be very glad to see me give the whole thing up as a bad job. It's not as if I'll be missed.'

'No, you're right. You won't be missed.' This was not the answer Trussell was hoping for. Stud knew that. 'After all,' he went on, 'You were only elected MP by one of the largest majorities in Parliament. It's not as if the people who voted for you at nine General Elections in succession will care one way or the other that their representative has seen fit to walk off into the sunset.'

'I am under no illusions, Stud. You know very well that if Richie Rich is replaced as lead singer of The Wreckage, it isn't The Wreckage any more. Even the absence of Julian Stud Lee might raise one or two eyebrows among the more discerning rock fans. But an MP is an MP is an MP. Pin the right colour of rosette on a pig and people will elect him. I am under no illusions. It isn't me they elected eight times – eight times, not nine – it's a Conservative.'

'Alright, now tell me...' Stud leaned over his friend, almost menacingly. The ageing rocker was still as tall and gaunt as in his heyday. His horse-riding, his walks round the estate, his dogs, his 'active lifestyle' all kept him trim. Acton saw Stud's long curly hair, thinning but still dyed a youthful brown, and wondered where the years had gone since he and Stud stood in the wings of the Free Trade looking out at the audience as they yelled wildly for another encore from The Wreckage and Stud was calmly discussing decibel levels with a local councillor.

'It's very simple, Stud. I got caught smoking.'

'You what?'

'Just like at school. I got caught smoking.' They both laughed and puffed their cigars ostentatiously.

'Where?'

'Outside a community centre in Slough. I was speaking at a debate on freedom. There was a break. I felt an overwhelming urge to smoke. I went outside and lit up. Unfortunately I was seen apparently.'

'It's unbelievable, isn't it? Five years ago, the Government depended on cigarettes for their income. Now the things are completely illegal. Nobody cares about bloody freedom of choice or the right to blow your brains out in your own way. God, it's easier to go hunting these days than it is to have a quiet smoke. Even the sabs have switched to hounding smokers.'

'And to think it was our Government which imposed the ban. Our Government.' Acton sighed and took another puff on his cigar. He tried not to inhale. All that raw tobacco would make him cough.

'I know. It's a tragedy and a scandal,' Stud went on. 'But surely, Acton, they can't make you quit for doing something which was still legal only a year ago. Surely. In that case, half the population will have to leave their jobs before the year's out.'

'The truth is no-one has actually said anything in so many words. They have just made it clear my position is untenable. I could have fought them but, you know, I just didn't have the strength. I don't really want to be a part of a Government which bans smoking and turns smokers into criminals. I still think we should live and let die, as they say. There are worse things in the world than hiding an occasional packet of Marlboro Lights in your briefcase. But it's all too late. The law was passed with a significant majority.'

'Just like they banned hunting. They do whatever they like and get away with it. The real scandal is the Government can dump you for something so trivial and get away with it.'

'I know. But let's face it, smoking is a disgusting habit and all smokers are anti-social pariahs. I am not at all sure people would vote to restore the right to smoke if they had the chance.'

'Maybe. But so's drinking. And drugs – yet they're legalising drugs.'

'Some of them.'

'Some of them. So why outlaw smoking? And, worse still, outlaw smokers?'

Stud was marching up and down the terrace now. He was on stage, performing to an audience of one tired ex-MP and three horses. Somewhere a night-bird screeched.

'It's a scandal, a liberty, a diabolical liberty. You should not go gentle into that good night, Acton, you really shouldn't. You should stand up for freedom, for liberty and the English way.'

Trussell laughed. 'The English way?'

'Like the American way. Only more... English.'

*****

Clifford Chambers arrived at Acton Trussell's back door at 8am on the Saturday morning. July was well-advanced and a light mist wafted over the fields. Acton was in his dressing-gown though Clarissa had been up for over an hour. She was sorting out clothes for the village bring-and-buy which she was determined to open even though her husband had resigned as the local MP.

Acton was at the table in the middle of the large breakfast-kitchen, near the Aga, tentatively sipping a mug of hot tea while trying to read the front page of the "Daily Telegraph". He wondered why he was struggling to absorb the words. Was this inability to concentrate a sign of ageing or was it something to do with his immense indifference to the news in general and the state of the Coalition in particular? He was re-reading an article about how the new Home Secretary, fat, boorish Rick Pickering, had been persuaded to press on with plans for a national identity card scheme despite the party's pledge to scrap it. 'We only said we would carry out a review,' the paper quoted an anonymous insider as saying. Acton wondered which of the spotty Old Etonian 23-year-old 'political advisers' that would have been.

Clifford Chambers knocked briefly. Hilda the dog barked and wagged her tail. Chambers let himself in. Acton Trussell did not stand up to greet him. Indeed, he barely looked up from the paper. Instead he sipped his tea again and wondered if he was suffering from a hangover after last night with Stud.

Chambers was wearing a sports jacket, a pin-striped shirt and a yellow and blue striped bow tie. 'Off to the polo, Clifford?' Acton had turned to the cricket scorecards in "The Telegraph" sports section. He liked the idea that his new inactivity gave him time to read the paper properly, though Clarissa was already beginning to complain he made the kitchen untidy.

'No.' Chambers stood in the doorway waiting to be asked to sit down and have a cup of coffee. Acton was unwilling to oblige.

There was a pause, embarrassing to the visitor though not to the ex-MP who noticed that Kent had made 479 for eight declared in their first innings. He wondered why they hadn't gone for 500.

'Looking at the cricket scores?' Chambers ventured.

'Yes indeed.'

'I was wondering whether I could have a word, actually, Acton.'

'Were you?'

'Well you have made life very difficult for us. For the association.'

'Have I indeed?'

'You know you have. Your behaviour has been quite unacceptable. Your resignation, without reference to the chairman of the association or any of its officers. We have to prepare for a by-election. The funds are depleted. It's the middle of the summer. Nobody's around. We have the whole selection process to go through. It's most inconvenient.'

At last Acton looked up at him, standing tall and thin in the doorway looking back down at the fat old man with his thinning hair. Clifford ran a finger through his short, parted black hair. Brylcreem boy, Acton thought, referring to the old fifties advertisements made famous by people like the great England batsman Denis Compton.

'Well I am very sorry to have put you to so much inconvenience.'

'Come on, Acton. You know how difficult this is. For all of us.'

'As I say, I apologise.' There was another pause. 'Is that it, only I was thinking of getting dressed?'

'Well, my difficulty is that we're having an extraordinary general meeting. To announce your resignation formally and to set a timetable for the selection of a new candidate and so on.'

'And?'

'Well, I mean, what am I to say to everyone?'

'About?'

'Why you resigned. What am I to say to them? No-one knows what's going on, what happened. I thought something was going to appear in the papers or on the BBC or the internet. But nothing.'

'No.'

'So?' Clifford ventured into the kitchen, drew a chair out from under the table and sat down. He smiled at the older man in a way he regarded as winning but Trussell thought of as irritating.

'My dear boy,' Trussell smiled and shrugged, 'What can I say? If the people who wished to see me resign have not seen fit to publicise their machinations, who am I to do it for them?'

Chambers was confused. He frowned and stared at the grain of the wooden table. Speaking to this uneven surface, he said, 'It's too bad of you, Acton, really it is. You have let everyone down. Badly let us all down. Even the Prime Minister. In the first few months of the new Government as well. Given the opposition a stick to beat us with. They're even talking up their chances at the by-election.'

'It wasn't entirely voluntary, you know. And anyway, Clifford, I am afraid I do not feel the need to defend my actions to you or anybody else. They rather speak for themselves, I should have thought.'

'But what am I to say to the association?'

'Tell them I have applied for the stewardship of the Manor of Northstead. That I have resigned my seat in Parliament. That they must find a new elected representative.'

'Don't you care?'

At this Acton rose and stood with his back to the Aga, his dressing gown flapping around as he spoke. 'Yes, Clifford, I do care. Of course I do. You don't devote over 30 years to a constituency and its people without caring about them. I know this constituency better, more intimately, than anyone. I know its people, their hopes and fears. I know their triumphs and disasters. I know a damned sight more about Barset and all its works than most sensible individuals would ever care to know. I have done my best to represent them in Parliament while, at the same time, doing what I have been able to support my party and my country. I may not have been a high-flier or had any great personal success. But I did my best and I do bloody well care.'

'So why resign?'

'If you don't know why, I am not the one to tell you. I am surprised the story hasn't got around by now. But the fact is that I have resigned because the party would no longer give me its support, whether or not I continued to support the party. It doesn't really matter why I resigned. The fact is I have done and I am no longer your Member of Parliament. You must find another one. I dare say they will be queuing from here to the castle ruins.'

'Well, your behaviour is most reprehensible.'

Trussell was angry now. Chambers' pomposity was unbearable. He turned his back on his God-son to examine the 'Homes and Gardens' calendar hanging on the kitchen wall. The picture showed a thatched cottage in glorious summer sunshine. He noted the hollyhocks. The picture was so sharp you could even make out a bumble bee on one of the roses.

'What am I to tell the members?'

'Tell them what you like. I've spoken to most of them already. The phone hasn't stopped ringing. I've spoken to Mavis Murcot, Henry Hardcastle, both the McPhersons on separate occasions – he offered sympathy and golf, she wanted to know who was going to take on her campaign for cleaner ditches. I've talked at length of Sybil and Beryl, Steve Prince and Steve Blunt. Even old Pinky Green called round demanding whisky and explanations. I think you will find they are all sufficiently well-informed.'

'And did they ask why you resigned?'

'They did.'

'And what did you say?'

'I said I did not want to go into the details but that I was no longer in sympathy with the direction the party was going, that I was no lover of Coalition, that the party had wanted me out before the last election and I was tired of fighting a losing battle.'

Clifford Chambers thought for a minute. Trussell looked out of the kitchen window and wondered whether he ought to dead-head the roses now he was retired or whether he could get away with leaving it to the gardener, a young lad called Mick Allardyce who had taken over from his uncle, Sam, after the latter won the lottery and emigrated to Spain.

'Don't you think we've got a right to know the truth?' Clifford said eventually. He was stroking his chin and looking perplexed. He hated not being in the know.

At that moment, Clarissa came into the kitchen from the hall, swearing loudly about the bloody fools running the food stall. At the same time, Vernon Small popped his head round the back door.

'Vernon,' said Acton, with relief.

'Vernon,' said Clarissa, with annoyance.

'Vernon,' said Clifford, with surprise.

'Morning all.' Vernon walked into a kitchen he obviously knew well and went across to the Aga, almost shoving Acton aside as he did so, picked up the kettle, filled it at the sink and replaced it on the hotplate. 'Coffee for four is it? Lovely day, don't you think? How's the bring-and-by by-the-by Clarissa? Morning Acton, how's unemployment? Hello again, Clifford. Surprised to see you here. Thought you were engineering the succession.'

There was a general commotion of people moving and chairs being sat on which gave Chambers a chance to cover his embarrassment before replying.

'As agent, Vernon, I am surprised to see you here.' Chambers sounded at his most official. 'As an officer of the association, I may feel the need to draw this to the attention of the executive committee.'

'Ignore him, Vernon,' said Clarissa, taking up "The Telegraph" and turning to the crossword, while shifting her position to gather more light and turn her back on the young man.

'I shall, dear lady, I shall,' said Vernon, unflustered. 'It is a lovely day, though, isn't it? I was over here to discuss the future with Acton but I can see that must wait.'

'Don't mind me,' Clifford said. 'I was just going. So, Acton, we will have to explain your resignation as best we may, then?'

'Explain his resignation?' said Vernon as he scooped spoonfuls of Nescafe from a jar and spooned them into four mugs. 'Aren't you staying for coffee, Clifford? Oh well.' He poured the coffee grains back into the jar and returned one mug to the cupboard. 'Waste not, want not. Anyway, what's there to explain? The association knows more than enough about why Acton chose to resign. He was hounded out because he was too old, too old-fashioned – he was a left-over, a blast from the past. Ain't that right, Acton?'

Trussell smiled at his old friend. 'That's a reasonable description of the situation,' he said.

'Very well then,' said Clifford. 'I must go anyway. We're playing Went-wood this afternoon in the Bliss Brewery League. Thank you Acton.' He offered a hand to Mrs Trussell: 'Clarissa.' And he nodded in the agent's direction: 'Vernon.'

*****

Vernon settled at the table and took a noisy slurp of his coffee. 'I know his father was a friend of yours but Clifford Chambers is what I would call a slithy tove.'

Acton looked up from the sports section. 'Slithy tove?'

'"Twas brillig and the slithy toves did gyre and gimble in the wabe. All mimsy were the borogroves and the mome raths outgrabe",' quoted Vernon.

'Ah yes, the "Jabberwocky".'

'Lewis Carroll was a friend of my great-great uncle, you know,' Clarissa said.

'Was he?' Vernon asked. 'What was he like?'

'Cold and austere, supposedly.'

'Rather like Acton's godson, then.'

'Godson? Clifford my Godson? Is he? I'd forgotten.'

'Acton, don't be so stupid. You remember the Christening, don't you?' Clarissa had abandoned the crossword and was gathering up various items of equipment – secateurs, twine, mobile phone, gardening gloves.

'Oh yes. The baby made such a row the vicar had to postpone the service until his mother could calm him down. We spent half an hour wandering around St Jude's churchyard while she took him for a drive.'

'Pity she didn't drown him,' ventured Vernon.

'Now, now, Vernon,' Clarissa said with a smile. 'Anyway, if you two are just going to sit here all morning then I have work to do. Bye, Vernon.'

He stood and kissed her on both cheeks. 'Dear Clarissa,' he smiled.

'Vernon, your socks,' she exclaimed, looking at his bright orange socks.

'Holland,' he said as if that somehow explained them.

'Explain.'

'They're taking part in the 20-20 Cricket Cup this weekend. I've got a bit of money on them to make the semis.'

After Clarissa had gone to work in the garden, taking Hilda with her, Acton put down his paper, finished his coffee, and led the way onto the terrace overlooking the rose garden. The flowers had been battered by the recent rain. The buds were tightly curled and rusting away but at least the morning was bright and reasonably warm. The clouds were high and, though thick, they were sufficiently fluffy they didn't threaten an immediate downpour.

'The expression "up his own arse" was, I think, designed to describe my Godson exactly,' Acton ventured, withdrawing a single cigarette and a lighter from his dressing gown pocket.

'You shouldn't do that, you know. Not only is it bad for you but it is also against the law.' Both men chuckled.

They sat in silence for a few moments as Acton took a deep draw on his first cigarette of the day. 'I never thought I would need a dealer,' he said. 'It's ironic, isn't it? Drug dealing is now perfectly legal because otherwise it means gangland killings but a harmless pursuit like smoking a cigarette is no longer acceptable.'

'It's for your own good,' Vernon replied with a smile.

The two had fought a long, hard battle against the introduction of the national smoking ban. They tried every manoeuvre, looked for every compromise, adopted the tactics of the Countryside Alliance and other oppressed minorities. They deliberately refused the huge sums of money offered to them by the tobacco companies – though their Liberation campaign was still accused of being in the pockets of the vested-interest 'dealers in death' as they were branded by the media, the party, the lobbyists and everyone else who thought smoking an obnoxious and irresponsible habit.

The financial argument hadn't worked. The lost revenue from smokers came to £8 billion not to mention the money saved by the premature death of the majority of those who enjoyed the habit. But the Party decreed the ban was a necessary step towards improved public health and, as the Leader declared, 'What's a few billion pounds lost to the Treasury against the priceless benefit of young children growing up fit and healthy?' He failed to add, though it didn't take much working out, that the revenue would be more than made up from the doubling of taxes on air travel and all forms of fossil fuels. This was supposedly justified by the pressing need to reduce Britain's CO_2 emissions.

The European Union was busy imposing a smoking ban of its own anyway. If the Prime Minister hadn't voluntarily introduced one, it would have been forced on him. One of the reasons for taking early action was to prevent the smoking ban getting caught up in arguments about whether Britain should withdraw from the EU. In opposition, the Party had always claimed to be sceptical about further integration; in Coalition with the Liberal Democrats, the Leader was adamant that Britain had to remain 'at the heart of Europe'. He couldn't have the EU undermining itself by imposing an unpopular smoking ban from outside – far better to pre-empt it by bringing in the ban first and claim to be on the side of the angels.

'Looks like we've lost and lost again,' Vernon said after a while. He was sitting with his elbows on the garden table looking across at Acton, who was enjoying the yellowish haze created by the smoke from his Marlboro ExtraL-ite. In this bright morning light, Acton did look elderly. His hair was grey and thinning. The bags under his eyes were puffy. His unshaven morning face was plump and sagging. His eyes were clouded. His expression resigned. How old was he? Sixty-four, sixty-five? Old and tired.

Vernon went on: 'We lost the freedom campaign and now you've lost your seat as well. Precisely what the Party wanted. "Do not go gentle into that good night".'

'That's what Stud said. And anyway, what are you doing quoting poetry at your age?'

'Well, are you going quietly?'

'What choice do I have? I told you. The party needs the seat for one of Our Glorious Leader's little chums.'

'Doesn't mean you had to resign.'

'Yes and no, yes and no. There wasn't much point in carrying on. An irrelevance. A bit of a joke. An old fool whose time had come and gone a long, long while ago.'

'All the more reason to stay. Thorn in their side. Pearl in their oyster. Manure on their rose-bed.'

'I'm tired, I'm old, I've had enough. I am yesterday's man. The day before yesterday's actually.'

Vernon couldn't tell if Acton was feeling sorry for himself or whether he was being ironic. After so many years working together, he still found it difficult to fathom the man sometimes.

Acton was one of those politicians who was slow to rouse. It took a while to discover what his true feelings were on any given issue. He was not one of those volatile men who spoke in screaming front page headlines. Acton thought for a long time before he reached a conclusion on something. But when he did, he was difficult to shift. Then he would speak in reasonable, measured tones without feeling the need to bludgeon his audience into submission. He preferred to lay out his stall and allow people to make up their own minds. Rarely did he become roused to real passion or fury though he had been known to express both on occasion.

'Well, I think it's a damned pity. For me as well as for you.'

'For you?' Acton sat up and looked over at his old friend: Vernon, short, bouncy, bald head shining brightly, eyes darting. 'You're still the agent. What difference does it make to you?'

'I was your agent, Acton. Yours. Not some other bugger's. Not the party's. Certainly not the ruddy councillors'. They've been wanting to get rid of me from about Day Two. They don't like me interfering in their cosy ways so I'm retiring. That's what I wanted to tell you. I am retiring as the agent of the Barset Conservative Association as of the end of the month. They can find a new agent as well as a new MP.'

'Clifford won't like that.'

'Which makes it all the more satisfying.'

'But why retire, Vernon? Why give it up? It was your life.'

'Listen to yourself.'

Trussell acknowledged the point. He stood up, threw his cigarette end into the rose bushes. 'I feel guilty now,' Acton said, turning back from the middle distance to look at his old friend, who was gazing up at him like an eager schoolboy, despite his advanced years. 'I never thought... I should have thought... I am sorry, Vernon. I really am.'

Trussell sat down again and deflated. There was a longer silence.

*****

Vernon's interview with Clifford Chambers was less amicable.

They were the front room of the house Chambers shared with his sister on the outskirts of Barset. The lawn was looking even more well-groomed than usual. 'Like Lord's,' Vernon observed.

Clifford's sister, Samantha, sat with her back to the men on a sofa looking out through the sliding French windows into the back garden. She read the paper and appeared scarcely to listen to the conversation.

Clifford offered Vernon a sherry and poured one each for himself and Samantha, who accepted hers with a murmur of thanks. Vernon was used to sherry at Clifford's house. At least it was dry.

Clifford sipped his daintily then sat down in the armchair placed to enjoy the best view of the wide-screen television. This was plainly 'his' chair. Vernon was forced to sit on the sofa and chose a place as far away from his constituency association chairman as he reasonably could.

Clifford had a pile of notes and minutes in front of him. 'If we press on,' he said, 'We can have all this sorted in a couple of hours.' He sounded cheerful at the prospect. 'There's only one real topic on the agenda, though, isn't there, Vernon? Selecting a new candidate.'

'Well, before we come to that, Clifford, I have an item of my own to place on the agenda.'

Clifford looked through his pile of papers, as if they would somehow yield the secret of Vernon's agenda item. 'You're not going to tell me you want to stand, Vernon, are you?' This was said as a joke, as if the prospect were too absurd to contemplate. Clifford even attempted a smile, something he rarely pulled off successfully without making him look like a lecherous old man.

'No, no. It's just that I have written to the party and I have already informed Acton, not that it's strictly relevant to him now, I suppose, but anyway I have handed in my notice. One month ago, actually. It means I leave at the end of next week – at the end of the month.'

'I don't blame you, Vernon.' This comment was thrown into the silence that followed the revelation and came from Samantha. 'I do hope you have a happy retirement – you deserve it.'

'Thank you Samantha,' Vernon replied. He had always liked Samantha. Clifford still couldn't speak.

Vernon took a sip of sherry. Then another. Then he finished the dregs in his glass and wondered if it would be reasonable to help himself to a second. Clifford looked through his pile of papers.

'Vernon, you're doing this deliberately. On purpose. Just to spite us. The party. Deserting us in our hour of need. You are a traitor,' his chairman complained.

'That's a bit harsh, Clifford. But I have no intention of arguing with you about it. Or putting up with insults. If I can be of service to you over the next few days then I will willingly do what I can. But anything longer-term is not possible I'm afraid.'

'Vernon, you can't. I mean. We've got to select a candidate, organise a by-election campaign. Who's going to do it all?'

'If you want my advice…' Vernon waited.

'Advice?'

'Advice on how to proceed.'

'From you?'

'Clifford, I have no wish to leave you in the lurch. Or at least not completely. And I do still owe some loyalty to my friends in the party, my friends in Barset. They will probably want another MP from the same party. Probably. Unless we can offer them an alternative.'

'An alternative? What on earth do you mean?'

'Oh nothing, I don't mean an alternative, I mean options to choose from. We need to give them options to choose from – which candidate to select. And you do need someone to organise it for you. That's what I would like to suggest.'

'What?'

'Who?'

'Who. Yes. I think you would be well advised to offer the post on a temporary basis to someone from the party's headquarters.'

'Anyone in particular?'

'Yes. Compton Dundon.'

'Compton? But he's in charge of… What is he in charge of these days?'

'He seems to be the Leader's fixer and gofer – gofer this, gofer that, you know. He'll want to be in the selection process from Day One in any case. So I suggest you tell him to make himself useful and run the thing for you. From the paper sift to the MP's speech of thanks on election night. By the way, when is it to be? Last I heard it was due to be on October 28, three weeks after the party conference.'

'You know more than I do, then. Oh God, Vernon, do you have to?' Clifford deflated like a long thin balloon pierced with a pin. He wanted to run the election and have Vernon at his beck and call. Compton Dundon was an unappealing alternative. 'Do you have to really? Couldn't you postpone your retirement for a couple of months?'

Vernon's plump and cheerful face suddenly became serious, which aged him instantly and reminded Clifford that this man was well into his sixties and beyond the usual retirement age anyway. Vernon placed his empty glass carefully on the mantelpiece. 'I couldn't do it, Clifford. Not for you, not for anybody,' he said. 'I have not said anything in public but I cannot bear the way Acton has been treated by the party and I know where my loyalties lie. I have worked hard for the party, locally and nationally, but I have had a great deal more respect for Acton than many other people. He is a decent, honest, diligent man and I think the party's treatment of him has been monstrous. I am afraid I cannot dedicate myself to work for the election of a candidate for a party I no longer believe in or care about. I'm sorry but there it is.'

Clifford looked perplexed and didn't know what to say. Vernon headed for the door to let himself out. As he was leaving, Samantha called after him, 'Bravo, Vernon. Bravo indeed' and he heard Clifford saying indignantly, 'Samantha…'

*****

Compton Dundon, in his tailored suit and open-neck shirt, wore the expression of a postman who has fled from a snarling hound once too often. His gold cuff-links were firmly in place, however, and, as if to compensate for the absence of a tie, he sported a spotted purple and white silk handkerchief in his breast pocket. He met Clifford Chambers outside the entrance to the Houses of Parliament and led him through the security queue to meet the party chairman for lunch.

August was a quiet month for politicians. The hubbub of tourists faded as the visitor walked through Westminster Hall. Clifford was wearing a natty green bow tie and his steel-tipped heels echoed around the vault of the medieval building where Charles I stood trial in 1649. They veered off to the right, towards the cafeteria which remained open during the political closed season to service the needs of those who bothered to turn up.

Dundon and Chambers greeted each other with their habitual suspicion. Chambers had called the meeting but Dundon wanted it anyway. The party chairman's presence was a small complication he could have done without. Dave Hersey had only been in the job three weeks. He was young, ambitious, impressionable and still had some sense that his job was to represent the views of the members. This would be knocked out of him soon enough but it made life a little more difficult for Compton Dundon.

They met in the food queue. Dave had just arrived as well. They all opted for some kind of vegetarian concoction with chips, accompanied by fair trade orange juice. Dundon paid. It wasn't much anyway, thanks to the generosity of the taxpayer's subsidies.

They found a table some distance away from two Labour MPs who were conferring in hushed voices. They ignored the intense young men with Parliamentary passes and i-Pads. They did not even nod to the well-known Baroness and her pretty companion. A reporter looked over towards them, nodded to Dave, who waved back, and walked on. Once they settled down, Dave began: 'This by-election is a wonderful opportunity to secure an early endorsement of our policies and approach.'

'He means we can't afford any slip-ups, Clifford,' Dundon interpreted.

'That is one way of putting it, Compton,' said the party chairman. He spoke like the barrister he was. Precisely, slowly, carefully. 'The Prime Minister himself will be taking an interest in the outcome and in the way the campaign is conducted. We must ensure it is run on the Government's performance to date and our promise for the future. We must ensure it is positive and up-beat.'

Clifford was nodding feverishly. He liked positive and up-beat. 'This is a message I am happy to take back to Barset,' he said happily. Then a cloud crossed his features. 'There is one problem, though.' They looked expectantly at him. Dundon was used to problems; Dave was frightened by them. 'The agent, Vernon Small. He's retiring at the end of the month.'

'Yes, we knew,' said Dundon, while the party chairman asked, 'Before the by-election? Surely not?'

Dundon explained, 'He and Acton Trussell go back a long way. He was Trussell's representative on earth. Anyway, we have a contingency plan.'

'We do?' the chairman asked.

'This election needs to be held on November 5. That means we have four weeks before the party conference to select a candidate and four weeks after the conference for the campaign with ten days in the middle for the conference.'

'November 5?' asked Clifford.

'We will move the writ on October 13.'

'But I thought the House wasn't sitting then.' Dave looked bemused. 'Can we move a writ when Parliament isn't sitting?'

'No but it will be. October 13 is the day after the leader's speech to the party conference. He will recall Parliament for an emergency debate. We'll move the writ then.'

'An emergency debate?' asked Clifford.

'What emergency debate?' asked the party chairman.

'We haven't decided yet. Anyway, that's my problem. There will be one, however, and we will take the opportunity to move the writ at the same time. Catch the opposition on the hop. They think the by-election won't be called this year. Steal a march on them. Get our retaliation in first, as they say. Anyway, by then we must have our candidate in place. And this is where we need your help, Clifford.'

'Yes,' Dave added, 'We need to make sure the process is open and inclusive.'

'As long as we agree now who the candidate will be,' said Dundon.

'You can't do that,' the party chairman started explaining to Compton Dundon. 'It's a free and democratic process. We may even open the selection up to every voter in the constituency – the primary system.'

'We can't afford a primary,' Clifford said. 'It can cost fifty grand and we haven't got that sort of money.'

'Don't worry about that,' said Dundon. 'There won't be any need. All we require is a fair and open contest which concludes in the unanimous selection of Lucy Loxley as the candidate.'

Clifford raised one eyebrow. The party chairman looked puzzled. 'Lucy Loxley? Who is Lucy Loxley? Have I met her? Is she on the candidates' list?'

'She is now, chairman. She is the sister of Robin Loxley, the trader.'

'Oh Robin. Yes, of course.' Dave registered the fact that the Loxley family trust was a major donor to the party through various investment vehicles and offshore trading companies. 'And Lucy?'

'Lovely girl,' said Clifford. 'Stunning looks.'

'Lesbian,' added Dundon.

'Lesbian?' Clifford was shocked. 'But she's so beautiful. Truly.'

Dundon laughed. 'Thought you were in with a chance, did you, Clifford?'

The party chairman looked at his watch. It was 1.34. 'I must go,' he said, standing up and shaking hands with Chambers. 'Good luck with the campaign, Clifford. I know the party can rely on you.' He dashed off, clutching various documents to his side as if they were liable to slip onto the ground and expose his innermost secrets.

'He can't hide it, can he?' said Dundon with a grin. 'He's off to see his girl-friend again. She's Asian too. Lovely girl. Works at a solicitor's in the City somewhere. Surinder. He thinks nobody knows but actually the only person who doesn't is Mrs Hersey. Yet.'

Dundon went on, 'So, Clifford, let me explain how the process will work. I shall take charge of the campaign. Don't worry about Vernon Small. He was hopeless anyway. We will advertise the vacancy this week and sift applications over the Bank Holiday. I shall put up at the Barset Sleepover Hotel for the duration – they have suites which are very comfortable and I shall make them my campaign headquarters. The Sleepover chain is owned by Lord Brothers, a friend of the Prime Minister, so we will be given every facility. This by-election is important because it will emphasise that the Party's modernisation is more than skin deep. We have changed, we have embraced change, we are change.'

'But what if the members don't want to select Lucy Loxley? What if they want someone else?'

'That will be your challenge, Clifford. I will help you. But you are responsible – you have to get her selected and then you have to get her elected. The party is relying on you.'

'It would be good to have a role on the national board of the party. One with a high profile.'

'Of course. When an opportunity arises I am sure the party chairman will be looking for people he can rely on to deliver for him. And so will Dick.'

'Will the Prime Minister be able to campaign in Barset during the election?'

'Clifford, really. You know Prime Ministers never sully themselves with by-elections. What if something were to go wrong?'

'Dave will be there, though, I suppose? And Amelia Browning? And Bud Brooke?'

'What's Trussell's majority?'

'Ten thousand seven hundred and forty three.'

'We don't want to go in for overkill. That would be taken as a sign of weakness. This is a low-key, local campaign in support of the values and beliefs of the Government.'

'So why all the interest from you?'

'We can't afford any slip-ups. This is our first by-election. The Lib-Dems are on board with the cessation of hostilities on the ground. It is an important statement for the future. And just to make assurance doubly sure, we'll be bringing Steve Thomas along for the duration as well.'

'He's quite some operator, isn't he?' Clifford rubbed his hands with glee. 'I remember Steve when he span that story about old Chester Itchington, the Lib-Dem who died on the job. 'Tragedy of family man's last moments'. No mention the woman he was shagging was a local tart. How did Steve secure her silence anyway?'

Dundon smiled. 'It's amazing how the word 'deportation' can help a young woman forget things.'

*****

The regulars at the Conservative Working Men's Club in Barset were neither Conservatives nor working men. The three-storey Victorian building round the back of the High Street consisted of a bar with velvet plush seats and teak-veneer tables, beer mats and a darts board. It offered lager, mild beer and a range of three different whiskies. It was run by Terry and his third wife, Finola. Terry was corpulent and tattooed. Finola was not dissimilar. The regulars were three retired dustmen and a couple of their colleagues, now approaching retirement and disinclined to trouble themselves over-much by the demands of the day job.

These gentlemen kept themselves aloof from what went on elsewhere in the building. The second floor had a couple of empty offices and a larger meeting room with a table and a few chairs. The top floor had two more rooms stuffed with election posters, banners and stands for long-defunct campaigns, boxes of accounts and minutes from a hundred old meetings, some trestle tables and collapsible chairs. There was a bathroom as well but nobody in living memory had ever taken a bath in it and few people were ever brave or desperate enough to avail themselves of its facilities.

The first floor meeting room had a large, framed print portrait of Winston Churchill in bulldog mode and a second, almost as large, photograph of a smiling Margaret Thatcher resplendent in purple. There was also a smaller picture of John Major and, oddly, another of Dr David Owen, the one-time leader of the long-dead Social Democratic Party which flourished briefly in the 1980s.

There was a small, signed photograph of a young Acton Trussell celebrating his first election victory by waving enthusiastically from the top of a Range Rover festooned with 'Vote Trussell' banners. The young man, sporting a huge rosette, a broad grin and a full head of lush brown hair, looked cheerful and enthusiastic. As he walked into the room, Clifford took the picture off the wall and placed it face down on the table.

Four tables had been pushed together in the centre of this dusty room, where Clifford Chambers presided over an emergency meeting of the local management executive, the governing body of the party association in the constituency.

Only four of the executive's six members had turned up. It was a rare hot evening towards the end of August and no doubt others had better things to do than attend a meeting in the dismal interior of the working men's club.

Clifford had brought with him a bottle of Le Clos du Château Château de Puligny-Montrachet as a special treat. He fished glasses from his briefcase and placed them in front of his colleagues.

'I think this occasion deserves to be marked, gentlemen, lady.' Clifford carefully opened the bottle, poured five modest glasses and distributed them in silence before raising his own glass to his nose, inhaling ostentatiously, and declaring: 'Fruity! Creamy! Beautiful! Lady and gentleman, I give you: The Party.'

The others, with varying degrees of enthusiasm, clinked glasses and mumbled, 'The party'.

'Very nice, Clifford. Very nice indeed. Most characterful, most characterful.' This was Quentin Quinton, the Treasurer, a small man with a dapper moustache. Like all of them except Chambers, he was retired. He used to be in metals. Some sort of salesman, though nobody was very clear what he sold. Beside him was Gary Atherstone, who organised an annual discussion of political issues with interested members. Only he and Clifford usually turned up, along with the MP. But Gary was meticulous with the minutes and anxious standing orders were rigidly adhered to, not to mention the constitution and articles of association.

Councillor Sue Alne, who represented the St Thomas ward in south Barset on the county council and the district council, was a member of the police committee and the local health authority. She rarely spoke but could be relied upon to vote whenever and wherever called upon to do so. This evening, Sue was busy trying to read a new planning guidance document.

Taking up the next two seats was Tony Grafton. Tony enjoyed politics. He was a dab hand at a leaflet and positively relished delivering them. A large, lumbering man, Tony couldn't stand Clifford, who he considered effete. He wanted to become the next chairman of the association and didn't mind who knew it.

Clifford surveyed his audience. 'Gentlemen, lady. There is only one item on the agenda tonight. The by-election and the selection of candidates.'

'Point of order Mister Chairman,' Gary interrupted. 'Would it not be appropriate first of all to sign of the minutes of the previous meeting?' He looked around. Sue ignored him, Tony looked restless, only Quentin smiled supportively.

'As this is an extraordinary meeting, I am not sure that is strictly necessary, Gary. And besides, I am not sure Tony has them written yet, have you Tony?'

'As a matter of fact, chairman,' Tony began, leaning forward and passing across a carefully typed sheaf of papers, 'I think you will find what you are looking for here. Though it is usual to distribute them in advance and give members the opportunity to read them before we come to signing. I would suggest…'

'Mister Chairman,' Gary interrupted. 'Mister Chairman. Can I suggest a short suspension of the proceedings while these missing minutes are copied, distributed and read?'

'I don't think that's really necessary,' Clifford began.

'Really, anyone would think the minutes were more important than the meeting,' said Tony.

'Can't we just get on with it?' asked Quentin. 'In my experience, these things come right in the end.'

'I think we should,' said Clifford, talking over further protests from Gary. 'I'm sorry Gary, no, I know, I know. Ultra vires almost certainly. But we have much to discuss.'

'Oh very well then,' Gary finally conceded.

'Thank you, Gary. Now, as I was saying, we are here as a result of the resignation of our Member of Parliament Acton Trussell after over 30 years' service to the constituency.'

'Shouldn't we organise some sort of event to offer him our thanks?' interrupted Sue. 'After all, he was our MP for a long time?'

'Yes, good idea Sue,' said Tony. 'I think we should. Maybe then he can tell us why he resigned. Why did he resign, Clifford? What explanation has he given us?'

'You saw his letter to the party members, now can we get on?'

'The letter just said "irreconcilable differences" as if he was talking about my divorce.' Tony grinned at his little joke and leaned back, almost breaking his chair as his considerable weight was shifted onto its already weakened plastic back.

'Can I suggest we come back to what, if anything, we may wish to do about our late, unlamented MP after we have discussed the way forward?' Clifford asked.

'Mister chairman, mister chairman,' interrupted Gary Atherstone. 'It is surely incumbent upon us in our position as the elected representatives of the membership to demand of our MP, or our ex-MP, or our departing MP, call him what you will, to demand, as I say, a complete and full explanation of the circumstances surrounding his hasty and, if I may say so, his ill-timed resignation.' Atherstone limped on, slowly and with unexplained squeaks and screeches, to say there could be no question of seeking a new MP until the last one had been properly dealt with and put to bed.

Considerable debate followed. Clifford tried to bring the meeting to order. Tony sided with Gary. Quentin was slow to stir. Sue was awaiting developments. It looked as if the meeting might achieve nothing but bad blood when Quentin finally spoke up, calling for a separate meeting to discuss the passing of Acton Trussell and demanding progress on the matter in hand. Gary and Tony conceded. Clifford decided against offering anyone else a refill.

Clifford thought it might be counter-productive, if not disastrous, to tell the committee everything he agreed with Compton Dundon. He confined himself to an outline of the process of selecting a candidate, announcing that the advertisement of the vacancy would be distributed to potential candidates within the next 48 hours with a ten-day deadline.

A sub-committee would be formed to consider the applications and reduce them to no more than a dozen candidates who would then present themselves for interview by the 62 members of the Barset executive committee. This group would select no more than four people – including at least two women and one BME candidate – to go through to the final selection meeting, which would be open to all members of the party.

'BME?' Sue suddenly piped up. 'What is BME?'

'Black and ethnic minority persons,' Clifford explained.

'That's BEM.'

'Yes but it's known as BME.'

'Why?'

'Don't know. Can we get on?'

'But why must one of the candidates be one of these ethnic people anyway? And if we have two women and an ethnic in the last four, does that mean ordinary men are wasting their time?' Sue asked.

'Need not apply,' put in Tony helpfully.

'Not necessarily,' Clifford answered. 'One of the two women could be a BME.'

'Two birds with one stone?' declared Tony in a voice which suggested a stoning was what he had in mind.

'As it were.'

Sue was now paying attention. 'So you are saying that a white man has only a one in four chance of getting to the final four?'

'Even less,' Tony added helpfully, 'If the best two ladies are both white.'

'No, that's not right,' said Atherstone.

Clifford Chambers intervened before the debate could drag on any longer. 'It is part of the leader's drive for greater inclusiveness and, if I may say so, a more-than-welcome, if belated, development in bringing the party into the 21st century.'

'Well I don't like it,' said Sue. 'Margaret Thatcher never needed any help.'

'She was more of a man than any of 'em,' Tony agreed. Gary scowled, Quentin looked perplexed, Clifford irritated.

'We don't have to accept these terms,' Sue said. 'We are independent of the party in London. We have autonomy.'

Tony laughed with heavy irony. Gary said, 'Strictly speaking I am not sure that is entirely correct, Susan.'

Clifford gathered his papers together. 'I think that's all we really have time for tonight. Thank you for coming. I look forward to our meeting at the paper-sift in two weeks' time. On the 29th.'

Tony stood, tall, bulky and menacing. 'You can't do that,' he said and sat, for emphasis and because the exercise was a little wearisome. 'We haven't agreed to this yet. You can't cut short our debate just because you don't like the way it's going.'

'I have to be away,' Clifford said, 'My sister is expecting me.'

'Oh your sister! In that case...' Tony laughed and surveyed the table for allies. Quentin could not suppress a small grin of complicity though Gary was not impressed and Sue was still absorbing the information about BMEs.

Clifford gathered the glasses, placed them carefully in his briefcase. 'I think we have gone about as far as we can for one night, gentlemen, lady.'

Sue Alne started packing her papers into her huge handbag. Quentin returned his to their ring binder. Gary stood and shook Clifford's hand. 'Good job, well done.'

Tony remained sprawled over the table in an impression of an incredulous faint.

*****

A large woman barred the way as Clifford tried to leave the working men's club. She stood in the doorway occupying most of the space, even though this was a high, wide late-Victorian doorway. 'Are you Conservatives?' she demanded in a strong Barset accent.

Clifford, having already offered her an 'excuse me' and tried to squeeze past, stepped back to view this obstruction more clearly in the fading light. The woman appeared to be middle-aged but was probably a little younger than that. She wore a pair of jeans, thick boots and a football shirt advertising Barset Albion's number 9 from the season before last, Jean-Luc "the Camel" Faivre, so-called because he took the hump so often. He was sold at a huge loss 18 months ago when 'The Stokers' were relegated.

'Yes,' Clifford said cautiously. 'I am the chair.'

'Chair? Good. I need your help.'

Clifford said he really was in a terrible hurry and would she like to e-mail him. He gave her his business card and, as she had somewhat foolishly stepped inside the building creating an opening, he was able to hurry past to the car park.

'Oi!' she called after him. 'Oi, come back 'ere. I've got to talk to you.'

'Sorry, running late,' Clifford called over his shoulder as the woman turned and started to run after him. He climbed into his red Audi Attractive and turned the engine on. But as he was looking to back out of his parking space, the woman banged on the roof and stood in his way.

'I was talking to you,' she called.

The window descended, Clifford looked out, the strains of Andrew Lloyd Webber seeping into the still evening. 'Well?'

'It's about my council house. It's burnt down. The gas exploded and we lost everything. Me, my husband and the kids, we're all living at my mother's. But there's not room for all of us and Hayley's gone to her boyfriend's.'

'Have you been to the council?'

'Course I have.' She folded her arms across her ample breasts and looked contemptuously at this young man in his expensive car. 'Bloody waste of time that was. My point is, what are you going to do about it?'

'Are you on a waiting list?'

'Course we are. Council have offered us temporary accommodation. Say it'll take nine months to refurbish our home. And they want to charge us rent. Bloody cheek. I told them, forget it.'

The others were drifting away. Quentin Quinton was first off in his Peugeot Esclavage, old but perfectly serviceable. Sue Alne was in her Renault Croche. Gary Atherstone walked to his Toyota Tonka, registration number GA 1, while Tony Grafton was already half way down the road on his way to the pub for a ward meeting.

Gary called over, 'All well, Clifford?' but his question went unheard because the woman was in full flow. As she spoke, she flung her arms wide, threw them towards Clifford in explanation and imprecation, ran her fingers through her short, dyed blond hair.

She was telling Clifford how the fire started, how she had thrown Kelly from an open window and Dean had rushed out with Hayley before her husband, Derek, had driven up in his van, realised at once what was happening and called 999 before even getting out of the car. He prevented the children's mother from going back into the flames to find the cat which, luckily, was out on the tiles. Anyway, the woman went on, what she needed to know from Clifford was what he proposed to do about it.

'Well, if you're living with your mother and you've been offered temporary accommodation, I am not sure there is much more we can do to help is there?' Clifford was becoming bored with this everlasting tale of woe.

'It's not that. It's Hayley. She's only 14 and I don't want her living with her boyfriend, getting pregnant and ending up just like I did. I don't want her to be a 32-year-old mother of three like I am. I need to get her away from Degsie before it's too late. Though it's probably too late already. Isn't there a law against it? Statutory rape? Isn't that what they call it?'

'Only in America,' Clifford explained. 'Here it's unlawful sexual intercourse. How old is, er, Degsie?'

'Thirty-four.'

'I think you should go to the police, Madam.' Clifford was firm. He turned the ignition, the woman stepped aside. 'I'm sorry, but I really do think this is a matter for the police. I'm sorry.'

The window slid closed and the Attractive slipped slowly backwards. Clifford shifted into first and headed towards the exit as quickly as he could.

Chapter 6

It was a mild, late-August afternoon. The sun was not quite shining but the milky white clouds were high and the breeze was pleasant. The trees in the woods swayed a little in the wind. They were still thickly coated with deep green leaves. The fields were cut to a stubble and smelt of straw. Apples were thick on the trees in the vicarage orchard, the other side of the wall from the village green where the Howard Michael Village Fete and Show was traditionally held.

Boys played "Splat the Rat" and threw each other onto hay bales while their sisters queued to have their faces painted by Mrs James or tried to win a cuddly toy. Their older brothers were in the beer tent or trying to outdo each other on the coconut shy and the ten pin bowling. Their fathers were manning the stalls, sitting outside the beer tent with glasses of cider or competing with their sons. The women were concentrating on the judging of flowers and produce on display in the main tent.

The interior of the marquee was thick with heat and the competing odours of watered earth, expiring plants and hastily sprayed perfumes. The judging party was making its way slowly round the various displays: the cakes, the fuchsias, the roses, not to mention the vicar's famous gladioli displays which always carried off the top prize. This year's event was in aid of the church restoration so it seemed a little unreasonable for the vicar to win again. Everyone secretly hoped the Rev Mrs Morris's display of gladioli would be pipped to the post, if only by Clarissa Trussell's roses, though even that seemed wrong, somehow.

The Rev Mrs Morris was a little over-anxious about her gladioli. At least, that was what Mrs Dorsington thought. The rock star's housekeeper kept an eye on the vicar. Mrs Dorsington was one of the judges, alongside Mrs Hughes and Acton Trussell himself. Across the marquee, the Rev Morris hovered beside her gladioli trying to talk to her flock, expiring in the heat as her normally ruddy complexion grew redder. She was wearing her Sunday surplice having presided at a wedding a little earlier.

'She hasn't bothered to change,' whispered Mrs Dorsington to Mrs Hughes. 'You'd think she might have made an effort.'

Mrs Hughes, a small woman in her early seventies, was wearing a straw hat with a purple ribbon above her best summer frock. Mrs Dorsington, a good ten years younger and a bad five stones heavier, was in a light cotton trouser suit. The ex-MP was in his usual pink trousers and white shirt. He was also wearing a straw hat, though he had taken it off since they entered the marquee and was discreetly fanning himself with it.

Several people were watching Acton intensely as he made his slow circuit of the marquee conferring with his fellow judges. They appraised him, discussed him, wondered about him. Nobody wanted to be the first to ask the question on everyone's lips.

Then, as the judging came to an end and Mrs Hughes was collecting in the scoring sheets to collate the results, Acton emerged into the muted afternoon light to cool off a little and enjoy some fresh air.

Sid Shipley, the former landlord of the now-closed village inn, the Fox and Trumpet, stood beside him and fished in his pocket for a packet of cigarettes. He held it towards the former MP and offered, 'Cigarette, Mr Trussell?'

'Come on now, Sid,' he said with a chuckle, 'You know better than that.'

'I know the first smoking ban killed off my business.'

'Yes, well, we've discussed all that before,' Action replied, putting his hat back on his head with a firmness which indicated the conversation was now at an end. They stood looking out across the green, where several boys were playing football using hay bales as their goals. A group of people was gathering around Acton.

'So?' said Sid, replacing the cigarette in its packet but making no secret about the guilty possession he was holding.

Acton wasn't a politician who enjoyed being coy and teasing his audience. He preferred to be straightforward. But he was not keen on going into the details. 'There comes a point in every career.'

'Yes but why now? You're in Government, you've been around for years, this is your time. Isn't it?'

'Not really, Sid. You know I fought the smoking ban.'

'And got nowhere.'

'And got nowhere. I didn't fit in any more. That's it really. Not the party I joined all those years ago.'

Several people started talking. Complaining there was no difference between this lot and the last lot, blaming the Liberal Democrats or accusing the Prime Minister of being a closet Socialist, asking why it was so metropolitan, politically correct and London-centric.

Acton was dragged back inside the tent by Mrs Hughes to discuss the awarding of prizes with Mrs Dorsington. It looked as if the vicar was heading for outright victory again and they wanted to see if there was any discrepancy in the voting which they could exploit.

By the time Acton re-emerged, searching for his wife and a cup of tea, the sky had cleared. Sunlight drifted across the field and sharpened the shadows under the horse chestnuts. He was making his way over to the tea-and-cakes stand for a well-earned rest on a bale of hay when he was accosted by a large woman wearing big leather boots, a flowery skirt, a T-shirt and carrying a motorcycle helmet.

'Are you Mr Trussell?' she asked accusingly.

Acton immediately found himself adopting the public persona of an MP. He smiled, he greeted her with a warm 'I am' and held out his hand to shake hers.

'My house burned down,' she announced in her strong Barset accent. 'And Hayley's in trouble.'

'Come and have a cup of tea.' Acton led her to the tea stall, greeted Mrs Higgins and Sarah Smallbrook, who were on duty, bought two cups of tea and led this belligerent woman over to a pair of bales. All the time Mandy Black was regaling him with the story of the fire, the devastation, the domestic upheavals it had created, her worries for Hayley's virtue and her own devastation over the way the council was behaving.

'You need to speak to Mr Rogers in the housing department,' he said several times, as the woman went on.

'Hayley's a lovely girl, don't get me wrong. Lovely. But she's headstrong. She's impressionable. It's not that I don't trust her, Mr Trussell, I do, it's just that I don't trust that bastard Degsie. Wouldn't trust him further than I could throw him.'

'Who is Degsie, exactly, Mrs Black?' Acton asked.

'Mandy, Mr Trussell, Mandy. I'm not actually married. As good as. But not. I told Derek, "I won't marry you until the Stokers get into the Premiership". So I don't think we'll ever actually get married. Anyway, Degsie's Derek's cousin. Two Dereks, see. Bloody stupid, excuse me, stupid if you ask me. Two fathers calling their two sons the same name, and not a year apart. But that's the trouble with the Wilkeses, mad the lot of 'em. Anyway, it's almost family. I warned Degsie, I warned him, if you lay a finger on our Hayley I'll have you. But I still don't trust him.'

Trussell looked more closely at Mandy Black. She was a tough-looking woman but she had a sparkle in her eyes which made her look more attractive than she at first appeared. She had plump arms, with a couple of tattoos on display, and a healthy stomach. At least she's not showing a pierced belly button or anything seriously hideous, he thought. As she talked, she took some cigarette papers and a substance which looked suspiciously like illegal tobacco from inside her helmet and proceeded to roll a cigarette then light it. She inhaled deeply then passed it to Acton. 'Rose petals,' she said. 'Not illegal. Not harmful. Not tobacco either, more's the pity.'

He took it and tried it just as Cordelia Quint focused her camera on him and snapped a picture. 'Mr Trussell,' Mrs Quint called from across the open tea-drinking enclosure, 'Caught on camera. How much is it worth?'

Acton looked up, alarmed for a moment. The cigarette tasted of bonfires and made him cough. 'It's rose petals,' he stammered, 'Here, try it.'

Cordelia, a woman in her thirties with three young children and a solicitor for a husband, came over to join them. 'Are you deep in consultation? Shall I go away?'

'We're just discussing Ms Black's domestic difficulties.'

'Oh, do tell.' Cordelia sat down beside Mandy and started pointing the camera at her.

'No close-ups, thank you very much,' Mandy demanded, laughing a little.

Acton made his escape but not before inviting Mandy to e-mail him with her address and details and promising to contact Mr Rogers in the housing department.

*****

Lucy Loxley's uncle Richard and his wife Ann lived in a former rectory called The Manor House, overlooking a golf course in what was once the village of St Clare's. The rectory was surrounded by a housing estate on the outskirts of Barset. The council had introduced street lighting, speed humps and an irregular bus service. Richard wanted to move somewhere quieter but Ann enjoyed the sense of living in the centre of things.

Lucy had set up a base for herself on the top floor of the rectory. She had a bedroom, a small bathroom and a large study, where she was creating what she called the 'nerve centre'.

She would need a campaign office in the middle of town, she explained to Clifford Chambers, her uncle and aunt over a pizza supper. It was late on Saturday evening. Clifford had returned from scoring a match between Barset and Upper Melksham. He had spent the tea interval taking a walk round the ground with Maggie Pride, during which he had suggested to her that despite his wholehearted support for her as an excellent local candidate, she shouldn't raise her hopes too high of actually securing the nomination. 'Party headquarters are taking this one on,' he explained.

'But you will have some influence, won't you Cliff?' she asked. She still couldn't decide if there was any point in trying to look attractive and feminine though she did her best just in case. Today, because it was still warm, she wore a thin summer dress and her long hair was allowed to remain almost naturally curly. Clifford thought it was too long for a woman of her age and noticed the brown dye had not been applied recently – her roots were showing.

Now, though, he was eating pizza and drinking Peroni with the lovely lesbian Lucy Loxley, all trim hair and trim body, her uncle, whose business had somehow survived the recession – perhaps because his practice concentrated on developments in India – and her curious aunt.

Lucy was appraising him carefully. 'I have the full support of the Winning Women campaign group,' she was saying. 'But I need to know about local issues and who I should be meeting. Of course, I have been here ten days already and Richard's a huge help.'

'You'll be perfect for this constituency,' Clifford assured her. 'Experienced, committed, supportive. You will add expertise to Westminster. The only point I think you should remember is to be statesmanlike. Statesmanlike. It's important to act the part then people believe you can carry it off. You are going to be the next MP for Barset and people want to have confidence in you from the outset. Do not make promises about anything, just give them your winning smile and promise to try. That's not the same as promising to achieve.'

Ann interrupted. She frowned and brushed a shock of black hair from her forehead. She looked perplexed. 'Clifford,' she asked, slowly and deliberately, as if she were thinking furiously, 'I do not understand. How can you say Lucy is going to be the next MP? There's a selection process isn't there? Won't a lot of people want the job?'

Lucy smiled. Richard nodded in support of the question. Clifford leaned back in his chair, master of all he surveyed. 'Well yes and no,' he explained. He wanted to appear enigmatic and powerful. 'There are wheels and there are wheels within wheels.'

'You're not saying it's going to be a fix, are you?' Ann was aghast. Richard smiled. Lucy looked at the tablecloth – a Cath Kidston number, a few years out of fashion now but popular in its day. Clifford leaned further back in his chair and clasped his hands behind his head. Ann wondered if he would topple over backwards and decided she wouldn't mind too much if he did.

'I wouldn't put it quite like that, Ann. Lucy is an excellent candidate and she will be an excellent Member of Parliament.'

Ann wasn't ready to be fobbed off. 'Clifford,' she said, the frown deepening, her expressive hands with their long musician's fingers waving in the air as she made her point, 'I am not a complete fool. I understand politics is not always straightforward. I read Machiavelli at university. I haven't forgotten Peter Mandelson. I know things are fixed from time to time and I am not complaining they may be fixed in Lucy's favour. But I don't understand how they can be. Not in this case. Doesn't she have to be voted for by a majority of members in a secret ballot? Isn't that how it works? So how can you be so sure she will be selected?'

'Well yes and no,' Clifford began again. His chair came back to the upright position and he leaned forward, as if conveying intimacy with his new friends. 'You see Ann, Lucy, this is a process. And as such, the formalities have to be observed. Unfortunately, in the past, the selection of Parliamentary candidates was something of a lottery. We have had some very strange people getting into Westminster over the years. Acton Trussell among them…'

'I quite liked Mr Trussell,' Ann interjected.

'He had his supporters, I accept. But he was really way off beam. He had no grasp of politics in the 21st century. The new paradigm.'

Ann tried to interrupt but Clifford talked over her. 'The new paradigm, the step change. The new contract between the people and their Government which we, as a party, represent and which is personified by the party leader.'

'The Old Harrovian,' Ann complained.

'It's not where you were educated that counts, it's what you learned. And that's what Dick personifies as Prime Minister. Naturally Dick wants likeminded people around him, people who will understand what he's about, who will support him and take the fight to the Labour Party. More to the point, he's determined to increase the representation of all minorities in Westminster. He's sick of middle-aged, middle-class men…'

'Men like him and Bud Brooke, you mean?' Ann interrupted.

'Middle-class men monopolising the Government benches – even the Lib-Dems stick to the stereotype. The media spotlight hits a by-election very hard. The glare means we have to ensure our candidate is entirely appropriate. Appropriate for the constituency, of course. But appropriate for the party and its aspirations for itself and the country. Lucy fits the bill exactly.'

Ann got up to make coffee, abandoning the debate because she didn't want to be rude to her guest and was not keen to damage Lucy's chances by provoking an argument. Clifford, like all politicians, had not actually answered the question. How can he be so sure she will be selected? How, for that matter, can Lucy? What do they know that she doesn't?

By the time he left, Clifford had given Lucy the names of a dozen people to meet in the next few days, ranging from Hampton Arden ('you really should get a car with a local dealer's name on it, Lucy. Makes people think you're from the same community'), Sir Oliver Williams, chairman of the cricket club ('fingers in a lot of pies, wealthy, good for introductions, definitely one of us'), Jimi Hunt and Newbold Whitnash, from the 'Barset Chronicle' ('don't trust Hunt but as he'll write about you anyway you might as well give yourself a chance. As for Newbold, he'll just love you'), Viscount Preston ('need the house for the fund-raisers'), Chatham Smith ('he'll support you, wants a knighthood') not to mention Sue Alne ('one of our more sensible councillors, never says anything') and Terry Page ('our glorious council leader, everybody hates him, he has no influence or power whatsoever, but you'll need to say hello to him some time so you might as well get it over with sooner rather than later').

*****

'No retreads.' Compton Dundon was sifting through the pile of applications. 'We need a shortlist of no more than a dozen. Half of them women, at least a quarter BMEs.' They also knew who would definitely be included in the shortlist. Lucy Loxley 'obviously', as Dundon said, but at least one local candidate because the party wanted to appear sensitive to the opinions of the members in Barset.

Steve Thomas, unfortunately sporting a prominent and ugly boil on his nose which made his usually-angry features particularly livid, was weeding out applications from men and placing one in every ten onto a second pile. Dundon, Thomas and Clifford Chambers were in the committee room at the Barset Working Men's Club on August Bank Holiday Monday. Each man had a cup of weak coffee which tasted even worse than it looked. They had a box of chocolates in the middle of the table, provided by Dundon. They each had a set of application papers.

Steve Thomas complained the whole exercise was pointless because they all knew what the result would be. Dundon said it was the price of democracy. 'And don't forget, Steve,' he added. 'Those 362 people whose applications we're going to throw away represent the backbone of the party. We need them to work for us, raise money, knock on doors. Who knows, one day we may even need them in Westminster? We have to give them a sense that we are being fair.'

'Due diligence,' said Clifford helpfully.

'Exactly.'

'Really no retreads?' Clifford asked. 'Not even Dilhara Mendis?'

'Mendy? The only man who lost a seat when the party won a landslide?' Dundon was contemptuous. 'Never met a lazier Member of Parliament. Too busy with his legal practice to bother with his constituents. No wonder he lost. No, definitely not.'

'He's a BME,' said Clifford coaxingly.

'Doesn't give him the right to lose his seat. And he can't complain about racism – he only got the seat because he was a BME. All the fool had to do was hold onto it and he couldn't even manage that.'

'Anthony Andrews?' Thomas inquired laughing.

'Andrews?' Clifford guffawed.

'Any man who resigns his seat, leaves his wife and children, takes up with another man, dumps that man for yet another man, then asks his wife to take him back and claims he was having a mid-life crisis cannot possibly expect to be taken back by the party even if his wife is foolish enough to do so.' They all chuckled over Andrews's fall from grace.

'Remember that dreadful photo-call?' Thomas reminisced as he consigned another dozen hopefuls to the reject pile. 'Andrews, three little Andrews sisters and Rocco or Rocky or whatever he was called. The lodger. Lodger? Ha!'

'We all knew about it months before it got on the internet,' Dundon told his colleagues. 'At least two people I know had enjoyed close encounters with him. But of course he was one of us – in every sense, I suppose – so we were honour-bound to sit on it.'

'Sit on it?' Thomas asked lewdly. Clifford looked uncomfortable at the direction the conversation had turned.

'Whatever.'

They worked on in silence except when one or another of them came across a candidate they knew of, when they would generally offer up disparaging remarks along the lines of 'too bald', 'smells', 'up himself' or 'a good Lord Mayor of Birmingham in a lean year', the put-down used by David Lloyd George to describe the wing-collared appeasement Prime Minister, Neville Chamberlain.

At mid-day they retired to the pub for fish and chips. The town centre was surprisingly busy. There was some sort of carnival and open air rock concert for the under-twelves in Throckmorton Park at 2pm.

Clifford didn't want to ask the question Ann had raised with him. Despite his impression of omniscience, he had no idea how they would engineer the selection of Lucy Loxley. He hoped Compton Dundon would explain, but the party fixer spent most of lunch on his mobile phone dealing with a backbench MP. 'Stupid bloody idiot,' Dundon complained at one point. 'Stupid fuckwit.'

Thomas, likewise, was on the phone dealing with the same fall-out. 'The moron,' he agreed. Neither of them explained what the MP had done or even who he might be. Clifford idly flicked through the Daily Mail on-line on his internet reader.

The MP in question was Hugh Lighthorne, aide to the chief whip. He had broken the rule that people in the whips' office were not allowed to comment on Government policy. They were 'enforcers' and were not supposed to have opinions. In Lighthorne's case, that wasn't usually a problem. Unfortunately he'd given an interview to 'Countryside Today' in which he said he thought the Government should stop wasting time with badger culling. It would never eradicate the problem of badgers carrying TB, he said. This was not Government policy. The official line was that there was a 'consultation exercise' followed by the establishment of an Office for the Protection of Rural Activities (already known as Opera) to be paid for by a tax on cattle. This was not straightforward or universally popular. Lighthorne would get carpeted and told to keep his mouth shut in future.

Back in the meeting room, Compton Dundon called for a review of the position so far. He announced he had seven BMEs, three men and four women. Chambers had seven women. Steve Thomas, rubbing his boil gently, had a dozen men. 'So, twenty-six candidates for a dozen places. Let's start with the definites. Clifford?'

He said: 'Lucy Loxley, obviously. Sharon Duggan. Wendy England.'

'The radio presenter? God no,' said Dundon. 'Did you hear her interview with Dave Hersey? Silly bloody woman asked him why the party was so keen on homosexuals. No thank you.'

Clifford suggested two other names who were also rejected. 'Well there's Maggie Pride, I suppose. Local woman. Used to be in TnA.'

'TnA? What the dancers?' Thomas looked interested.

'Yes but she's put on weight since those days. Still, we do need a local candidate.'

She was added to the shortlist.

Thomas ran through his candidates, throwing out anyone who had previously held elected office. As he said: 'We can't have any more professional politicians, can we?' They reduced the men to two, a retired army officer, Colonel Tim Buckley, and Conor George, the round-the-world backpacker and green activist.

Dundon ran through his names and concluded, 'So, we've got seven BMEs, four of them women, three white women including one lesbian, and two WASPs. Excellent, that makes 12 in total, seven of them women, seven of them BMEs. You can't say fairer than that. Plus we've got none of the usual suspects.'

'Except Parvinder,' Clifford reminded him.

'Yes, well her time will come.' Parvinder Singh was a party employee, excessively pretty and desired by most heterosexual men in the party headquarters. The difficulty was that she appeared on TV game shows whenever she had an opportunity and there were several popular clips of her on YouTube wearing little or nothing and a description of her as 'Bombay's answer to Paris Hilton' was trotted out whenever her name appeared, as it did all too often, on the gossip web-sites. 'She'll cheer everyone up at the selection meeting,' said the party fixer.

He was wrapping things up. He took the pile of rejections and said he would get Emma Loveitt, his personal assistant, to e-mail the unlucky candidates. He would also get her to send out the interview invitations and supervise the timings. It would be a long day if they were to crack through all 12 people in one session but it was better to get it sorted.

The mood was lifting so Clifford ventured to ask, 'How are we going to make sure the process delivers the result we all desire?'

Dundon sat down again and sighed heavily. Steve Thomas groaned. 'I don't believe I'm hearing this,' said Dundon. 'Clifford...' The party's chief of staff stared at the association chairman. Thomas's eyes blazed with a strange contempt.

'Well?' Clifford was non-plussed.

'Do we have to spell it out? Tell him, Steve.'

The press officer was at his most curt. He spoke with contempt. 'That's what you're here for, Clifford. You know what we need. You have to deliver. That's the deal. You get us the candidate, we deliver the MP. We don't need to know how you manage it.'

Clifford stared. 'You mean I have to fix the selection?'

'No, no, certainly not,' said Dundon. 'We leave election-fixing to the Opposition. We cannot fix elections. Think of the trouble it would cause. Luckily, Clifford, we have selected you a shortlist of candidates who will not prove particularly challenging. As chairman of the association you will be in a position to draw attention to their shortcomings. One way or another. Won't you?'

'Yes, of course. Of course.' Clifford was unconvinced. What was expected of him? How should he go about it?

'The party's management board is looking for talented younger members,' Dundon added, as he resumed packing up his papers. 'Knighthoods are not for sale these days, you know, Clifford. Not that most of us could afford one anyway.'

*****

Barset Borough Council's offices were modern, bright and clean. In the original artist's impressions the building was peopled by attractive-looking, well-dressed young men and women. The drawings held out the promise that the council would enjoy a building with the same status as the headquarters of a multi-national information technology business or a first class hotel in a Middle Eastern city state.

The impression was not borne out by reality. Once the visitor passed through the turnstiles beside reception and made his way through the double doors, already bruised and scraped by boots and trolleys, he was confronted by long corridors of the sort familiar from visiting older hospitals and schools. The offices were small, cramped and filled with files and computer screens. Their denizens seemed to be buried under paperwork. The corridors stretched, seemingly without end, past signs directing the visitor to various sections, ranging from Treasurer to Diversity to Enterprise.

Acton Trussell, well-known in these corridors of power, made his way purposefully towards Housing. There was a time when most of the staff here knew their local MP and would be interested in having a chat with him. Those times were long gone. These days, local government workers were so bogged down in directives and strategies, and were so cynical about their political masters, both national and local, that their aim was just to get through the day. One or two people nodded acknowledgement to Acton as he passed but nobody stopped to greet him, not even those few he had known and worked with for 20 years or more. Maybe, he thought, it's simply the result of no longer being an MP. I am nobody to them any more.

But it wasn't the case when he finally reached the Housing department and found Bill Rogers, its deputy head. Bill had been with the council for 30 years and was still only 51. He had no intention of taking early retirement. He sat with his feet in the desk drawer, his Barset Albion mug next to his scruffy computer keyboard, chewing an old biro. A box of nicotine-substitute chewing gum sat on the desk while gobbets of used gum wr1apped in pieces of paper piled up in and around the recycling bin.

'Bill, how's it going?' Acton knocked on the outer door of the glass-partitioned office and let himself in uninvited.

'Oh it's you. I might have guessed.' Rogers did not rise to greet his guest nor did he remove his feet from the drawer. Acton noticed his elderly Hush Puppies were placed underneath the desk. Rogers was in his socks.

'You're looking well, Bill.' And he was. Last time Acton met him, a few weeks before the smoking ban came into force, Rogers was sallow, coughing and his hair was a greasy mess. Now his complexion was definitely clearer and healthier-looking. There was no immediate coughing either.

'Ha!' Rogers pasted some gum into a piece of paper and lobbed it into the recycling basket near the door. He missed and the paper joined two or three other little packages which had so far failed to hit the target at the first attempt. 'Gum?' Rogers offered a stick of 'Quit-or-die heavy-duty life-saving tobacco substitute chewing gum' to his visitor.

'No, no, thank you Bill. I don't.'

'Ha!' the other man replied, devoting his attention to his keyboard and computer screen. 'You'll have to give me a minute, Acton, I'm just e-mailing the chief executive. Stupid bugger.' Rogers tapped away laboriously, eventually clicking 'send', removing his feet from the drawer, slipping into his Hush Puppies, sitting up, running a hand through his still-greasy hair, taking a slurp of cold, weak tea and eventually saying to Acton, 'So, what can I do you for, Mr Trussell? Bearing in mind, of course, that as you are no longer Member of Parliament for this rotten borough you have no power, no sway, no authority and no credibility any more.'

'And it's always a great pleasure to see you too, William.'

'Are you going to tell me, then?'

'About why I resigned? One day mabe, Bill, but not today. I can see you're busy.'

'Busy? Have you heard what that idiot Councillor Claverdon has decided now? We are supposed to carry out a house-to-house audit of our entire estate to establish whether there is any overcrowding. As if we don't know the answer already. Of course people are living in overcrowded houses but what do you expect? Some people have too many children. Then they expect us to give them bigger homes. Which we haven't got. So they say they're living in slum conditions and blame the council. It's all ridiculous.' Rogers chewed furiously on a new piece of gum and slurped some more cold tea before remembering to offer his guest a cup, which was declined. 'Well?' he said.

'In my capacity as not-an-MP-any-more I said I'd have a word on behalf of a constituent. Or should that be a former constituent? Either way,' Acton checked his e-mail print out, 'Her name is Mandy Black.' Rogers groaned. 'Ah you know her? Good. That saves a lot of time.'

'Acton, if she's got her talons into you too, you won't escape. Actually it's very difficult. We should re-house her.'

'But?'

'The health and safety people say they have to complete their inspection of the premises and the fire investigation people say they have to write a report and the police need to conduct a thorough inquiry and the insurance loss adjustors have to adjudicate. And until that's happened, we can't offer to re-house the family. In case, you know, it's arson. In case they did it themselves. Deliberately.'

'And is there any suggestion that they did?'

'No. Gas leak.'

'Well then?'

'Procedures.'

'Bill, isn't there anything you can do to speed it up a bit?'

'Out of my hands, old boy.'

'William.' Acton looked at him with amused scepticism.

'I'd love to help if only to get her off my back. Calls me three times a day.'

'Well?'

'Councillor Claverdon.' They both groaned. Langley Claverdon was the 'portfolio holder for social inclusion' which, apparently, meant head of the housing committee. Claverdon was trying to privatise the whole estate of 7,500 houses and 1,500 flats. He was not interested in individual tenants. 'Claver Clogs has announced there will be no re-housing at all until he has completed his review. So we need all the excuses we can get to fob people off. And in Ms Black's case, we've got plenty of them.'

'Has this policy been announced? In public, I mean?'

'Of course not. There would be hell to pay if it was. Nobody is to know about this. Claver Clogs calls it a moratorium. Not sure half the other Cabinet members know yet.'

*****

Acton took himself off to the 'Traveller's Rest', Councillor Claverdon's small hotel, which he sometimes visited for a drink when he was in town. It was a Monday so he was not surprised to find Langley there, behind the bar, discussing business with three fellow Rotarians.

Claverdon was a short, clever, lively man in his early thirties who had inherited a family business six years ago and seen it reduced to just the one hotel in the Great Recession. He was determined to build it back up again. His housing privatisation plans were part of this, as was his election to the council three years ago.

'Acton! Gentlemen, our former Member of Parliament. What a pleasure, Acton.' Trussell could never tell whether this man was sincere but assumed not.

'Langley,' he acknowledged and shook hands with the others, all of whom he knew vaguely. It was one of the curses of politics: Acton knew the faces but had no idea where, or how often, if at all, he had met these three men. He'd spoken at Rotary lunches many times over the years and really should have tried harder to put names to faces. But he relied on Clarissa to help him out. He resorted to the old tactic of offering his hand and shaking them one by one announcing 'Hello, Acton Trussell' in the hope that they would respond by offering their name in exchange.

Today, though, the first man, a tall, fit looking chap who could well be a rugby player, replied, 'Of course I know who you are, who could forget the infamous Acton Trussell?' The others laughed and Acton chuckled politely.

'So come on then Acton,' said the shortest of the trio, 'Is she really such a terrible woman?'

More chuckles as Claverdon asked what he was drinking and the ex-MP skirted around the main points of his resignation while remaining polite, diplomatic and non-committal.

The conversation moved onto the Government's record and the personality of the Prime Minister. 'He's a good bloke,' declared the rugby-type. 'Tough but compassionate. I like what he's doing.' There was general agreement that he was on the right track. Claverdon beamed with pleasure and handed Acton half a pint of Barsetshire Superb, one of the weaker local beers.

It took some time for Acton to get a chance for a quiet word with Claverdon but when the opportunity arose, he decided to be straightforward. 'Your housing moratorium, Langley. I need you to lift it in the case of Mandy Black and her family, the woman whose house burnt down. I called to have a look at the ruins on my way in. I gather there's no question of arson, her daughter is at risk and the family deserves help. I take it we have suitable voids.'

'We do but that's not the point, Clifford, we are carrying out an audit.'

'Does the "Chronic" know about it?'

'Of course not.' Claverdon looked horrified and gripped the beer pumps with both hands, as if to steady himself. 'God, imagine.' He imagined and frowned.

'I am not sure you will be able to keep it from the "Chronic" indefinitely, you know, Langley. Ms Black is not the sort of woman who takes no for an answer. She's bound to talk to the paper sooner or later. And if she does, well, who knows what they may uncover? It only needs one housing officer to breathe something off the record and then where's your moratorium?'

Acton looked at the man behind the bar. He was clearly ambitious, with a name and a fortune to make. He would cut corners and do deals when he could. He was obviously worried. The frown deepened across his narrow forehead. His hands continued to grip the pumps though the bar was now empty of customers except for Trussell and the chill-effect meant Claverdon's hands were becoming gradually colder and damper as water dripped down onto them. His stubby fingers were turning white.

'So you're saying...' Claverdon began cautiously.

'I'm saying it would be wise to nip this in the bud. Do the right thing for the woman and her family. And get on with your audit as quickly as possible. I don't think the 'Chronic' would take kindly to the news that council houses are standing empty while the waiting list gets longer just because you have called in the accountants.'

Trussell wondered if he was threatening Claverdon or simply alerting him to the dangers. But it was plain the councillor took this as a friendly word of warning. 'You think it might be wise to do something for the Black family?'

'Wouldn't do any harm.'

When Acton left, he was grinning to himself. I may be an ex-politician, he was thinking, but I have learned a few things over the years. At least Mandy Black and her daughter would be reunited. My good deed for the day.

*****

'Why do you want to become a Member of Parliament, Loose?'

Lucy Loxley was standing in the lounge of her uncle's home being questioned by her brother Robin, uncle Richard, aunt Ann and girlfriend Joanna.

Joanna was lying on the floor wearing a track-suit, doing sit-ups, her short black hair bobbing about as she exercised. She was preparing for her next triathlon in Frankfurt. It was she who asked the question, which prompted murmurs of support from uncle and aunt.

Lucy had asked them to act as an interview panel. She had treated them to a speech on the political state of the nation, the problems of Third World debt and her concerns over the situation in Kashmir. Ann had already asked her whether she would do anything to revive Barset town centre. Lucy's response was generally agreed to be unsatisfactory – she had gone on about economic revival. Richard said she should talk about rate relief and suggested redevelopment.

And now this. The killer question. 'Why do you want to be a Member of Parliament?'

Lucy, who was expecting them to tell her how marvellous her performance was, played for time. 'What? Isn't that a bit too obvious for them to ask?'

Everyone agreed it wasn't necessarily obvious. 'I know the expenses stuff is history now but politicians still have a terrible reputation,' said Ann.

'God yes,' added Robin. 'You wouldn't want them to think you're some spivvy estate agent like that bloke what's his name? The local chairman?'

'Oh I think Clifford's quite nice.'

'We all know he thinks you're quite nice, don't we?' chuckled Joanna in between grunts. She was up to 154 and the sit-ups were becoming a bit of a strain. 'He likes the idea of two women... you know.' Ann was shocked but pretended not to be. Richard chuckled. Robin smiled. 'Anyway,' Joanna went on, 'Answer the question. We know you're a politician and never answer the question but you've got to say something more than just 'isn't it obvious?' 'cos it isn't.'

Lucy stood before them, in front of the fireplace with its big gilt mirror. She was wearing jeans and a white blouse, a single string of pearls and her hair was messy because she had been moving files and computers in her office upstairs. The lid below her left eye twitched. Nerves or lack of vitamins, Joanna thought.

'Why do I want to be an MP? Well, it's a natural progression, isn't it? I've always been interested in politics. I'm a councillor in London. I have been a member of several important committees. I've been the Cabinet portfolio holder for economic development. I support our party leader in his campaign to modernise the party. I want to…'

Joanna stopped her exercises, sat up straight and interrupted Lucy. 'I, I, I, me, me, me. Come on Loose, if that's the best you can do they really will look for someone else.'

Robin took up the theme. 'Joanna's right, Lucy. What you say is all well and good. But what can you offer these people that singles you out from the other candidates?'

Ann, whose frown was deepening again, added, 'It's not even that. It is what can you bring to Barset which is unique to you? To the town, the constituency, the voters? Why should they choose you rather than any other Tom, Dick or Harriet?'

'She's right, Loose,' Joanna added. It looked to Lucy as if Joanna was actually enjoying her discomfort and she felt for a moment as if she might burst into tears and behave like a spoilt child who has been told off by the grown-ups. But that was a ridiculous reaction.

'I would like to be the MP for Barset because I will be able to use my talents to benefit this town.'

'It's a start,' Joanna admitted. 'What are these talents, exactly?'

'I am a successful, young businesswoman. The skills I have acquired will be devoted to the economic and social development of a cohesive town according to the vision set out by our party leader, who I know personally and have nothing but admiration for.'

Uncle Richard was frowning. He'd been leaning back on the sofa apparently not paying much attention. He now pronounced, 'I am not sure that explains why you want to become an MP. You could, after all, use those talents on behalf of Barset without becoming a Member of Parliament at all.'

'Especially if you actually lived here,' Ann added under her breath.

Richard repeated the question, 'Why do you want to become an MP?' He paused and went on, not critically but as if he were holding a debate with himself, 'We all know why people become politicians. It's show-business for ugly people. You want the attention, the fame, the notoriety. You want to be noticed, it's probably some kind of thwarted childhood Oedipus complex. Did you feel ignored as a girl, Lucy? Don't answer that. The point is, the real reasons you want to become an MP are not reasons you can possibly admit to in public. The traditional answers are always bollocks. 'Public service'. Isn't that what they usually say? 'Giving something back?' 'For the good of my country?' What you need to think about, Lucy, if I may say so, is an answer to this question that isn't bogus, isn't all about you, and has a modicum of credibility. Everyone knows the real reasons. Don't we folks?' Everyone chuckled, except Lucy, who again felt tears pricking her eyes. 'I think you need to work on that one, Lucy.'

The would-be MP stopped holding court and squatted on a stool to one side of the fireplace. 'Anyway,' she asked, 'What do you think I should wear for my interview?'

*****

They were all there. Nobody would miss an opportunity like this. To select your Member of Parliament, to sit in judgment on a dozen wannabes, to influence the course of history.

The meeting room at the working men's club had been set out in a horseshoe of desks around a small table where each candidate would have to sit or stand, depending on her choice. She would be led into the room from the bar, where candidates would be offered a cup of tea or coffee by Terry or Finola and might choose to peruse their copy of 'The Sun' as a piece of last-minute revision to make sure they understood the views of working people. They would then be summoned to the meeting by Compton Dundon and given half an hour to sell themselves. Each member of the local executive committee was provided with a timetable and scoring sheets where they were asked to rate the performance under a number of headings: Ability and credibility; Presence; Local knowledge; Political knowledge and commitment. On each seat, Clifford Chambers placed a set of the candidates' CVs.

The committee was summoned to attend at 8.30am on the dot for a briefing by Clifford Chambers under the supervision of Compton Dundon. The first members were there by eight o'clock. The last were still five minutes early. Nobody wanted to miss the fun.

There were 15 people, apart from Chambers, Dundon and Steve Thomas, whose nose was still red and livid and who placed himself in a corner, slightly detached from the proceedings. He said he wanted to be there because, if he was to have responsibility for selling 'this joker' to the voters of Barset, he needed to see how they performed under pressure. He was also looking for flaws the others might not notice. While he and Dundon had already decided who the candidate should be, it was felt wise to keep an eye out for an alternative if things went wrong.

The young, thrusting, entrepreneurial wing of the party was represented by Hampton Arden, the car dealer, who spent all day fiddling with his i-Phone. The youth wing was personified by Matt Simpson, the somewhat overweight and leaden-footed vice chairman of the Barset St Leonard's ward when he wasn't at university in Exeter studying human geography. Matt was disappointed he wasn't allowed to bring his potential girlfriend Rosie with him. Rosie had recently been talked into joining the party and Matt hoped he might have made some progress with her if he'd got her into the meeting but Clifford was adamant. Clifford was very forceful, Matt thought, and it didn't do to get on the wrong side of him.

Gary Atherstone was there, carefully scrutinising the paperwork and laying his pencil, pencil sharpener and fountain pen like knife, fork and spoon, on the desk before him. Quentin Quinton sat beside him beaming at everybody and discussing the prospects for the one-day cricket international with the leader of the local council, Terry Page. Trying to muscle in on the conversation was Tony Grafton, whose bulk made the others feel uncomfortably claustrophobic. Page was not interested in cricket. He wanted a word with Langley Claverdon before proceedings got under way. But Claverdon had buttonholed old Pinky Green, the secretary of his ward party, to discuss their plans for a Hallowe'en drinks and nibbles party. Pinky was still in his 70s while Mavis Murcot and Henry Hardcastle, who were chatting about begonias, were well into their 80s. Alan McPherson and Beryl Bishop were discussing their impressions of the candidates, based on their application forms, with Samantha Chambers and Sybil Whitney.

Clifford was nervous about his older sister's presence. She, of all the assembled company, was someone he knew he could not control. Worse than that, she had the power to cause his reputation real harm if she chose to use it. They had already fallen out over whether she should attend at all – she explained that as a member of the executive in her own right, she would be failing in her duty if she did not – and over Clifford's announcement that he would be relying on her to help ensure the committee reached the right decision. 'At this moment, Samantha, all we must agree on is that Lucy Loxley goes through to the next round.' She was not receptive to the idea, arguing they should select a local man. 'We can't select a man, Samantha. How many times do I have to explain it to you?'

Clifford reminded everyone that if they wanted any coffee or biscuits they should get them now. This took almost ten minutes. He then called the meeting to order. It was ten to nine and they still hadn't discussed the ground rules.

Just as Clifford was about to launch into his speech, the door was flung open and a young woman rushed in. 'Sorry I'm late, everyone,' she announced in a confident and well-spoken voice. 'Daddy told me I had to come. I know it's all a bit embarrassing but one must do one's duty, as a member of the executive, I suppose.'

The woman wore a flowery skirt, a brightly-coloured top and leather boots. She had a shock of red hair tied in an artfully untidy bundle on the top of her head, a yellow handbag hung from one shoulder and she manoeuvred herself into an empty seat beside Tony Grafton, who beamed with satisfaction at her arrival and greeted her with an unexpected kiss on the cheek. 'I wondered if you'd make it, Livvy,' he said in a stage whisper. 'You're looking lovely.'

'I'm sorry, Mister Chairman.' It was Gary Atherstone, his voice already rising to a squeak as indignation got the better of him. 'Mister Chairman. Chair. Is this not ultra vires? Surely it must be ultra vires? This cannot be acceptable.'

Several voices broke out at once, as the new arrival looked about her with a serene smile, which suggested perplexity also suggested a certain satisfaction at the stir she had caused.

Clifford fished his gavel out of his briefcase. He had brought it in case of emergencies. This was an emergency. He banged it three times on the table, cracking the Formica slightly. Compton Dundon, sitting on his right hand side, leaned over and whispered, Chambers thought somewhat superfluously, 'You need to sort this, Clifford.'

'Olivia,' Clifford said in his most authoritative voice. 'Olivia. I am not sure it is appropriate for you to attend this selection meeting. In the circumstances. I think I speak for the majority of those present if I say it would be more appropriate if you were to withdraw.'

'Are you saying she should resign?' asked Tony Grafton, his Barset accent coming to the fore. The question sounded more like a threat.

'No, I am not asking Olivia to resign. But in the circumstances...'

'Mr Chair,' said Councillor Claverdon. 'I do think this is not really appropriate.'

'Inappropriate. Entirely inappropriate. Entirely,' agreed Chambers. Further debate and discussion followed. The new arrival sat serenely, her long fingers stretched out on the table before her, gazing across the room at the space where the small photograph of her father, Acton Trussell, used to hang.

Compton Dundon stood up and, taking Chambers's gavel, tapped the table a couple of times. 'Ladies and gentlemen. For the benefit of those I have not had a chance to meet yet, my name is Compton Dundon. I am Chief of Staff at party headquarters and I am here representing the party chairman and the leader himself. I am also here to adjudicate on issues arising in relation to the party rules. There is no rule to cover this eventuality. If Miss Trussell will not withdraw...' He looked towards Olivia, who remained calm and would not meet his eye, 'If she will not withdraw then it is a question for the rest of the committee whether you wish to work alongside her or not. I propose we resolve this immediately. The first candidate is already waiting downstairs and we have a long day ahead of us. So, would those in favour of Ms Trussell remaining on the selection committee please indicate their support now?'

Quentin Quinton was the first to raise his hand. He beamed towards Olivia as if to say, 'I am doing this for your father.' Terry Page raised his hand, followed almost immediately by Alan McPherson and Pinky Green. Tony Grafton raised both his hands high over his head. Clifford was counting. Five. Sybil Whitney raised her hand tentatively. Six. She's out.

'Those against?' asked Dundon.

Immediately Matt Simpson, Gary Atherstone, Hampton Arden and Langley Claverdon raised their hands. Four. Clifford raised his. Five. Sue Alne reluctantly raised her hand. Six. 'What about the others?' Clifford asked.

'Abstentions?' asked Dundon. Mavis Murcot, Henry Hardcastle, and Beryl Bishop all raised their hands.

'Samantha?'

'Miss Chambers, it seems you have the casting vote,' said the party fixer. Samantha smiled. 'If you force me to vote, I will, but I would prefer not to.'

'Samantha?'

'I think it would be helpful,' said Dundon.

'Very well then, I vote for the motion. Olivia should stay.'

'Samantha.' Clifford felt the blood drain from his face.

Olivia stood up. 'Samantha, thank you very much. I am sorry my presence has been the cause of this conflict. I think it would be better if I were to withdraw. I am sorry. Thank you all.' With that she collected up her papers and left the room.

Samantha smiled ruefully. Clifford tried to make a joke of it. 'Perhaps we can make a start. Now the Trussells have finally resigned.'

*****

The selection committee was given a briefing by Compton Dundon; Clifford Chambers felt the need to re-interpret it. There were several confused questions to be answered. The first candidate was ushered in half an hour late.

As the young man before them started to thank the committee for inviting him to attend and explain that he wanted to tell them what he would do when he was the MP for Barset, a perplexed Sue Alne, who had been scrabbling desperately through the papers before her, interrupted. 'Mister Chairman, I thought we would be interviewing a white lady first called Viv Arnold. This gentleman is neither white, nor is he a woman.'

The candidate was obliged to explain, 'No, you see, my full name is Vivek, which is an Indian name, but it has been shortened to Viv for years. And as for my surname, Arnold is actually quite a common surname in the subcontinent.'

Viv Arnold was a London lawyer. He was smooth, sophisticated and immaculately dressed. He charmed the ladies with his belief in the importance of marriage. Beryl Bishop said afterwards he was lovely though Terry Page said grumpily, 'He's a bloody lawyer. Can't trust any of 'em.'

Next up was Sharon Duggan, a middle-aged woman six feet six inches tall and broadly built. She was the leader of a local authority in the North of England who devoted her time to improving the situation for 'my people'. Asked why she would want a seat in Barset when she was clearly so devoted to Northern folk, she said it would help consolidate her power base. This did not impress many people.

Conor George was the son of an Earl. He had recently left Cambridge, where he failed to become President of the Union. He was still chairman of the party in the city, on the party defence think-tank, knew the leader and his family socially and expected to be given the seat. His priorities included the preservation of ancient buildings. He had noted the valuable Georgian facades on several shops in the High Street were in need of renovation and hoped, as MP, to secure the necessary funding. He added that if he were to be selected he could promise his campaign would benefit from the active participation of his childhood nanny.

Parvinder Singh arrived so late that, even though the proceedings were running late anyway, the committee had to sit around for twenty minutes before she made an appearance. They almost asked Lucy Loxley in ahead of her. Just as Dundon was giving up hope, she breezed in wearing a beautiful pink and turquoise blue silk sari. She apologised, smiled at all the men, chatted about what a lovely constituency this was, dropped a few names and said if she had to be stuck on a desert island the one thing she would take with her was a traffic-free motorway.

The men all sat up and paid attention when Parvinder was in the room. She was petite, flirtatious and full of energy. She could not stand still even when she was giving her ten-minute speech, preferring to wander around and stand behind the shoulders of the committee members, breathing exotic perfumes down the necks of Gary Atherstone and Tony Grafton.

Lucy Loxley was fifth. Clifford deliberately put her in that position because it was close to lunch, everyone would be eager for a break and would be pleased with her if she was brief and to the point. That's what he had instructed her to be.

'Looks are everything,' Robin reminded his sister the night before. 'Never mind what you say, it's how you look that matters.'

She was nervous. As she waited for her interview, staring at a weak cup of coffee Terry had provided for her, she was shaking and her left eyelid was twitching furiously. Her hand couldn't lift the cup or put it back in the saucer without upsetting some of the coffee. Luckily it didn't spill on her dark blue silk dress. She tried reading the paper but couldn't even absorb the headline in "The Sun" – something to do with a love-rat soap star. She fumbled for the notes in her businesslike blue handbag, tried reading them, closed her eyes and imagined herself speaking. And couldn't. Nor could she speak to the hideously cheerful West Indian who introduced himself as Wesley Small and was due on after her. The best she could manage was a weak handshake.

Dundon came to fetch her just as she decided she needed another visit to the ladies'. He was forced to hang around outside and this delayed the interview process for another few minutes.

Once she launched into her speech, Lucy relaxed a little. This was familiar territory. The interviewers were types she knew well, old-school party stalwarts. Admittedly they were more down-market but they shared the same prejudices. Up to a point, at least.

'Our future,' she was telling them, 'As a country lies in international trade and co-operation, we must work for social inclusion and integration. The Prime Minister is determined to lead us to a prosperous and inclusive future and I am determined to play my part in helping to bring about this future world.'

There was a short silence when she finished. Clifford looked at Dundon who looked at Thomas who frowned. Mrs Murcot asked the first scripted question: 'What brought you into politics?'

Lucy said the opportunity to be serve, to help people, her abiding interest in creating a climate of opportunity for all. Clifford smiled encouragingly.

Did she agree women and ethnic minorities were under-represented? She did, but she did not approve of positive discrimination. She would like to be their MP but she would like to be selected on merit not to fulfil some quota system. Clifford nodded approval.

What would she take onto a desert island? Her web-enabled laptop because then she could communicate with anyone she wanted to from wherever she happened to be. She believed communication was the key to success in politics. And she could keep in touch with her family, her mother and father, her brother, all her relatives. There was nothing more important than families.

Clifford looked around him beaming. Does anyone have any last question they would like to ask Lucy? Tony Grafton caught the chairman's eye, got the nod and asked, 'You haven't mentioned Action Trussell, Ms Loxley. What is your view of our former MP?'

'I know Acton and like him very much indeed, I respect him and he has had a very successful career in politics. He has been an excellent servant to this constituency. He has some notable achievements to his credit – saving the Cottage Hospital for one – and I would be happy if I could be as devoted a servant to Barset as Acton Trussell was.'

'But what about his resignation?' Grafton asked before Chambers could silence him.

'Well, that was a matter for Mr Trussell. I do not pretend to know the circumstances surrounding it. I just know it will be hard to fill his shoes. But I would like to be given the chance to try.'

And that was it. Lucy fled to the ladies'. She saw a flustered young woman whose cheeks glowed bright red. A blue vein beat out across her high forehead. Her short, blonde hair still looked stylish, though, and her dress was perfect for the occasion. She unnecessarily adjusted her mascara, ran her wrists under cold water and looked around for a dryer only to be disappointed.

She headed for the car-park to discover this September day was mildly warm and sunny. She was looking for her Jaguar then remembered she'd borrowed Ann's Golf instead. She thought a Jag might be a bit ostentatious in such a poor town.

At least nobody had asked about lesbianism.

*****

The selection meeting went on all afternoon. Helen Panesar, the business-woman who ran a small chain of discount Web 3.0 stores was followed by Antara Muthupalanialpan who caused consternation because nobody could pronounce her name and who did not have a sense of humour. Sonia Prassana was a short, fat woman who worked as a lecturer in economics. She impressed everyone with her story about attending a meeting in New York on the day the terrorists flew into the 'twin towers' of the World Trade Centre and she was only a few hundred yards away drinking coffee with a colleague who would otherwise have been in his office in the 75th floor. She told the story to impress on the committee her anti-terrorism credentials. But she did lose marks by declaring that 'Moslems are not to be trusted'.

Ravi Viraj was another London lawyer, like Viv Arnold but less handsome and more interested in helping the poor and dispossessed than in multi-million-euro deals. Colonel Tim Buckley drew on his experiences in the army and appealed for a future based on the values of the past. He confessed he had never visited Barset before but said he had heard a lot about the place and was looking forward to becoming better acquainted with the city.

'Town,' Terry Page corrected him. 'No cathedral.'

It was well after seven o'clock when Maggie Pride was finally summoned. Everyone was tired and few were able to concentrate on what she said. Several of them glanced surreptitiously at their watches whenever they thought no-one else was looking. They all knew there was a voting session to come and dreaded the idea of a long battle over who might go through to the next round.

Clifford had placed Maggie last for this reason. He assumed not only that nobody would be listening but that they would dismiss what she had to say because they were fed up and wanted to go home. Maggie had other ideas.

She wore leather jeans and a frilly white shirt with a red scarf at her throat. She managed to conceal some of her excess weight and, by the lavish use of make-up and the advantageous services of a push-up bra, succeeded in making herself look surprisingly interesting. Not attractive, necessarily, but at least worth a look, Terry Page thought. A bit like that old pop singer, what was her name? The one who got lost in France? Bonny somebody-or-other.

Maggie appealed to the locals to select a local. 'I know this town inside out,' she said. 'I have been involved in many of our major annual events like the dance festival, with Clifford,' she said, smiling at the chairman. 'I am known here, a little, thanks to my past career. 'The Chronic' has featured me once or twice and I know the people on the paper. I can secure good publicity for us. I am concerned for the big issues affecting Barset – single mothers, worklessness, the decline of our shopping centre, the disappearance of major employers. I want to help with the economic development of our community.'

At last Quentin Quinton asked the question he had wanted to put to the other women but never had the chance. 'Mrs Pride,' he said, smiling. 'You are, how old, forty-two, three? You are married. You have a successful husband and three young children. If you are away in Westminster for the whole of the week, no doubt you can deal with the child-care issues. What worries me, though, and this is something I really wonder if you have properly addressed yet, what worries me is that if you were to become our Member of Parliament and live half your life in London, what on earth would your husband do?' Maggie looked puzzled. 'What would your husband do for sex, I mean? What would he do for sex? We wouldn't want him to end up like Jacqui Smith's husband watching pornography and charging the taxpayer for it, would we?'

Clifford interrupted. 'Don't answer that, Mrs Pride. That question is wholly inappropriate. I really must apologise. Thank you. Compton, would you show Mrs Pride out please?'

Maggie was shocked. She tried to leave with dignity intact but as soon as she was outside she turned on Dundon. 'How dare he? How dare he? How dare he?' It was all she could say.

Dundon had the decency not to laugh. This was one for the boys back at party HQ. Stupid little cow, if she'd got any sort of a sense of humour she could have dealt with that well enough. But Pride by name, he supposed.

By the time he quietened Maggie down and trudged back upstairs, the committee was in uproar. Clifford was remonstrating with Quentin, Tony Grafton was arguing in favour of the question, Henry Hardcastle was discussing with Pinky Green where they would go for sex in similar circumstances, Terry Page was laughing at Beryl Bishop because Beryl hadn't understood the question in the first place.

Dundon stood by the door and announced, 'We will reconvene at 11 am tomorrow to make our decision. This meeting is now closed.' He looked at Clifford, daring him to issue a challenge but Clifford was only too pleased to be able to beat a retreat. 'Come along, Samantha, let's go. If we hurry I can just get a quick mow in before it gets dark.'

Several people protested that they could not make it tomorrow as they had other things to do. Dundon told them to leave their appraisal sheets with him and he would make sure they were taken into account.

Tony Grafton stood up to make a loud speech of protest but then thought better of it. Even he'd had enough for one day.

*****

The committee reconvened at 11am, or at least nine of them did: Compton Dundon and Steve Thomas, who had spent the night drinking in the deserted bar of the Barset Sleepover Hotel, Clifford Chambers and his sister Samantha, Gary Atherstone, Tony Grafton, who was looking particularly grumpy, Mavis Murcot, Henry Hardcastle and Councillor Sue Alne.

As soon as they sat down, Dundon announced: 'I have already totted up the votes of the other members of the selection panel. If you could let me have your own score sheets, I will complete the count and announce the winner.'

Tony Grafton stood up. 'Mister Chairman,' he demanded, while simultaneously waving away the score-sheets proffered by Sue Alne and Mavis Murcot on his left. Compton Dundon got up to collect them. 'Is this acceptable? Surely we are entitled to a discussion, a debate, some sort of collective consultation. Surely we don't just hand in our scorecards like we're on 'Strictly Come Dancing'.' He went on in this vein for some time as Clifford tried, and failed, to interrupt him and Compton Dundon started adding the scores of the others to his master sheet.

Gary Atherstone began to speak as well. He and Grafton traded constitutional amendments and accusations of trickery. The word 'gerrymandering' was spoken several times, each time a little more loudly than the last though Atherstone's nasal whine made it more and more difficult to understand what point he was making, while Grafton's heavy accent, in keeping with his lumbering body, grew thicker and more indignant. It wasn't so much the sally and riposte of refined debate, more like the lumbering broadsword of Grafton's heavy cavalry versus the rat-like cunning of Atherstone's fierce stiletto jabs.

Each felt wounded though neither was hurt. Clifford Chambers grinned stupidly and shook his head. Steve Thomas checked his i-Phone, Samantha Chambers discussed flower arrangements with Mavis Murcot, Henry Hardcastle was straining to hear what Grafton and Atherston were saying and Sue Alne was poring over the report for the next planning committee meeting.

Compton Dundon announced: 'With the exception of Mr Grafton's votes, we now have a complete set. Mr Grafton, are you prepared to hand me your scoresheet?'

Grafton said he was not.

There was a silence. The big man turned on the agent from party headquarters and repeated: 'Where's the debate? How do we know the figures you have there are accurate? What's the point in asking us to draw up a shortlist if all you plan to do is sit there like some bloody accountant adding up the scores and ticking all the boxes?'

Gary Atherstone slowly rose from his seat. 'You may be a big fat bully,' he said, slowly and deliberately, his voice rising to its habitual whine, 'But you can't intimidate me. You oaf.'

Grafton clambered over the desk and headed for the smaller man. Towering over Atherstone, he suggested they settle their dispute outside.

Mavis Murcot leaned forward, eager to watch the fight develop. 'I love a good scrap,' she told Henry Hardcastle, 'It's just like the war.'

Hardcastle nodded while Sue Alne looked up from her reports to ask what was going on and Samantha Chambers said, 'Clifford, this really is too bad'. Steve Thomas stepped forward, as if to intervene, then thought better of it. Clifford grinned. Compton Dundon raised his voice. 'If there is any further argument, I am authorised by CCHQ to cancel the selection process entirely and institute the usual by-election procedures which, in this instance, means choosing the candidate without reference to the constituency association,' he said.

The party fixer stacked his papers in front of him, picked them up with some deliberation, said 'Come with me' to Steve Thomas and Clifford Chambers and walked from the room leaving Grafton standing over Atherstone with a look of incredulity on his chubby face while the smaller man grinned in triumph.

In the pokey room next door, Dundon announced the winners. He said those going through to the second and final round would be Viv Arnold, the London lawyer, Parvinder Singh, the beauty in the sari, Lucy Loxley and Maggie Pride.

Clifford nodded sagely. Thomas noted the names on his i-Phone. Dundon deliberately and carefully tore up the score-sheets and the sheet he had used to make the calculations, leaving nothing but a piece of paper with the four names on it.

'Happy?' he asked Clifford.

'Maggie Pride?'

'She came top of the poll. Almost everyone gave her higher marks than any of the others.'

'Don't worry,' Thomas said with a sly grin. 'By the time that story about her husband's sex life has appeared in a couple of diary pieces, she won't pose much of a threat.'

'I can't believe they went for Viv Arnold,' said Clifford.

'Oh they didn't,' Dundon said breezily. 'Actually he came pretty near the bottom but that's OK. We needed a man and we needed a man who wouldn't win. So he was the natural choice.'

Clifford chuckled. 'But Parvinder?'

'Beautiful, beautiful,' Dundon agreed. 'But don't worry about her either. I think you'll find she will not be here next week.' Thomas grinned again. 'Shall we go back?'

In the larger room, the remnants of the selection committee were sitting around waiting for something to happen, not sure whether to stay or go. Compton Dundon handed the piece of paper to Clifford Chambers, who cleared his throat officiously and announced, 'After due process, we have selected the following four candidates to go forward to the second and final round of the process to select a Parliamentary candidate for the constituency of Barset in place of our former representative Mr Acton Trussell. Viv Arnold, Parvinder Singh, Lucy Loxley and Maggie Pride.'

'Who?' asked Sue Alne.

'Good for Mags,' said Henry Hardcastle.

'Good Lord,' declared Gary Atherstone.

'What?' demanded Tony Grafton.

Chapter 7

Aston Cantlow began worrying several days after he'd handed his DVD to Acton Trussell. Nothing had happened. No reaction. No thanks – obviously. But, apart from the MP's resignation, silence. He trawled the web day after day but nothing new appeared. He tried the illegal sites as well as the obvious ones. He hacked into the party's own database and inspected its private files on the departing MP. He discovered, among other things, a briefing paper prepared by someone called Compton Dundon saying that his successor was to be a woman called Lucy Loxley, that the by-election would be on November 5, that the main opposition parties were not expected to put up a fierce contest and the Liberal Democrats had agreed not to field a candidate, as part of the 'power-sharing' agreement between the Coalition partners. Even this document was vague about the precise reasons for Trussell's resignation. It only said he quit 'amid unspecified scandal'.

Aston clicked on his own version of the short piece of footage he had obtained in a random trawl of security camera databases. There it was: the MP comes out of the side door of the community hall, the security lights go on and he can be seen quite clearly looking up at the camera. He then walks into the shadows. There is a brief illumination followed by a red glow which rises and falls from time to time as a dark figure raises it to its lips. The smoke from Trussell's cigarette billows back towards the brightly-lit area. That, in itself, might not be enough to prove completely the MP was smoking an illegal cigarette. But the crucial moment comes when he returns into the light, takes a last quick drag on the almost-finished cigarette, drops it on the concrete, stubs it out, picks up the butt and carefully places it in a metal container which he slips into his pocket before taking out a can of breath freshener, squirting it into his open mouth, brushing down his coat to remove imaginary signs of ash. He looks briefly around him into the gloom, opens the door and returns inside the building.

Aston believed he was the only person to own a copy of this three-minute sequence. He'd got hold of it illegally. In his opinion, far too many CCTV systems were now connected to a central server where the images were retained for months before being archived. Once you gained access to the server, you had access to every spying eye the security company possessed.

Of course, it took a long time to find anything interesting on the cameras if you didn't know what you were looking for but Aston Cantlow didn't mind; he was working on a program which would do the filtering for him. It could go through hours of images in next to no time and tag what it thought might interest him. That was how he'd found Acton Trussell's crafty fag.

He wasn't the one who had betrayed the MP. He couldn't explain who had done. He didn't believe Solid Oak Securities, the company which operated these cameras, had ever been through the images. Maybe someone had spotted it at the time, someone in the control room who didn't have access to the data itself but who was responsible for monitoring the cameras in case a crime was committed. That monitor may have noted the incident without taking action and later passed on some information to a contact, a journalist, say, or a member of the Opposition. That way they could have made trouble, spread rumour and gossip, without ever getting hold of the footage itself.

It might explain why the MP had been forced to quit – the threat of exposure was enough.

Aston Cantlow thought this was very unfair. Acton Trussell seemed like a decent bloke. He'd never even been reprimanded over the great expenses scandal. He had tried to help Aston's mum when she needed re-housing. He was always in the "Chronic". And what he'd done was legal only 12 months ago. Why should he be forced to give up his job just for having a crafty cigarette, even if it was against the law these days?

Aston had never smoked. He'd never even tried. But he hated the way the Government told everyone what to do, all the time. And, while he had never actually flown, Aston liked the idea that he could hop on a plane and travel the world. It was so unfair the Government had decided to impose a 100 per cent tax on air travel.

They said it was to save the planet and prevent global warming. Aston Cantlow wasn't stupid. He may be only 17 but even he could work out that the real reason for the new 'environmental surcharge' on flying was to make up for the money the Government had lost by banning the sale and consumption of cigarettes and other tobacco products.

It was all bollocks. That was what he said when he was discussing it at school the other day though everyone laughed at him, telling him he was a know-nothing loser. Aston did have Miss Hendricks' support, though. Miss Hendricks used to smoke and she had found abandonment particularly difficult. Even now she was on patches, as she reminded her students every morning when she lost her temper and said, 'Don't blame me, blame the bloody Prime Minister and his attack on civil liberties'.

Aston rather liked Miss Hendricks. He only got taught by her for one lesson a week because he was studying physics, maths and chemistry and Miss Hendricks taught politics. But he was in her citizenship class on Thursday afternoons. He looked forward to these lessons because it gave him a wider perspective on the world. It was also nice to watch Miss Hendricks, who was bright, bubbly, with rosy cheeks and a glint in her eye. She also had large round breasts and sometimes Aston would fantasise about them in the privacy of his own bedroom.

That's where he was now. In his bedroom listening to his father's old Wreckage audio files. Aston loved The Wreckage. Usually he listened to bands like Scumbag Vomit, Avenger and Death Howl but sometimes he liked the old classics: The Wreckage, Free, Megadeath, Metallica, stuff like that.

He couldn't understand why Acton Trussell had been forced to resign without the reason ever becoming public. He had tried to present the MP with the information in person, but it seems Trussell never looked at it. He certainly doesn't seem to have done what Aston Cantlow wanted him to do with it.

Aston's idea was that the footage should be posted on the internet – Youtube would do – and the public's support for Acton Trussell would be so overwhelming nobody would be able force him out of his job. Everybody loved a smoker. Trussell was a victim of the police state. It was time to fight back. If he wouldn't make use of the smoking gun to defend himself then Aston Cantlow would do it for him. It was so unfair Barset's MP should have been hounded out of his job. Miss Hendricks would approve of his plan. It was a question of civil liberties. Aston was defending them.

It only took a few minutes to upload the file onto his website. It sat alongside Aston Cantlow's musings on life, death metal and the pursuit of happiness. But somehow it didn't look right so he removed it again. There had to be a better place.

He Googled various combinations of 'no', 'smoking' and 'freedom' until he found smokersareevil.com and its forum pages which allowed users to upload comments. It didn't take long to by-pass the supposed security on the site and upload the file. He added the comment: 'Smokers are oppressed. Fight for liberty. Why did Acton Trussell have to go? Just for this? Scandal.'

He added a web link to a "Daily Mail" story about the resignation then his mother called him down for tea so Aston added a heading, "The Smoking Gun" and hurried off to eat.

*****

Unusually, Olivia Trussell was first up. She was due at rehearsals in Bristol with her folk group. She was in the kitchen making tea when the phone rang. She answered immediately – her parents were still asleep. After all, it was 6.30 on a Saturday morning. The voice asked to speak to her father. She explained the situation. The voice introduced himself as Jimi Hunt from 'The Chronicle' and referred to the video on smokersareevil.com.

Olivia told him to call back later. He said he would come over to Howard Michael immediately, with a photographer. She put the phone down and it rang again. The BBC wanting to speak to her father. She said he could not be disturbed. They said they would be sending a camera crew. She put the phone down again and it rang instantly. Her mobile also started to play the opening bars of Gershwin's "Rhapsody in Blue" while her mother's mobile, lying by the toaster, started to vibrate. She answered the land line. It was Sky calling from outside the house asking permission to set up in the driveway. She went to the dining room, looked out and, sure enough, there was a mobile broadcasting unit. She told them to go away. They said they would wait. When the phone rang again she left it to the answerphone and ran upstairs to wake her parents before fetching her laptop.

Her father wandered in wearing his old dressing gown, the one they used to refer to as his smoking jacket, looking rumpled and confused. 'What's going on?'

She said, 'Look at this', showed him the website and took him to a bedroom window from which they could see the Sky crew and another unidentified individual, presumably a reporter.

Acton groaned. 'Caught smoking. At my age. It reminds me of when I was at school. Oh well.'

Olivia had seen her father under pressure before but on this occasion he really didn't seem bothered. 'Tell them I'll be down in half an hour and offer them a cup of tea,' he said to his daughter adding, 'Please, darling' before he kissed the top of her head and squeezed her shoulder reassuringly. 'Don't worry. Nothing to lose now. Nothing to lose.'

The phone continued to ring and Olivia answered it, telling anyone who wanted to know that her father would be issuing a statement in an hour's time. It would be available on the internet.

She went outside. It was a chilly morning with a breath of autumn in the air and the promise that it may yet warm up a little. She offered coffee to the three Sky people and the other reporter, who turned out to be from "The Sun".

Dan Adams from Sky asked her to see if she could get her father out there and gone again before the BBC and ITN turned up. He added that, as an ex-smoker, he had a lot of sympathy for her old man. She said she'd see what she could do.

Olivia, barefoot, in her baggy pyjamas, her hair tousled with sleep, gave off an aura of calm. She did not rush anywhere, she seemed to glide. On the way back into the house, she stopped and cut half a dozen roses – three white, three pale pink – to place in a vase. She made coffee. She rang Dave to say she might be late. She checked her own messages and started to draft a statement for her father to place on his website. She was well aware that he wouldn't be able to do it himself but she thought it was necessary, given the amount of media attention they seem to have attracted.

Her mother had thrown on jeans and a jumper. She was worried this 'ridiculous nonsense' would harm Acton's reputation.

'But it's why he resigned, mummy,' Olivia reassured her. 'It can't really do him any more harm.'

'What if he's prosecuted?'

'Prosecuted?'

'For smoking.'

'Mummy, a first offence is a £100 fine. Even if he is prosecuted, it won't matter. We can afford £100, can't we?'

'That's not the point, Livvy. He'll have a criminal record. His career will end in disgrace.'

'Mummy, it's like a speeding fine. It's not like he's raped somebody.'

'They may deny him medical treatment.'

'You're on a private scheme, aren't you?'

'They might cancel the insurance.'

'Oh come on mummy, now you're being ridiculous.'

'Ridiculous?' Celia was about to start shouting at her daughter when Acton finally came downstairs in a pair of brown trousers, an open-neck shirt and a smart, light brown jacket.

'Man at Boden, eh?' his daughter laughed. 'Some things don't change.'

'Where are they then?'

Olivia led her father out into the front garden. The TV crew were set up on the lawn, which was still damp with dew but gave them a good shot of the house. A photographer from 'The Chronicle' snapped away as soon as Acton emerged, smiling, with his beautifully-dishevelled red-headed daughter at his side.

Dan Adams introduced himself, though he and Acton had met several times in the past. Acton smiled and said he didn't see what all the fuss was about. Dan pointed out that he was the first MP to be found flouting the ban. Acton pointed out that he was not an MP any more. They did the interview.

'Acton Trussell, do you admit that earlier this year you broke the smoking ban?'

'Yes, I do.'

'Is this the reason for your mysterious resignation as an MP?'

'Yes, it is.'

An aeroplane flew overhead. The cameraman said they'd have to do it again because the sound of the jet engine had drowned out Acton's answer. They waited for the plane to head eastwards out of earshot. Dan Adams asked if this, indicating Olivia, was his daughter. She smiled at him from where she stood, just out of shot near the 'Chronicle' photographer.

They began again. 'Acton Trussell, do you admit that earlier this year you broke the smoking ban?'

'Yes, I do.'

'Is this the reason for your mysterious resignation as an MP?'

'Yes, it is.'

'Why did you feel it necessary to resign? Surely a breach of the new smoking laws isn't a resigning issue.'

'Some people thought it was. Other people pretended to think it was because they realised they could get rid of me.'

'It doesn't really make sense. You wouldn't resign if you were caught speeding.'

'No, you're right. But I'd had enough. I couldn't face a full term in parliament under this Coalition and this leader. Too many compromises. It's not the party I joined nor is it one I wish to belong to. When they made it clear they wanted me out, I decided to leave. It's as simple as that.'

'What's wrong with this Government, then, in your view?'

'Well,' Acton looked towards the woods where a few weeks earlier he had been taken for a 'chat' by portly little Compton Dundon and his spotty, slimy sidekick Steve Thomas. 'Let's just say the world seems to have moved on and left me behind.'

'Is this really just about the smoking ban?'

'Not really. But the ban is an example of what's happening to us. Don't forget we are not only banned from smoking, we are now more or less banned from flying because the taxes are so high. We're told this is to save the environment. We all know it's to make up for all the lost revenue caused by the ban on smoking. It's about freedom really.'

At this point, Olivia walked into the shot and took her father to one side. The cameraman was irritated and Dan Adams tried to hold her back. 'No, please, only another couple of questions,' he pleaded. But Olivia was determined. She walked her father towards the front door.

'Daddy, what's going on? Why are you saying all this when until now you've said nothing at all? Are you sure this is sensible?'

Acton looked into her dark, lovely eyes and saw the image of her mother at her age. He saw her mother's protective belligerence and intelligence. He said he couldn't really explain his change of heart.

'I think it's the anger of defeat, darling,' he said with a rueful smile. Acton kissed her on the cheek and marched back to the TV camera. 'I'm sorry, Dan, my daughter wants to protect me from myself – I think it's a bit too late for that, don't you?'

The newsman, still keen to wrap up his interview before anybody else arrived, glanced over his shoulder as a vehicle could be heard driving down the lane. It was just a huge tractor heading to the fields.

They polished off the interview with one more question. 'Are you seriously saying we should have the freedom to kill ourselves with cancer-causing nicotine and the freedom to pollute the globe with cut-price flights?'

'It's more complicated than that, Mr Adams. On the smoking ban, we have successfully turned England and Wales into a bootlegger's paradise, boosting violent criminals and the black economy. And for what? It's still legal to smoke in Northern Ireland. In future, when I'm desperate for a smoke, I shall nip over to Belfast. If only I could afford to travel that far now it's too costly to fly.'

And that was it. Dan Adams and his weekend outfit of Barbour jacket and green cords was on his mobile promising the newsdesk an interview any moment now. The BBC still hadn't appeared. It was a result.

Now it was over, Acton didn't know what to do with himself. He looked to his daughter for reassurance but Olivia was frowning.

She took him by the arm and led him round the side of the house, away from the cameras. 'Why talk to them at all, daddy?' she asked. 'You've given it up now. So why worry yourself unnecessarily?'

He wasn't sure about the answer. Acton looked at the sunlight shining off his daughter's tousled red hair and said, 'I did alright really. Your mother and I, anyway, didn't we?'

'Daddy, what are you on about?'

'Making a daughter as lovely as you?'

'Oh for God's sake.' She strode off into the kitchen to make more coffee.

Acton stood in the garden looking at the thin sunshine on the roses. Their petals were starting to fall like leaves from a horse chestnut tree. His thoughts wandered back to one particularly vicious TV debate when he was attacked by the new Health Secretary, some 29-year-old ex-consultant called Lizzy North.

'You're the 21st century equivalent of a slave-owner,' she said. 'People like you fought tooth and nail to prevent the abolition of the slave trade. But they could not stand in the way of enlightenment and progress. In 200 years' time, people will look back on the days when smoking was legal with incredulity. They'll want to know what kind of people existed in the early 21st century who were prepared to encourage their fellow human beings to become trapped into an addiction which would cause them and their families untold misery. You and your vile little campaign are like so beneath contempt.'

Olivia returned with coffee and a smile. 'Daddy, the BBC's arrived. They want to film you in the garden. I said I'd ask.'

*****

'My God, what a prat. What a complete dickhead. The old fool.' Compton Dundon was wearing a shirt and boxer shorts. He lay back on his bed watching TV and laughing.

At the dressing table sat Steve Thomas, dressed in a pair of black jeans and a black T-shirt. They were in their 'executive suite' at the Barset Sleepover Hotel to discuss tactics for the candidate selection. They were waiting for the association chairman.

'Look at him. Trussell you loser,' Dundon roared at the television. 'Oh it was all about freedom. Freedom? Pull the other one you idiot. My God but the man's got some nerve. He takes on the whole party over a very clear and open policy, he loses, he breaks the law, he gets found out, he is forced to resign and what happens? He goes on the telly talking about freedom and liberty. Bloody hell the man's a prat. Prat, prat, prat.'

Dundon's chubby cheeks were turning red. Thomas sat and watched, quietly drinking his coffee. 'Don't you think you should get dressed?' he said eventually, 'The pompous arse will be here in a minute.'

Thomas was searching for the video clip on the internet. It had already been deleted from the smokersareevil website and transferred to YouTube. It was being replicated by bloggers here and there. Someone had even set up a new site: thesmokinggun.co.uk and people were starting to comment on it.

'Funny,' Thomas added, 'Most of the comments so far are in favour of the old git.'

'That's just from the lazy and the lost,' said Dundon, pleased with his alliteration. He rolled off the bed, removed his clothes and waddled into the bathroom for a shower.

'TPA will be here in five minutes, you know,' Thomas called after him.

'He'll have to bloody wait, won't he?'

Eventually Dundon re-emerged, shaved, dressed in a pair of fawn chinos and a city shirt without the cufflinks in or a tie. He wore a pair of black city shoes which belied the attempted casual look. He made Clifford Chambers wait in reception. It was very modern, very red and very badly lit. The cricket club scorer was irritated at being made to hang around; he had to get off to the away match and it was so gloomy in the hotel he could scarcely make out the stories in the Sunday papers he had taken up to pass the time. Chambers decided not to stand to greet Dundon and Thomas and did not even offer to shake their hands. He'd let them know who was boss, he thought.

'Right I don't have much time,' Chambers began. 'What are we here for anyway?'

'We are here, Clifford, to ensure the selection process goes smoothly.'

'It's all pretty straightforward isn't it? They've all been told to turn up at the Free Trade Hall by 6pm. Members have until 6.30. Each candidate gets ten minutes to speak and 20 minutes for questions. Then we vote. Simple majority wins it.'

'That's not how it's going to be,' Dundon said. 'Alternative vote, order of preference, that sort of thing. Everyone gets a ballot paper and chooses the candidates in order of preference.'

'Now hang about...' Clifford was upset, not because he objected to a different system but because nobody had consulted him. 'I have already explained the system to several people.'

'Never mind,' said Dundon. 'They will soon understand this system is fairer. More equitable.'

'And to ensure impartiality, Dundon and I will be responsible for the onerous task of counting the votes cast and revealing to you who the winner is,' added Steve Thomas with a sly grin.

Clifford looked at him and was about to protest. But there was something in the grin, coupled with Dundon's air of satisfaction, that persuaded him not to complain.

*****

The man from the BBC asked, 'Mr Trussell, how did this get onto the internet in the first place?'

When he heard the question, Acton Trussell frowned. His high forehead wrinkled and he squinted. His eyes widened. His mouth fell open but no words came out. He involuntarily raised both hands, about to hide his face in them before realising he was being filmed by a camera. So he lowered his hands and frowned again. The first time he looked surprised and perplexed. The second time he was starting to look angry.

'Do you know,' he told the interviewer, 'That's a very good question. It had never occurred to me.'

Back in the sanctuary of his kitchen, with the newshounds back on the leash and their big satellite vans trundling away down the early autumnal lanes, Acton posed the question to his wife. Clarissa was trying to bake a cake and could have done without her husband taking up room in her kitchen. And she was listening to Mozart's "Requiem".

She sighed, wiped her hands on a tea towel, put the kettle on and sat down at the large breakfast table. 'Are you serious?' she asked. 'Haven't you wondered how somebody got hold of that film in the first place?'

Acton said it never really occurred to him. He had known of its existence. It was why he resigned. But how did the party know about it? Where had it come from? Who had seen it and when? And why was it now all over the internet? 'Oh dear,' he sighed, 'I must be getting old.'

Clarissa told him not to be so stupid. It was obvious. The video had been obtained by the party and placed on the internet by his enemies. 'They're determined to finish you off once and for all,' she said. 'No doubt you'll be getting a summons to appear in court next. It may only be a small fine but they will want to make an example of you.'

Olivia came downstairs. She cancelled rehearsal with her friends in the folk group. They understood. The lead singer had been a dedicated smoker – told her to give her father his love. She wasn't sure that was quite appropriate but said she'd pass on a message of support.

'I've been talking to Amanda and Polly. They're both furious with you, dad. You know that, don't you?'

'Polly isn't, darling. She hardly ever did any work for me and she really wasn't interested you know.'

'That's what you think. I talked to her today, we were chatting for ages. She says you're one of the best MPs she ever worked for. Organised, clear, friendly, not demanding, polite, respectful. And she is so angry about you resigning. Says you were pressured into it. Says the party was out to get you. And Amanda is just the same.'

'Yes, I'm sorry about Amanda.' She had been Acton's constituency secretary, a job she'd worked at part-time for the last seven years. She was a young married mother who lived on the outskirts of Barset and fitted in her work for Acton in between looking after her two young children. He was paying her until a new MP was elected and he hoped to persuade his successor to keep her on but nothing could be guaranteed and he couldn't afford to keep employing her for ever. Acton felt guilty about Amanda.

'Oh daddy!' Olivia was exasperated. 'She's not feeling sorry for herself. She's angry for you.'

Clarissa was suddenly irritated. What did it matter who got hold of what or how or why? The thing was out there on the internet now. Acton looked a furtive fool sneaking out for a quick drag – like a fat, overgrown schoolboy. He may be a victim of some sort of dirty-tricks campaign but he had only himself to blame.

Olivia was indignant. Her father had clearly been stitched up by party headquarters. He was an old fool and a troublemaker – 'Thank you very much,' huffed Acton – they wanted to get rid of him. This was an issue of privacy, the snooper-state, the misuse of information, a clear and gross infringement of daddy's civil liberties.

Clarissa said she'd never heard such nonsense. Acton had been caught with his trousers down, his hand in the till or at least red-handed with a cigarette in his mouth and he deserved what he got, stupid fool.

Mother and daughter were close to falling out quite seriously. It wouldn't be the first time. Clarissa was not used to being contradicted; Olivia had a fiery temperament and a self-belief which worked on most people, though rarely on her mother. Acton saw confrontation in the offing and announced he was going to watch the cricket.

Unfortunately it did not free him from his daughter. No sooner were they settled in front of the TV (England were taking on New Zealand) than Olivia was worrying away at him again while poring over various websites on her laptop and quoting them at her father.

The Campaign Against the Police State had taken up the cause. Its spokesman was demanding explanations from the Home Secretary about how the video had come to be in the public domain at all. The news websites were starting to follow up this line though most of the headlines still dealt with Trussell as the most prominent person yet to fall foul of the nationwide smoking ban. 'Stubbed out!' said one headline. 'The smoking gun' said another. 'Politics is such a drag' said a third.

There were pictures of her father when he was campaigning against the ban, including the first 'charity smokeathon' he took part in while the legislation was still going through Parliament. Several thousand smokers had gathered in Trafalgar Square to smoke, listen to speeches and – hypocritically, everyone said – raise money for cancer research. They were universally condemned and Acton was among those MPs 'named and shamed' for standing out against the Government. The worst of it was that several smokers refused to use the ash-trays provided and left their butt ends on the ground as a protest. These were later picked over by the pigeons, leading to several deaths. 'Smoking kills' headlines did not help the cause.

'We should put out a statement,' Olivia was saying as the England batsmen set about New Zealand's opening bowler. 'We should call on the party to explain how and why this film found its way into the public domain. And we should say we refuse to believe them if they say it had nothing to do with them.'

'Livvy, dear, I'm trying to watch the cricket. Haven't you got any homework to do?' She slapped him, quite painfully, on the leg and started typing furiously.

*****

Steve Thomas was working his way through the third bottle of wine with Compton Dundon when the panic text came through. They had decided to spend the week in Barset trying to find an office to set up as the campaign headquarters. They also thought they might do a little sightseeing, play some tennis, use the hotel's gym and swimming pool and maybe take in a show if there was such a thing to be had in this barren area of the northern Midlands.

The wine was house plonk – the party's expenses had been reined in since the good old days before MPs' perks became front page news. Though they were not politicians as such, their political masters were no longer willing to tolerate staff living in the lap of luxury while they were on what some of the richer and more pompous MPs called 'starvation rations'.

The text read: 'Call CW immediate' so Thomas rang the Chief Whip, Amelia Browning. She was at home. It was late on Sunday evening. She was getting calls from the BBC and the Sun alleging dirty tricks. She was putting all further calls through to Steve Thomas.

Dundon's phone rang while Thomas was listening to Mrs Browning complain. It was Dave Hersey, the party chairman. His voice, too, had an edge of ill-humour in it. 'Get back to London straight away. We need to meet at eight am tomorrow,' he demanded. Dundon tried to protest but Dave went on, 'This is a crisis. The Leader himself has demanded to know if there is any truth in it. Of course we've issued a denial. But is the denial true? And even if it is true, do we want it to be true? Or should we deny our denial and admit the denial was a lie? What is the truth anyway? Did you do it?'

Dundon still wasn't sure what the problem was but he didn't want the party chairman to realise. He explained he was busy setting up the by-election. 'Bugger the by-election,' Dave exclaimed.

Amelia Browning was explaining to Steve Thomas, 'Why is this a crisis? Because I say it is. That should be good enough for you. What do you mean there's no need to panic? Panic? Who's panicking? Are you accusing me of panicking?' As her voice grew louder, Thomas held his mobile further and further away from his ear, hoping Dundon would hear the hysteria and share the joke. Unfortunately Dundon was frowning seriously into his mobile and speaking in such a low voice Thomas couldn't hear a word of it.

Luckily, the dimly-lit bar of the hotel was empty except for a Croatian barman who looked as if he had better things to do than hang around waiting for two middle-aged drunks to wend their way to bed. Thomas started searching his pockets and the briefcase at his feet, while Mrs Browning continued to harangue him about why she was not panicking when she said there was a crisis on and his services were required immediately to kill it off, nip it in the bud, put it to bed and close it down. He realised he was unconsciously searching for a cigarette.

Eventually the two calls came to an end and the two officials had a chance to compare notes. They worked out quite quickly what the trouble was. The media were accusing the party of dirty tricks: of invading Acton Trussell's privacy, posting the CCTV footage on the internet, attempting to discredit him and exercising a petty revenge on a good and faithful public servant.

Their phones rang. Thomas found himself talking to the "Mirror", never the party's friend, while Dundon was dealing with Amelia Browning.

The "Mirror" said the incident showed the truth behind the party's lies about openness and honesty. Thomas was asked what he had to say to accusations that the party had blackmailed an MP into giving up his seat and that, when he did so, it couldn't resist the petty vindictiveness displayed by this abominable use of the police state for party political purposes. If the party could shaft its own MPs, nobody was safe. It was worse than a police state. Even their Coalition partners in the Liberal Democrats were asking questions.

Mrs Browning told Dundon to mount an immediate inquiry into how this footage came to be on the internet and demanded a personal assurance from him, personally, that he, personally, had never been involved in dirty tricks of this nature and that, specifically, he had not personally had any involvement in, or knowledge of, this particular dirty trick.

'Are you suggesting, Chief Whip, that you believe the allegation to be true?' Dundon asked, as smoothly as he could after one and a half bottles of Barset's breeziest Chardonnay.

She exploded. Of course she was not. But everybody else was. She had denied it to anyone who asked. Even her husband had suggested this was a bit below the belt. And her son Aaron (named after Elvis, apparently). How dare people tarnish her reputation like this? How dare they? She wanted to know who was responsible and she wanted to know fast.

'That assumes, Chief Whip,' Dundon replied suavely, 'That the party has, or might have had, some knowledge of this video and its antecedents.'

'Antecedents? Antecedents? Don't give me bloody antecedents.' She rang off.

Meanwhile Steve Thomas was pacing the room listening to the "Mirror" reporter outline the rest of his story. The party hated Trussell for opposing the fag ban and the holiday tax – 'you mean the green duty on air travel' Thomas corrected him somewhat futilely – had threatened to expose him as a hardened smoker willing to break his own Government's laws, forced him to quit but couldn't resist exposing him anyway, even when there was nothing to be gained. What did the party leader have to say about it? the 'Mirror' man wanted to know.

'The Prime Minister is in Dubai on a finance and trade mission, as you well know.'

'Yeah but what did he know when Trussell was shafted?'

'Does it not occur to you that Acton Trussell may have posted the video himself in order to discredit the party?' Even as he asked the question, Steve Thomas knew it was a mistake.

'Ah so you're saying that Acton Trussell brought about his own downfall, quit as an MP, obtained the CCTV footage, posted it on the internet and then alerted the world's media to it as some sort of revenge on the party? Is that what you're saying? Are you accusing him of dirty tricks and sour grapes?'

Thomas back-tracked rapidly. No, no, that wasn't what he was saying.

'Then you admit the party is responsible?'

No, he wasn't saying that either. He did not know who was responsible. It was not the party, though, of that he could be sure.

'And your Glorious Leader, the Old Harrovian himself, Lord Snooty, he doesn't know anything about it either?' the Mirrorman demanded.

'Of course not.'

'On the record?'

'No, not on the record. Off the record.'

'Why off the record?'

'Because, off the record, I have not had a chance to talk to the Prime Minister's staff.'

'So, off the record, you don't actually know if the Prime Minister knows anything or not?'

'Off the record, no.'

'And on the record?'

'The Prime Minister knows nothing about this and is certainly not involved in any way.'

'That's the official on-the-record statement?'

'Yes.'

'So if we discover at a later date that the Prime Minister did know about it, he will resign for lying.'

'He's not lying.'

'But you're lying on his behalf.'

'You'd better speak to Number Ten.'

Steve Thomas rang off and immediately called the Prime Minister's Chief Press Officer. As he did so, he was working out that Denzil Duxford would be fast asleep. It was half past two in the morning in Dubai. Denzil would not take kindly to being woken up.

Compton Dundon, meanwhile, was talking to the man who had tried, and failed, to persuade Acton Trussell to give up his seat in the Commons and take a knighthood like a good boy. Sir Michael Watford was at home in Berkshire rather than on his island off the coast of Antigua – he preferred Britain during the cricket season especially as it meant he could avoid the Caribbean during the hurricane season. Sir Michael was calling to congratulate Dundon on his success in exposing that idiot Acton Trussell. Dundon was trying to deny any responsibility and persuade Sir Michael that it would be extremely damaging if he tried to put it about that the party had a hand in this fiasco.

'But Trussell's an utter shit,' Sir Michael insisted. 'Wanted a Peerage. I mean, the bloody cheek of the man. After all he did – or should I say didn't do. Pompous arse if you ask me.'

'That's all very well,' Dundon was trying to explain, 'But if anyone in any kind of official or semi-official position in the party suggests we were responsible for this, it'll do us serious damage. The Home Secretary might have to resign.'

'The Home Secretary, why on earth…?'

'Because he's in charge of security. We said we would bring an end to the Big Brother surveillance state. If our enemies can make the charge stick that we are somehow responsible for this….'

Dundon was searching for the right words. Sir Michael filled the pause, 'Trussellgate' he said with a chuckle.

'This Trussellgate, then all the civil libertarians, the freedom people, the crusties and rusties and dusties and the rest of them – not to mention the die-hard smokers – will be at our throats. They will scent blood. And besides, we've got a by-election to fight.'

*****

By the time Compton Dundon and Steve Thomas arrived at the party's rented riverside office-block a stone's throw from the Houses of Parliament, seven TV cameras had been set up in the concrete space outside, where fountains played when there was still enough money about to meet the cost of the water rates and the official anti-global-warming policy didn't dictate it wasn't acceptable to waste water – even in one of the wettest summers for years.

On the seventh floor, the party chairman was pacing up and down, staring out of the window, checking his Blackberry, spilling his coffee and barking at Bindy, the Hon Belinda Cooper-Price, his PA. Sitting at the table were Dave Hersey's 'aide-de-camp', Stan Stanley, a spotty new graduate from Clare College with a First in Politics, Philosophy and Economics, who had been given the job by his uncle, Simon Stanley, the internet millionaire and MP for somewhere plush in Surrey. Stan fancied Bindy but she knew he was just a spotty oik with a parvenu uncle; her sights were set on the man sitting next to him, the party paymaster Sir Michael Watford.

Sir Michael was trying to reassure Dave Hersey. 'Dave, old boy, what does it matter? We've got rid of the old fool and he's been exposed as a lawbreaker. What could be better?'

Dundon and Thomas had only just sat down when Amelia Browning bustled noisily in, greeted Sir Michael with a kiss on his balding head, threw a sheaf of papers on the table, demanded a coffee and asked, 'Come on then. Who did it?'

Hersey took his seat at the head of the table. 'This is a party matter, Amelia. As chairperson I think I should chair this inquiry.'

'Inquiry?' asked Dundon, flustered. He was pale from lack of sleep and still a little flushed from alcohol. Thomas was slumped in his chair hoping someone would take pity on him by supplying a strong black coffee. He could not ask for one in this company. He knew the merits of obsequiousness.

'We must wait for the arrival of the Home Secretary,' Hersey announced before starting to chew his finger-nails.

'Rick Pickering?' asked Amelia Browning in surprise.

'Pickers?' said Sir Michael, enjoying everyone's anxiety. 'What's he coming for?'

'This could be a criminal matter,' the party chairman said sententiously.

At that moment the Home Secretary arrived. He was the new John Prescott, a big burly bloke from up north who thought he was the workers' representative and spoke with all the bluster and bullying that went with the job.

'Mornin',' said the MP for Bingley North. 'Where's bloody coffee? Bindy my love, coffee? Three sugars please love. Now, what's this all about?'

Pickering flung himself into a chair at the opposite end of the table from the party chairman and set about running the meeting. 'What's to report? Amelia?'

The Chief Whip explained the situation. Acton Trussell had resigned. The party had, indeed, put pressure on him to do so. It had been known there was some sort of compromising video in circulation though nobody actually knew what it was. Not even Trussell.

Compton Dundon added, 'As you know, Home Secretary, we are in the process of selecting the by-election candidate.'

'Lucy Loxley,' said Sir Michael.

'Indeed,' Dundon smiled back. 'Lucy is about to be included in the final shortlist. But we now have a complication.'

'The media are accusing us of dirty tricks,' Thomas volunteered, unfolding his pile of morning papers with headlines like 'Dirty Dave' and 'Smoked out'.

Pickering reached for them. ''Dirty Dave' – that's good eh Mister Chairman. I remember Dirty Den from Eastenders.' He chuckled then slurped at the coffee which the chairman's PA had just slipped onto the table in front of him.

'Would anybody else like any coffee?' she asked.

Thomas sat up straight, smiled wanly at her and was about to speak when Pickering went on, 'Well who's the genius behind this then? Who is responsible? And should we fire him or hire him?'

Sir Michael chuckled. He liked Rick Pickering's heavy-handed jokes, especially when they were referring, however obliquely, to his ex-business rival, the Labour Peer Al Demerara, who was notorious for a TV programme called 'The Trainee' in which one contestant was fired every week.

'We do not believe we are responsible at all,' said Amelia. She did not like Pickering. He was far too old-school for the new party – if he'd not been such a figure of fun, he could easily have gone the same way as Acton Trussell. Instead the Prime Minister kept him on – exhibit A, the fat northern working-man-made-good.

'Aye, 'appen. But that's not how it looks though, is it Amelia dear?'

The Chief Whip did not like being called 'dear'. She delved into her papers, as if looking for something. There was a pause. Everyone watched and waited. She emerged without anything. The pause continued.

'I'll tell you how it looks,' Pickering resumed. 'It looks like we shafted Trussell, hung the bugger out to dry then shafted him again just for the hell of it. It makes a mockery of my plans to deal with the surveillance state. I promise people more privacy, then this. It's as if someone planned it. Just to have a go at me.'

'I think, if I may say so Home Secretary, that seems highly unlikely,' Dundon tried to mollify him. 'It's just an unfortunate coincidence.'

Pickering's voice went quiet. He lost his working class accent and the voice of the public schoolboy he really was forced its way through with menacing clarity. He leaned across the table towards Dundon and whispered, 'I don't believe in coincidence, Mr Dundon. In politics, there is always something going on. Some plot, some scheme, nobody's to be trusted. Your job is to find out who has done this, why they have done it and what we are going to do about it. Is that clear?'

Before Dundon could respond, the party chairman intervened. 'I think you will find, Rick, that Compton reports to me as party chairperson, not to you as Home Secretary. It would appear you are confusing your role in the Government with the exigencies of the party machine.'

The volume and accent returned as Pickering stood up and gazed at Dave Hersey with a look of contempt. 'Ex-ig-encies? Ex-ig-encies? Not only have you got the wrong word, you tosser, but you seem to miss the point entirely. This is a plot to undermine me and I intend to get to the bottom of it. Dundon, I want a report by this evening. Now I have a country to run.'

With that, Pickering swept out and slammed the door. The glass partitions shook. Various party employees looked in at the goldfish-bowl meeting room with frank curiosity.

The party chairman resumed as if nothing had happened. 'We need to issue a press statement. Has anyone spoken to the Prime Minister about this?'

Thomas said he'd discussed the situation with Denzil Duxford, who had refused to wake the Prime Minister up in the middle of the night just to ask him if he knew anything about an ex-MP being caught smoking on CCTV. They had discussed the question again this morning and Duxford had told him this was not something the Prime Minister would be dealing with.

'And someone needs to say something to those TV people outside,' Amelia Browning said. 'I do think that's a job for the party chairman, don't you Dave? After all, this seems to be a party issue, not a Government question whatever our Right Honourable Friend might think. Steve, what can we say?'

'No comment?' he offered optimistically.

Ms Browning pursed her lips. 'I don't think so, do you? Shouldn't we simply deny any involvement?'

'Yes, of course.'

'Assuming nobody in the party did have any involvement,' Sir Michael interrupted, 'Though I'd still like to shake their hand and congratulate them on their initiative.'

'Shouldn't we announce some sort of inquiry into the confidentiality of CCTV data?' suggested Dundon.

'Suggest that to Pickering. That's a Government question not a party one,' said Ms Browning.

'Very well,' said Hersey, 'I'll go out there and deny everything. This is nothing to do with the party, we have no knowledge of anything.'

'Have we carried out an inquiry?' asked Dundon.

'Obviously not.'

'Shouldn't we?'

'Only give the story legs,' said Thomas. 'Announce an inquiry and it lives on and on. Witnesses, investigations, claims and counter-claims. It just goes on and on.'

'So, no inquiry,' said the chairman.

'But what if we deny everything and then some idiot proves we did have a hand in it?' asked Dundon.

'Then you're buggered,' Sir Michael announced with a smile, looking at the chairman. 'You'd be advised not to make an official statement without either knowing it to be true or at least knowing that if it's not true nobody will ever be able to prove it's not true. Deniability, my dear Dave, deniability not liability.'

Thomas checked his Blackberry. Dundon sketched a few notes on his pad of paper. Ms Browning started to pack away her papers. Sir Michael gazed blandly out of the window. The party chairman tried to catch someone's eye and failed. He sighed. 'Any suggestions?' Nobody responded. 'Steve?'

Thomas looked up from his mobile phone. 'It says here we are in crisis talks. BBC website. They're calling it Cigarettegate.'

'Why does everything have a gate in its name?' asked the party chairman.

'Ever heard of Watergate, Dave?' asked Ms Browning contemptuously. 'Look, I've got to go. My car is downstairs so I won't have to walk through the rabble.'

She left, followed closely by Sir Michael. Dave Hersey, the party chairman, looked at the remnants of his meeting.

Stan Stanley, who had kept as low a profile as possible, now offered his suggestion. 'Why don't we accuse the Opposition of doing it to undermine our policy of rolling back the Big Brother State? If we don't know who did it, they don't either. We can pin it all on them.'

'No,' said Thomas.

'God, no!' exclaimed Dundon.

'Excellent,' said the party chairman, 'That's just what we shall do. Stan, draw me up a statement would you?'

'Mister Chairman,' protested Dundon, 'This will get us even deeper into the shit.'

'Don't be ridiculous, Compton, it's perfect. We don't need an inquiry, we can accuse the Opposition. They'll be outraged. It's perfect.'

Chapter 8

Olivia Trussell accepted Clifford Chambers' invitation to an evening of Puccini arias at the Barset Free Trade Hall because she wanted to listen to the music. She also wanted to find out what part he had played in her father's downfall.

Clifford was reluctant to turn up at Howard Michael and bump into her father. Instead Olivia drove her elderly, but immaculate, green Renault Romantic to Rosepetal Avenue and found Clifford in his thick gardening gloves gently pruning the roses.

Later, in the cramped bar of the Free Trade Hall, over a tasteless cup of coffee, Clifford was complaining, 'It's such a pity Nessun Dorma's become a football song. It was quite exquisite, back in the day.'

Olivia, who still rather liked the song and didn't mind its Three Tenors, football World Cup connotations, gazed into the middle distance where a poster advertised a 'Back from the Wreckage' tribute band. 'My Godfather Julian was in The Wreckage,' she said, nodding towards the poster.

'Oh you mean Stud Lee. I know. What an abominable man,' Clifford replied. 'Sex, sex, sex.'

Olivia laughed and shook her tousled red hair. It was such a familiar gesture it reminded Clifford of how long they had known each other. She was looking as lovely as ever, he thought. No make-up, just a pair of jeans and a soft Cashmere jumper, a bright pink scarf and various pieces of cheap jewellery rattling away at her wrists and from her ears. Bohemian, he thought, but not excessively so. He wondered if she had any tattoos.

Halfway back to Rosepetal Avenue, Clifford pulled into the Barset Arboretum car park. They had been talking about the selection process for Acton's successor and he'd explained that, for some reason, party headquarters had decided the winner would be Lucy Loxley whether or not she was the best candidate for the job. 'I suppose it's because she's a lesbian,' Clifford said before bringing the car to a halt, turning off the engine, turning to Olivia, leaning over towards her and adding, 'You're not a lesbian, are you Livvie?'

'Clifford!' she said indignantly, leaning away from him as she inhaled his coffee-tinged breath. But he was pursuing her and soon his lips found their way onto hers, his hand was groping for her breasts and she was trapped by her seat belt.

'Clifford! Get off! What are you doing?'

'Oh you are a lesbian then.' He withdrew to the driver's seat. 'I knew it. I knew it.' Clifford punched his right palm with the fist of his left hand, for emphasis.

'Clifford?' Olivia didn't feel threatened, or even angry, but she was confused. What on earth was this fool playing at? There had never before been any suggestion that she might fancy him. Why did he think she would now?

'Well if you weren't a lesbian…'

'I'd be willing to have sex with you on the front seat of this tiny but expensive car even though we've never come within a million miles of this sort of thing at any time in the past? Is that what you're saying?'

'Well, I've always had a soft spot for you, Livvy.'

'And it can stay soft, Clifford. Come on, let's go home.'

Clifford sighed and she wondered if it was not so much in resignation that his attempt on her virtue had been rebuffed and more that he was relieved to have tried and failed.

'Anyway,' he said, immediately starting the car and changing the subject, 'How has your father been? I suppose he loves all this stuff about the conspiracy theories. Cigarettegate.'

'He does rather. He thinks it's probably all true, or most of it. Nothing is strange in politics.'

*****

Back at their temporary headquarters in the bar of the Barsetshire Sleepover Hotel, Compton Dundon, Steve Thomas and Clifford Chambers convened the following day to discuss their two problems – selecting a candidate and dealing with the 'Cigarettegate' fall-out.

The papers were full of Opposition outrage at the suggestion they had somehow tapped into private security systems to snoop on an MP and then leaked the information to the media. There were calls for a public inquiry. The Prime Minister had issued a statement denying any knowledge of anything and reiterating his view that the tobacco ban was for the health and well-being of the whole nation.

Newspaper columnists dusted down their prejudices and were full of reminiscences about the good old days when people were allowed to smoke themselves into stinking, coughing, unhealthy happiness and the health service benefited because so many people consigned themselves to an early grave. In future, hospitals faced an even tougher time coping with a healthy, ageing population – all those ex-smokers would now live into their nineties and beyond rather than conveniently dying at 74. Pretty soon the Queen would have to stop sending telegrams to centenarians – e-mails would have to do.

The civil libertarians were also on the march. They hated the smoking ban from the day it was first suggested – everyone had a right to smoke, it wasn't the Government's job to tell people how to live their lives, they argued. Now, though, they could seize on the evidence of the Police State – not only was everyone subject to perpetual surveillance but their every move would be scrutinised by sinister forces, the secret police, they suggested, for instances of deviant behaviour. To this Government, the libertarians said, Acton Trussell was deviant because he smoked an illegal cigarette after the imposition of a ban. He was therefore fair game for the surveillance state. He had been subjected to private blackmail followed by public humiliation. The treatment he suffered was a form of mental torture. It was wicked totalitarianism.

The Prime Minister's supporters, as well as the forces of health who had campaigned for the smoking ban, argued that, on the contrary, Acton Trussell had brought everything on himself for breaking the law. How the video made its way onto the internet was beside the point. The truth was out there. He had been exposed as a law-breaker. We couldn't have law-makers who chose to be law-breakers as well. Trussell had made himself vulnerable to blackmail through his own stupidity in breaking the law. CCTV cameras were deployed for the very reason that they detected crime. In the case of Acton Trussell they had just been doing their job in exactly the same way as if he had been a gang of vandals or a serial rapist.

Both sides of the fence were fully represented. Few reporters chose to sit on it. Everyone took sides. The overwhelming consensus seemed to be that Acton Trussell should not have been hounded from his job as an MP, should not have been blackmailed, should not have been subjected to exposure on the internet and should not have been treated like a criminal for committing a 'crime' which a few months ago had been perfectly legal.

Even supporters of the ban and advocates of CCTV were unhappy. They questioned how the footage had been obtained, by whom and why it had been placed on the internet. What role did the Government have in all of this? Denials were not accepted though the idea that this was an Opposition tactic to discredit the Prime Minister was given some credence, at least in those parts of the media which supported the Government and abominated the other lot.

'That stupid idiot,' Compton Dundon was declaiming as he flicked through the papers. Dundon was referring not to Acton Trussell or the Prime Minister but to the Leader of the Opposition, Sally Bloxham. She had been a strong supporter of the smoking ban, claiming slavery to the cigarette oppressed women. Not only was she outraged at the accusation her party was involved in spying on Acton Trussell – 'Acton who?' she asked in her piece for the "Sunday Mirror" – she was complaining about the destruction of the traditional liberties the 'snooper-State' was responsible for. 'As if her lot hadn't been responsible for 99.999999 per cent of it,' Dundon went on, spitting droplets of cappuccino over the newspapers spread out on the table before him.

Steve Thomas looked as if he could do with something stronger than his luke-warm latte. He had been ordered onto the wagon several weeks ago after an unfortunate incident with an intern in the media office and had to avoid booze occasionally for form's sake. He had only given up smoking three weeks before the ban. His sallow, pitted face looked even more pale and ill than usual. He was reading something on his i-Phone, then he checked his Blackberry. 'Looks as if Fag-gate has cost us six points in the polls according to partypolitics.com,' he announced wearily.

'Six points? That's nothing,' Clifford Chambers answered. 'We were 21 points ahead last week. Six points won't make any difference. Certainly not here.'

'No,' Thomas replied, 'But suppose it's just the start.'

'Well, the erosion of our power-base was an inevitable fact of life once we were forced into this bloody Coalition with the Lib-Dems. I know you're a Lib-Dem, Steve, but you've got to admit we make strange bedfellows,' said Clifford.

'Oh my God,' declared Compton Dundon. 'Can you cut the party political crap, both of you? We have a by-election to fight and we have to regain the initiative. We need to ensure we select the right candidate and that she – the candidate, that is – is properly on message. This was a high-profile election anyway; now it will be under huge scrutiny. *We* will be under huge scrutiny. Do I really need to remind you, Clifford, that your political future, and yours, Steve, are bound up in this?'

They looked like sheepish schoolboys. Dundon asked Clifford, 'Now, what has Lucy been told?'

'Nothing yet,' said Clifford.

'Nothing?'

'Well I was wondering, are we sure she's the candidate we want?' Clifford looked uncomfortable and squirmed in his seat. 'Maggie Pride would be a good local candidate and Parvinder ticks all the right boxes.'

Dundon and Steve Thomas both chuckled sarcastically. 'Tell him, Steve,' said Dundon.

'Fact is, got to be Loxley. Fact is, got to be,' said Thomas.

'You look puzzled, Clifford,' Dundon said.

'Well, I know you want her to be given a fair wind…'

'Fair wind!' Dundon and Thomas laughed.

'…A fair wind. But surely the other candidates…'

'Window dressing. Go on, Steve, explain it to him. But Clifford, this is in confidence. In absolute confidence. If this gets out into the media or any-where else, you will be a dead man. A dead man.'

'Not literally, I trust,' Clifford said with a nervous chuckle.

'Well, dead man or not, do you want to tell him, Compton?' asked the press secretary.

Dundon sighed heavily and leaned forward in his uncomfortable, designer seat so his face was only a few inches from Clifford's. 'Actually Steve is right. It would be wrong to tell you. It would put you in an invidious position. It would be wrong of us to burden you with such knowledge. Just take my word for it, the party, the chairman, even the leader, desires, requires, that Barset selects Lucy Loxley as its candidate and elects said Ms Loxley to Parliament, God bless her and all who sail in her.'

'Come on, Compton,' Clifford replied, with what he considered to be a winning smile. 'Come on, you can trust me. Don't I need to know? Don't I deserve to know?'

'Oh for God's sake, Clifford, it is in your best interests not to know. It is also in your best interests to ensure Lucy Loxley is selected as our candidate. Let me tell you we've already ordered the posters and leaflets. She looks very sexy in the picture.'

'Christ, Compton.' Chambers was wringing his hands and looking at his two companions with a mix of bewilderment and despair.

*****

Stud was gazing out across the garden into the middle distance where his horses were grazing in the park. He was alone, again. His latest girl-friend, Marinka, was on a modelling assignment somewhere. Bermuda, he thought, or was it Belize? He was enjoying a gin and tonic and listening to Brahms's clarinet sonatas.

There was a time when Stud would only listen to 70s rock. Then he grew bored of it all and branched out into World Music. He tried listening to Oasis and Blur in the 1990s but they sounded like bands from the '70s. By the time the 21st century dawned, Stud had heard enough. Age, he supposed, had withered him. It had certainly made him jaded. He'd heard it all before. If anyone ever again told him there was something remotely original or even cool about Coldplay, he would be forced to write a letter to "The Telegraph" in protest. Coldplay were, to Stud and his memories of how a rock band ought to be, an insipid imitation for a feminised age. They were a bunch of wimps who whispered and moaned when, in the good old days, they would have swaggered and yelled. That's how The Wreckage behaved and all their contemporaries – Free, Led Zeppelin, Deep Purple, Humble Pie, Rod and the Faces, the Stones before they became laughable.

These days Julian Lee preferred Brahms's sonatas as the sun sank slowly in the west. It was more peaceful, with a melancholic air and a warm tone which suited the mood of an early autumnal evening.

Olivia Trussell was curled up on the carpet listening quietly to the music. She had been there all afternoon. Julian wasn't quite sure why, though he enjoyed her company. They had talked to the horses. They had spent a little time in his studio – a converted coach house – where he accompanied her on bass as she whistled away on the flute and sang him one of the songs she had written recently. He'd liked it and they had fiddled around with the digital recording equipment trying to turn it into a disco dance tune. Julian enjoyed playing with his technology more than he enjoyed playing his bass guitar these days and as he watched Olivia pursing her lips to kiss the embouchure, various thoughts had occurred to him, few of which related to the playing or recording of music.

They'd gone into the house for mugs of tea and he'd sought out the Brahms. Olivia, in her jeans and baggy jumper, looked lovely. Stud kept reminding himself he was old enough to be her father. In fact, her father was one of his best friends. He was her Godfather and would have attended the Christening if the band hadn't been away on tour. He had known her all her life. He could remember holding her crying in his arms and patting her back in an attempt to calm her down. It would be wrong. Even he, Julian 'Stud' Lee, rock star (ageing), had scruples. He couldn't. He wouldn't.

As she lay on the thick carpet staring up at the ceiling, Olivia asked, 'What are we going to do about daddy?'

'Nothing we can do, my dear.'

'Don't call me 'my dear'.' Olivia sat up and stared with mock ferocity at Julian. 'It's so condescending. It makes you sound so old.'

'I am old, Olivia. Very old.'

'You are a Rock God. Rock Gods never age.' She stood up and walked over to where he sat and began to stroke his thinning grey hair.

'Rock Gods don't sit in drawing rooms listening to Brahms, drinking gin and tonic and looking out over country estates. And they definitely do not have thinning, grey hair.'

'But they do have the lines of experience in their faces and a lust for life.' Olivia bent towards Julian and placed a warm, soft kiss on his lips. Her thick hair, scented with a perfume which was vaguely familiar, wafted over him and he found it impossible not to place a hand on her warm, thin back and seek the flesh beneath the jumper.

'Olivia, really,' he protested, half laughing.

She drew back, looking slightly puzzled, slightly hurt. 'Come on, Stud,' she said, putting on a voice she fondly regarded as 'tarty', 'You know how to make a good groupie happy.'

Julian stood. At six feet two inches, he towered over Olivia. He thought he could use his height to put some distance between them but instead she looked up at him with warm, pleading doe-like eyes and he could scarcely tear his own eyes away from them. 'Olivia, you are lovely. Lovely and beautiful. But you are my best friend's daughter. Acton's little girl. I may be an old lecher and believe me there is nothing I would like more than to take you upstairs right now and give you the benefit of my experience. But it would be wrong. We've known each other so long, all your life...'

Olivia raised herself up on tiptoe and kissed him again on the mouth. 'I don't think we need to worry about that. Daddy will understand. You can always say I made you. It's true, anyway, isn't it? I am making you. There is no escape. Come with me.'

She took his hand and started to lead him upstairs. Julian knew he should resist. But how could he? It would ill-mannered. And, after all, she was particularly lovely.

Later, as they were lying in bed with only a light from the landing to illuminate them, Olivia said, 'I don't want you to say anything about anything. OK. I know what's what. I'm a big girl. You don't have to feel guilty, profess love to me or anything. But can we do it again, soon?'

Julian forced himself to stay awake. It was rude to roll over and fall asleep, though these days that was his preferred activity after making love. Olivia deserved more respect. He looked at her sleek back and smooth buttocks and smiled. 'My God but you're lovely,' he said, kissing the back of her neck.

'Corny.'

'Leslie Phillips. I don't suppose you've any idea who he is. Was. Have you?'

'Leslie? A man?'

'Famous actor.'

'Anyway, what about daddy?' Olivia sat up displaying her luscious breasts. Stud turned on a bedside light, mainly to get a better view.

'I know, I don't think we should mention this to him, do you? Could be the end of a beautiful relationship. Or your mother.'

'No, I mean, what about daddy and politics? Now all this stuff has come out about him being sacked for smoking – it's so ridiculous – we should get him re-elected to Parliament as an independent. Just to show the bloody party and all those fucking hypocrites what bloody fucking hypocrites they are. I mean it Julian. You've got to persuade him.'

Julian looked doubtful and murmured something about not thinking he should interfere.

'Otherwise I'll tell him about us,' she added with a giggle.

*****

'No!'

'Daddy.'

'No''

'Daddeeee daddddeeeee daddddeeeee….'

'No, Olivia! No! Tell her Clarissa.'

The Trussell family sat round the kitchen table with their mugs of tea. Olivia has taken her shock of thick red hair and gathered it up in a rough bun on top of her head. Strands fell over her forehead and she ineffectually blew them away.

It was Sunday morning in Howard Michael. Acton was still in his dressing gown trying to read 'The Telegraph'. Clarissa was about to go to church, dressed in a purple jacket and skirt made of some woollen fabric that looked rather hot for a warm September day. Olivia was just back from Julian's, looking pale and tired and dressed in yesterday's jeans and jumper.

Olivia was about to continue when Vernon Small knocked on the back door and walked in, making a noisy fuss over the dog, which wagged and jumped up to greet him. 'Morning all,' he said cheerily. 'Have you heard the news?'

'I would have if I'd got the chance to read the paper,' Trussell complained.

Vernon ignored him. 'The Prime Minister has ordered an inquiry into Nicotinegate.'

'Nicotinegate? I thought it was called Cigarettegate,' said Clarissa, crossing the kitchen to kiss Vernon gently on the cheek and run a hand down his arm in affectionate greeting.

'Now it's Nicotinegate or, on some of the websites, CCTVgate but that seems a bit of a mouthful to me. No, the PM, our great friend, says it's nothing to do with him, his government or any dirty tricks department which the party hasn't got anyway so it couldn't carry out any dirty tricks and to prove it he's ordered an inquiry into this issue and into the issue of the security of CCTV data and the liberty of the individual.'

By now, Vernon was filling the kettle to make himself coffee. Olivia turned to her father, 'It doesn't make any difference, daddy, you've still got to do it. Tell him, Vernon, tell him he's got to stand at the by-election as an Independent.'

'Ohhh,' Vernon declared, putting the kettle down to clap his hands in glee. 'What a lovely idea. Isn't it Cliss?'

'Really, Vernon! Don't encourage her. Or him. Acton has retired from politics and that's that.'

'Ah but has he, dear? Has he really?' Vernon turned to Acton. 'Have you, Acton? Have your really?'

Trussell paused to think. He didn't like making decisions swiftly. He worked on the theory that decisions should only be made if and when they had to be made. Usually, if you didn't make any decision, the right answer would somehow present itself and happen anyway or the whole dilemma would just go away or sort itself out. He believed that as far as possible one should always try to muddle through. Decisiveness was rarely called for and there was never any reason to exhibit this trait just because someone else wanted you to make a decision. On the other hand, he thought maybe he had a better idea than either Vernon or Olivia.

'I think,' he said, as slowly as possible to ensure their rapt attention, 'I think that insofar as Barset needs an alternative to the official party candidate and taking into account the impact of a by-election fought on the issue of privacy and freedom, it would not be desirable for the man at the centre of the storm to face down his enemies...'

'But daddy,' Olivia interrupted, swinging her long red hair, which had fallen out of its makeshift bun, and leaping up from her chair to make her point.

'Allow me to finish, darling,' Trussell went on. 'This is an opportunity. An opportunity to take a fresh look at politics and state our case with a clear conscience.'

'Acton, you are sounding absurdly like a political broadcast,' Clarissa complained.

'Well, the long and the short of it is this: I think Olivia should stand.'

'Daddy!' she exclaimed as her mother said 'Don't be ridiculous' and Vernon clapped his hands in delight and declared. 'What a wonderful idea.'

*****

Clifford Chambers was unhappy. How could he be expected to secure Lucy Loxley's victory? There would be dozens, maybe even hundreds of members at the selection evening. Was Compton Dundon seriously expecting him to fix the voting? How could he do that? Were there three or four people he could trust to ensure the vote-counting went according to plan? Could he coach Lucy enough to secure her a win without the need for anything odd?

Gerrymandering was the word, wasn't it? Fixing the voters in advance to make sure they gave you the result you wanted. It wasn't fraud. But mis-counting the votes would be. He wasn't sure he was up to fraud.

On the other hand, Clifford realised, his future in the party would depend on whether he was able to deliver the needful. Compton Dundon was a fixer. He could fix things for Clifford if he wanted to – or fix things against him if he didn't.

Clifford found himself envying tubby little Dundon. He wanted to be in a position one day to hold Dundon's fate in his hands. He wanted to make or break Dundon's career just as Dundon could make or break his now.

Clifford had to see Lucy Loxley.

He poured himself a gin and tonic with lime and crushed ice and rang Ms Loxley, summoning her over to Rosepetal Avenue. Lucy had been sitting in the last of the afternoon sun reading a novel in the garden of her uncle's house wondering why Joanna was sulking with her and vaguely considering whether to up-date her website with some of the pictures she'd had taken of her visit to the Euthanasia Centre (motto: 'Drop in, drop out, drop dead') so she was pleased to have something to do.

She wasn't very keen on Barset. Richard and Ann were nice enough but usually she only saw them at Christmas and they were beginning to irritate her. Maybe she should get herself a house now. But how could she? If she bought a house, it would show insufferable arrogance which might cost her the election. When she was elected she would get a flat and visit the place once a month. Joanna could probably live with that.

While he waited for her to arrive, Clifford set out a pair of mats depicting scenes from the Italian lakes on the coffee table, put on some background music – Michael Buble, he thought, was appropriate to the occasion – and sat perusing the Cigarettegate write-up on the 'Times' website via his i-Pad. That prat Acton Trussell. If he hadn't been a family friend, Clifford would have withdrawn his support years ago. He realised now he should have done.

Lucy turned up in hot pants and a baggy T-shirt with the slogan: 'Lesbians do it without men.' Clifford was appalled. She looked good. Very sexy. There was something androgynous about her. She looked like a young boy. Clifford was scandalised.

He explained their meeting was intended to prepare her for the selection. 'You can't go round dressed like that,' he told her. 'It just won't do, Lucy. You have to remember the members, especially the elderly ladies who make up at least half your electorate, may not be prejudiced against homosexuals but they really do not like having your sexuality thrust down their throats as it were. You need decorum. You must be statesmanlike.'

'Statesmanlike?' Lucy curled up on the sofa, long brown legs on prominent display, sipped gin and tonic and looked like a naughty schoolgirl. She could not conceal her grin.

'Lucy, this is not some sort of game or joke. If you want to become a Member of Parliament you really must start taking it seriously. Do you want to become a Member of Parliament?'

'Of course.'

'Then you must behave like one.'

'What, you mean take bribes, claim expenses, sit on the boards of defence firms, charge thousands of pounds for speeches at marketing conferences for multi-nationals?'

Clifford rose and stood with his back to the log-effect fireplace looking down at his guest. 'This is serious,' he said, slowly and deliberately. 'This by-election will be the focus of national attention. The media will be down here en masse. There will even be foreign interest in it. This is the first real public test of the Coalition since the General Election. We are lucky the electoral pact is still in place so we don't need to worry about the Lib-Dems. But we need to win and we need to win convincingly. This smoking business won't help. It got rid of Trussell and created the opening, of course. But now we have to prove the policy was popular and we have to make it clear we were in no way involved in this breach of security. This is not some dirty trick by the Government but an unfortunate freelance operation. By the way, you don't smoke, do you?'

'Not since I was thirteen. I smoked a lot at school but that was just because it was the thing to do. Luckily it made me sick and my girlfriend at the time made me promise not to try them again.'

'That is not something you should tell people when they ask. It would not be helpful. They do not want to know you were breaking the law when you were thirteen – especially the bit about your girlfriend.'

Lucy looked up at Clifford. He was nervous. He was fiddling with the ice in his glass, swirling it around and sipping the melting water, dipping a finger into it and licking it. He put the glass on the mantelpiece and then picked it up again. She took pity on him. 'What's the matter Clifford? Don't worry, I'm not as stupid as I look you know.'

He sighed and sat down beside her, turned to look at her and took her hand. 'Lucy, the party wants you to become the next MP for Barset. My job is to ensure you are selected next weekend and then to ensure you are elected on November 5.'

'November. But it's only September now. You mean the election is still eight weeks away?'

'It's the earliest date we can get. And even that is going to take a bit of manipulation of the Parliamentary timetable. In the meantime, your job is to meet everyone in Barset who matters.'

'I've been doing that, going through your list of contacts like a good girl.'

'We need to prepare your literature, distribute a newsletter, get you into some schools, make sure you visit the hospital, have some pictures of you in the "Chronic", set up a letter-writing campaign, find a local issue for you to campaign on. We've got a head start. The Opposition haven't even bothered putting together a shortlist of candidates. We can expect four or five minority parties to complicate things for us but basically we can ignore them because they'll all lose their deposits. No, Lucy, the first task for Lucy Loxley is to secure the selection. You will have to change, Lucy. You will have to become a nice, sedate middle-class lady if you want to win over the locals. And you will have to do better in your speech and your interview than you did last time.'

'I thought I did alright. I got through, didn't I?'

'Yes but only thanks to your friends and your connections. By the way, is there anything you want to tell me?' Clifford looked closely into her grey and innocent eyes. What was their secret? Why was the party so keen on her? She had few achievements to her name and even a lesbian had to have something else going for her. The quota system was working well. A third of the party's MPs were now women. A full 12 per cent of them, male and female, were gay – more than twice the national average. Nobody could accuse the party of being unrepresentative any more. Of course, it was still true that 86 per cent of its MPs had been educated privately at expensive fee-paying public schools but, as the Prime Minister often said, that was due to the failings of State education. Once he had improved that, there would be no need for people to educate their children privately. The whole sector would wither away and die, he said, it would just take time.

Clifford resumed his headmasterly pose before the fireplace. 'Lucy,' he asked, 'Why do you want to become an MP anyway? It's the first question people ask, especially as voters have nothing but contempt for politicians and distrust all of them. You must have a good answer.'

'Because I want to change the world,' she said with a light laugh.

'That's not an answer.'

'Because I care?'

'About what?'

'I don't know. Everything, I suppose.'

Clifford groaned and sat down again. 'No Lucy. Why not start by telling me really why you want to become an MP?'

'I don't know, Clifford. Because it's there, I suppose. Isn't that why Mallory climbed Everest? Because it's there. It's a challenge, it's fun, it's something to do.'

Clifford groaned again.

*****

Howard Michael was shrouded in damp morning mist. Yesterday's bright autumn evening had been replaced by low clouds and moisture in the air which wasn't quite rain or even drizzle but left dewdrops all over Hilda's coat as the dog and Acton Trussell lumbered slowly up the hill outside the village towards the woods.

He needed a walk. He needed to think. He needed to escape the scepticism of his wife and the enthusiasm of his daughter. He also needed a cigarette.

The papers were still worrying away at the story about his exposure as an illegal smoker. They had turned on the Opposition, refusing to believe its outraged denials of a dirty tricks campaign. Several websites now carried profiles of Acton himself. Most of them said the same sort of thing. An obscure backbench MP for far too long. Never achieved anything of note. Now regarded as a voice of reason, defender of liberty, much-missed champion of the underdog, the poor and the oppressed. It was remarkable how one's fortunes could change without one actually having any hand in the thing. Journalists did not present people with facts any more, just opinions. And, as those opinions changed by the day, the journalist's art was to take the acknowledged facts and transform them to support whatever side of the argument they chose to adopt. Thus Acton Trussell, for many years dismissed as an out-of-date dinosaur fighting for lost causes and frozen out by his own party, had been transformed into an iconoclastic champion of individual freedom, a dauntless Saint George doing battle against the dragons of an over-mighty State machine on behalf of all the innocent citizens of this once-great nation.

Acton felt old. He was exhausted by all this attention. It wasn't nice waking up to find TV crews on your lawn. But it was just as bad to discover your daughter was suddenly so enthusiastic about the whole bloody mess. Had he been serious when he suggested Olivia stand at the by-election? She had gone very quiet when he said it. Vernon was jigging about excitedly and drawing up election slogans. Clarissa had gone off to church without comment – always a bad sign.

Could he let Olivia do this? Could he put that genie back in the bottle? Would she enjoy it? Would he wish it on his own worst enemy? What should he do now? There was only one way he could spike her guns and that would be to stand himself. Would she rather he did that or would she actually wish to have a go herself?

What was the point? Would she win? Would he win if he stood? Which of them would be most likely to succeed? Did he want to have a go? He had to admit he was tempted. Why? Just because. Because what? Because he had been ill-used. He did, truly, believe that Governments should be there to set people free not lock them up in chains. We had the right to go to hell in our own way. Didn't we? Maybe we didn't. Maybe Governments should protect us from ourselves. Lots of people had no idea what was good for them. If they didn't have family and friends to guide them properly, perhaps they needed civil servants to lay down the law for them instead.

Acton trudged up the hill while Hilda sniffed at the undergrowth and trotted along behind him. The damp blanket of cloud showed no sign of lifting.

In the clearing where, a few weeks ago, Trussell had given the slip to Compton Dundon and Steve Thomas, the ex-MP made for an elderly oak tree with gnarled roots. He removed a strategically-placed branch and fished underneath it into the wet earth until he laid hands on a plastic bag. The bag itself was rare enough, he considered, given that no shops were prepared to enlarge their carbon footprints by issuing such things these days.

Trussell slid out from its underground lair a 'Prague Airport Duty Free' bag. Inside were two intact packs of 200 Marlboro Light cigarettes and a third pack which contained six unopened packets of 20 cigarettes and a seventh. He took out the seventh and inspected the contents. It still contained three cigarettes and a cheap lighter. He returned the bag to its hiding place and carefully laid the branch over it before crossing to the felled tree where, in the damp of morning, he sat down and proceeded to light one of the cigarettes.

Trussell inhaled deeply and exhaled with a satisfied sigh. He felt the nicotine rush through his veins. He felt a little light-headed and was pleased he was sitting down. Last time had had attempted to smoke a cigarette standing up, he had staggered and almost lost his balance. It just showed, he realised, how powerful these dreadful things were. The Government was right to discourage people from smoking. It was dangerous and addictive. It was a drug. And, like any drug-user, he was more interested in getting another fix than in the rights and wrongs of legislation.

He looked about him. The woods were still, the only sound a faint hiss as the drizzle made contact with the still-green leaves. There was no birdsong. No sound of traffic. There were no people. This spot was Trussell's safe haven, where he could retreat to think and enjoy one of his diminishing supply of cigarettes without interruption or fear of prying CCTV cameras.

He had no idea what he would do when his supply ran out but he only visited the copse about three times a week so it should keep him going for a while yet, though he did make the most of his visits. He thought it reasonable to smoke all three of the cigarettes left in this packet.

Trussell tried to wrench his mind back to the problem. Should he encourage Olivia to stand as an independent? Should he do so himself? Should neither of them do any such thing?

What were the chances of success? Normally, zero. Independent candidates had a long and unheroic history of failure at parliamentary elections. The big parties carried all the weight with voters. It was almost impossible to make a mark against them. But there had been exceptions over the years. Local campaigns occasionally propelled a local worthy to Westminster in spite of the combined might of the main parties. It could be done; it had been done.

There was more chance of success, Trussell thought, at a by-election than at a General Election. In a by-election the focus was more on the candidates as individuals than on the parties or their leaders. The voters were aware they could make an impact, change things for the better or register their disapproval, in a way which would force the Government of the day to pay attention. But usually their protests were local – against a hospital closure, against the imposition of an outsider as the candidate for the favourite party, against a motorway or in favour of a by-pass. Over the years, there had been a few dissidents who succeeded in fighting by-elections on national issues and winning. But they were rare and mostly in the past.

Still, Trussell could imagine a by-election fought on the issue of freedom and liberty might possibly attract a few voters away from the main parties. The down-side was that many people who professed a belief in freedom were at the same time vehemently opposed to smoking. They would argue that the freedom of the individual to kill himself had to be subordinated to the freedom of everyone else to live their lives unpolluted by the vile evil of nicotine in its various forms.

Against that, though, Trussell realised, would be the ex-smokers who simply felt unfairly victimised. For them, debates about freedom or responsibility were academic. They had been singled out as pariahs and resented it. They were down there with motorists and air travellers, among others. People who felt increasingly marginalised and despised by Government, the media, society as a whole. Yet these were ordinary, decent people. They didn't deserve persecution. They might well support a candidate who spoke up for them.

Who should that candidate be? Trussell knew well enough the nastiness of politics. He'd been woken in the middle of the night by silent phone calls. He'd seen gossip and lies about him appear on websites and in newspapers. He'd been subjected to leafleting campaigns, had paint thrown over his car, endured bomb threats, the fury and bad breath of nutters on the streets of his home town, the contempt of perfectly nice people, the disdain of others. He had endured the plots of his colleagues and the manoeuvrings of his friends. He'd seen his salary, expenses and tax bills pored over on websites as clever-clever critics asked what he wanted with a non-executive directorship of a local engineering company or why he felt it necessary to attend a trade conference in Delhi at the expense of the Indian Chamber of Commerce.

As he stubbed out his first cigarette and lit the second, Trussell reflected that an MP spent all his life trying to justify his existence. Why bother? Why bother again? Why not let Olivia discover how awful it is for herself?

On the other hand, should he expose his beautiful and beloved daughter to the misery and unhappiness of life as an MP? Even if she were to win, she'd only be an MP until the next election. Then the old system would reassert itself and she'd be out – an ex-MP at the age of 25 or so. That was not a fate he was happy to contemplate.

Trussell didn't see or even hear the stealthy footsteps of the 'Barset Chronicle's' ace reporter Jimi Hunt as he crept towards the clearing, enticed by the smell of tobacco on the air. Hunt fancied himself as a photographer and, as this was his day off, he had ventured out towards Howard Michael in search of the buzzards said to be there. When he caught sight of Acton Trussell through his telephoto lens, he realised he had stumbled on serious money. He set the camera to silent mode and snapped away.

*****

As her father was enjoying his secret cigarette, Olivia was saddling a horse in Julian Lee's stables. She and Stud were off for a hack round the estate and towards the Goodbye Hills. It was all a bit awkward. Olivia wasn't sure where she stood. She had kissed Stud hello when she arrived but he was reluctant to kiss her back. She suggested the ride because she wasn't sure what they would be doing otherwise.

Olivia hadn't seen Stud since the night she spent with him, nor had she spoken to him. He wasn't the sort of man you just rang up for a chat nor was he the sort who would be interested in long conversations of the deep-and-meaningful sort. That's one of the things she liked about him. He was plain, straightforward and practical. He was also invariably cheerful – as if he could never quite get over his great good fortune.

'I think you should get your hair cut and stop dying it,' Olivia told him as they were riding slowly down the drive.

Stud smiled. 'My flowing locks don't seem to have put you off that much, young lady. How's your father?'

'Is that a question or an invitation?'

'Very good but as we are on horseback I think you can probably work that one out for yourself.'

'He thinks I should become an MP.' Olivia laughed but was secretly anxious to know how Stud would react to the idea. She valued his opinion, he would know if it was the right thing to do. He laughed, turned through an open gate into a field and started to trot off up the hill.

They didn't return to the subject until much later, when they went to The Miller's for a pub lunch together, still in their riding clothes and both a little flushed from the exercise and the chill in the air.

'So, daddy wants his little girl to inherit his constituency, does he?' Stud asked. His hair was flattened by his riding hat but he still looked every inch the ageing rock star, down to his deep tan, lined face and single diamond ear-stud. Olivia wondered if he even remembered they had made love only two days ago but she was determined not to be the first to mention this. It was up to Stud to decide if this was a one-off or something more significant. She wasn't going to be clingy, desperate or pushy. But she did want him to acknowledge what had happened and, ideally, suggest it might happen again some time soon. She was playing it cool. Meanwhile there was this idea of becoming an MP to talk about.

'It's not like that. I was telling him I thought he should fight as an Independent and he turned the tables on me. Said if I was so keen on the rights of the individual, I should do it instead.'

'Have you ever smoked?'

'Yuck, no! It's disgusting. Had enough of that watching daddy coughing himself to death. Can't stand them.'

'But you think the Government was wrong to ban them?'

'Yes, I suppose so. It's like the time they tried to ban hunting, do you remember? They didn't care about the countryside. They just trampled over the rights of country-folk.'

'Country-folk?' teased Stud, 'You sound like an extra off "The Archers".'

'Well, people who don't live in big cities. You know. Ordinary people like us. You, me, Mrs Barton behind the bar. Poor old Sid Shipley who had to sell up when the Fox and Trumpet couldn't make any money and ended up in one of those council houses in Howard Michael.'

Stud couldn't help but be amused. 'You are certainly not an ordinary person, Miss Trussell,' he said. Olivia was a lovely, lively, intelligent young woman and he was surprisingly fond of her. He was not sure what kind of relationship he should have with her – he certainly didn't want her parents to discover how close they had become. He was still looking for a way of broaching the subject of their relationship but she seemed reluctant to discuss it. Had he done something to upset her? He thought it best to stick to the subject in hand. 'Do you want to become an MP, Livvy? That's the real question, isn't it?'

'Oh God no. I can't imagine anything worse. All those miserable misfits, those long, tedious debates, all those horrible stories in the papers. Why would anybody want to become an MP? Of course I don't.'

'Then why are you asking me if I think you should fight the by-election?'

'Because daddy suggested it.'

'And you don't want to disappoint daddy?'

She smiled sheepishly and threw a twist of red hair off her face and over her shoulder.

*****

Compton Dundon was sitting at his laptop in the bar of the Barset Sleepover. Steve Thomas was in his room looking at pornography on the internet. Dundon was e-mailing the candidates about the selection meeting the following Saturday.

His e-mails to the London lawyer Vivek Arnold, Lucy Loxley and Maggie Pride congratulated them on being short-listed for selection for the seat of Barset. Dundon asked them to attend a selection evening starting at 6pm on the evening of Saturday, September 7. He told them to be prepared to give a 15-minute address to the members on 'Why I would make a good MP for Barset'. He said the meeting would be chaired by Clifford Chambers, the association chairman, and the winner would be declared the same evening after a vote of all eligible members present, in accordance with the party rules. His e-mail to Parvinder Singh said exactly the same thing except that he told her the selection evening was on the following Saturday, September 14.

*****

Maggie Pride called into the offices of Alveston Pink in Barset to see Clifford Chambers.

Business was still slow. The meltdown of global capitalism may have been staved off but that didn't mean the housing market had picked up. Prices were ten per cent or more down on ten years ago. People were reluctant to trade up. Nobody wanted to sell at a loss. Everyone was frightened of paying over the odds. First-time buyers were a rare breed – graduates were too broke paying off their student loans to think about getting on the housing ladder which, in any case, was these days seen more as a slippery slope than a route to riches.

Clifford sat at his desk with its glass partition looking out over the quiet, carpeted silence of the main office where one young woman was laboriously typing up the details of yet another house which was 'unexpectedly back on the market' after the sale fell through when the purchaser's business, a car dealership, called in the receivers.

Maggie greeted the girl with a smile and stood chatting about the state of the market for a while before making her way through into Clifford's inner sanctum and, without being invited to do either, she shut the door and sat down opposite him.

Maggie was all business. She wore a neatly tailored jacked and skirt in grey with a small silver brooch on one lapel and carried a neat, shiny black handbag. She did not wait for him to speak. 'Clifford, good morning, I do hope you don't mind my disturbing you at work," she said. 'I gather from Alice you are not terribly busy this morning.'

Chambers, who had been playing a new computer game, smiled, nodded, said, 'That's quite alright' while raising one eyebrow to suggest it was far from alright for Maggie Pride burst into his office without a by-your-leave. He prided himself on his ability to say one thing and mean another. It was one of his greatest strengths.

Maggie sat on the chair opposite Chambers and launched into her speech. 'What I want to know, Clifford, is this: Am I to be given a fair and equal chance of selection on Saturday or am I wasting my time? Is it all a foregone conclusion? I've spent the last week and a half going round everyone I know in Barset canvassing for their support, whether or not they are party members and whether or not they intend to turn up on Saturday evening. And I can tell you that, as the only local candidate on the shortlist, I feel I am definitely in a strong position. Strong enough to carry the day. That's how I feel. But. And it is a big but, Clifford. But everyone who says they know what's what – that means people like Chatham Smith and Reg Wootton, Jim Dutton and even Tony Grafton...'

'Quentin Quinton?' Chambers smiled at the memory of his outrageous question.

'That man. I still haven't got over his "what would your husband do for sex?" line. Haven't you kicked him out of the party yet?' Maggie didn't wait for an answer. 'Anyway, I've been talking to people, supporters, you know, friends. And they all say the same thing. They say it's been fixed already. There's no way I can win, they say. It's all arranged.'

'All arranged?'

'They say that Parvinder Singh woman with her yellow saris and her scent has got it in the bag. They say she's got everything going for her. BME. Woman. Beautiful. The men can't keep from dribbling whenever she's in the room, they say. More to the point, they say the party chairman has already decreed she shall be the candidate. Is it true, Clifford? Am I wasting my time?'

Clifford smiled complacently. He was very good at telling the truth. 'Maggie. Margaret. Maggie, my dear. Maggie. I can assure you, Maggie, I can tell you categorically. There is no plot to give this constituency to Parvinder. You are right that she did make quite an impact at the first round of selections. Several members were highly impressed by her presence, her ability to get to grips with the issues, her charm. But she is not a shoo-in. This is not a staged selection process, there is no stitch-up in Ms Singh's favour, there is no fix. No deals have been done behind anybody's back to get her selected at all costs. She will take her chances alongside everyone else. We – that is to say, your association committee officers and the team from HQ – we are quite neutral in all of this. We have to be. We will have to work with whichever candidate the members see fit to select. It could easily be Parvinder Singh, but then it could just as easily be Maggie Pride. 'Putting the Pride back into Barset' – it's got a ring to it. It's a good election slogan, Maggie. Very good, very positive.'

Clifford looked at the woman across the desk from him. She was plump. He would go so far as to describe her as dumpy. He couldn't imagine a time when she had been a successful dancer in TnA. He had once caught a glimpse of the troupe prancing around to some Bryan Adams song on one of the dozens of music video channels and had noted, even then, that she was perhaps a little too curvaceous for her cat-suit. Clifford wondered if she'd ever tried lap-dancing. He presumed not.

'Well I'm very pleased to hear it.' Maggie's indignation had been deflated but she was still sceptical. Clifford wasn't entirely trustworthy, she knew that now. 'And what about your little chum Lucy Loxley?' she asked accusingly.

'Lucy? No chum of mine. As I say, Mags, it's a level playing field. Everything to play for. May the best man – or woman – win.'

Maggie got up to leave. She now wished she hadn't marched in on Clifford. She had gained nothing, no knowledge, no insight. If anything, she had made herself look just a little foolish. But if she did get selected, the first thing she'd have to do is get rid of this buffoon anyway. Clifford Chambers was old before his time, Maggie thought, he'd have to go.

Chambers stood to shake her hand. They no longer kissed in greeting or parting, any reminder of their brief intimacy erased by common consent. 'One piece of advice, though, Mags, which I think may be helpful to you on Saturday night. This is a by-election, it will be fought on national issues with national questions to the fore. The party won't want – and the voters won't want – too much emphasis on the local, parochial, parish-pump stuff. Less trading estate, more balance of trade if you see what I mean. If I were you I'd steer clear of local issues and local committees. Think global – Europe, the Far East, the war in Afghanistan, that sort of thing – not the Barset Festival or the board of the hospital trust. Avoid painting yourself as the little local worthy up against these sophisticated London types.'

'But I thought that's what people wanted most – a local woman who understands local concerns.'

'No, Maggie, trust me, that's the last thing they want. Barset elects statesmen – stateswomen – not parish councilors. Think national, Mags, think international. Don't think parochial.'

Chambers told the same thing to Vivek Arnold when the lawyer telephoned him a couple of hours later. And when he met Parvinder Singh he gave her similar advice – 'use your exotic origins to emphasise your status as a global statesman,' he said.

After he took Lucy Loxley to meet the Barset Fire Station crew and before he took her to a beer and chips evening at the cricket club, where she was to make a short speech and present the prize to the Young Player of the Year,

Chambers stopped the car in a lay-by and, with rush-hour traffic rumbling by, turned to her with a serious frown and said, 'You know what the members will want most, don't you, Lucy? Someone with strong local connections, with real concern for the constituency and its people. They don't want an MP who will spend her life globetrotting. They don't want some international trouble-shooter. This is a parish-pump place and we like parish-pump politics. If I were you, I'd talk about the local economy, how to revitalise the trading estate, the decaying town centre shops, about how important it is to defend the local hospital and improve our schools – have you been to King Arthur's yet? When it comes to abroad, just tell them how much you hate the European Union, that it's a Franco-German plot to rob us of our liberty, and say how you pray every night the war will soon be over and we can bring our boys home at last. Stick to the parish pump and you won't go too far wrong.'

*****

Newbold Whitnash was early into the office. He had the morning papers spread out on his desk. Several were sporting a picture of the local ex-MP Acton Trussell sitting on a log of wood in a clearing smoking a cigarette. There were several versions of this. One showed him exhaling with a look of satisfaction on his face. Another showed his lips tightly pursed together as he drew deeply on the cigarette. A third showed him gazing into the middle distance while the cigarette rested between his fingers. All the pictures depicted a chubby, elderly man in a battered wax jacket and all of them showed his faithful Labrador lying at his feet. Only one of the papers correctly named her as Hilda.

None of these pictures had been made available to the "Barset Chronicle". The first its editor had heard of them was when he saw a review of the day's papers on TV. The show had acquired the pictures as well and was holding a discussion with its tame doctor and a talent show winner about whether the pictures should have been taken, whether they should have been published and whether Trussell, who had already been caught flouting the smoking ban once, should be prosecuted for his crime.

Whitnash didn't care much about any of these questions. He was much more bothered about where the pictures came from and why he hadn't known in advance. He called in his chief reporter. 'Jimi, I know it was you,' he said.

'What was me?' Jimi Hunt was wearing jeans and a filthy shirt, open at the collar.

'And why the hell can't you dress properly? This is a newspaper office not a doss house. Where were you last night?'

'I was up all night.'

'Selling these bloody pictures. Don't try to deny it. They've got your prints all over them. I haven't got any choice, Jimi. I'm going to have to let you go.'

'Let me go? Go where?'

'Jimi, I am sacking you. That's it. End of a glorious career. You're out. Pack your things and leave. You will be paid until the end of the month but don't expect anything else. No tribunals, thank you very much.'

'You can't do it.'

'I can and I have. You are fired for gross misconduct. It is not acceptable to sell stories – or pictures – to rival media outlets. You know that Jimi.'

Hunt shrugged and left without another word. He did not bother to say goodbye to his colleagues, mainly because he knew they knew about the pictures as well and they would feel the same way as their editor. He didn't mind. He'd already got a freelance contract with a national website to be their man in Barset. And he'd earned more in the past 24 hours than the "Chronic" paid him in six months. This wasn't the end of the road, it was the start of an adventure.

*****

The Home Secretary rang the party chairman.

'Dave? Rick. Pickering. The Home Secretary. God this bloody man's a fool. Dave are you there? It's Rick. Yes, Rick-the-Home-Secretary-Rick. Your Cabinet colleague. Have you seen the papers today? The papers, man, the bloody newspapers. Have you seen them? No? Christ! Has anyone in that hell hole seen today's papers? Stan? Stan who? Stanley? That spotty youth? Alright, put him on. Stanley? Pickering. Get onto Dundon and that fool Steve Thomas and ask them what they're doing about these photos. What photos? The bloody photos of Trussell of course you bloody fool. The ones in the bloody papers. Well have a look at the bloody papers then call Dundon then call me back. Bloody hell.'

The Home Secretary rang Bingley Ortega, the Chief Constable of the Trent Constabulary.

'Bingo, Rick. 'Ow are you, man? Still after that knighthood? It's a joke, Bingo, don't be so sensitive. I know how you feel. How's the handicap? No, I don't mean Mrs Bingo, I mean are you under ten yet? No? Too busy? Pity. We must have another game some time. During the party conference? Ideal. Get your people to fix it with mine. Look forward to it. Now, Bingo, have you seen today's papers. You have? Thank Christ for that. Now you will have seen the prima facie evidence against Acton Trussell? The ex-MP actually, Bingo, ex being the operative word. Prima facie evidence, yes. The felon has committed a felony. Well a misdemeanour anyway. He's breaking the law. Yes I know it's sensitive. Tell me about it. Have you seen the stick we've been getting lately thanks to the bloody Opposition's treacherous breach of the privacy laws? No, of course we can't prove it. They're not that stupid. Mind you, maybe they are. Nothing's too dumb for dumb animals. Anyway, Bingo, listen. Do you think you could make it your order of the day for our man Trussell – not our man, your man, your man Trussell – to be taken into custody, questioned, charged and bailed? Maximum publicity, obviously. Yes, maximum. We need to issue a warning that this Government will not tolerate such blatant flouting of the law. Fuss over nothing? Of course not. He's broken the law and it's our job – your job, if I may say so, Bingo – to detect law-breakers and bring them to justice. A £60 fine? Well that's something, isn't it? But this is a second offence. Maximum fine £2,000 or seven days imprisonment if I remember correctly. Imprisonment? Maybe. If you see fit, Bingo, if you see fit. Wouldn't do for a politician to interfere in the judicial process. But it would be a pity if the CCTV evidence which is, after all, in the public domain, were to count for nothing in such a blatant instance as this, don't you agree? I am so pleased. Well, Bingo, see you on the links in a few weeks' time. Do let me know if there's anything my people can do to aid you in your quest to bring a little law and order to the good people of Trent.'

*****

Detective Chief Inspector Hazel Snitterfield was late for work. Again. Child care was always difficult now the schools were back. Little Sammy didn't like Terrible Tots but it was the best in the area and at least she had personally checked the criminal records, DNA prints, police national computer, DVLA computer, immigration records and bank account details of all seven of its employees so she was reasonably confident it was secure.

On DCI Snitterfield's desk was a note from her secretary, Heath, to call the Chief Constable immediately. She did as instructed and listened carefully to the instructions she received before asking, 'Won't it seem a little like overkill if we go round in squad cars with the sirens blazing? And should a DCI really be deployed in what is, after all, a fairly trivial offence? I'm sorry, sir, of course, sir, if the Home Secretary has ordered it then of course sir. Immediately sir.'

DCI Snitterfield called in her team and issued her instructions. 'We won't need a search warrant. I can't see a man like Trussell objecting to a search of the premises. If we mess it up a little, well dear, dear. No doubt he can afford a cleaner.'

*****

Compton Dundon called Jimi Hunt and 15 minutes later the out-of-work reporter was crouching down behind the headstones in the churchyard of Howard Michael with his camera and an excellent view of the Trussells' home. The police arrived 20 minutes after the reporter. Five squad cars with sirens wailing and lights flashing as if they were racing through the streets of New York. Several officers were dressed in riot gear. Hunt thought he saw a couple of machine guns but he was so busy clicking away he couldn't be sure. He'd check later.

A woman in civilian clothes – a bright blue skirt and a beige cashmere pullover – with dyed blond hair and a mystified expression, marched up to the front door, knocked and waited. There was a brief conversation between the policewoman and the woman who answered the door. The latter was holding the end of a Dyson vacuum cleaner in one hand and shaking her head.

The policewoman turned to her colleagues. Her look had changed to bafflement. She took out her mobile phone and made a call.

The police officers reluctantly returned to their cars. The woman in charge had a long conversation with a man in a suit and a sergeant before they, too, returned to their cars. There was a pause, as if they were trying to reach a decision, then the vehicles dashed off, once again lights blazing, sirens wailing, until gradually peace descended again on the small village of Howard Michael.

Hunt called Dundon. 'Not at home. They've disappeared again. Any idea where?'

Dundon called Clifford Chambers, who said Clarissa's mother was very unwell and they could have gone to St Barset's Royal Infirmary.

Hunt did not arrive in time to see the police descend on the hospital but he was there to see Acton Trussell led away, in handcuffs, by half a dozen uniformed officers. His wife stood in the entrance to the hospital quietly talking to the policewoman in charge. Hunt, sitting at the wheel of his Vauxhall Viagra VX, snapped away, recording it all.

*****

It made the one o'clock news. Jimi had used his camera's video facility and the picture quality was surprisingly good. He went to Sky first because they paid the most. Pretty soon all the other news outlets were clamouring for pictures, still and moving. He was doing deals – good deals. This was becoming his story. Acton Trussell was his man.

Jimi eventually made it to police headquarters in time to see an attractive young woman with thick red hair arrive accompanied by someone he thought he recognised but couldn't place. Unfortunately they disappeared before he could park or get out his camera. He waited.

Inside, Acton was sitting in a dreary interview room with DCI Snitterfield and a tall Rastafarian called Detective Constable Yardley Wood. Mr Wood sat on the edge of his seat fiddling with his dreadlocks and looking uncomfortable while Ms Snitterfield did the talking.

Did Mr Trussell accept it was him in the pictures seen in various newspapers that morning? He did. Would he admit that he was actually smoking a cigarette? He would. Would he admit these photographs were recent? That they had been taken since the ban was imposed and that he was therefore breaking the law? He would not. He had no idea when the pictures were taken. He often used to enjoy a cigarette in that copse. If it was since the smoking ban it would be up to the police to prove it. He was certainly not prepared to admit to a crime he may not have committed purely on the photographic evidence displayed in the newspapers.

But if that was the case, asked DCI Snitterfield, would he be suing the newspapers for libel. Surely they were insinuating that he had been caught breaking the law. If he had not then, as a public figure, he would have to clear his name by suing them in a court of law. He didn't see any reason to do so. If they wanted to print ridiculous pictures, how could he stop them? The only people who gained from libel cases were lawyers and he saw no reason why he should enrich them further.

DCI Snitterfield persisted. These pictures proved he had broken the law. Just as the CCTV pictures proved the same thing. Taken with his resignation as an MP, in advance of public exposure and humiliation, he had to admit he was an incorrigible recidivist and deserved the full penalty of the law.

Trussell laughed and reminded Ms Snitterfield that he was present when the legislation in question had been debated in the Houses of Parliament. He knew how serious his alleged offence might be in the eyes of the law. And it was not that serious. Indeed, it could be counted as trivial. Furthermore he questioned why it was necessary for someone of her rank, accompanied by five squad cars full of officers, some in riot gear, to march into a hospital and arrest him at his dying mother-in-law's bedside for such a trivial cause.

'But I shall not be lodging a formal complaint, you may be relived to hear, Detective Chief Superintendent Snitterfield. This is all too trivial for words and I do not suppose you are acting entirely on your own initiative.'

She left him and ordered her officers to track down the photographer. They needed proof the pictures were taken recently. Otherwise how could they prove Trussell had broken the law? She rang the Chief Constable, who was disappointed. He rang the Home Secretary, who was furious. He told the Chief Constable to detain the ex-MP overnight and find the evidence. The Chief Constable relayed the order. DCI Snitterfield told her DI. Acton Trussell was led down to the cells, invited to hand over all his possessions, remove his belt and shoelaces, given a cup of tea and a copy of that evening's 'Chronicle' and told he had better make himself comfortable for the night.

DC Yardley Wood went to the offices of the 'Chronicle' and asked Newbold Whitnash where the pictures came from. Whitnash gave him Jimi Hunt's name, address and mobile phone number, explained he had been sacked that morning and asked what the story was. Wood told him they had arrested Trussell but couldn't prove when the pictures had been taken.

'Ah, a fatal flaw,' said Whitnash.

When the officer had gone, he immediately wrote a new story for the website. 'Police baffled by Trussell case' said the headline, explaining the arrested ex-MP may not be charged with breaking the smoking ban because there was no proof of when the picture was taken.

He then called Hunt.

'Jimi, the police are looking for you. Can you prove when you took those pix of Trussell?'

'Fuck off, you've just fired me.'

'Yes but I'm trying to help you. Can you prove those pix are new?'

'What do you mean?'

'Well, unless you can prove the date you took them was after the ban came into force, the police can't charge him with breaking the law, can they?'

'Of course I can.' But could he? The computer files would show when they were first created but was that enough? No doubt some clever lawyer could cast doubt on that. It would be for him to prove Trussell was breaking the law. All the fat fool had to do was say nothing.

It *was* him, it *was* the day before yesterday, he *was* breaking the law. But it would be his word against Trussell's. What was the point in that sort of a fight? Was there any money in it for Jimi Hunt? Of course not. So why bother?

He was still sitting in his Vauxhall Viagra outside the police station when he spotted the odd couple he'd seen earlier emerge. The young woman was clearly agitated and gesticulating wildly at her older companion, who was trying to calm her down. Jimi took a few snaps, though the light was fading fast and he wasn't sure how good they would be. Then he thought he might as well get out of the car, cross over the road and find out what was going on, whether they were in some way connected with Acton Trussell.

The young woman was complaining. 'It's scandalous. They can't keep him locked up in a prison cell all night. He's done nothing wrong.' Her companion tried calming her down but she shook him off. 'No, Stud, we have to do something. Find a lawyer. Find a lawyer. Now!' she was almost screaming.

'Calm down, Livvie. Calm down, darling.'

'Can I help?' asked Jimi Hunt innocently as he walked over to them.

'Who are you?' Olivia demanded, angry at having her anger interrupted.

'No, we're fine, thanks,' said Stud. 'We're just leaving, aren't we Olivia?' He took her by the arm and started to lead her towards his old Land Rover.

'Olivia? You're not Acton Trussell's daughter, are you?' asked Jimi innocently.

'They've bloody locked him up. The police have arrested him and jailed him.'

'I know.'

'How do you know?' Olivia turned blazing eyes on him. 'Who are you?'

'Jimi.'

'How do you know?'

'It's on the TV.'

'Bastards. You know they arrested him in the hospital. Right next to my granny's bed. How could they?'

It was starting to drizzle again. The grey day had become a grey evening. 'Come on, Livvy. We'd best be off.'

'I want a lawyer. I'm not going anywhere. Mummy's really upset. They won't even let us talk to daddy.'

'I'm a journalist.'

'Good, then print this: the police have arrested my father. Took him from my grandmother's hospital bed. Locked him up. Won't even charge him. Won't let him go. It's not as if he's a criminal. It's not as if he'll skip the country.'

'Come on, Olivia,' Stud said, this time more firmly, seizing hold of her arm and starting to march her towards the Land Rover. 'Come on. We'll call Arty Welford, he can sort this out if anyone can.'

'Sorry mate, do I know you? I'm sure I recognise you from somewhere?' Jimi asked.

'Sorry, we need to go now,' Stud replied politely. But Jimi finally remembered.

'You're Stud Lee, aren't you?'

The man did not deny it as he walked briskly away with the young woman, still protesting, at his side.

Jimi had his story.

Chapter 9

DCI Snitterfield and DI Wood were outside Jimi Hunt's flat when he finally returned home. They invited him to accompany them to the police station.

Olivia stood at his side prompting, complaining and ordering as Julian Lee called his lawyer Arthur Welford.

The Home Secretary called Compton Dundon: 'What the bloody hell are the police playing at? Arresting the man in a hospital? Lodge a formal complaint against the Chief Constable. What do you mean it's not for us to complain? Of course it is. We are defending the rights of our citizens to be treated with care and consideration.'

The Home Secretary threw a pile of papers angrily across his office.

Jimi Hunt admitted he was, indeed, the photographer who had taken the pictures of Acton Trussell on a fallen log enjoying a Marlboro Light. When had he taken them? Was he under arrest? Was it illegal to take photographs? No? Then he wanted a lawyer. Why was he there at all? They should let him go.

DCI Snitterfield called Bingley Ortega. The Chief Constable was with his girl-friend, PC Sandy Freshwater, who was still wearing most of her uniform, when his mobile rang out with to the tune of 'Hawaii Five O'. He did not answer the call. DCI Snitterfield consulted DC Wood. It was Yardley Wood's view that there was really no serious crime here and it would be best to take Mr Hunt back home and release Mr Trussell sooner rather than later. His boss said she was late for picking Sammy up from Terrible Tots and she couldn't hang around all evening just to charge some ex-MP with smoking. She told DC Wood to sort everything out and said she was off home.

DC Wood went back to the interview room, thanked Mr Hunt for his co-operation, offered a car to take him home and said he was free to go. He then visited Acton Trussell in the cells below the police station. Trussell was sitting on the mattress concentrating on the sports pages of the 'Daily Mirror' which another officer had offered him to while away the time.

'We can't charge you, man,' said DC Wood with a broad grin. 'Looks like you're off the hook.'

At that moment, Arthur Welford arrived at the reception desk of Barset Police Station demanding an immediate audience with his client Acton

Trussell. Welford was a hard-drinking man with a red nose and a reputation as one of the finest property lawyers in Barsetshire – at least in part because he was one of the few left after the Great Crash had seen dozens of law firms go to the wall.

Arty had explained to both Stud and Olivia that he hadn't practised criminal law for decades. But Stud insisted. Arty hoped an efficient and determined demeanour would work. He had no idea what he would do if the police started quoting the law at him.

The officer on the desk called through and eventually tracked down DC Yardley Wood, who presented himself at the reception desk while Acton Trussell was being given back his wallet, tie and shoe laces.

'This is an outrage,' blustered Welford. 'I demand you release my client immediately, release him or charge him. You cannot possibly keep him locked up in a cell all night. This is police brutality. It's an outrage.'

Tall and gangling, Wood leaned against the wall and smiled a languid smile. 'Cool, man. He's on his way up here already. We're letting him go.'

Welford was non-plussed. 'You're letting him go?'

'Without charge.'

'Without charge?' The lawyer was used to getting his own way but not that quickly. He was suspicious. 'Why?'

'Lack of evidence.'

'Lack of evidence? It's in all the papers, it's on the TV, it's all over the internet.'

'We can't prove when the picture was taken. The man who took the photographs won't co-operate.'

'Can't you force him to?' Welford realised this was a stupid question. Was he trying to undermine his client?

'Could do. Could force him to give evidence. But Mr Trussell won't say when the picture was taken. Actually says he has no idea when it was taken. Not as if he was posing for a publicity photograph after all. And Jimi Hunt won't say either.'

'Jimi Hunt, the Chronicle reporter?'

'Ex. Been sacked. Won't tell us when the pictures were taken. Don't know why. Anyway, the Chief Constable will just have to live with it.'

'The Chief Constable?'

'He ordered the arrest personally. Ordered the raid, the publicity, everything. Orders from the top. The very top.'

'The very top?'

'Wherever that is.'

Trussell emerged looking none the worse for his ordeal. 'Sorry about dragging you out of the hospital, sir,' said Yardley. 'It was insensitive, it was wrong. But you know how it is… orders.'

'Don't worry old boy. Nothing to worry about. Evening Arty, what brings you here?'

'I have been appointed as your criminal lawyer by your daughter Olivia, Acton. Sorry.' Welford looked apologetic, conscious that Acton could start quizzing him about his qualifications for such a role.

'Looks like you've done an excellent job, Arty. Come on then, are you taking me back home?'

It looked like 'Cigarettegate' still had some way to run. By the following morning, Acton Trussell had become the victim of a vendetta by his political enemies, the country had become a police state and all lovers of liberty should beware of the fate that would await them if they stepped out of line. There were pictures of DCI Snitterfield marching Acton out of the hospital. Questions were being asked about whether she was acting on her own initiative or under orders from above. And, if from above, how far above.

DCI Snitterfield was summoned to see the Chief Constable. He was furious. Why was Trussell not charged? Why was he, Bingley Ortega, not consulted? Why had she been so stupid as to get herself plastered all over the front pages?

The Home Secretary called the Chief Constable. Pickering was furious. Why was Trussell not charged? Why was he not consulted? Why had Bingley Ortega been so stupid as to allow Trussell to be arrested at the bedside of his dying mother-in-law?

Compton Dundon summoned Clifford Chambers and Steve Thomas. Dundon was worried. The selection meeting was only 48 hours away. Acton Trussell was headline news. The Government had endured its worst couple of days for months. It was being accused of heavy-handed bullying and worse. There were rumours the arrest was ordered by the Home Secretary himself. This was not the atmosphere in which to fight a by-election.

'Get it postponed,' Clifford Chambers suggested.

'You stupid prat,' Dundon replied. 'That's the last thing we can do. It would be an admission that we were guilty of something. I'm not sure what of but of something. No. What we need is a local campaign. Something that matters to the people of Barset but which is boring to everyone else in the country. We want to make this by-election so dull that everyone stays away except for the voters. We can only do that by concentrating on the parish pump. What is there, Clifford?'

'The future of the Barset Festival?' he suggested.

'Nobody cares.'

'Decline of shopping.'

'Same everywhere.'

'The trading estate and jobs.'

'Hmmm. What about it?'

'Well, most of the units are empty and in decline. We need to revitalise the trading estate but where's the money? Nobody wants to build anything any more. The coffers are empty, as you know. We need a Vision for Barset. At least, that's what Newbold Whitnash said and I think he's right.'

'A Vision for Barset? What sort of vision?'

'Something that involves money, investment, jobs, prosperity, the future.'

'Good words, Clifford, good words. Steve, work on that.'

*****

As well as the latest on "Cigarettegate", the "Chronic" carried news of the Opposition's selection plans for the forthcoming by-election. The locals were not happy. The Liberal Democrats had been ordered not to fight the seat at all and some of them were furious. The Labour Party's proposals for an all-elderly shortlist of candidates had two long-serving councillors and a prominent trade unionist complaining it was 'the worst kind of ageism – prejudice against the young, fit and healthy'.

A party spokesman explained an all-elderly shortlist was a logical extension of the party's policy of ensuring fair representation of every section of society. The party had pioneered all-women shortlists from which to select candidates in the face of fierce opposition from within its own ranks. But all-women shortlists were now universally acknowledged to be necessary if Parliament was to be properly representative.

Since then, the party had pioneered other innovations. It was the first to insist at least 10 per cent of candidates should be gay or lesbian, by introducing all-homosexual shortlists in one tenth of its safe seats. It insisted four out of every six people put forward for selection as MPs should be non-white. So far, the party had refrained from imposing all-Afro-Caribbean or all-Asian shortlists because the members accepted the need for diversity. The days when MPs were all white, middle-aged, middle-class, heterosexual men were long gone.

But if Parliament was to be truly representative, the time had come for all-elderly shortlists. Pensioners made up an even larger minority than gays, Muslims and the disabled put together. Diversity and fairness demanded pensioner-power and the Opposition was the only party prepared to promise it.

The Pensioner Power policy meant the Barset Labour Party would be offered only six names from which to choose its candidate. To make that shortlist, the hopefuls had to be aged over 63. This was considered elderly enough though some critics pointed out there were plenty of MPs over 63 already and, in order to be truly representative, the lower limit should be raised to at least 67, if not 70. Only then would the voice of the elderly be truly heard in Parliament – especially now the House of Lords was an elected assembly.

The plan was widely welcomed by organisations representing the elderly. The pressure group 'We've Still Got All Our Marbles' proclaimed the decision a victory for the ageing population. It pointed out that politicians kept on talking about how important it was for Parliament to be 'representative' and how they rejected the old ideas of 'elitism'. But how could Parliament be 'representative' when the elderly – at least 15 per cent of the population and growing by the day – were without a real voice in the Corridors of Power? How could young men and women, no matter what their faith, colour or sexuality, share the concerns of the old?

Some old people thought it outrageous and patronising. 'We don't want to be treated like an oppressed minority,' complained Harry Buck, the chairperson of the Amalgamated Union of Retirees, Pensioners and the Third Age. Buck had once been a shop steward. He had led signalmen out on strike on three notorious occasions. Now he fought to defend the rights of the elderly but he despised 'We've Still Got All Our Marbles' as a middle-class, Government-subsidised quango. The real militants in the fight for the rights of the elderly stuck to AURPTA and didn't need the patronising condescension of an all-elderly shortlist in an unwinnable seat at a by-election. They demanded real change not cosmetic, politically-correct nonsense.

'Perhaps I should send them a CV,' Acton Trussell joked. 'I'm old enough to qualify.'

He was in the sitting room trying to read the paper. Clarissa was beside him on the sofa. They were being interviewed by their daughter. Olivia was still outraged by her father's arrest and scandalised at the thought it had been ordered by the Home Secretary. 'We must do something, daddy. We must stand up to them.'

The house was no longer under siege. The TV crews had turned up again that morning and Acton had been obliged to perform for them. He said he was 'disappointed' by the behaviour of the police but they had treated him well and he was not willing to admit to any crime given that he had no idea when the photograph was taken. He said he certainly used to enjoy a quiet cigarette while out walking the dog. It was one of the few pleasures he had left in life before the ban was imposed.

A couple of TV crews made the long walk up Howard Hill to find the very spot where the photograph had been taken. Luckily, nobody reported finding a secret stash of Marlboro Lights.

One of the neighbours, Cordelia Quint, was organising a petition to the parish council calling on the Trussells to leave Howard Michael. The village should be a haven of peace and tranquillity but since Mr Trussell's criminal activities had been exposed in the papers, it was pandemonium. Mrs Quint had taken photographs of the TV crews' vehicles churning up the grass verges. She would present the evidence at the next meeting.

Clarissa was calm. 'They should not have invaded my mother's privacy,' she said. 'On the other hand, Acton is an old fool and you, Olivia, should have enough sense to realise this is not a battle worth fighting. It's certainly not one anyone will win. Haven't you seen what happens? Look at all this fuss, darling. It really is demeaning.'

'"Demeaning"? Oh mummy, what on earth do you mean "demeaning"?'

Clarissa had never liked the compromises involved in being married to a public figure. Even when Acton was an obscure backbencher, he had been subjected to occasional, apparently motiveless and generally random, public humiliation at the hands of the media. Every time it happened, she recoiled and wished he would stop this nonsense once and for all. Yet, for reasons best known to Acton, he persisted in the pretence that he could somehow do some good for someone. She was tired of all this – especially as she was physically exhausted from all the time spent at her mother's bedside.

'I do not understand,' Clarissa began, in her most cut-glass voice, 'Why we should subject ourselves to these public indignities.'

'But we must do something, mummy.' Olivia, still in her jodhpurs and riding boots, having spent the morning riding with her new man-friend, was striding around the room again. She couldn't sit still. 'Stud says we should fight back.'

Her parents both sat up and looked at her. 'Oh no, Olivia,' said her mother. Her father just groaned and his shoulders slumped.

'What?'

'Julian Lee? Oh Olivia,' said her mother.

'Oh dear,' said Acton.

'Daddy, talk to him. Talk to him. Stud knows what he's talking about. Don't forget it was Stud who got Mr Welford to sort the police out.'

'Oh Olivia, really. Julian Lee has always been a bad lot. I've never known why your father took such a shine to him. The glamour, I suppose. But not you, Olivia, surely you've got more sense than that. Surely, Olivia?'

'He is old enough to be your father,' added her father. 'Think of that. Fat, flabby, elderly, infirm. Incontinent for all I know.'

'Daddy!' Olivia flounced out of the room, slamming the door.

'Actually, Julian isn't fat at all. Unlike some of his contemporaries,' Clarissa observed quietly.

*****

Barset Free Trade Hall was created at the time of the Chartist riots when the workers campaigned for the right to vote. It was the venue for Unionist rallies against Mr Gladstone's plans for Home Rule in Ireland. It mustered volunteers to the cause of the Empire against the Boers and, not long afterwards, for the King against the Kaiser. The Free Trade Hall even staged a couple of sparsely-attended Suffragette meetings though trade union assemblies had to take place on the Hall steps outside during the General Strike. The Hall was the venue for recruiting sergeants, Women's Institute workers and Home Guard units throughout the Second World War. Most political party leaders had spoken there at one time or another before television made great rallies redundant.

Since then, the Free Trade Hall had been a venue for amateur dramatics, arts festivals and the occasional gig by itinerant rock bands. The Beatles played there once, before their fame, and The Wreckage staged their first public performances there, low on the bill beneath the likes of PJ Proby and the Tremeloes, when they were still known as Richie Rich and the Ravens. And there was the time The Wreckage returned to their home town at the height of their fame and Councillor Trussell was deputed to monitor the volume following concerns expressed at a meeting of the General Purposes Committee of Barset District Council.

Refurbished, revitalised and generally revived, the Free Trade was too big for a party political selection evening but Clifford Chambers insisted it was the traditional venue for such meetings and tradition mattered, even in an industrial town like Barset. So Compton Dundon booked it, at great expense, and party members were encouraged to attend.

The rules were strict. Nobody admitted after 6pm. Nobody to leave before the end. Nobody to vote if they missed any words from any candidates. Nobody to be admitted if they were not fully paid-up members. The definition of fully paid-up being that they had subscribed a minimum amount of money and that they were no more than three months in arrears. Several elderly ladies who could afford only £10 a year were barred from entry and sent unhappily away.

'Nobody told us that £10 wasn't enough,' one of them complained. 'You still took the money. You should have said. You took the money, you took the money.' But tubby Compton Dundon, who had placed himself on sentry duty, was adamant.

'I am very sorry, madam,' he would say, 'The rules are very clear on this point.'

'And where might I find these rules?'

'On the party's website, madam.'

'But I haven't got a computer.'

'I'm sorry, madam.'

'That's ridiculous,' she complained to her companion. She stared furiously at Dundon and said, 'Come on Betty. We are not wanted here.'

Dundon was assisted by Tanya Arden, who was wearing thick red lipstick and a voluminous dress which was the height of fashion in 1955. Tanya was standing at a trestle table covered with a Union Jack tablecloth taking people's names, ticking them off against her list of members and greeting the people she knew by name. There were few she didn't know. When Vivek Arnold arrived she looked at him as if he were from another planet. He introduced himself as one of the candidates and was immediately handed over to Clifford Chambers, who ushered him through the big hall, up onto the stage and off through the wings into a small dressing room furnished with a plain Melamine table and some rickety wooden chairs. He drew Vivek's attention to the Thermos of hot water, tea bags and biscuits and promised a briefing when all the candidates arrived.

He dashed back to the foyer in time to greet Lucy Loxley. She had taken his advice and was wearing an elegant grey dress with a small gold brooch. Her blonde hair had been neatly cut and combed into the epitome of charming sophistication. She carried a slim black handbag which looked expensive. It contained her speech. Joanna was conspicuous by her absence.

Lucy was greeted by Clifford Chambers, who had chosen a bright yellow bow tie to set off his best blue suit. He guided her through the auditorium. When they were alone, he asked, 'You've memorised your speech, haven't you? You won't be reading it, will you?'

'Well,' she said doubtfully.

'It makes all the difference, Lucy. And don't forget – local, local, local.'

Vernon Small checked in with Olivia Trussell. Compton Dundon thought about asking them to leave then thought again. Sid Shipley, formerly land-lord of the Fox and Trumpet in Howard Michael, was behind them and observed, 'This shouldn't be happening, Olivia. Your dad should still be our MP.'

It was a familiar refrain as other members filed slowly in. Mavis Murcot was complaining this was a terrible waste of a Saturday night, especially as a new series of 'Celebrity Job Swap' was on. Henry Hardcastle agreed but Sybil McPherson didn't hear her properly and Beryl, her sister, had to explain it to her somewhat laboriously and then had to explain that 'Celebrity Job Swap' allowed famous people to exchange their jobs – a pop star would become a TV presenter for a week, the TV presenter became an actress, the actress became a dancer and so on. Sybil said, 'What is the point of that?'

Chatham Smith arrived in his suit. He had been doing a deal, he explained to Percy Preston. Chatham was the only person who ever called Viscount Preston Percy. Reg Wootton had forgotten to change out of his gardening things even though Gloria, resplendent in red, had reminded him to do so several times until it was either change or be late for the meeting.

Tony Grafton was already complaining to Terry Page about the ridiculous waste of money involved in holding the meeting in such a big venue when they'd be lucky to get a hundred members to turn out. Sue Alne was trying to persuade Gary Atherstone that the contribution to party funds from her branch had already reached its quota and he was arguing that holding money over from one year to the next was not in the spirit of the rules.

Maggie Pride arrived with her husband Doug. He was a short man wearing a leather bomber jacket. His greying hair curled over his collar. Doug Pride was surprised to find himself a member of the party at all, given that he had never consciously joined. He considered it a party for Philistines. They only recognised culture when they saw it growing in a laboratory, he always said. But Doug wanted to be a supportive husband. It made life easier. If Maggie got selected it would be a nightmare but he wouldn't tell her that. He'd just vote for someone else and hope the majority of the others did so too.

Clifford swooped on Maggie, who was busily greeting all her acquaintances and said, 'Come on now, Maggie, no electioneering. I need you, please.' He led her through the cavernous hall, where 300 chairs had been set out to accommodate the members. Even that number seemed lost in the space available but Maggie wondered if it wasn't still a little optimistic.

She was wearing a neat two-piece suit in dark blue with modest heels and a white blouse. She had managed, to some extent, to tame her thick, curly hair which was remarkably similar to her husband's except that hers was regularly dyed and he only dyed his when he remembered to.

Maggie, Clifford realised, was remarkably relaxed. She looked as if she was enjoying herself. That was a worrying sign.

At ten to six, Clifford tried to hurry everybody into the auditorium. 'We will commence proceedings at 6pm precisely,' he announced in a loud voice, first to the people lingering in the foyer and then from the stage to the assembled company. 'I shall be briefing the candidates shortly and then we will begin.'

Back in the dressing room, Maggie, Lucy and Vivek were trying to make polite conversation. The weather was the main topic. It had, they all agreed, been a dreary sort of a day. Vivek sat at the table, a bland smile on his thin, handsome face. He betrayed nervousness by constantly checking the knot of his purple silk tie. Someone had told him purple was statesmanlike. Maggie stood beside the Thermos clutching her handbag. Lucy was shaking. The others could see a quiver in her left eyelid, her hands looked as if she were suffering from delirium tremens, her eyelids fluttered, her left foot tapped the floor impatiently. She could not settle.

Clifford Chambers and Compton Dundon arrived together. They were just closing the door when Steve Thomas squeezed in as well.

'Where's Parvinder?' asked Maggie.

'Late,' said Clifford.

'Again,' said Thomas.

Dundon looked at his watch. 'If she is not here by six o'clock for the candidates' briefing, we will be forced to carry on without her. The rules are the rules.' It was five to. The six politicians stood or sat in agitated silence. After two minutes, Dundon sent Clifford Chambers back to the foyer to check. He returned at precisely six o'clock to report there was no sign of Parvinder Singh.

'What a pity,' Dundon said, smiling. 'Still, ladies, gentleman, the good news for the three of you is that it increases your chances of selection.' He stood with his back to the door, to prevent anyone gaining entry. 'Now, good evening. I take it you all know each other?' He was greeted with vague nods. My name is Compton Dundon. I am the party's Chief Political Agent and I am here to ensure the procedures are followed according to party rules and I am the representative of the party chairman. I am responsible for ensuring a fair selection.

'The procedure for this evening is that, in a moment, you will be asked to draw lots to decide the order in which you appear before the members. You will be given ten minutes to make an introductory speech. No more than ten minutes. If you exceed the allotted time, I will turn off your microphone. You will then be asked a series of pre-agreed questions by our chairman, Mr Chambers.' Dundon nodded at Clifford, who failed to conceal his grin. 'Then there will be five minutes for questions from the floor. In all, you will each be given half an hour. At the end of that time, you will be asked to return to this room and the next candidate will be invited to speak. When you have all been given an equal opportunity, the members will be asked to vote. As you know, the winner must receive at least 50 per cent of all the votes cast. If there is no clear winner after the first ballot, the process will be repeated with the candidate who received the fewest votes dropping out.'

'Will we be given another opportunity to speak at that stage?' Maggie asked.

'No. Once the voting process starts, you will have no contact with the members until the final results are known.'

'Where will the counting take place?' Maggie wanted to know.

'It will be carried out by Mr Thomas here under the supervision of Mr Chambers and myself.'

'Will we be able to see it take place?' asked Maggie.

'No. We have decided it would place candidates in an invidious position if they were able to see in advance of the outcome how they were faring.'

'But I thought the party rules required the count to take place in front of the candidates.'

'Ms Pride.' Dundon put as much contempt as he could muster into the word 'Ms'. It was spat out like a hiss. 'Ms Pride. The party rules require the responsible person to make that decision at the time and, as the responsible person, that is my decision.'

'I'm sure we'd all agree to an open count,' Maggie persisted, looking at Vivek and Lucy for support. They nodded vaguely, not really interested in the issue and preferring to get on with the whole business.

'Well I'm sorry. That is what has been agreed and that is how it shall be.'

*****

The political website itsmyparty.com was said by the papers to be 'influential'. That meant a few members of the party checked it obsessively and lazy journalists used it as a source of stories. itsmyparty.com was set up by two 'ex-staffers' formerly employed at party HQ who claimed the "rank and file" deserved a greater say in the running of the party.

What that meant was the website ripped off every item of news about the party and its members – the Prime Minister, Cabinet Ministers, MPs, councillors, financial backers and so on – pasted it onto the front page with various comments from its editors telling the members whether they agreed or disagreed with the views expressed, why so-and-so was wrong or why such-and-such is not just correct in every detail but also a jolly good bloke because one of the editors went to school with his ex-wife's brother.

The website and the journalists who relied on it created a merry-go-round of 'news'. A story appeared on the site, it was reported on by the papers and on their own websites, and itsmyparty.com then reported on their reports with added comment. Sometimes the stories were true.

Beyond that, the site contained long articles by a few of the party's leading lights and many of its dimmer bulbs as well. Attached to these were the comments of the members. Careful analysis would reveal the site had about 50 regular commentators, at least 15 of whom were political opponents taking advantage of the new openness to add snide comments and sideswipes in the knowledge that the editors, in their desire for inclusiveness, would not censor them.

The level of debate was dubious. 'That's typical of Dick.' 'Why can't Amelia Browning get a new dress? We've seen that one seventeen times?' 'I cnt blv u thnk rik pik is populr – man's a prik.' 'Wn r we gng to brng bk hanging??????'

The site also carried constituency news. It had been reporting on the Barset by-election for weeks and the 'Cigarettegate' scandal allowed the editors plenty of opportunity to develop their themes of freedom, liberty and the pursuit of happiness. They were temperamentally against the smoking ban but supported it because it was party policy. They were furious about the CCTV leak but defended the Government from accusations of involvement. They did their best to prove the Opposition was to blame. itsmyparty.com was sympathetic over the arrest of Acton Trussell and outraged that it took place in a hospital. It was the first place where allegations were aired in public suggesting the Home Secretary may have had a hand in this. As itsmyparty's Barsetshire correspondent, who went by the name of Pravda, a not-altogether-ironic reference to the Soviet newspaper 'Truth', pointed out, Rick Pickering and Bingley Ortega had been at Oxford University together. They had even appeared together in the same production of 'Julius Caesar on Ice'. itsmyparty was sent a photograph of a young, much thinner Rick Pickering with most of his hair, dressed in a bed-sheet that purported to be a toga, smiling at the camera as he stood beside a tall, strong West Indian dripping fake blood from a toga while performing a pirouette of assassination in the sparsely-filled ice rink.

The site announced the shortlist of candidates to replace Acton Trussell. It noted the day, time and place for the meeting. At 6.15pm, the editors received an e-mail. 'Am in Barset FTH for Trussell selection. Parvinder Singh has not arrived. They have started without her. Is this constitutional?' It was signed Pravda.

One of the editors, Gervaise Thynne, had been at university with Parvinder's brother. When he received the e-mail, he not only published it as a new story on the website, he e-mailed Parvinder herself.

By this time, Vivek Arnold had come to the end of his half-hour. He had been impressive when discussing the military situation in the Middle East. He was knowledgeable on the subject of the global economy and the risk that China might implode as a result of civil war and democracy protests. He even demonstrated a sense of humour over Acton Trussell's plight – 'I admired your former MP and it's a shame he has been forced to resign. I suppose you could say his career was stubbed out prematurely which is a bit of a drag, as a smoker would say.' This didn't go down well. Most of the members liked Acton Trussell. Anyway, everyone knew Arnold was there just to make up the numbers.

The last of the set questions put to him by Clifford Chambers elicited one of the few spontaneous rounds of applause Viv received. 'If you came top of the Private Members' Bill ballot and you could propose any new law you liked, what would you choose?'

Viv did not hesitate. He knew the question would crop up – it always did. And he knew the crowd-pleasing answer, too. 'I would turn April 23 into a Bank Holiday. It's about time we English had the chance to celebrate St George's Day properly. St George is the Patron Saint of England and we should promote our Englishness and show we are proud of our country.' The members liked that – especially from a man whose family came from India. Members liked nothing better than a born-again Englishman.

'Pravda' was sitting with Tony Grafton and Sally Hardcastle in what Compton Dundon immediately identified as the troublemakers' corner. He sent a second e-mail to itsmyparty.com. 'Vivek Arnold no chance. Nothing local in his speech. Next up L lox.'

Lucy Loxley looked out from the high stage at the audience beneath her. Only about 80 people had actually turned out even though the association had a nominal 250 members. The hall was big enough to accommodate 3,000 for a rock concert. The 300 chairs, placed at the front of the auditorium fairly close to the stage, were sparsely populated. Groups of friends spread themselves out across several seats but still couldn't give the impression this was a well-attended meeting.

Clifford Chambers and Compton Dundon sat at a desk on the stage. The candidates were given a lectern to speak from. Lucy was led on from the wings to a smattering of polite applause. She placed her speech on the lectern and grabbed its sides with both hands to steady herself. Her legs were quivering as if she had a bad dose of flu. She smiled down at the party members, wished them good evening, received no response, thanked them for this opportunity and proceeded to announce, 'I have a vision for Barset.'

She read out her prepared speech about reviving the town centre, attracting new shops, developing small businesses, expanding the trading estate and rebuilding the run-down railway station. The town needed a new hospital capable of dealing with even the most serious illnesses – it wasn't good enough for people to be sent 50 miles away for cancer treatment. The time had come to improve the schools, deal with troublemakers and vandals and clean up the streets.

As she proceeded, Lucy started to relax. But her hands still shook in her hands and she found it difficult to lift her eyes from the words and look out at her audience. She knew she should catch people's eyes and make it look as if she was speaking to each one of them individually but it was difficult, if not impossible, while she was stuck with her speech. She couldn't abandon it now, even though she felt she was gaining in confidence, so she ploughed on. She tried to modulate her voice, to go fast and slow, high and low, to avoid being boring. It didn't seem to work. It all came out as a fast monotone. She knew she was being boring and she couldn't do anything about it.

Still, when it came to the questions, she had no choice but to speak off the cuff. She talked about her career as a councillor in London. How she had been instrumental in the decriminalisation of parking. She did not add that taking responsibility away from the police and giving it to private contractors had proved deeply unpopular and crippled trade. She talked of her love of Barset and the surrounding countryside. She spoke of her deep roots in the area and her long family associations in the county. She added that if she became their MP she would have an open door to Number Ten because the Prime Minister was a family friend and it would be beneficial to the constituency to have the ear of the man in charge. 'I want to be your Member of Parliament because I want to build a better Barset,' she declared.

Clifford Chambers asked a series of questions culminating with, 'If you came top of the Private Members' Bill ballot and you could propose any new law you liked, what would you choose?'

Lucy knew the answer to this question, at any rate. 'I would turn April 23 into a Bank Holiday. It's about time we English had the chance to celebrate St George's Day properly. St George is the Patron Saint of England and we should promote our Englishness and show we are proud of our country.'

Exactly half an hour after it started, it was over. Compton Dundon announced her time was up, thanked her for taking the time and trouble to attend the meeting and explained that she would be informed of the results of the voting in due course.

Pravda sent itsmyparty another note: 'LLox nbg but at least sh is local. Mags next.'

Maggie Pride walked onto the stage with a purposeful air. She looked calm, efficient and confident without being arrogant. She stood to one side of the lectern so the members would notice she was speaking without notes, not reading.

Clifford noticed and groaned inwardly.

Maggie spoke of the global challenges facing the Government. The drain of money and manufacturing to China and the Far East. The endless war in the Middle East. The importance of the European Union as a defender of democracy and a bulwark between the United States and unstable former Communist countries. She spoke of terrorism and Islam. She reminded everyone the most important challenge facing the Government was to rebalance the economy. She added that the party needed to care for the spiritual, cultural and emotional well-being of the country as well by supporting education, hospitals and the arts.

Clifford Chambers asked a series of questions culminating with, 'If you came top of the Private Members' Bill ballot and you could propose any new law you liked, what would you choose?'

'I have wondered about that,' Maggie said. 'I know a popular answer is to make St George's Day a national holiday and I have some sympathy for that. But if I had this one opportunity to change the law in a way that might have a lasting impact, I would prefer to introduce legislation making it compulsory for all school pupils to take part in organised sport on at least three occasions every week. We don't have enough sport in our schools. Both parties were guilty of selling off playing fields. We need to encourage young people to become healthy and discover sports which can give them a lifetime's enjoyment. Too many kids spend too much time in front of televisions and computers. There's nothing intrinsically wrong with either of these but we need to make sure they are aware of all the other options available to them.'

Maggie won a ringing round of applause.

The last question from the audience was posed by Trevor Lancaster, 'Pravda' himself. He looked up from his Blackberry long enough to ask, 'Maggie, you have told us a great deal about the national and the international picture but if you were to become our Member of Parliament, what would you do for Barset? Isn't that the most important thing of all?'

She smiled. 'I'm delighted you asked me that question, Trevor. As you know, my heart and soul are in Barset. I was born here, I live here, my children go to school here. Nowhere is more important to me than Barset. This constituency would be the focus of all my efforts and concerns. The people of Barset would be my first priority. I do believe, though, that Government action to rebalance the economy, for instance, will do more for Barset than any fiddling about with planning permissions on the trading estate or local council inward investment initiatives, important though they may well be. At heart, Trevor, I'm a local girl and this is where my heart will always be – even if I am away at Westminster.'

Maggie won another ringing round of applause. Pravda e-mailed itsmyparty.com, 'Mags is the pride of Barset. She's sure to walk away with the nomination. C'mn Mags.'

There was a commotion. Maggie was returning to the dressing room and Compton Dundon was inviting members to use the ballot papers they had been given on their arrival when Parvinder Singh marched in with two men at her side. She made her way to the stage, climbed up to face Compton Dundon, waving a piece of paper and declaring, 'What is the meaning of this? What is the meaning of this?'

Parvinder was angry. Her two large, Sikh bodyguards looked angry. They stationed themselves just below the stage, arms folded, and stared fiercely at the members. Dundon took the paper and saw it was a print-out of his e-mail to Parvinder inviting her to a selection meeting a week hence.

'Good Lord,' Dundon said, loudly, so that everybody could hear. 'It looks as if some terrible mistake has been made, Ms Singh. I cannot understand it.'

'Well?'

Dundon looked surprised. 'Well what?'

'Do I get an opportunity to address the members?'

'I am sorry, Ms Singh. That would not be fair on the other candidates. You can't just march in two hours late and expect to be given an equal chance at a selection meeting. We are just about to conduct the voting.'

'This is an outrage,' she said and slapped him, hard, across the cheek. Turning to the audience, she announced, 'I have here an invitation to a selection meeting to choose the candidate for Barset due to take place next Saturday. Next Saturday, ladies and gentlemen, not tonight. I was only informed of tonight's meeting twenty minutes ago, by a friend in the party. This is unfair, contrary to natural justice. I ask you to give me a hearing. Please.'

There was a chaos of voices, people demanding to be heard, calling out their opinions. Clifford Chambers returned to the stage and took in the sight of Parvinder, in her black jeans and white shirt, her two fierce-looking bodyguards, the panic on Compton Dundon's face and the breakdown of order among the members.

Chambers had a hurried word with Dundon. Steve Thomas joined them. They agreed a course of action. Dundon went to the lectern. 'Ladies and gentlemen, we have an imposter here. Ms Singh was not invited to the selection meeting tonight. For some reason, some people believed she was on the shortlist but that is not, and never was, the case. I cannot explain where this e-mail may have come from but it is clearly a cruel hoax. I am very sorry, Parvinder, but you are the victim of a prank. Would you please withdraw from the stage now so that we can continue with the process of selecting a candidate?'

'Mister Chairman! Mister Chairman! Point of order Mister Chairman,' boomed Tony Grafton, rising laboriously to his feet. Beside him, Trevor Lancaster was e-mailing itsmyparty.com with the latest news.

'Oh sit down you stupid man,' said Gary Atherstone.

'What? What?' asked Sue Alne, waking up.

'Good God,' declared old Pinky Green. 'Good God indeed.'

'Mister Chairman,' boomed Tony Grafton.

'Sit down, Tony,' called Terry Page. 'We don't want her as our MP anyway.'

'Ladies and gentlemen, ladies and gentlemen, we shall conduct the voting now, if you please,' declared Compton Dundon as loudly and firmly as he dared. 'Clifford, Mr Thomas, would you please go around the room collecting up the ballot papers. Ladies and gentlemen, if you have not cast your votes, please do so now as we will be collecting them up immediately.'

'Mister Chairman! Point of order! Point of order!'

'Good God.'

'What? What?'

'I demand to be heard,' Parvinder declared and 'You will be hearing from my solicitors.'

*****

Only 37 completed ballot papers were collected. Most people were too preoccupied with the interruptions and arguments to make a choice before Clifford Chambers and Steve Thomas asked for them. Several members handed in blank papers forgetting that they hadn't voted. When Chambers, Thomas and Dundon withdrew to a second dressing room, they had 68 ballot papers, 31 of them blank.

'We won't be needing these,' said Clifford, indicating another batch of blank papers he had in his pocket.

'Do you think someone should keep an eye on what's going on out there?' asked Dundon. 'Clifford, go and make sure some sort of order is maintained and try to get rid of bloody Ms Singh will you?'

'If you're sure you're alright in here.'

'Quite sure, thanks. Oh and look in on the candidates, too. Reassure them everything is progressing as expected.'

When he was gone, Dundon laid out the papers in three piles. The two votes for Lucy Loxley, the five votes for Vivek Arnold and the 30 votes for Maggie Pride. He and Thomas added another 31 votes onto Lucy Loxley's pile, placing Xs on the papers with their left hand using a variety of pens.

The final scores Loxley 36, Pride 30, Arnold 5. 'That's lucky,' said Dundon. 'It means Lucy's got a clear majority on the first ballot so we won't need a second round. Probably just as well. Go and tell the candidates. I'll go back to the stage and see if order has prevailed.'

Thomas announced the results, shook hands with the two defeated candidates and asked Ms Loxley if she would be kind enough to return to the stage to hear the results announced and then give the members a little pep-talk. He added that they may find the situation had deteriorated a little since they spoke to the members. An imposter had gate-crashed the meeting and disrupted proceedings.

Maggie and Vivek, united in defeat, stared at each other wordlessly as Lucy followed Thomas back to the stage. They decided to follow and stand in the wings to watch the event come to its conclusion. 'I'm amazed,' Vivek told Maggie. 'I was sure you would win. You were easily the most confident of us. And I could tell you thought it had gone well.'

'I did,' she admitted. 'But you never know what it is the members will want. Maybe I said the wrong thing. Maybe I didn't talk enough about the constituency. I don't know. How can you tell?'

'Well I am still amazed. I knew I was just the token bloke but you... I really don't see what Lucy Loxley's got going for her at all.'

'She is a lesbian.'

'Yes but even so, haven't we got enough queers in Parliament now?'

Maggie slapped him playfully on the arm. 'You can't say that,' she said in mock horror.

Back on stage, Clifford was arguing with Tony Grafton, Trevor Lancaster and Sonny Hatton about whether Parvinder Singh should have been allowed to speak. Gary Atherstone was citing standing orders and the party constitution to rebut their allegations. Several other groups were having arguments of their own. Parvinder was holding court in one corner with half a dozen sympathisers. Clifford gratefully gave way to Compton Dundon.

He called for quiet several times. Gradually the hubbub died down enough for him to pretend he had everyone's undivided attention and announce in a sententious voice, 'Ladies and gentlemen, I am delighted to be able to report that there is a clear winner in the first ballot. Ladies and gentlemen, you have overwhelmingly selected the new Parliamentary candidate for Barset. The new Member of Parliament for Barset. Ladies and gentlemen, congratulations go to – Lucy Loxley.'

Lucy stepped up to the lectern. She giggled. She started to speak. 'I don't know what to say,' she said. 'Gosh! It's like winning the Oscars isn't it?' She giggled again.

Tony Grafton's voice boomed out. 'Mister Chairman! Mister Chairman! I cannot believe… Are you asking us to accept this, this, this,' he cast around for the right word. All eyes were on him. 'This farce?' he said finally. 'This farce?'

Lucy was lost for words. A few people applauded her. Several cried out that Grafton's comments were a disgrace. Gary Atherstone started to quote the constitution in defence of the decision. Sue Alne wanted to know what all the fuss was about. Clifford took Lucy firmly by the arm and led her off the stage to talk to Terry Page – the council leader could be relied on to do the right thing. He congratulated her, shook her hand and started discussing the impending decision to increase car parking charges. Doug Pride sought out his wife. He looked angry. 'It's a fix,' he told her, 'It's a fix.'

Maggie, who had been quite prepared to believe she had lost fair and square, looked at him with incredulity.

Pravda was sending a long e-mail to itsmyparty.com

*****

The report on www.itsmyparty.com read:

Farce and chaos in Barset selection

I am told the selection of lesbian Councillor Lucy Loxley, the daughter of Sir Edmund Loxley and sister of city entrepreneur Robin, as the replacement for controversial MP Acton Trussell in Barset has not been without controversy.

Ms Loxley survived a three-way battle with Vivek Arnold, the Old Harrovian human rights lawyer, and a local candidate, Maggie Pride. But only after the fragrant Parvinder Singh was excluded from the final selection meeting by what has been officially described as 'an administrative oversight'.

It seems Parvinder, who was our candidate in Luton North at the last election and is tipped for the top, was originally invited to attend a selection meeting a week after last night's meeting. She only discovered the mistake after being contacted by itsmyparty.com and arrived in time to present her case before the members voted.

However, party supremo Compton Dundon, the chairman's representative in Barset, ruled that she was not in the final shortlist anyway and should never have received an invitation to attend the final selection, whatever the date on the invitation.

This was not the only controversy surrounding the selection. My spies at the meeting report that Ms Loxley was plainly a weaker candidate than the local candidate, a former lap dancer. Whether or not that is the case, Ms Loxley won on the first ballot, with a clear majority over the other two candidates.

Personally I am delighted Ms Loxley has secured the nomination. The party needs more gay and lesbian MPs if it is to be truly representative in the 21st century. I was at school with her brother and worked with Lucy briefly at party headquarters when I was a staffer and she was on vacation from university a few years ago.

Ms Loxley is young, successful, attractive and very much the vision of the party we need going forward.

Congratulations, Lucy.

The comments of the website's readers were less enthusiastic.

"Pravda" said: 'What a farce!!! L Loxley, lovely though she is, was definitely not the first choice for most of us. We don't care about her sexuality but why should we have some brainless totty imposed on us when we have a perfectly good candidate in Maggie Pride. And she was never a lap-dancer. Get your facts right.'

"Littlelady" replied, 'Sexist pig. Get real.'

"Adam Smith" complained: 'Local candidates are nothing but trouble. We need people who will toe the party line.'

"Minesapint" disagreed: 'Brainless automatons, then, Mr Smith?'

Clifford Chambers, using his real name, wrote: 'As chairman of the Barset association I wish to congratulate Lucy Loxley on her victory and wish her well in the forthcoming campaign. Our task now is to focus on ensuring she becomes the next MP for Barset and put any complaints or recriminations behind us. Well done, Lucy, I am sure you will make a wonderful MP for Barset.'

"Ex-smoker" asked: 'Have we forgotten Acton Trussell in all this?'

"Dream-maker" replied: 'What, the criminal ex-MP? Least said soonest mended.'

"Ex-smoker" hit back: 'Acton Trussell is an honourable man who has been stitched up by his own party three times over – they made him quit by blackmailing him, they exposed him by releasing illegally-obtained CCTV footage onto the internet (and blamed the Opposition for this appalling piece of trickery) then they ordered his arrest by screaming squads of police cars as he visited his dying mother-in-law in hospital. How sleazy can this Government get?'

"Dream-maker" responded: 'He got what he deserved. He's just a parasite growing like a cancer on the body politic – a lung cancer at that.'

And so it went on as people who had nothing to do with Barset and little, if any, connection to the party, bandied insults on a website and called it informed debate on an issue of public concern.

After a while Olivia Trussell decided she could not stand the anonymous insults. She was at Stud's house though he was out at the pub. She was feeling angry with everyone. Her father and mother for questioning her relationship. Stud for allowing her to enter into a relationship with him without actually explaining if it was serious or not. Herself for getting involved with someone so plainly untrustworthy. The party for slinging out her father. The Government, the police, the media, in fact just about everyone, for attacking him and dishonouring the family name. For some reason which she couldn't explain, Olivia decided the family name should be restored – it should command respect, people should hear the name Trussell and know it represented honesty, integrity, decency. She felt as if the name had been trampled in the mud. It felt dirty and sullied. It made her angry.

And then there was her brother Sam, out in California working for his IT company and not giving a damn about what happened back home. She had called him to discuss her various problems. He had not been much help. 'Be true to yourself,' Sam advised. 'Be true to yourself.'

'What the hell does that mean?'

'It means be honest with yourself. Be your own best friend. Love your weaknesses. Nurture your insecurities. Believe in belief.'

'What?'

'That's what my shrink says.'

'Your shrink needs a shrink.'

*****

Rick Pickering, the Home Secretary, was at home in bed with his own wife. He was woken at six o'clock in the morning by his press officer telling him about a story in the "Sunday Times" accusing him of personally ordering the arrest of Acton Trussell. The Home Secretary rang Chief Constable Bingley Ortega. 'Bingo, Pickering. Now look, Bingo, say nothing and deny everything. That understood? Good. See you on the links.'

The Home Secretary rang the Party chairman. 'Dave? Pickering. Get that useless sod of yours in Barset or wherever it is to create a diversion. Understood? Good.'

Pickering went back to sleep. His wife, awoken by the calls, was unable to follow suit because of his snoring. She made herself a cup of tea.

*****

'Compton,' said the party chairman, 'I see we have lumbered ourselves with Ms Loxley then?'

'As requested, Mr Chairman,' said Compton Dundon.

'Yes, yes, as requested. I see from it'smyparty it wasn't all plain sailing. Will there be any come-back?'

'I don't think so, chairman. Just the usual grumblers grumbling, you know.'

'Good. Now, you need to swing the campaign into operation as soon as you like. There's not much time. I am drawing up a schedule for Cabinet Ministers to visit the constituency. I shall let you have it in due course. Now, what about Mr Bloody Trussell?'

The party chairman explained what was in the 'Sunday Times' – a two-page 'investigation' describing, in worryingly well-informed detail, what it called 'the web of intrigue spun to trap the ex-MP at the behest of the Home Secretary himself, if not the Prime Minister'. The party chairman went on, 'Of course we are denying all of it. Steve Thomas should already have issued our statement. But that's not enough. We need to discover who really did put that video on the internet. The police are refusing to cooperate claiming it is a party political issue not a criminal one. I think they're upset old Bingo Ortega seems to have come a cropper over all this. Of course, privately Bingo is seriously pissed off but he can't exactly blame Rick Pickering in public can he? Anyway, we need to contain the situation.'

'Throw up a bit of ack-ack?'

'Precisely. Fill the sky with red herrings.'

'Did you have anything particular in mind, Mr Chairman?'

'No, you're supposed to be the one with the ideas.'

Compton Dundon called Steve Thomas back from Milton Keynes, where he had gone for the night to see his girl-friend. He summoned Clifford Chambers and told Lucy Loxley to report for duty at 9am. 'I have an idea,' he said.

*****

'That's ridiculous,' said Steve Thomas. He resented being wrested from the arms of 17-year-old Kylie and ordered back to Barset even if this was a crisis.

'Well, I don't know,' commented Clifford.

'I am having nothing to do with it,' said Lucy Loxley. 'Suppose it turned out to be true after all.'

'Suppose it did,' said Compton Dundon. 'Then what?'

'Then, well, I suppose it wouldn't be spin after all, would it? In which case, I suppose, it would be OK because it was just, what, anticipating the truth?' said Lucy. She was willing to please Compton Dundon because, while she had no idea how or why, she realised her selection owed a great deal to his influence. He was the man to guide her. He'd already explained he was tasked by the party to guide her safely into harbour.

'I still don't like it,' said Thomas. 'Isn't it tempting fate? Mightn't it backfire on us?'

'What, you mean we might get found out?' asked Clifford.

'No, idiot. If we put it out that Trussell is planning to stand as an independent candidate at the by-election, what happens if the old fool decides to do just that?'

'He won't,' said Dundon confidently.

'No,' agreed Clifford, 'I've known him all my life. He's very cautious. He doesn't like taking risks.'

'Except for breaking the no-smoking laws,' joked Lucy. Nobody laughed.

Clifford went on, 'Acton Trussell is very old-school. He is loyal. He will accept what has happened and keep his head down. He may have caused trouble over the years in Parliament but he is, au fond, a decent man. He won't abandon the party.'

'Even though the party has abandoned him?' Thomas asked. 'I wouldn't bet on that. If I were Acton Trussell I'd have a lot of anger to get off my chest. Making life difficult for Lucy would be one way of letting off steam.'

'But he couldn't win, could he?' Lucy asked anxiously.

'No, no, of course not,' said Clifford.

'Probably not,' said Compton Dundon.

'I wouldn't bet on that,' cautioned Thomas. 'He just might, you know. He just might.'

They called a press conference to introduce Lucy to the media and sent her home to change. Jeans would not do, they said. From now on it was business suits, well cut but not showy. Grey, navy or black would all be appropriate. Nothing flouncy, nothing that reminded anyone of Margaret Thatcher and certainly nothing that said 'I am a lesbian'.

It was agreed they would take no questions about Acton Trussell or the stories surrounding "Cigarettegate". But they knew that was the only subject any reporters would be interested in. So Dundon and Thomas went to work, taking a few friendly hacks aside one by one and breathing confidences into their ears.

By two o'clock, Acton Trussell was receiving his first phone calls asking if it was true that he was standing as an Independent and that he had maliciously placed the story about the Home Secretary to boost his campaign and undermine the Government. Vernon Small heard the news at ten past two and called Acton. 'Now you'll have to stand, old boy. Bloody marvellous.' By half past, it was all round the pub where Stud was drinking with some of the locals. He called Olivia and told her. She was still angry with him and with her parents but she called her father and said, 'Well, daddy, this is what we wanted, isn't it?'

Acton Trussell decided to take the dog for a walk.

*****

By the following morning, it seemed as if Acton Trussell had become the Independent candidate for Barset at the forthcoming by-election whether he liked it or not. It was in all the papers, it was on television, it was all over the internet. And it was receiving general acclamation. His phone hadn't stopped all evening. His answerphone was full, his e-mail inbox had 450 unanswered messages, his mobile was full of texts, not that he could work the damned thing properly.

Olivia and Stud had a heart-to-heart. He pointed out to her that he was living with someone he was really very fond of. Marinka was sweet and loving and had no interest in music or horses, which suited them both very well. Stud admitted he was extremely fond of Olivia. Indeed, he said, he was more than fond of her but he did not want to hurt her. She mattered more to him than anyone. He had known her since she was a little girl. He was a friend of her father's. 'You need a good guy you own age, Livvie darling, you know you do,' he said, stroking her face gently.

She refused to cry but she did anyway. 'You're so old,' she said.

'I know, darling. Too old for the likes of you.' She tried to laugh. He got her a glass of whisky, twenty-year-old Glen Hoddle. 'Here, have a dram.'

'Oh Stud,' she cried. 'What will I do now?'

'I have an idea.'

*****

Stud arrived in Howard Michael at the same time as Vernon Small. It was only then, as he leaned against a tombstone keeping an eye on the comings and goings, that local journalist Jimi Hunt remembered the picture he'd taken of the ageing rock star and the ex-MP's daughter outside the police station. There was money in that. How had he managed to overlook something so valuable? God he was slow. But he excused himself on the grounds that he had been rather busy these past few days. Anyway, now he remembered it would be a great new angle to keep the pot boiling.

Would Trussell confirm all the rumours now he'd been outed? Would he admit he was plotting to undermine his former party and its candidate in Barset? Why was Stud Lee visiting him and who was that dapper little man in the Renault Renard? Jimi Hunt didn't know but snapped a picture of him anyway, just in case.

Stud took Acton into the sitting room while Celia, Olivia and Vernon fussed over the coffee in the kitchen.

'Acton, listen. I owe you an explanation. An apology, even.' Stud could see his old friend was angry with him. 'I am sorry if I have upset our relationship or done any damage to you, or Clarissa, or, of course, to Olivia herself. She is a beautiful young woman with a mind of her own.'

'Don't I know it,' Trussell said ruefully.

'But if you feel I have undermined our friendship or caused Olivia any lasting pain then I really am sorry. The truth is, Acton, I am very, very fond of your daughter. She is beautiful and lovely and if I were twenty years younger...." Stud trailed off and there was a moment's silence before he went on, "Alas I am not twenty years younger and you know how awful it would be if she ended up stuck with an old man like me. It just wouldn't do. It would ruin her life. I won't ruin her life, Acton, and I am sorry I allowed myself to get involved with her. I really am sorry, Acton. Really.'

Trussell looked at his old friend with his dyed, ringleted hair and his lined face that betrayed the days of debauchery he'd enjoyed at the height of his fame, and did not know what to say. He felt the betrayal but his daughter was old enough to make up her own mind and live with the consequences.

'I don't have to acknowledge you any more as an acquaintance,' Trussell said, slowly and formally.

'Maybe not, Acton, but I have an idea and I need to run it past you. Now. Before things get out of hand.'

The ex-MP sighed. 'You know, Stud, I am just about sick to death of things at the moment. There's this open warfare with my party. I seem to be in all the papers. I get arrested. Everybody's talking about me. Then you debauch my own daughter. Treat her like just another of your bloody groupies. You aren't 22 any more, Stud, you aren't a Rock God any more, you're just an ageing old fool with ridiculous dyed hair.' Trussell seemed to slump in his chair. 'I give up. I am defeated. I have retired hurt.'

Stud sat cross-legged on the floor at his feet and stared at the carpet. The central heating grumbled and ticked as it turned itself off. The room was warm in the sharp September sunlight. The house settled back to wait for autumn. Stud traced the pattern on the carpet with one long index finger. He waited.

'Well?' Trussell asked eventually.

Stud looked up at his old friend and smiled ruefully. He was back again. 'It's like this, Acton. The way I see it, we should put someone up in this constituency against the party. What's happened to you should not be allowed to pass without any resistance. And your cause...'

'Not my 'cause',' Trussell protested.

'Some are born to fight causes, some have causes thrust upon them. You have a cause thrust upon you. Anyway, the cause, the cause of liberty, is a cause worth fighting for.'

'The freedom to kill yourself by smoking?'

'No, freedom from the police state, freedom from interference and intrusion, freedom to live your own life as you see fit. That cause.'

'Oh, that cause.' Trussell gave a brief, ironic laugh.

'Yes that cause. Anyway, there is a cause worth fighting for and someone should take the fight to the party – the enemy.'

'The papers seem to thing I am going to stand but I'm not. I really haven't the heart for it any more. I just can't face it.'

'No, Acton, not you.'

'Not you, Stud?' he said facetiously.

'No, Acton, not me. Olivia.'

'Olivia? We've already discussed that and I have ruled it out. It's too much for a young woman. '

'You've ruled it out? What about Olivia? Has she ruled it out? She would be ideal. Young, attractive, enthusiastic, idealistic, incredibly intelligent, articulate...'

'Heartbroken when she loses and damaged by the process.'

'Come on, Acton, you know it's the answer.'

'You are a bastard, Stud,' he said, but this time with a hint of a smile. 'I must admit a part of me does rather like the idea but even so...'

'Come on, let's talk to her,' Stud said with a grin, standing up and leading the way back into the kitchen.

Chapter 10

Vernon Small called Newbold Whitnash at the 'Chronic' and Polly Greeb, news editor of 'Radio Quark 104.8fm for Barset and Barsetshire'. He invited them to coffee at Starbucks in the town centre because he had some news he thought they would find interesting. Neither accepted the invitation but both sent along a minion. In Polly's case that meant a work experience youth called Dan with spots and a big tape recorder he couldn't work properly. Whitnash at least managed a reporter who had been doing the job for six months, a media studies graduate called Leicester Cape.

Vernon ordered four cappuccinos, introduced his guests to each other and led them to a corner of the empty café where he introduced them to Olivia. 'This, gentlemen, is the next Member of Parliament for Barset, Olivia Trussell, the Independent candidate.'

It made the lead news item on Radio Quark that lunchtime and the front page of the 'Chronic' that evening. Pictures of Olivia were in demand. Jimi Hunt exploited his opportunity. The 'Daily Beast' bought up exclusive use of the pictures of Olivia with Stud and used one of them on its front page the next morning under the headline: 'I love you for your mind... not your body'.

The story said: 'Ageing rock star Stud Lee pictured with 23-year-old flame-haired beauty Olivia Trussell, who has just announced she's hoping to replace her controversial father Acton Trussell as MP for Barset in the forthcoming by-election. More on Page 3.'

It was all over the internet, of course. Olivia suddenly had hundreds of Facebook friends. Her musician friends told her she must be mad but promised to campaign for her as long as she promised to buy them tea on the Commons terrace when she won.

The Home Secretary called the party chairman. 'What the hell's going on?'
The party chairman called Compton Dundon. 'What the hell have you done?'
Compton Dundon called Clifford Chambers. 'You know the Trussells, stop them. Now.'
Clifford Chambers called Lucy Loxley. 'We need a campaign meeting.'
Lucy Loxley called her brother Robin. 'It looks as if we've got competition.'
Robin Loxley tried to call the Prime Minister. He couldn't get through.

Acton Trussell had counselled Olivia on all the reasons not to do this. He said politics was a nasty business. People would be rude about her, unkind, vile. They would investigate her private life and ask questions which even her best friends would never dare to pose. Everything she said would be taken apart and put back together in ways she would never recognise. It was no career for a young woman with a talent for making music.

But Olivia had the bit between her teeth. She said she was sickened by the way her father had been treated, it was about time someone stood up to these people. Anyway, she didn't have a thing to lose. 'It's not as if anyone's ever heard of me, is it, daddy?'

Clarissa said she should do as she pleased, she always had done so why stop now? But, added Clarissa, she shouldn't come crying to her when it all went wrong. Vernon was ecstatic, rubbing his hands with glee and planning his campaign leaflets. 'All we need are some funds,' he said. 'And we need to start spending now, before the writ is moved and the date is set. The limit on how much you're allowed to spend at an election doesn't come in until then. At the moment we can spend what we like. Have we got any money?'

Olivia looked at her father and at Stud. 'Have we?' she asked.

'Tell us how much you need,' Stud told Vernon. 'Send me the bills.'

Stud was less relaxed when he returned home. Mrs Dorsington was at the front door looking worried. 'Stud, thank goodness you're back,' she said in a hurried whisper. 'Have you seen the "Daily Beast"?'

He lowered his voice to imitate her apparent urgency and secrecy. 'No, Mrs Dorsington, I've been busy all morning.'

'Marinka has.' She handed Stud her copy of the paper. Stud took a quick look at the picture and the headline.

'Oh no.'

'She's upstairs. Packing, I think.'

Stud ran off shouting, 'Marinka, Marinka…'

*****

The town of Barset had seen better days. At the height of the railway boom in the 1850s and 1860s, it was a grand junction linking lines which ran north to south with others travelling east to west. Barset Main Line Junction railway station had a fine glass roof spanning twelve platforms. It had a busy market where produce from the surrounding county was bought and sold and transported on to London and the bigger industrial cities of the North and the Midlands.

Around this, Barset built up an industry. For almost a century it had a successful line in china, making lavatories and baths for the Empire. The Barset Blaster was one of its most revered objets d'art. There was a vast goods yard and engine shed. There were coal mines. Barset made nuts and bolts, nails, corrugated iron roofs, tin trays and toys. The town sold its produce around the world and provided work for thousands of men, women and, until it became illegal, children.

The town prospered. It had a fine Victorian Council House and the Free Trade Hall. But in the 1940s, the railway yards were regularly targeted by the Luftwaffe. Their bombs put paid not just to the railway station but to much of the old town centre, including the one or two historic buildings which had survived from the days when Barset was mentioned in the Domesday Book. There wasn't much of old Barset left by the time Hitler took to his Berlin bunker.

Rebuilding was cheap and cheerful. A small ring road was thrown around the town centre and several concrete multi-storey car parks were constructed. Within them a shopping centre was built, with an open air market and a branch of Woolworth's. For several months after the grand opening, it was clean, functional and attractive. Outside the inner ring, the suburbs were a mixture of council tower blocks of the same vintage as the town centre, more leafy suburbs and a few large houses on the fringes of the town.

The surrounding villages had kept Acton Trussell in Parliament. Places like Howard Michael, Lacy Newton, Harbingale, The Luftons and the medieval settlement of Munckton Proctor. In these places settled the prosperous middle classes who flocked to support their party and their MP come rain or shine. They ensured Acton's victories at the polls.

In the town centre itself, indifference to politics was almost universal. The locals rarely stirred themselves to vote. They would argue, if asked, which they rarely were, that politicians were all the same, it didn't make any difference who they voted for, and one lot was just as bad as another. Several of them, if pressed, would acknowledge they had heard of Acton Trussell, even before his recent notoriety. Some might go so far as to admit he had actually done something for them, personally, or for a member of their immediate family. But they would add that this didn't make him any different from the rest. Politicians were all out for what they could get so why encourage them?

The centre of Barset had deteriorated since it was opened by Alderman Albert Huxley in 1964. Woolworth's was swept away in the great recession. Many other shops had gone as well. The rest staggered on under the pressure of rising taxes, rising rents and falling demand. Plans for a big out-of-town shopping centre would be the final death knell for Barset though Terry Page told Lucy Loxley he had a vision of turning the centre into a 21st century residential retreat when the shops had all gone. 'We could make it a village once again,' he suggested.

Lucy was depressed by the sight of Barset. She hadn't really thought about the fact that, if she became an MP, she would be stuck with the place for years to come. She could not avoid visiting it sometimes. She could not escape being forced to be nice to people like Terry Page, who was OK she supposed, but also people like that gargantuan trouble-maker Tony Grafton or that old dear Sue Alne. No wonder Joanna refused to support her in her campaign. Joanna was a London girl and London was where she intended to remain, with or without Lucy Loxley. Lucy's London friends promised to come up and help when they could, nearer the time of the election, if their diaries allowed and, of course, they joked, if they could find their way that far up north.

'It's right next to the motorway. There's an intercity service to London,' Lucy protested, but her friends just laughed at the bizarre hilarity of it all.

'You must be mad, Luce,' they said.

Lucy also discovered that her committee of supporters, the dozen active councillors who were capable of staying awake throughout an entire meeting, were not the unified fighting force she might have thought. In fact there were at least three competing factions.

Terry Page was, indeed, the leader of the council and, nominally, the most important member of the party in Barset. But he had only become leader because the councillors were divided between the two real powers behind the throne, Sally Hardcastle and Langley Claverdon.

Hardcastle and Claverdon used to be allies. He had campaigned to secure her victory in a marginal ward. She had supported him to become deputy leader a couple of years later. They both ran small businesses, they were both in their 30s – younger by a couple of decades than most of their colleagues – and they both despised Councillor Page. But when Sally announced two years ago that she would challenge Page for the leadership, Claverdon said he was shocked and angry and refused to support her. She lost. She tried again a year later with the same result. Claverdon had not spoken to her since.

'If Sally and Langley ever agreed to work together, Terry would be yesterday's news,' confided Trevor Lancaster, the Pravda of itsmyparty.com, 'As it is they just sit on the sidelines and snipe at each other. I shouldn't be surprised if Claverdon's faction doesn't walk out any time soon. Declare themselves independents. The others won't like his plans to privatise our housing stock.'

Lucy was ordered to get a flat, set up an office, organise literature, raise funds and start campaigning. Her committee of helpers tended to melt away whenever the word 'canvassing' was mentioned.

Canvassing meant trudging round housing estates, knocking on doors, asking the people who answered whether they would support the party at the forthcoming by-election, handing them a leaflet, shaking hands and, if possible, escaping as quickly as possible. 'Don't get drawn into conversation with them, Luce,' Clifford counselled her. 'Wastes time. And do not get drawn into political argument or discussion. All we want to know is whether they will vote for you. If not, they can bog off.'

Canvassing took place on increasingly dark evenings or at weekends. Few people wanted to go out in the rain or miss the football. Even fewer wanted to answer the door after 8pm to be asked about politics. Yet this was a necessary method of garnering support and introducing Lucy Loxley to the locals.

It wasn't long, however, before people started to say, 'Sorry, love, I'm voting for Olivia Trussell.'

The Trussell campaign got off to a flying start thanks to the massive publicity she and her father received. Acton accompanied Olivia all the time, renewing acquaintances and chatting happily with political friends and former foes as he went. He found it was much more enjoyable to campaign for someone else, especially as he no longer had to defend some of the daft and indefensible policies his party had adopted over the years let alone apologise for a coalition with the Liberal Democrats. When people criticised, he could say, 'Yes, I agree' with a clear conscience and without it getting back to the whip's office. This lightened his mood and put a spring in his step.

Vernon found an office on The Parade, close to St Olaf's, the biggest church in Barset and the building which would have become the cathedral had the local worthies' attempts to have the town elevated into a city ever come to fruition. The office windows were plastered with posters of Olivia Trussell looking fashionably windswept but approachable. Passers-by were encouraged to go in for a cup of coffee and a chat. Vernon manned the office full-time though others joined him from time to time including some of her band-members, who descended on Howard Michael and set up camp in the back garden.

'They're not real gypsies, daddy,' she explained. 'Just electric gypsies.'

On the first Saturday after she declared her plan to stand for Parliament, Olivia and her band took to the market square and performed an impromptu gig for the passing shoppers while Vernon and Acton handed out leaflets explaining who she was and what she was doing. People queued up to talk to their ex-MP and offer support for his daughter. They wanted to help. The campaign was taking off.

Yet the election date had not even been announced.

*****

'She's useless, she's clueless,' complained the local party chairman Clifford Chambers.

'We can't dump her,' said the candidate's minder, agent and chief-of-staff Compton Dundon.

'We have to.'

'We can't.'

'Why can't we?'

'Haven't you worked it out yet, Clifford? Christ, it's fairly bloody obvious isn't it? Lucy Loxley is the party leader's preferred candidate.'

'Yes but why? Why?'

'Oh God, I suppose you could look most of it up on the internet. But basically her father is, let's just say, her father is a good friend to the party. And to the leader in particular. They went to the same school.'

'But not at the same time, surely.'

'No, not at the same time. But Loxley has always been a supporter of Dick's. From the days when Dick was still at university. Christ, Sir Edmund Loxley funded his campaign to become President of the Union. He's funded everything ever since.'

'Until it became illegal to make an individual donation of more than £50,000 anyway,' added Steve Thomas.

Chambers would not be put off. 'Well if we can't get rid of her, can we at least get the by-election postponed? Let the Trussells run out of steam while we stay in it for the long run. February, maybe?'

Dundon sipped his cappuccino. It was cold and left a moustache of fluff and foam over his flabby top lip. 'We could try, I suppose. I'll talk to Dave.'

This wasn't a conversation he could have on the phone so Dundon took the train to party headquarters. He found Dave Hersey worrying over the running order for the party conference. He was in no mood for a debate about the party's prospects at the Barset by-election.

'Haven't we had enough of bloody Barset?' he wailed. 'Can't you just go back there and do your job for me for once?'

'The Trussell campaign seems to have gained a little traction.'

'Traction? Traction? What's traction?' Dave tired of jargon surprisingly quickly for a politician. Like many well-educated Indians, the problem was that he had a far greater command of the English language than most of the people he talked to.

'They seem to be attracting some support among the voters. She's a very credible candidate. More so than our ours.'

'Listen, Compton, your job is to get Lucy Loxley elected to Parliament. We can't get rid of her and we have to win the seat. Christ, what was our majority there at the election? Over ten thousand? We can't possibly lose that. And anyway, if the Trussells want to make an issue of it, surely we can turn it into a referendum on the smoking ban. That was a hugely popular law, let's not forget. All the polls gave it a 60 to 70 per cent approval rating. I don't imagine the good people of Barset are untypical.'

Compton Dundon nodded slowly. The party chairman was not always the most straightforward politician. Dundon had a feeling there was something he didn't know.

'I'll bring her to Blackpool next week, then, shall I?' he asked, closing his mind to the possibility that he might not be in the loop. 'Do we need her to do anything?'

'She could take the stage behind the leader during his conference speech. I'll get him to introduce her by name. All she's got to do is smile nicely. She can do that, can she?

'So we're stuck with Ms Loxley? And are we stuck with November 5?'

'Yes.'

'So Parliament is being recalled?'

'Yes.'

'Do I want to know why?'

'I think you will find we have another fiscal crisis on our hands. The gilt markets have bombed, the Barklloyd Bank fiasco has driven investors abroad, the Lehron report is about to be published and it doesn't make for happy reading. There's talk of criminal negligence by the regulators – our regulators not theirs. Our Chinese debt is about to be renewed under unfavourable terms. We have to do something about it all. The leader has a plan, an emergency Budget – it's still not too late to blame everything on the last lot, you know. We think we can get away with it. He'll make the announcement in his conference speech, the House will sit the following week, the writ for your bloody by-election will be moved and we can look forward to welcoming Ms Loxley onto the back-benches on November 6 or thereabouts.'

'Are we part of the diversion?'

'My dear Dundon, of course you are.'

*****

Clifford Chambers appointed himself Lucy Loxley's minder. He would spend every waking hour with her if he could. He needed to win this by-election. He had ambitions. This was his chance to make his mark. He paraded her around Barset, of course, but he needed a bigger stage. Blackpool was ideal.

The party had reverted to the drab seaside town for its annual conference after some successful meetings in Birmingham and Manchester. The cities were too sophisticated for the members – their hotels and restaurants were too expensive and the members preferred a windswept walk along the chip-smelling prom to a saunter along a revitalised canal basin through the gay quarter. Accommodation in Blackpool was plentiful and cheap. The people who attended party conferences were not interested in luxury or even decent food, they just wanted somewhere to sleep for a few hours in between breakfast meetings and late-night bar-room debates.

Lucy Loxley was shocked to find cigarette burns on the carpet of her bed-and-breakfast. She was surprised to discover the cold tap would not turn on and the hot tap would not turn off. She was scandalised to find the bedspread made of nylon, curtains so thin they allowed even the pale autumnal sun to seep through at daybreak, and tea bags which had been sitting in a tooth mug since Easter at least. None of this was as bad, though, as the noise from the bedroom next door. On the first night there, she was awoken at 3.30 am by the sound of man vomiting copiously into what, in this part of the world, they would call 'the toilet'.

Lucy's accommodation, 'The Irish Sea Guest House', was half a mile from the conference centre and its adjoining conference hotel. Booking two years in advance, Clifford Chambers had secured a room on the same floor as the Prime Minister. He was determined to make the most of his foresight. Lucy wondered if she could offer to share the room; there would be no danger of anything untoward.

Her orders were clear. Meet Clifford at the hotel at 8am for breakfast and he would guide her through the fringe meetings, conference events, bar-chat, meals and freebies not to mention the accidentally-on-purpose bumpings into people which collectively made up a satisfactory day at a party conference. It was called networking. Her job was to smile, collect people's cards and hand out her own. Never say anything, certainly nothing interesting or controversial. Smile, be nice, try to remember people's names in case she ran into them again.

Clifford was in his element and Lucy realised he was something of an expert in the art of putting himself about. As the proud possessor of a desirable room on the same floor as the Prime Minister, he was in demand for late evening consultations, meetings and get-togethers. Clifford was able to ingratiate himself with several journalists, other association chairmen, MPs and even a couple of Cabinet Ministers, by inviting them up to his room for cocktails before dinner and for bacon sandwiches later in the evening. This was all very expensive but Clifford knew Lucy wouldn't mind footing the bill – this was her introduction to the big time.

Lucy had been to party conferences in the past. She had always stayed at decent hotels and only remained for 24 hours in order to show her face, renew a few acquaintances and make it look as if she cared about Brussels' plans for bailing out Turkmenistan. This time she had to stay for four long days. Chambers let her off the leash long enough for her to chat with a few of her council colleagues and one or two MPs she knew from the 'Women On Top' action group. They congratulated her on being selected for Barset and issued her with instructions about what she should do once she was in Parliament.

One evening she even met her brother and her father. 'Lucy darling, how are you my dear?' Her father ran a hand over her short, blonde hair. 'I meant to congratulate you, darling. How are you getting on in Barset? How are Richard and Ann?'

'They're fine. How's mummy?'

'I haven't seen her, Luce. You know what she's like. We're never on the same continent these days.'

Robin marched over to them where they were standing in the coffee bar, amid stands and exhibitions set up by the dozens of companies lobbying for lucrative Government contracts, think-tanks hoping to change the world and charities looking for funds from the taxpayers. 'Father, Lucy. Have you heard?'

'Yes,' said his father. 'Of course.'

'Good,' said Robin.

'Heard what?' asked Lucy.

At that moment, Clifford Chambers bore down on them, wearing his specially-commissioned Conservative Party bow tie with the oak tree logo and launched into a speech about how wonderfully the campaign was going in Barset and how much he admired Lucy before the other two men made their excuses and left. Together. Deep in discussion.

The highlight of Clifford's week was when the Prime Minister himself popped into the room, stayed all of two minutes, sipped a glass of orange juice, had a quiet word with Lucy and said, 'Thank you, Chambers, jolly good luck to you' on his way out with his wife Janine, who featured regularly in the papers as a fashion icon and last word in chic elegance.

The highlight of the party's week was always the leader's speech on the closing day. When the leader was also the Prime Minister this was a slightly trickier affair because, instead of simply attacking the other lot and promising to do better if and when he was elected, he had to explain why things had not, yet, turned out the way everyone hoped and hold out the promise of better things in future as long as everyone held their nerve.

For journalists sent all the way from London to this bleak northern outcrop, the leader's speech was rarely a highlight. Typically it lasted at least 55 minutes and said little that hadn't been said a dozen times already. The hard part was finding something in these speeches which was interesting enough to report as if it were real news. Party leaders, their advisers, colleagues and speech-writers, tried hard to avoid saying anything important. Instead, they sent out spin-doctors whose job it was to explain before, during and after the leader's speech exactly what he meant by those words and which words, in particular, were important and which were window-dressing.

Usually, only about half a dozen words in the entire speech really mattered, according to the spin-doctors, and most of them didn't mean what they said and had to be closely examined and re-interpreted before they came to mean what the Leader intended them to mean. It was one of the reasons why party members who attended conferences and then read about them in the papers were baffled to discover the news and events being reported bore no resemblance to the speeches and meetings they had heard or attended.

The Smoking Gun

Clifford Chambers reminded Compton Dundon. Dundon reminded Dave Hersey. Hersey persuaded Rick Pickering. Pickering asked Amelia Browning. Browning ordered Hugh Lighthorne and Harriet Standing. They were both bumped off the platform for the Leader's speech. In their place, in the front row, between the Environment Secretary and the Secretary of State for Wales, Scotland and Northern Ireland (one person, these days, though she represented Penzance) sat Lucy Loxley and, at her side, Clifford Chambers.

A crashing electronic beat with undertones of 'Land of Hope and Glory' coupled with a swirling light-show resembling a rock concert preceded the arrival of the Leader and his lovely wife. The words of the old Coldplay song, now re-worked into a suitably crashing, up-beat, crowd-pleasing anthem started to ring out. 'We live in a beautiful world, yeah we do, yeah we do.'

Prime Minister Dick stood and smiled, acknowledged the applause, ran his fingers through his thinning hair and indicated the crowd should allow the rapture to die down a little. He waited as silence descended.

'We live in a beautiful world, yeah we do, yeah we do,' he began. 'And we plan to keep it that way. Yeah we do, yeah we do.' This was the cue for more applause. And so it went on for the next 55 minutes.

Dick was a polished performer. Tall and imposing, he spoke fluently, without notes, from the heart. His admirers reinforced their admiration. His critics searched for things to dislike. They disliked the fact that he wasn't wearing a tie. They hated his constant references to global warming. They were unimpressed by his talk of 'change we need' and 'all sharing the same planet'. The reporters searched the handout of his speech for anything new, anything they hadn't heard before, and compared it with what Dick actually said in case there were revealing discrepancies.

Dick said 'change' 12 times and 'radical reform' seven times. It meant nothing would change. He mentioned the Liberal Democrats five times, waiting each time for a brief outbreak of 'spontaneous' applause.

Three-quarters of the way through, looking back at the party's achievements since winning power, he said, 'Yes, we introduced the smoking ban. I make no apologies for that. We will save thousands of lives every year as a result. We have changed Britain for the better. And yes, we have introduced a new air tax. That is because we live in a beautiful world, yeah we do, yeah we do. And we want to keep it that way. And let me tell you, it's policies like this that are at the heart of our radical reform.

'That is why I am delighted to introduce to you today our prospective parliamentary candidate for Barset. Lucy Loxley. Stand up, Lucy.' She did as instructed, beamed at the Leader and the audience, received their applause and sat down again, suddenly overcome by heat. 'I hope to welcome Lucy to the House of Commons very soon,' said Dick. 'She is the radical new face of reform.'

Then he came to the real news. 'I propose to recall Parliament next week to pass some important new legislation. We have done much to meet the health needs of our people – the smoking ban and the flight tax have created a cleaner environment for us all. Now is the time to tackle the nation's growing problem with obesity.

'Now I know some of us are a little over-weight.' Here Dick tapped his stomach and won an easy laugh. 'But obesity is costing the National Health Service billions of pounds a year. In a land of plenty – and we are living in a land of plenty, don't let anyone tell you otherwise – in a land of plenty, we are all at risk of over-indulgence. Snacks of crisps, cola, chocolates – we all enjoy them. And in moderation, they're fine. They are little presents we give ourselves when we think we deserve them. They still the pangs of hunger and provide a little lift in our busy days.

'But we can eat too much of them. Too many burgers and chips, too many cans of fizzy pop, too much sugar, too much salt. We are building a healthy nation and we must do so in every way we can. We have limited air travel. We have rid the country of the scourge of the cigarette. We can do the same with the snack.

'Of course we shall not prevent people from enjoying life's little luxuries. But they are luxuries, my friends, and luxuries come at a price. Therefore we shall legislate appropriately. I am determined – we are determined – to build a healthy society. We live in a beautiful world and we intend to keep it that way. Yeah we do.'

The reporters had their story. Compton Dundon, Steve Thomas and their colleagues swarmed into the massive media centre with briefing papers. The headline "Sheer Snack Attack" was on websites around the world before Dick sat down. Not spelt out in the Prime Minister's speech, but revealed to journalists later, was that the Government intended to impose VAT on fattening foods. The purchase tax rate of 20 per cent would apply to fast foods, chocolates, fizzy drinks and so on.

'Biscuits?' asked the fat man from "The Times".

'Depends on the definition of a biscuit,' the equally rotund Compton Dundon replied. 'Some will fall within the parameters of the legislation but others, which are defined as health foods or as basic foodstuffs, will not.'

'A loophole, then?' observed the man from "The Times"'.

On the way back to Barset in Clifford Chambers' Audi Attractive, he was full of enthusiasm for the 'fat tax'. About time people were forced to slim down a bit. The streets of Barset were full of porkers stuffing their faces. Then they were surprised their arteries clogged up and they had heart attacks. Of course, it was a question of class, really. The people at the bottom – what Chambers called the 'can't-be-arsed-to-be-working classes' – had nothing to do all day but gorge themselves stupid. When they weren't drinking, of course. They had to be priced out of that market. They couldn't be trusted to stick to a healthy diet so the Government had to force it on them whether they liked it or not. The 'fat tax' was a brilliant idea. And it would bring in billions. Perhaps now the party could abolish the top rate of tax and reward its loyal supporters.

As he rambled on, Lucy was wondering what it was she had missed.

Chapter 11

Parliament was duly recalled. Bud Brooke, the Chancellor, announced a new VAT rate of 20 per cent for fattening foods. 'This is a great day for the healthy future of our nation,' he declared. The Liberal Democrats cheered. He also mentioned that it would raise £6 billion in revenue for the Treasury.

The Opposition, which had toyed with just such a tax last time it was in power but thought it couldn't get away with it, denounced the move as a new tax on the poor. Health professionals and lobbyists welcomed the move as a major step in the right direction. The CBI said it would have only a modest impact on British industry. The National Farmers' Union said its members needed subsidies to grow healthier alternatives. The National Federation of Retailers said it would devastate corner shops and warned hundreds of small businesses would go bankrupt, destroying local communities.

The news was received with stunned acquiescence among the voters of Barset. Fat people said they were glad something was being done to help them overcome their disability. Thin people said it was a pity they'd have to pay a little more for occasional treats but they understood. Two fish and chip shops told the 'Chronicle' they would have to close but the town's only biscuit factory celebrated that its products were classified as 'health foods' by increasing its workforce and inviting Lucy Loxley for a visit to maximise the publicity for both parties.

'My father is one of your competitors,' she told the Managing Director.

The writ for the by-election was moved on the same day Bud Brooke announced his mini-Budget. The date was, indeed, to be November 5 – three weeks away.

This did not set Barset alight. The voters' indifference was palpable. When Lucy and the few supporters she could muster went out on chill, damp evenings to knock on people's doors and ask for their votes, few Barsettians were interested in what they had to say or were disconcertingly interested in their own hobby-horses rather than Lucy's policies.

Several people said they would definitely be voting for her. But it was beginning to worry Clifford that many more still said they would be supporting 'our Acton's daughter'.

The constituency, not just the town but the outlying villages as well, became fair game for reporters and TV crews from around the world. "The Straits Times" and the "Washington Post", the "Toronto Post" and "Le Monde" all agreed this would be a test of Dick's leadership, the popularity of his policies and a crucial referendum on his measures to boost the health of the nation.

The Trussells, meanwhile, were frequently denounced. Newspaper columnists decided they were mischievous, interfering and only in it for themselves. How could they be so self-indulgent? What rights should smokers have anyway? Wasn't Acton Trussell just a common criminal?

However, Vernon Small's town centre office was busy. The Labour candidate popped in one morning to express her support. Mrs Abbey Luddington knew she would be lucky to hang on to her deposit. 'I used to be a smoker,' she told Vernon. 'Still would be if it wasn't against the law.' Mrs Luddington was 72 and had been selected from the all-pensioners shortlist because she was local, had served on the council for 20 years and was a stalwart of the local Immigration Support Network.

She was a cheerful woman. When she met Olivia she told her, 'I shouldn't be here, I know. But I've always rather admired your father, dear. I felt so sorry for him when he was made to resign. Dirty tricks, my dear, dirty tricks. I do hope you can keep up the good work.'

The Communist Workers' Party candidate, Mick Mickleton, dropped by to declare he thought the new snack tax was a direct assault on the working classes and hoped that when Olivia was elected she would do her best to fight back against it.

The Independence for Britain Party candidate, Cherry Bussage, said the smoking ban was all the fault of the European Union, as were the air tax and the fat tax. 'If we weren't in the superstate we could make our own laws in our own way and we wouldn't have to put up with these politically-correct impositions from Brussels,' she told Olivia. 'I do hope when you are elected you will keep up the resistance to Eurocreep in our legislature.'

The Totally Monstrous Raving Mad Party candidate, Senor Philosophus Mayhem (name changed by deed poll from Ron Smith) stood outside the office for an entire day entreating passers-by to vote for Olivia Trussell – 'Vote for Trussell, Vote for Freedom,' said Senor Mayhem. It got him on the TV and an invitation to present a half-hour of his favourite music on Radio Quark so he was happy.

Olivia was enjoying herself. She liked talking to people and finding out about their lives. She suddenly discovered what her father had been doing all these years and why he had never been at home when she was growing up.

Clifford Chambers announced there would be no more door-to-door campaigning. It was a waste of time. The internet was the way to connect with the voters. And the party's national call-centre would be doing its job as well. He spent hours every day in front of his computer up-dating Lucy's campaign website and sending her out to get her picture taken in every corner of Barset. He e-mailed newsletters to his database of voters. He sent them personalised e-mails. He invited them to take part in on-line polls about measures to brighten up the town centre, what they thought about the state of the railway station and whether they agreed with the party's campaign for a healthier Britain.

Lucy fretted. She was interviewed almost every day by passing journalists. She had been given comprehensive notes from Compton Dundon and Steve Thomas about what she could, and could not, say. One of them sat in on each of these meetings to make sure she stuck to the script and, if she ever deviated from it, to explain to the reporter what she actually meant to say.

Various party officials and Cabinet Ministers came and went. They would arrive half an hour after the appointed time, in a desperate rush, spend twenty minutes chatting to a few hastily-summoned party members who acted the role of the general public, and disappear again wishing Lucy the best of luck. Occasionally, a TV camera arrived at more or less the same time and relayed a nanosecond of this performance to the waiting world.

Acton Trussell spent his time conducting Olivia from one meeting to the next. On each occasion, he received sympathy for his plight and support for his daughter. Acton was enjoying himself. He sat in on interviews with his daughter and threw in casual observations with the air of a man who thought deeply on these matters and had valuable things to say about them.

It was difficult to tell what would actually happen on election day.

Newbold Whitnash called Clifford Chambers. 'We're carrying out an opinion poll. Our canvassers will be in the town centre on Wednesday and Thursday.'

Chambers alerted Thomas and Dundon. They made their arrangements so that, on the days in question, dozens of party members from all over the country descended on Barset, apparently by accident and just to go shopping. 'This isn't scientific,' Dundon told them, as they passed one by one through his campaign headquarters in the Barsetshire Sleepover Hotel.

Dundon had taken over the whole hotel for the duration and offered passing journalists free accommodation if they needed somewhere to stay while covering the by-election. The party fixer even provided them with fake receipts so they could reclaim the cost of dinner, bed and breakfast on their expenses. It was the least he could do.

'It's not an election expense, this place,' he would say if anyone questioned the cost of taking over such a large establishment for so long. 'This is nothing to do with Lucy's campaign. Her headquarters are in the heart of Barset.' Some people suggested that might not be how the Election Commission would see it but recognised it would not be in the Commission's best interests, at a time of significant public spending cuts, to inquire too closely into the governing party's activities in the backwater of Barset. Besides, the chief commissioner was being lined up for an OBE.

Hampton Arden asked if it was quite ethical to distort the outcome of an opinion poll. Clifford Chambers told him, 'Hampton, the aim is to ensure the party is properly represented in the poll. All we are doing is maximising our presence. We need to make it clear there is no threat to Lucy. We need a result which proves the Trussell campaign is floundering. It will give our campaign a boost just at the right time and demoralise the Trussells.'

'Yes, I see that,' Arden said doubtfully.

Others were even less convinced. 'I'm sick of this,' Tony Grafton declared when he was chatting with Sonny Hatton, Trevor Lancaster, Jim Dutton and Sally Hardcastle in the Plough and Arrow. 'Should we tell the Independents?'

'No,' Lancaster said, 'But perhaps Pravda might have something to say on itsmyparty.com. What do you think?'

They debated the merits of this for some time, oblivious of the fact that Jimi Hunt was sitting close by listening in to their conversation.

Jimi had been enjoying himself since parting company with "The Chronicle". He'd made a lot of money out of his photographs and now regarded the Trussells as his passport to fame. He thought it would be in his best interests if Olivia won though he didn't mind either way. He'd spent the past couple of days trying to establish what had happened to Stud Lee. Since his picture appeared in 'The Beast' alongside Olivia Trussell, he hadn't been seen anywhere. Not at home, apparently, not in his local pub, not on horseback in the fields and lanes near his house and certainly not alongside the young candidate.

It was rumoured that Acton Trussell knew his whereabouts but there was no way Trussell would talk to Jimi Hunt. He had tried tracking down Marinka, but she was on an assignment in the Maldives. Jimi even had the nerve to knock on the front door of the former council house where Mrs Dorsington, Lee's housekeeper, lived. She threatened to call the police if he came nosing round there again.

Jimi spent a whole day stationed in the churchyard opposite the Trussells' home monitoring the comings and goings. There was no sign of Lee, though he did note the arrival of a couple of Government MPs. He sent the pictures to 'The Beast' which duly published them to the embarrassment of the politicians and their party. They denied offering support to Olivia Trussell at the by-election and claimed they were simply tying up some loose ends with their former colleague. Nobody believed them.

He retreated to the Plough and Arrow to regroup and resume his search for Julian 'Stud' Lee. Now, though, he had a new angle to pursue. The Tories were planning to rig the first – and, quite possibly, only – opinion poll to be conducted during the campaign.

Was that possible? He supposed it was, especially given the local paper's need to do these things on the cheap. Rather than employ a reputable polling organisation, he knew, the "Chronic" would use its own market research staff. It would be about as scientific as artificially inseminating a cow and hoping it would bring forth lambs.

On the Friday, "The Chronicle" published the results of its 'scientifically-conducted, authoritative test of public opinion in Barset'. It gave Lucy Loxley an overwhelming lead over her nearest rival, who was identified in the report as Labour's pensioner candidate Mrs Abbey Luddington. The headline declared: 'Trussell's trouncing' above a smiling picture of Olivia holding up a placard which read, 'Set Barset Free, vote for me'.

'I don't believe it,' said Vernon. 'It's simply not true.'

'I don't believe it either,' said Acton Trussell.

'It's such a pity,' said Olivia.

'Don't be disheartened, dear,' said Vernon.

'No, don't,' said her father.

'We might as well give up now,' she said.

'No, Olivia, this is when we need courage and a show of determination,' said Acton Trussell. 'This is where we hit back.'

'How?'

'Well, there are a couple of things,' he said.

*****

It didn't make the front page but, even so, Jimi was satisfied. "The Beast" ran with the headline: 'Can we fix it? Yes we can' and went on to disclose that the first opinion poll in the Barset by-election had been rigged by the simple expedient of filling the town centre with party loyalists on the two days when researchers were out asking about people's voting intentions.

Dave Hersey rang Compton Dundon. 'Is this true?'

'Is what true? That we are streets ahead in the polls? Yes. That the polls were in some way falsified? I have no idea, you would have to ask 'The Chronicle'.'

Steve Thomas said much the same thing to journalists who scented a story. 'Is this another dirty trick against Acton Trussell?' they asked.

'The paper says the survey was scientifically conducted and we have no reason to doubt its veracity,' Thomas replied. 'The results are in line with our own private polling.'

Mrs Luddington expressed herself surprised and gratified. Olivia Trussell put out a statement which said, 'While we have no wish to query the integrity of the "Barset Chronicle" we are nevertheless surprised by the results of its recent opinion poll which seem to be at odds with every other test of public opinion.'

'What other tests of public opinion?' the journalists asked.

'Our own polls,' Vernon told them.

Newbold Whitnash found himself at the centre of the story. TV crews demanded a statement. Jimi Hunt doorstepped him outside his own home. Newbold was not happy. He called his head of market research, Jan McEwan, and asked for an explanation. She insisted the results were faithfully recorded.

'The only risk would be if someone let Lucy Loxley know in advance when and where we would be conducting our field research,' she said.

Whitnash ordered a second poll. This time he decided not to alert Clifford Chambers in advance.

A week before polling day, Lucy Loxley and Olivia Trussell met for the first time. They were both invited to participate in an open forum organised by the Barset Combined Churches Union which was held in the Baptist Church in Mitchell Street. The two women shook each other's hands politely and sat at opposite ends of the public platform, separated by all the other candidates.

Lucy told the audience of about 55 people, all aged over 55, that the election was about 'building a better Barset'. Olivia agreed but said that would only be possible if people were free to make their own choices and the Government was prepared to leave them alone to live their lives as they saw fit.

Gary Atherstone, who was in the audience, asked with slow deliberation, 'Would you agree, Ms Trussell, that living your life as you see fit is only acceptable if you do nobody else any harm? Freedom is contingent? We don't have licence to do whatever we like? There must be constraints? Would you agree, for instance, that how one behaves in one's private life has a bearing on what one says in public? Especially for an aspiring politician? Would you agree, therefore, that it ill behoves a young woman to preach freedom when she has exploited that freedom to undermine the relationship of a man and a woman who were, to all intents and purposes, happily married?'

It took Olivia a moment to understand what he was getting at. When she realised the question referred to her relationship with Stud Lee, she blushed redder than her hair, stammered and blurted out, 'How we conduct our private lives is a matter for the individual.' But Atherstone knew he had won his point and smirked with satisfaction.

Lucy Loxley took up the theme. 'We all want to have freedom but none of us has absolute freedom. We are not free to hurt, murder, rape or steal. And we never shall be. Thank God. Freedom has to be freedom within the law. And Parliament makes the law. We elect MPs to represent the views of the people about how far a law can go and how much liberty an individual can expect. Freedom is not a right, it is a privilege which has limits placed upon it by Parliament.'

Acton Trussell could stand no more. He had arrived late because he didn't want Olivia to be constrained by his presence. He had planned to stay unobserved. He wore a dark overcoat and a thick scarf partly because he knew the hall would be cold and partly as a disguise. Now, though, he stood up and turned to Lucy.

'Thank you, Ms Loxley, for that eloquent disquisition. You are right, of course. However, I have a question for you. If you cannot answer it now, I am sure we would be delighted to receive an answer later. My question is this: If we are to have a new tax, a fat tax or a snack tax or whatever it may be called, and we are to have it in order to reduce the nation's obesity problem, can you explain why some types of biscuit are exempt from this new charge? You will tell me some of them have been designated 'health foods' and that is quite right. But is it a pure coincidence, I wonder, that one of the biggest beneficiaries of this apparent concession just happens to be Big Bite Biscuits plc? And is it pure coincidence, Ms Loxley, that the major shareholder in Big Bite Biscuits is a long-standing friend of the Prime Minister? And is it pure coincidence, Ms Loxley, that this long-standing friend happens to be your father? In short, Ms Loxley, has the Prime Minister fixed this new legislation in order to favour your father's company?'

It was Lucy's turn, now to blush and stammer. 'The other day, I had the privilege of visiting Newton Nibbles, here in Barset,' she said. 'As you will know, Mr Trussell, Newton Nibbles is a major local employer and they are among the many food manufacturers to be exempt from this new tax. I don't see how you dare stand there and cast such terrible accusations about in public.' Lucy was recovering her composure. 'This is libellous, Mr Trussell. You are guilty of the filthiest form of dirty trick, the most wicked innuendo, the most disgraceful slurs. Are you saying the Prime Minister would sell his integrity? The Prime Minister is a decent and honourable man. And so is my father.'

By the end of the meeting, both the main candidates were in tears. Olivia was comforted by Vernon and her father, Lucy by her uncle Richard, while Clifford Chambers and Compton Dundon consulted in a corner of the room. The vicar who convened the meeting was offering everyone plastic cups of orange juice and being ignored for his pains.

'There, there dear,' Abbey Luddington told Olivia and, later, Lucy, as she shuffled between the two young women trying to cheer everyone up. 'It's only politics.'

Mick Mickleton was composing an e-mail to the Workers' Party website. 'Corruption and big business at the heart of 'fat tax' revealed'. He rang Jimi Hunt.

Tony Grafton told Gary Atherstone, 'I suppose you think you were very clever, you idiot. Look what you've done now' and made to punch him in the face.

*****

The story, when it hit the papers, was written by the heavyweight business and political journalists. It was based on high-level briefings and serious inquiries into the balance sheets and financial interests of some of the country's leading businessmen and politicians. The consensus was that the exemption offered to 'health foods' had been extended to cover a range of biscuits including 'Jim-Jams', 'Yummies', 'Inca' bars and even the thick toffee and chocolate 'Pluto' range. 'How can a 'fat tax' exclude some of the country's most fattening snacks?' asked the papers. The Prime Minister's office denied doing any deal with anybody. The Trade Secretary admitted, however, that the impact on British industry and British jobs had to be taken into consideration when framing new legislation. But that was not the same thing, he said, as doing deals with individuals. And it was irrelevant whether they were supporters of the party or not.

Then a new poll was published in "The Chronicle" announcing 'a massive boost to the Independents'. Ms Trussell was running neck and neck with Ms Loxley. The paper loved being able to announce the result was, as they say in America, 'too close to call with everything to play for'.

'God it's all so disgusting,' Olivia complained to her father over breakfast.

'I'm sorry, dear,' said her father. 'I shouldn't have let you do this.'

'No, you shouldn't,' said Clarissa.

'Oh I don't know,' said Sam Trussell, who had flown in for the last few days of the campaign. 'It's quite good fun, really.'

At the Barsetshire Sleepover Hotel, Compton Dundon was in deep conversation with Steve Thomas and Clifford Chambers. Before them on the table were several cups with frothy white or brown stains that once contained cappuccinos and a full array of the day's papers, ruffled and read. Thomas had also printed out the front page of several leading websites. They all told a similar story – the party was selling its flagship policy to the highest bidder.

'Well?' asked Dundon.

'Well what?' asked Chambers.

'What do you propose to do to retrieve the situation, Clifford?'

'What do I propose to do?'

'This is your campaign, old boy.'

'My campaign? Since when?'

'Always has been,' said Thomas. 'This is your chance to pull something out of the fire. If Loxley loses now, it won't be about Cigarettegate or any of that crap. It'll be all about this new business.'

'Biscuitgate?' Dundon suggested helpfully, with a chuckle.

'Biscuitgate. And that reflects directly on the Prime Minister. This is now a referendum on his personal integrity. Bloody Acton bloody Trussell.'

'What do you want me to do?' Clifford asked. His chances of preferment in the party were receding before his eyes. He imagined he would never again be invited to sit at the same table as members of the Cabinet or get to call the Prime Minister 'Dick'.

'Fix it, Clifford. This is your constituency, your association, your candidate. You fix it,' said Compton Dundon the party fixer.

*****

Clarissa's mother Daphne Beauchamp died in her sleep. The family had been summoned to her bedside on the Tuesday evening because doctors feared the worst. Daphne looked frail and her breathing was fitful, laboured, distressing. She was rigged up to a range of machines to monitor her progress. Doctors looked in at regular intervals. Nurses fussed around. There was nothing they could do.

Clarissa, matter-of-fact even in the face of death, said the sooner it came to an end the better. This was no way for her dear mother to live. The woman had been the life and soul of the party. A great huntswoman in her day, a beauty in her youth, she would hate it if she knew she was reduced to this pitiful state.

Daphne Beauchamp died at about nine o'clock in the evening with her family around her. Olivia held one hand and wept silently. Clarissa and Acton quietly discussed funeral arrangements. Sam held his sister's hand as she sat beside their grandmother.

The family returned quietly to Howard Michael at about midnight. The funeral would be the following Monday, to give other family and friends time to make their way to Barset. Olivia determined to give up her political campaign. Her father said he would do a bit of work on her behalf but he quite understood.

Jimi Hunt knew one of the nurses. Honey Fullready drank at the same pub sometimes, when she came off duty at 10 pm. That night Honey felt the need for a little chat. She still couldn't treat a patient's death with the professional disinterest she needed to survive. She ordered a pint of lager and nodded to Jimi, who was sitting in a corner with Clifford Chambers. He beckoned her over. He knew Daphne Beauchamp was one of her patients. 'Seen the Trussells lately, Honey love?' Jimi asked and so she told him.

Hunt and Chambers exchanged glances.

*****

The news was in "The Chronicle", on TV and on the world's websites by lunch-time the following day – the eve of polling day. 'A smoker's death' ran the headline in "The Chronicle". It went on to describe the 'final days of agony' of 40-a-day fag-addict Daphne Beauchamp. Journalists took great pleasure in recounting the whole 'Cigarettegate' scandal as well as reminding readers that Daphne's grand-daughter was standing at the Barset by-election as an Independent candidate dedicated to promoting 'freedom and liberty'.

Newbold Whitnash wrote an article asking, 'Is this the freedom Ms Trussell is campaigning to protect – the freedom to smoke ourselves to death? If that's the freedom she wants, we can confirm to Ms Trussell that this is not the kind of freedom the people of Barset want. Her grandmother's untimely death should be a lesson to this young woman and a warning to the rest of us.'

Acton Trussell stood once more in his front garden answering questions from TV crews. His daughter was not available, he was very sorry, she was too distressed by the passing of her grandmother. Yes, Mrs Beauchamp had smoked occasionally. But as she lived to be 97 it was not necessarily the cigarettes which killed her. She had lived a long, good life and would be sorely missed.

'I must add,' he said, 'That my whole family is deeply distressed by the way this tragic personal and private situation has been allowed to dominate the media in a purely partisan political campaign to undermine my daughter's bid to become the MP for Barset. She is upset by her grandmother's death but she is enraged by the personal and vindictive nature of this gratuitous attack.'

*****

The party chairman rang Compton Dundon. 'Bit of luck, eh, Compton?' he chuckled.

'Luck had nothing to do with it, Mr Chairman,' Dundon chuckled.

'You don't mean..?'

'Good God, no. What do you take us for down here? No, but we did give the story a bit of a shove, as it were.'

'Excellent. All ready for the last push?'

'Yes, indeed, Mr Chairman.'

Dundon told Steve Thomas to prepare and print a new last-minute leaflet. It was to be in the shape of a coffin. And it was to read: 'Choose Life. Vote Loxley'.

Clifford Chambers was feeling a little guilty. 'I was their friend,' he said to Dundon. 'Acton is actually my god-father.'

'You'd better go over there, then, and offer your condolences.'

'I can't do that.' But he did. Unfortunately, only Sam was at home. His mother had gone to the undertakers. Olivia had gone to see Stud, who was back at home without Marinka and without any explanations, and their father had gone into Barset to help Vernon in the office and see if there were any volunteers left willing to dish out some last-minute leaflets.

Clifford Chambers and Sam Trussell hadn't seen each other for years. They had always been friends. They were much the same age, they enjoyed musicals and they loved the theatre. They went off to the pub together to catch up.

*****

Acton Trussell spent the last evening of the campaign walking the streets of what had once been his constituency delivering leaflets on behalf of his daughter. He had no idea where Olivia was and didn't really want to know. She was anguished by her grandmother's death and by all the publicity. He was trying to remember why he had gone into politics in the first place but couldn't remember. Idealism? Ego? Boredom? He really didn't know.

He trudged alone up footpaths of crumbling concrete, through the detritus left outside by families with young kids, to the letterboxes with spring traps to sever the fingers of the unwary. Nobody was about. It was dark. He was pretty certain the impetus of Olivia's campaign had been lost like water disappearing into the sand. People were confused by scandals and accusations. They just wanted a Government which would keep the country on an even keel and offer them a bit of peace and prosperity. It wasn't too much to ask, was it?

'Mr Trussell! Mr Trussell!' a woman was calling his name. Acton turned and saw someone large approaching him from across the street. 'Mr Trussell!' she said again. 'I'm so glad I've seen you.'

Acton tried to recall her name. 'Ah yes,' he said, holding out his hand to shake hers, 'How are you?'

'Wonderful,' she said. 'And it's all thanks to you. Come and look.'

She led him across the road to a neat terraced house built in the late 1920s with a small piece of grass at the front, a concrete wall dividing it from the pavement and a battered old Ford Fandango parked on the kerbside.

'Hayley's back with us now and Kelly and Dean have their own rooms as well. Derek says he loves it.'

'Oh yes.' It was all coming back. 'Mandy, isn't it? Mandy Black?'

''Course it is Mr Trussell. What are you doing here at this time of night?'

'Delivering leaflets. Here.' She looked at the picture of Olivia and read the headline, 'Freedom for Barset – Vote Olivia Trussell, Independent'.

'Is that your girl, Mr Trussell?'

'It is, Mandy?'

'And what's she doing?'

'Standing for Parliament.'

'When?'

'At the by-election. Tomorrow.'

'By-election? Tomorrow? Nobody told me.'

'Well I hope you remember to vote, Mrs Black.'

'Oh I will do now, Mr Trussell, don't you worry. We'll vote for your Olivia. But aren't you our MP Mr Trussell?'

'Not any more, Mrs Black.'

'Oh what a pity. Never mind, I'm sure your daughter will do just as well.'

'I'm sure she will, Mrs Black, I'm sure she will.'

Chapter 12

Polling day dawned dull. It was, after all, Guy Fawkes night so it was bound to rain. Turnout was slow. People made their way to vote in dribs and drabs throughout the morning. Clifford tried to persuade elderly ladies to squeeze into his Audi Attractive so he could drive them to the polling stations. Olivia stayed with Stud, though they slept in separate rooms.

The newspapers were excited at the prospect of 'the first test of the Government since the imposition of the smoking ban and the new fat tax'. Lucy Loxley wore her simplest black suit, her ridiculous rosette and her sensible shoes and toured the various wards where, in each place, a few elderly members had set up their 'campaign headquarters'.

At each stop she was plied with coffee and biscuits and listened to reminiscences of elections past. From time to time, someone would come hobbling in clutching pieces of paper which recorded who had voted so far. Someone, usually a man, took these and officiously crossed off the appropriate names on a sheet listing all the voters in the area.

At the Barset Sleepover Hotel, Compton Dundon and Steve Thomas sat back amid piles of papers and leaflets with nothing to do except wait for the polls to close. Dundon was already investigating the lie of the land in South Hope, where another by-election was likely to be called before Christmas. Thomas spent most of the morning on the phone to his 17-year-old girlfriend trying to persuade her to go away with him to Amsterdam for the weekend.

'Well, we've done our best,' Dundon said when Thomas finally came off the phone. 'Can't say we haven't tried.'

As she toured the campaign offices, Lucy started to appreciate there was, indeed, a possibility she would win and become a Member of Parliament. She hadn't really thought about the consequences of being elected. What was she to do if she became an MP? Call for an inquiry into her father's relationship with the Prime Minister? Vote against the fat tax? No, she would keep her head down and wait. She was young. She had a political career ahead of her. She just hoped Joanna would understand. After all, they would be back together in London soon and things could go on pretty much as usual but for an occasional visit to Barset to keep an eye on things.

*****

The polls closed at 10pm. The last couple of hours were supposed to be spent 'knocking up' which meant tracking down supporters who hadn't bothered to vote and asking them to get down to the polls before it was too late. Vernon Small sat in his office making telephone calls. Acton stood beside him trying to help. Nobody else bothered much.

Most of Lucy's supporters, including Clifford Chambers and Lucy herself, were having a bath, getting changed and having dinner before presenting themselves at the Free Trade Hall to watch the count unfold.

Security was tight. Everyone was searched. Firecrackers were confiscated from Senor Philosophus Mayhem. A couple of Lucy's members were turned away for having the wrong accreditation. Olivia arrived at 11.45. She was determined to be cool and casual. She wore jeans and a pretty top. Her hair was piled up on her head with its thick red strands occasionally brushing over her face. She couldn't help it, she was excited. She seized her brother's hand as they made their way into the hall, past the bright lights of a 'Newsnight' team transmitting a live report which said counting was about to start.

Acton Trussell led the way into the hall. It was busy with council officers poised to open the ballot boxes. On the stage there was a lone microphone. Before it, in an area roped off from where the council officials would be counting the votes, half a dozen reporters and a couple of camera crews had been corralled. When the result was announced, they would be in pole position but at the moment they were cut off from the rest of the world and generally ignored.

A little group of Olivia's supporters, wearing their white rosettes, was standing around the coffee bar in one corner. Lucy Loxley's supporters were gathered round the water-cooler opposite. Mrs Luddington came over to join the Independents. 'I was sorry to read about your grandmother, my dear,' she said, placing a consoling hand on Olivia's arm. 'And not in the least surprised to see that Ms Loxley's family connections being looked after by her party leader.'

Mick Mickleton, the Communist Workers' candidate, was trying to interest the reporter from 'The Chronicle' in the plight of some travellers who couldn't find a site to set up camp over the winter.

From outside, the sound of explosions and bursts of light filtered into the hall as a few bonfire night celebrations came to a conclusion. Vernon Small told Olivia, 'We've checked the postal ballots. Do you want to see them, Olivia, or are you happy for me to deal with it?' She had no idea what he was talking about and said she was happy to leave it to Vernon. Her father explained he was checking for spoiled papers. Sometimes there were disputes about who the voter had intended to support; sometimes they crossed out all the names in a green-ink fury.

A hush descended. A look of concentration came over the council officials as the metal ballot boxes were opened and the voting slips were poured onto trestle tables. The papers were unfolded, placed in piles by candidate, then, eventually, counted and bound in bundles of one hundred.

Last to arrive, long after the count began, was Julian 'Stud' Lee. He wore biker boots, tight jeans, an AC/DC T-shirt, a leather bomber jacket and a white rosette. Everyone stopped to look. Even the council officials paused momentarily. Some of them lost count and had to start again. Before Stud could reach Olivia, he was waylaid by Senor Philosophus Mayhem who asked for his autograph and when there would be a reunion.

Stud was soon surrounded by fans, political opponents united in their admiration for the local rock legend. 'No reunion, mate, we're all too old to relive those glory days. Besides, I'm working on a new project at the moment.'

It wasn't until half past two that the council officers sat quietly with nothing to do while a couple of officials summoned Vernon Small, Clifford Chambers and the other candidates' agents for a discussion over spoilt votes and dubious decisions. They agreed with the Returning Officer's verdicts amicably and suddenly the candidates themselves were being summoned to the stage. Olivia felt a surge of excitement and terror.

The Returning Officer lined the candidates up along the stage. The TV crews turned on their lights and activated their cameras. The photographers began snapping away. When she was satisfied everyone was ready, the Returning Officer stood in front of the microphone and announced, 'As the Returning Officer for the Barset Parliamentary constituency, I hereby declare the results are as follows: Burbage, Cherry, seven hundred and sixty two; Luddington, Abbey, two thousand one hundred and eleven; Loxley, Lucy, fourteen thousand, seven hundred and six; Mayhem, Senor Philosophus, seventy three; Mickleton, Mick, ninety one.' There was a pause. 'Trussell, Olivia, fourteen thousand, four hundred and two. I therefore declare that the aforementioned Lucy Loxley is duly elected as the Member of Parliament for the constituency of Barset.'

There were gasps, followed by half-hearted cheers from Lucy's supporters and from Olivia's. Thomas was busy on his i-Phone and his Blackberry. Dundon was immediately on the phone. Acton Trussell turned to Clarissa and they kissed. Clarissa was in tears. 'Thank God,' she whispered to her husband.

There were speeches and kisses and commiserations.

'First is first, second is nowhere,' Compton Dundon told the party chairman.

'A win is a win,' Steve Thomas said in his e-mail to the Home Secretary.

'Check the scorebook,' Clifford Chambers said smugly to one of Olivia's supporters who said they thought there should be a recount. 'It's there in the scorebook. A win by 304 votes. No second innings, I'm afraid.'

'Darling,' said Acton Trussell, throwing his arms around his daughter.

*****

On the way home, Stud said to Olivia, 'Sweetheart, that was fantastic but I don't think politics is for you. And I don't think I am either. Olivia, you are beautiful, talented and so bloody young I can't stand it. I am old and gnarled and washed up. But I have a proposition for you. I think we should make an album together. You and your chums and me and mine. We'll form a band and go on tour. What do you say?'

Olivia smiled for the first time that day.

*****

Lucy Loxley called her father and her brother to receive their congratulations. Then she called Joanna who said she was really not interested and if Lucy had to have a career in politics, she would have to find another partner.

*****

Maggie Pride left her husband and children and married Sir Chatham Smith, who was knighted for services to industry. Lady Pride was made the Coalition's "dance tzar" and later she was given a seat in the House of Lords.

*****

The party chairman congratulated Compton Dundon and ordered him down to South Hope where the party was defending a majority of just 2,400. Steve

Thomas was ordered back to headquarters to spend the next few days explaining to the press why the party had been given such a bloody nose at the by-election and why there was no truth whatsoever in the allegations that the fat tax had been fixed to favour the Prime Minister's cronies.

*****

After her mother's funeral, Clarissa Trussell got on with preparing for Christmas in Howard Michael. She made her husband join the choir. Acton found he had a surprisingly decent singing voice for someone of his age.

*****

Clifford Chambers met up again with Sam Trussell. And again. And several times after that.

*****

Shortly after 2.30 am, as soon as the by-election result was announced, Home Secretary Rick Pickering called Chief Constable Bingley Ortega.
'Now, Bingo. Go now.'
Ten minutes later, police officers in riot gear and carrying machine guns beat down the door of the house a young man shared with his mother. They kicked him out of bed in the dark, pinned him to the floor, threw a few punches for good measure, and dragged him screaming to a heavily armoured vehicle parked in the suburban road.
Aston Cantlow was paraded before the world's press three days later, accused of plotting acts of terrorism and subversion. He was tried in secret, on the grounds of national security, and never heard of again.